SADISTIC MATES

SAVAGE SERIES
BOOK TWO

JESSICA HALL

Cover by MCDamon Design

Format design by CED

Edited by Gabrielle Gerbus @incubix

Art work by Athira on insta

BLURB

Blurb

My name is enough to send most people running. Those that don't are fools, and for that, they will feel my wrath. I am the King of Darkness. The Dark Tribrid is what they call me. Destruction is what I am, what I bring, and what I am known for. Countries have fallen by my hands. A world changed by me and the blood I have spilled. People now fear the dark, fear the Dark Ones.

My mother thought she was protecting me by keeping my magic from me. That betrayal is what hurt the most. She took a piece of me, and I nearly killed her for it.

Growing up, I knew I was different. My outlook on life was different. My childhood was filled with love and everything a child could desire. But despite my upbringing, I always felt like I was lacking something. Something vital was missing from my life.

From the outside, we appeared to be the perfect family. Our lives were great until I turned sixteen, and I came back into possession of my magic. The darkness sucked all parts of me away until I became the person I am today. I used to fear the darkness, but now I embrace it.

For decades, I roamed the Earth, struggling to find meaning, and that was how I stumbled across my mates. At first, they feared me. By then, everyone had heard my name, not a country left intact as I made my way through each one, trying to figure out my purpose.

I met Ryland first. He was just as sadistic as me and a werewolf. We continued our reign of terror until we met our other mate. I was hoping for a woman, not that I was uncomfortable with my sexuality. It is what it is. I would fuck anything with legs to fulfill my needs and my mates.

Orion was different, weaker. He disagreed with my past and the things we had done. He was much older than both of us and knew of my grandfather. Orion is a vampire and a little old-fashioned, but he is mine even though he annoys and frustrates me.

He hated me at first, but he came to see reason. He has remained by my side, even when he disagrees, trying to talk me down and change me. Yet now I think he has given up.

Then, there is her. I thought I was complete until I met her. Evelyn Harper, the light in my darkness. I want her, crave her. She is a human and perfectly made for us. Evelyn is everything I never realized I desired, and exactly what I was searching for. The moment I laid eyes on her, I knew she would be ours. She just didn't know it.

CHAPTER ONE

Thaddeus

Sitting on the balcony of my penthouse apartment, I look over the city. My eyes scan the street below as I watch the crowds of people go about their night, unaware of the monster watching them.

As the sliding door opens, the sound of movement behind me makes my eyes snap to the glass doors. Bianca steps out and hands me a smoke. Taking the lighter from her, I light it, breathing in deeply, enjoying the burn in my throat from its harshness.

"When do you intend to return home? Haven't you punished them enough? They did it to protect you. It is time you stop doing this, whatever it is that you are doing." She says while leaning on the railing as her blue eyes watch me with caution.

"And what am I doing?" I ask her, looking back toward the city.

"The destruction. What are you trying to prove? Who are you looking for?" She asks, and I sigh.

Only she can get away with questioning me like this. I have always had a soft spot for Bianca. She listens and doesn't judge, no matter how much I fuck things up.

"I am not trying to prove anything. I don't need to."

"Then why, Thaddeus? Why all this?" She asks, motioning with her hand toward the city below.

"Because I can, that is why," I tell her.

Bianca shakes her head. Tears brim in her eyes as she looks away from me, folding her arms across her chest. "Your mother said there was still good in you. We just had to find it. She claimed that we could pull you back from the darkness, but I am not so sure anymore. I can't watch you destroy yourself, destroy everything you put your hands on. Sorry, Thaddeus, but I can't do it anymore. I am going home. Come and see me when you see sense," she says, as she pushes away from the railing and moves toward the door.

"You're leaving already? You just got here," I ask.

In an attempt to hide my disappointment, a painful growl tears out of my throat. As much as I don't want to show any weakness, her rejection hurts. Bianca is leaving me. She is leaving me like the rest of them did.

Frightened by my reaction, Bianca steps back. "I'm sorry, Thaddeus, but please just go home. They will forgive you," she says, before turning her back on me and opening the glass sliding door.

"Tell mom I am not coming back," I tell her, peering over my shoulder at her.

A sad smile spreads across her lips as Bianca nods, acknowledging my words. Then, I just listen to her walk inside, closing the door behind her, leaving me all alone.

A few minutes later, the glass door opens again. I don't pay attention until Orion appears at my side and plucks the smoke from my fingers. He leans against the railing, looking at the main street of the city. In the meantime, my eyes run the length of him.

He is wearing dark blue jeans and a black long-sleeved shirt. His muscles tense as he turns his head to look at me. He runs his fingers through his dark brown hair before drawing back on my smoke.

"What did you say to your Aunty Bianca that upset her?" he asks, passing my smoke back to me.

"I told her I am not going back," I tell him the truth.

Orion sighs loudly and looks over the railing again. I move behind him, press myself against him and reach around. My hand slips into his pants while the other roams over his hard-muscled chest. At my touch, his dick twitches in my hand. That's all it takes for a lewd groan to leave me as I tug at his belt.

"Not tonight, Thaddeus," he says, smacking my hand away.

All I can think of is his obvious rejection. Hence, I can't help but voice the hurt and frustration with a growl. If this is how he is going to act, fine by me. I shove Orion away from me and he actually has the gall to glare at me.

"Fine," I snap at him, turning on my heel and heading back inside. Bianca is gone, and only her faint, lingering scent remains as I step into the living room. "Ryland?" I yell but get no answer. "Hurry up; we're going out," I add.

Ryland walks out with a mischievous grin on his lips. He is dressed in a gray shirt and black jeans. He grabs his leather jacket and tugs it on as he approaches me. His eyes flicker black, and his excitement smacks into me at the invitation.

Ryland stops beside me just as the sliding door opens and Orion steps inside. He curses under his breath, shaking his head at us before strolling over to the couch. Ryland growls and rolls his eyes at the look of disgust Orion is giving us.

"Where are we going?" Ryland growls and leans into me.

I grip his belt, tugging him closer. My lips crash against his and he groans, shoving me against the dining room table I stand next to. His tongue fights mine for dominance, and I growl at him before gripping his arms and reversing our positions. He laughs as I pin him against the table and his arousal presses against my stomach. I pull my lips from his and grip the front of his jacket. "I just want out of this house, and I need blood," I tell him.

Ryland nods and I let him go. I won't risk feeding on him. My hunger is insatiable and as intoxicating as his scent is, I know I won't stop once I start. Marking him was a nightmare. I nearly killed him, nearly killed my mate. Orion was different. He is a vampire, so I didn't struggle as badly with him.

Ryland looks over at Orion expectantly, but Orion wants no part of our endeavors, as usual. I turn and walk toward the elevator. Ryland is quick to follow.

I enter the lobby and proceed to the exit door. Ryland shivers beside me as we step out of the building. The snow crunches under our feet as we walk down the street, looking for my next victim. When the breeze shifts, I pick up the most mouth-watering, intoxicating scent I have ever smelled. "Hmm, whatever that is, I want to take a bite out of it," Ryland says, picking up the same scent.

I follow it before I hear an ear-piercing scream. Something twitches inside me, something I haven't felt in a long time. Fear. Fear races through my cold veins as I hear the woman's voice. Ryland, who is also feeling it, looks at me as we walk around the corner into an alleyway. The alleyway is dark, the ground is covered in snow. There are some dumpsters near the end, and I can see a man standing over a woman.

The woman thrashes violently as the man tries to pull her pants down. Her following scream makes my blood boil, but before I can even move, Ryland is ripping him to pieces with his bare hands. The woman moves and I can't take my eyes off her, hypnotized by her.

As I step into the alleyway, her head whips in my direction and she whimpers before the sound of Ryland slamming the man on the ground makes her cower away. Ryland is bashing the man, his face now utterly unrecognizable as human, his blood seeping into the snow.

As the woman tries to pull her pants up, looking between Ryland and me, I can smell her fear. She thinks we are here to harm her. Ryland stops and stands upright, panting. He turns toward her, looks at her fear-stricken face, and reaches for her. The girl slaps his hands away, shuffling away from him.

Her entire body is shaking with fear, and her heart is beating rapidly, I am sure even she can hear it. The cold is biting at her skin, making her lips a little blue. She is in a waitress uniform, not appropriately dressed for this weather. The closer I get, the stronger the scent becomes. Her scent is the most addictive, mouth-watering smell I have gotten a whiff of. She makes my heart race faster.

All this time, I didn't think I needed anyone besides my mates. Yet, I want her, need her with every cell in my body. My gums tingle as my fangs slip out, I want to taste her. Want to see if her skin is as soft as it looks.

She cowers back as I kneel before her, her hazel eyes filled with nothing but fear. I can tell she knows what we are. I extend my hand to her, but she slaps it away, her knees pulling to her chest as she cringes away from me.

"Please, I won't tell. Just let me go. I saw nothing, I promise," she stutters, with tears trekking down her pale face. Her voice is like music to my ears; I could have listened to her talk all day.

I sweep her light brown hair out of the way so I can see her face. She averts her gaze when it meets my onyx eyes. "Ours," I gasp.

She shakes her head, and I feel Ryland touch my shoulder, making me look at him. "We are scaring her," he murmurs, and for the first time, I can tell he doesn't enjoy the scent of fear, at least not from her. The mate pull is intense.

Looking back at her, I get up and step back to give her some space. "Go," I tell her, and she gets up, grabbing her handbag before running off.

We watch her run when I notice her wallet lying in the snow. As I examine it, I notice the material is worn and fraying. Pulling out her bus pass, I read it - Evelyn Harper.

I have never craved anyone as much as I do her, never desired another person more than I do her right now. She is ours, and yet we can't have her. She is light while we are dark. We are monsters of the night to her, and I have to fight with myself to stop from chasing her down and claiming her.

"Thaddeus?" Ryland says, gripping my shoulder.

I turn my head to see him still staring at the end of the alley where she ran. "I want her," I mutter.

"She is human," he whispers, and I can feel his sadness bleed into me. Ryland wants her, too. No doubt Orion also will when he meets her.

"For now! She is ours. She will be ours," I growl, looking at her frayed wallet.

"What if she doesn't want us?" he asks, and my brows pinch together at his words.

"That's not her choice to make. She belongs to us. She will come to realize that," I tell him.

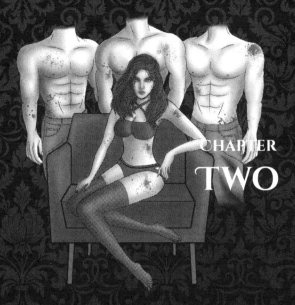

CHAPTER

TWO

E velyn
I just finished my shift; my sleaze-bag boss swiped my tips once again. At this point, I'm not sure if I should be as surprised as I feel anymore. Should I wait for anything better from that scummy man?

Walking through the cold streets, I shiver. Something is off. The streets are too quiet, suspiciously so, and a feeling of unease settles over me.

However, I ignore the feeling and keep walking. I don't have time to waste second-guessing everything. As I walk, the cold snow sinks into my flats, making my toes go numb. I have worked at the same cafe for two years now. It doesn't pay much, but given the state of the economy, I should be grateful I have a job. Work is scarce these days, and finding a job is hard when half the city is in ruins.

It never used to be like this. When I was a child, this city flourished.

In fact, most had never heard his name before, but everyone had heard the rumors of the Dark One. The man, or should I say monster, that destroyed the world. No one stood a chance against him. The human government tried for years, banding together, trying to rid the world of his evil.

He slaughtered not just towns, but countries; burning cities filled with families and people, to the ground, along with his two mates. Rumor has it he is trying to find something that he isn't even sure exists.

Walking between two abandoned buildings, I can see the alleyway that leads to the trailer park. One more block, and I will be home. Well, I'm not sure if that rusty tin can is a home in other's eyes. For me, it's not much, but it is mine. And in fact, I am quite proud of what I have accomplished, never knowing a good home.

When I was born, my parents gave me up; I don't even know their names. Apparently, I was dropped off in front of a church, only a few days old. The nuns took me in, and I bounced from one foster home to another, until I eventually aged out of the system. My age left me homeless and living on park benches. Just me and my plastic bag full of clothes.

I remember walking the streets, looking for a safe place to sleep when I stumbled upon the cafe. The sign in the window caught my attention - they were looking for help. To this day, I believe I must have been in the right place at the right time because when I walked in and asked about the job, the owner just tossed me an apron and told me to start straight away as they were overrun with the lunch crowd. I have worked there ever since.

A little lost in my thoughts, I carry on walking, eager to get back home. As I reach the corner of the building, I'm about to turn up the alleyway when I see a man, leaning against the side of the building.

The smell of his smoke hanging from his lip's wafts to me. He moves off the wall he is leaning on, and I quickly turn up the alleyway. I can hear his footsteps coming behind me before I feel a tug backward.

I scream, as I feel his gloved hand go over my mouth.

"No. Come now, pretty, be a good girl and stay quiet."

I nod my head, thinking he is going to rob me. Reaching into my handbag, I feel around it and pull my wallet out. It has little in it, but he can have it.

I wave it in front of his face, and he knocks it out of my hand. His next words make my blood run colder than the snow sinking into my shoes. "I don't want your money; I want something else," he whispers, his whiskey-filled breath wafting over my face.

I struggle against him, realizing he has more sinister intentions than just robbing me.

He throws me to the ground, and I let out the loudest scream I can muster, hoping that someone will hear me, he slaps my face. My head whips to the side as his palm connects with my cheek, making my vision blur for a second.

He starts ripping my black slacks down, and I fight, kicking, hitting, and scratching anything I can. All I can think of is the need to escape him, so I dig my fingers into his eyes. He grunts, grabs my hair, and slams my head into the pavement. The force makes my teeth rattle, but I continue to thrash, as he continues trying to undress me.

As the cold snow seeps into my clothes it makes my muscles ache, and fighting against him becomes harder with every passing second. But then, all of a sudden, his weight is gone. I stare, shocked for a second after he completely vanishes.

When I hear the grunting and obnoxious sound of flesh on flesh, I start yanking my pants up my legs.

As I look toward the alleyway, I see a man, or perhaps that is the wrong word for him. I didn't think I would meet a bigger monster than the man that just tried raping me, but I also don't know what else you would call him. He is literally ripping the man to pieces. I have to hold my stomach as I feel it lurch when I see one of his arms fly off and hit the snow.

Blood coats the ground, as the man punches his face until it is unrecognizable. The snow turns red. I clench my eyes shut, unable to handle what I am witnessing.

It is like something out of a horror movie. I shake like a leaf, my teeth chattering from the cold as I sit frozen with fear. Fight or flight is kicking in, and here I am, paralyzed by my fear. Scared that I am next, I keep my eyes closed, waiting for death.

The noise stops, I look up and two men are staring down at me. One holds his hand out and I smack it away, covering my head with my hands, fearing him belting me and inflicting what he just did to the man in the alley.

"Please, I won't tell. Just let me go. I saw nothing, I promise," I beg them, as sobs wrack my body.

The biggest man kneels in front of me, moving my hair away from my face and brushing it over my shoulder. Looking up, I see pitch-black eyes staring at me; eyes so dark I am afraid they will swallow me whole. I turn my gaze to the ground, not wanting to see my death through his eyes. He holds his large hand out for me to take and I cringe away from him, flinching as he tries to reach forward.

"Ours," he gasps, and I almost think I heard it wrong. Are they going to finish what the other man couldn't?

"We are scaring her," the man who brutally slaughtered my attacker says, making me look at him. He is drenched in blood; it is dying his skin a scarlet color. The smell of death is so pungent on him that I can almost taste it.

"Go," the man with onyx eyes says. He is watching the other man, who I see nod to him.

I take off running down the alleyway, thanking God, they let me go. I run the entire way home, like my ass is on fire. I bolt through the trailer park until I finally reach my tin can. Never in my life have I been as thankful to see my shitty, graffiti covered van. It's falling apart, but it's screaming safety right about now.

Just as I reach the door, I finally lose my stomach, doubling over and puking the contents into the snow. I retch for a few minutes, trying to rid my mouth of the taste. My face grows hot from throwing up, and the back of my throat burns from my stomach acids.

I must be making a fair amount of noise because I see the trailer beside mine flick on its lights, and I quickly slip inside before my neighbors see me through their window.

Stepping inside, I see the familiar surroundings of my humble abode. I shut the door and slowly slide to the floor as my legs give out from under me. What the fuck just happened? How the fuck am I still alive?

Whoever they are, they aren't human. I can't get the picture of his dark eyes, staring at me, out of my mind. Those eyes are so dark I could see my reflection in them.

Yet, they let me go. Why? I could have run to the...well, no one.

You don't last long as an officer in this city. Most law enforcement are dead, the only justice found in the city these days is vigilante justice or the underworld trades. With the way that man tore my attacker apart limb from limb, I doubt anyone could match up against them. He didn't even break a sweat!

Closing all the curtains, I quickly make sure all the doors are locked. I've never been this paranoid before. I grew up in this city and know it like the back of my hand. Sure, every city is dangerous, but growing up here, I know all the do's and don'ts, and which streets to avoid.

My area is mostly considered safe; nothing much happens around here. Never have I been attacked on my way home. Few people live on this side of the city because there isn't much left. Even the homeless refuse to live here because the place is abandoned; there aren't many places to beg or dumpster dive.

After what happened, I feel like this is just the start of something bigger. I have always been pretty intuitive, but I have this nagging feeling something bad will happen, and I pray this feeling is just because of today's events. Once I am convinced, I have locked up completely, I walk into the bathroom and turn on the shower.

Stripping off, I hop in. The water burns my skin, making me jump. My skin is so cold the water feels like it is blistering it. I only know it is my skin that is cold by the shaking of my hands and the fact that my toes are blue. Easing myself in slowly, I let the water warm my freezing body, inhaling the smell of my two-dollar straw-berry shampoo.

When I hop out, I grab my fluffy towel and walk into my room, quickly getting dressed before hopping in bed. I have to be back at work by 5:30 am for the breakfast shift. Wrapping myself up in my comforter like a human burrito, I close my eyes, drifting off into the darkness of sleep.

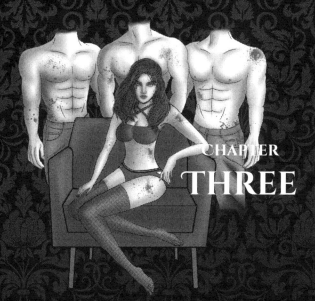

THREE

E velyn
     I sleep terribly. Nightmares plague my sleep, making me toss and turn, and I wake in a sweat. My anxiety forces me to get up and check all the locks again.

Then, lying in bed, trying to go back to sleep, my mind won't stop questioning if I really checked the lock on the windows or the door. And that, in turn, makes me even more paranoid, so I'm forced to get out of the bed to check again.

By the time the noise of my alarm blares next to my head, I feel like a zombie. Dragging myself to my feet, I make my way to the bathroom and turn on the faucet. Only nothing comes out. The pipes shudder and groan, but no water. "Fuck!" I scream, annoyed, realizing the water has frozen in the pipes overnight. This has to happen in the morning when I need a shower to wake myself.

Walking into the kitchen, I pick up the kettle to find it empty.

"Not today, Satan!" I yell, flipping him off with both hands, as I march to my room and grab a fresh blouse from the closet and some black slacks.

Quickly getting dressed, I throw on my flats only for my toes to go straight through the end. "Really? Can this day get any worse?" I groan, as I get up and dig through the kitchen drawer.

Duct tape. Duct tape fixes everything. Grabbing a roll of black tape, I tape my flats that now have a mouth for my toes to play peek-aboo. Giving my toes a wriggle, they seem to hold, but just in case, I wrap more around the end of my shoes to make sure they hold in the snow.

Buttoning up my blouse, I go into the bathroom and brush my teeth. Then, I make the mistake of looking at my reflection. My god, I look like shit.

I haven't slept in a good week, which is easy to prove by the huge, dark bags under my eyes. Any bigger, I could smuggle my wallet in them. When I think of my wallet, I quickly rinse my mouth, drop everything, and run to get my bag. I reach into it and dig around for the wallet.

Panicking, I tip my bag upside down and the contents spill on my bed. My wallet is gone, and I don't remember picking it up.

I could try going back the way I came to see if I can find it. The thought alone makes me shiver in fear.

Throwing my phone into my bag, I toss it over my shoulder before grabbing my sweater and pulling it over my head. Pulling my hair into a high ponytail, I unlock my door and take a deep breath, willing myself to leave the safety of my trailer. When I swing the door open, I quickly rush out before locking it. As I turn around, I see something sitting on the top step. Looking around, I eye the package suspiciously. It is a cardboard box. Bending down, I pick it up and open it.

My blood runs cold, and my heart hammers in my chest so hard I think it might bounce out. My breathing comes in short pants, as panic takes over. Anxiety is my biggest weakness. It takes nothing and everything to set it off. Nothing feels worse than the adrenaline that pumps through your veins, just because your brain becomes a little irrational.

I know I'm not being irrational this time, though. As I look down at my wallet, I know I have a reason to panic and burn bridges in fear. They know where I live.

What if they come back to finish off the job? I look around to make sure they aren't lurking around.

Gripping the handrail of the stairs, I try to ground myself. Something I can feel: the wooden handrail. Check. Something I can see: snow. Check. Something I can taste: my toothpaste. Check, check, fucking check. Yep, very much alive still.

I will my heart to stop racing and beating erratically. Forcing my feet down the stairs, I practically run the entire way to work, bursting through the glass door.

The bell jingles loudly, as Lisa spins around from serving someone and stares at me, bewildered. "Geez, Evelyn, the way you burst in, I thought we were being held up again," she says, coffee pot in hand.

"Sorry," I gasp, trying to catch my breath as I place my hands on my knees.

Standing up, I look around. The cafe is retro, with its red and white checked flooring, brightly colored bench seats, and table decorations. I notice the person Lisa is serving is watching me. I drop my eyes, but I can feel his eyes on me as I walk behind the counter and grab my apron.

Lisa sets the coffee pot down and I grab a mug, filling it before gulping down the liquid gold.

"Rough night?"

"You have no idea," I tell her, finishing my cup and pouring another.

"Vick isn't in yet. Hopefully, he doesn't stop in today," Lisa says, walking past and squeezing my shoulder.

The morning is abnormally quiet. Like, no one comes in, except the man that Lisa served. When I watch him from behind the counter, he looks up and I avert my gaze. Something is off about him.

He is gorgeous, with dark hair, thick lashes, and a strong jawline. He is bigger than most people in this area. This man clearly works out; by the size of his biceps alone, I assume he lives at the gym. He is dressed nice too, which is a little odd for this side of town. He doesn't fit in; he stands out like a sore thumb. His button-up shirt hugs him tightly, and I can tell his chest is just as muscular as his arms. Lisa pulls me out of my daze when she taps me on the shoulder.

"It's quiet, I am going for a smoke. You all right on your own with Mr. Hotty?" she says with a wink.

I chuckle and watch her leave out the front, placing her apron on the empty table next to the door. As soon as she walks out, the man moves, making my eyes snap to his. They are emerald, green, and I can't look away as he approaches, sitting on the stool at the counter. I watch his lips move but don't hear what he says, hypnotized by his eyes.

"You okay?" he asks with a smirk on his face.

"Huh?" Good going, Evelyn.

"I asked if I could have some more coffee," he says, pointing to the pot behind me.

"Shit, sorry, I spaced out," I mumble, turning around and grabbing the pot before refilling his cup.

"Evelyn," he says, looking at the name tag attached to my shirt.

I nod before looking to the door for Lisa, hoping she will be back in soon to save me from my awkwardness.

"I'm Orion," he says, making me look at him. Hmm, that surely is one weird name.

"Nice to meet you, Orion," I tell him, and Lisa walks in.

She puts her apron on before tossing me her smokes, giving me a wink. I take my apron off and walk outside. As I walk around the side, the chill in the air blasts my face. I sit on the milk crate, light up a smoke, and inhale deeply.

"Smoking is bad for you."

I hear his familiar voice before I see him. The sound makes my eyes snap open. Not creepy at all.

"Gotta die of something," I tell him, waiting for him to leave. He leans on the side of the building, watching me. "Can I help you with something? Are you lost?" I ask, a little annoyed.

"No, I was looking for you, actually," he replies, looking down at me.

"Well, you found me, so you can leave now." I wave him off, and he chuckles.

"That's not very nice," he says, raising an eyebrow at me.

"Last I checked, you're invading my personal space, so I don't need to be nice," I tell him, quickly finishing my smoke and putting it in the ashtray. Walking back toward the entrance, I groan when I see my boss's yellow car pull up out the front. Orion opens the door and waits for me to enter.

Quickly stepping past him, I put my apron on and warn Lisa that Vick is here. She walks out to the front counter, while plastering on a fake smile. I don't bother hiding my disgust for the man, especially after yesterday when he told me I had to blow him if I wanted my tips. Filthy asshole. I am the same age as his daughter.

The bell jingles and Vick walks in. He is a middle-aged man who is overweight and balding. His white shirt is covered in grease, probably from last night's dinner. Oh, and he is ripe today. I have to fight the urge to gag when he walks past and I catch a whiff of his body odor.

"Ladies," he says, walking out the back. I roll my eyes, and Lisa groans loudly once he is out of sight.

I notice Orion watching us. A strange look crosses his face as his eyes follow Vick. Then, all of a sudden, I hear Vick shout out my name, and I look past the kitchen to his office with a groan.

"Maybe we can make a run for it?" Lisa jokes, light-heartedly.

"Evelyn!" Vick screams from his small office.

I grab a mug and fill it with coffee to take to him. I hope he is distracted with something and doesn't remember me calling him a perverted pig before I stormed out of work yesterday.

As I enter his office, Vick is sitting at his desk. He runs his hand over his bald head, a cruel grin on his face. "Shut the door," he snaps, as he reaches forward and snatches the mug from my hand. Coffee sloshes all over his desk. I grab the tea towel tucked into my apron, mopping it up.

"Do you have anything to say about yesterday?" he asks, raising his unibrow.

"Nope, I am pretty sure what I said was pretty accurate," I tell him, crossing my arms over my chest and glaring at the vile man before me.

"You should watch who you are talking to, girlie. I am not firing you only because we are understaffed, but I am cutting your shifts as punishment."

"Who are you punishing, Lisa or me? She can't run the place by herself," I state.

"She will manage. Unless..." he says, uncrossing his legs and looking at his pants zipper.

I walk out, no way am I degrading myself for my shifts. I need the job, but I will manage without it. I have some savings to last a week or two till I find another job if need be. Slamming the door, I walk back out to Lisa.

"What does he want?" she asks, staring at me worriedly.

"He is cutting my shifts because I wouldn't blow him," I whisper, and she frowns.

She knows what he is like, but mostly, he leaves us alone. He used to be only touchy-feely, but he has taken it to an entirely new level of disgustingness since his wife passed.

"So quiet this morning," Lisa says, looking out the front windows.

I turn to look out and notice Orion glaring at the office door. His anger confuses me, as he shoots daggers at the door.

"Probably because they spotted the dark ones," I tell her, taking my eyes off him and turning to Lisa.

She nods. "Yeah, I heard they destroyed the north side of the city. They need to just fuck off. This world is hard enough to live in without them killing everyone and destroying everything. I heard a hundred people died when the bank collapsed because of that psycho," she whispers.

Suddenly, the office door opens, making us look toward the kitchen. Vick strolls out, a cruel smile on his face. He walks over to the register and retrieves the tip jar before walking out.

"Vick, that's bullshit!" Lisa calls out to him, but he ignores her and keeps walking out. We both huff.

"Not like much was in it. I haven't seen one customer besides him," I say, looking in the direction of the man named Orion. Only, he is gone. I look around, but he isn't anywhere. "Where did he go?"

Lisa looks up, noticing him gone too. She walks over to the table he was at before coming back.

"I have no idea where he went, but he left a $500 tip!" she says, waving the cash in front of my face.

I chuckle as I walk to his table to clean it.

Once he left, after an hour or two I notice the place was filling up with customers again. We're run off our feet for most of the day. Lisa and I take turns cooking and serving, because the place has no cook after Miranda left. She was sick of Vick's constant harassment.

By closing time, we both notice Vick never came back, which is odd, considering he always stops by before the dinner rush. When closing time comes, Lisa empties the new tip jar and gives me half of it. I place the cash in my wallet, toss it in my bag and help Lisa lock up the place.

Lisa catches a bus to and from work, which pulls up out the front as we walk out the door. "Shit!" she hisses.

"I will lock up," I tell her.

She tosses me the keys and quickly races over, just before the doors shut. I pull all the shutters down and quickly place the padlocks on before locking the screen door. Once I am done, I turn around. It is dark now, seeing that it is nearly nine o'clock. Wrapping my arms around myself, I start walking. I have this strange feeling I am being watched, which makes me pick up my pace. I keep looking over my shoulder every few minutes, convinced someone is following me. When I come to the alley, I freeze, and look down at it. I look further down the street, deciding whether to take the shortcut or the long route, which will add twenty minutes. I opt for the street-lights, taking the long route. When my trailer comes into view, I start jogging, wanting to get inside to safety. Closing the door, I quickly lock it. The first thing I do is check the taps.

I do a little victory dance when I see the pipes are no longer frozen. Tossing my bag on my bed, I walk into the bathroom and turn the lights on.

My phone buzzes just as I am about to enter the shower. After letting the water heat up, I walk over to where I left my phone and pick it up. Vick has sent a text.

Going on vacation, you and Lisa will take over the cafe until I return.

Wow. To be honest, I am a little taken aback after the day's events, and this message just adds to it. Yet, I am glad I won't have to see him for a while. Lisa and I are more than capable of running the cafe. At least for now, we won't have to put up with his sexual advances.

Sure, Vick, have a pleasant vacation. I reply, before dropping my phone on the bed and walking to the bathroom so I can have a shower.

CHAPTER
FOUR

Thaddeus

A week goes by. I sent Orion to watch over her, to find out more about her, yet each day, he comes back with the same answer - nothing.

He even tried to compel the girl, Lisa, I think he said her name is. Not even Lisa knows much about her, despite the fact that they have been working together for almost two years now.

All Lisa could tell him is that Evelyn lives in the trailer park a couple of blocks away from the cafe. Orion claims he pressed for more information, but all he got about her background, from Lisa, is that our mate just showed up in that cafe, looking for a job.

Her answers, and the reluctance, makes me wonder what Evelyn is hiding. And if there is anything Lisa is helping her to hide.

Orion managed to steal her keys while she wasn't looking and already made a copy of them. So today, while Evelyn is at work, Ryland and I are planning to see what we can find out about her.

Watching Orion leave and waiting for his call to tell us she has arrived at work feels like the hardest part of this morning. But now that it's out of our way, I grab my keys and walk to our apartment door. Ryland is straight behind me, following on my heels. Both Ryland and Orion are just as curious about who our little mate is, as I am. We all are eager to find out more about her.

Thankfully, it doesn't take us long to drive to the trailer park. It looks abandoned. There's nothing besides the few trailers that remain, and the front office. The entire place comprises of around twenty trailers, so finding hers is a piece of cake. I pull up and notice an old woman sitting out the front. I am sure she lives next door. That much is clear by how her eyes follow us as we walk up the stairs.

I nod to Ryland, and he unlocks the door. His eyes don't leave the wrinkly old hag's face as she watches us with suspicious eyes.

"You're not worried she will tell her?" Ryland asks, opening the door.

We haven't even stepped inside the trailer when we are instantly hit with her scent. My mouth waters as the intoxicating aroma wraps around us. My body relaxes the same instant; her scent calms me as we step inside and close the door behind us.

"You can deal with the woman when we leave," I tell him, and he nods his head, looking around.

Evelyn doesn't own much. I think it's a bit weird that she has no personal belongings besides clothing, even though this is where she lives. We start opening drawers and find some bills with her name, a make-up bag, and a hair straightener. But other than that, there isn't much here.

No photos, no albums, no paperwork, nothing that could show what her personality is like, or where she comes from. Nothing.

As we walk into her room, Ryland instantly lays on her bed and just as quickly, jumps to his feet. "God, she might as well just sleep on the springs," he mutters to himself, as he turns and opens the bedside drawer.

While he goes through it, I notice a shoebox under the bed and bend down to reach for it. The moment it's in my hands, I open it. Inside, there is a small amount of cash, maybe around 500 dollars, and a newspaper clipping. The paper looks old and has fold lines in it.

I squint my eyes at it, it's a photo of a church and a nun holding a baby. The title of the article is asking for information on a baby that was dropped out the front of the very church. "I wonder why she has this?" I ask, turning the clipping and showing it to Ryland.

His eyes scan the paper for a second, but he just shrugs. "Well, this was a waste of time," he mutters and opens the top drawer of the dresser.

As soon as he does, he growls in the back of his throat, making me raise an eyebrow at whatever he might have found there. Before I can question him, Ryland turns around and, in his hand, he has a pair of lace panties.

I roll my eyes at him as he dangles them in front of my face. To his dismay, I snatch the panties from his hand and place them back in the drawer. No matter how annoyed he might be, Ryland has to understand we must leave everything as Evelyn had it before we came here.

He still complains under his breath as I place the shoebox where I found it and push him out of the trailer. Then, we lock the door and leave.

"What now?" Ryland asks.

"Hungry?" I ask, and he nods.

I am getting sick of waiting and being patient. When we first saw her and the fear in her eyes, the thought of having her scared me. Now, all I can think about is her. Every waking moment of the day, she is in my thoughts, and I know it is the mate bond. But we all already decided that she will be ours, one way or another.

We let Orion go first. He is trying to get to know her and woo Evelyn, but she shows no interest in him. In fact, she has shown little interest in anyone. Orion claims she does her job and heads straight home. According to him, she has no hobbies and doesn't wander far from home or work.

Those facts just make us more curious about why she keeps her private life so hidden, even from someone who's seemingly close to her. What is she hiding or running from that not even her co-workers are aware of? Or is she really that mundane?

As we pull up out the front of the cafe, both of us look inside the windows and we instantly notice Orion, sitting on a stool at the counter. The girl, Lisa, appears very animated as she talks to him. However, I don't see Evelyn around anywhere. She must be out in the back or somewhere near; Orion wouldn't sit there if she weren't around at all.

Evelyn

The week goes by quickly. Reaching the cafe, I quickly unlock it and apologize to Lisa who is already waiting outside for me. She has a smoke between her fingers as she greets me with a smile.

She isn't the only one waiting, though. Orion is also waiting for the cafe to open as he leans against the hood of his car, looking graceful despite his enormous size. Lisa heads straight inside to turn everything on and heat the stoves along with the deep fryers.

Shoving the key in the first padlock, I unlock it, lift the roller shutters on the window, and quickly move to the next one. However, much to my annoyance, the key doesn't go in this time. The lock mechanism appears to be frozen. I jiggle the key for a few seconds, a feeble attempt to fix the mechanism without really trying. It still doesn't work, so I drop my bag off my shoulder and crouch down so I can see the lock better.

"Let me try," Orion says, suddenly standing next to me. He bends over and inspects the key. Then, he jams the key in, and it does the same. Lisa comes out to hand me my apron. I glance at Lisa and then the next moment, I hear metal hit the ground and realize the padlock is broken apart on the ground.

"Whoops," Orion drags out with a mischievous grin on his face.

I raise an eyebrow as I hold out my hand for the keys, which he places in the center of my palm. Somehow, his fingers graze my wrist, making me jump, when I feel sparks rush up my arm. I pull my hand back, eyeing him, and he has a lazy smile on his lips, which confuses me more.

Lisa's voice pulls me out of my awkwardness. "Cheap bloody locks. I have to go to the store to grab bread. Do you need anything?" she asks, looking at me.

"Yeah, can you grab me some smokes?" I tell her as I focus on rummaging through my handbag. Finally, with a smile across my lips, I hand her some cash.

Lisa takes it and leaves the cafe, walking toward the corner store.

Throwing the broken lock in the trash, I walk inside and head behind the counter. The first thing I do is turn on the coffee machine. Once it is done, I pour three coffees, one each for Lisa and myself, and then hand Orion his one. He sits at the counter, watching my every move, making me nervous.

"Must you always stare?" I ask, as I turn around to pull the cash tray out from the safe and drop it into the register.

"No harm in looking," he says.

I roll my eyes at his answer, but thankfully, Lisa is here to get him off my case. As soon as she enters the cafe, she throws the pack of smokes at me.

"When are you going to get an ID so you can buy them for yourself?" she asks.

"One day when I get a day off," I tell her.

"You are the only person I know that didn't rush to get their ID the day they turned of age. Don't you go out or anything?" she asks, pressing the subject of the lack of my ID.

"And do what?" I ask, with my back to her.

"You know, drink or party - like people our age do," she states.

"No, I prefer my own company," I tell her.

"Why?" she asks, and I suddenly wonder what it is with her questions.

Usually, we chit-chat, but not about our lives, though I know a lot about her because she isn't exactly a private person, but I am, so her questions feel a little off to me. Like she is prying too deep into territory which isn't her business.

"Because I don't like people," I tell her, and she pretends to be offended.

"You don't like me?" Lisa gasps, sarcastically, placing her hand over her heart.

"No, you're different. I know you," I tell her.

"Then explain. Your answer makes no sense," she says, as she places her hand on the counter and stares at me. I notice that Orion has eavesdropped on our conversation and is waiting for my response.

"It's just easier that way. It's pointless to make friends for them to disappoint you when they walk out on you."

"Well, that's depressing," she states.

"No, it's the truth. Everyone leaves. Eventually, they realize you have nothing more to offer," I tell her and stop explaining myself once I notice someone else walking in.

For the sake of killing this rather odd interrogation, I focus on work and walk over to the newcomer to serve him. I can hear Lisa happily chatting to Orion behind me, and I quickly jot down the man's order before handing it to Lisa. I watch as she darts out the back to start cooking while I bring him his coffee.

I find Orion following me around while I do things. "Don't you have a job or something? Why are you hanging around here so much?" I ask, as I walk outside to have a smoke.

"Lisa doesn't seem to mind?" he says, crossing his arms across his broad chest as I sit on the milk crate, lighting my smoke.

"That's because you tip big, which leaves me wondering... Clearly, you have money, so why are you slumming it on this side of the city?"

He doesn't answer, so for a brief moment, I hope this interaction is over. However, of course, given my luck, it's far from over because Orion has questions. Of course, he does.

"Did you really mean what you said that people just disappoint you?"

"Look at the city, the world; everything has gone to shit," I mutter under my breath.

Honestly, at this point, it looks like he has landed on the wrong planet. Might as well say so because he clearly doesn't fit in this bullshit world, I call my home. Orion fails to see everything wrong with this place, wrong with the people that surround us.

"That wasn't what I asked, though," he argues.

"Then yes, I do believe that." I groan. Maybe now that he has his answer, he will leave me be.

"Why do you believe that?"

"That's none of your business, and you really shouldn't listen in on people's conversations," I snap at him. Can't he just back off? I really hate it when people think they have a place in my business.

"You have an attitude, you know that?" he says, stepping closer, making me look up at him.

"And you are in my personal space again," I tell him, standing up and flicking my smoke in the ashtray.

I am about to walk around him when his hand on my arm stops me, as he pulls me back in front of him. His face is close as he leans in; so close I feel his breath fan my lips, and I suddenly forget how to breathe. I am stunned by his manly good looks.

"Does my closeness bother you, little one?" he asks in his husky voice.

And just like that, I suddenly lose all focus as his lips move closer to mine and I see him smile, while I struggle with getting my brain to function instead of going foggy and blank. He pulls me closer, his hand sending tingles shooting up my arm, making me gasp as his other hand wraps around my waist, pulling me flush against his chest. His breath brushes my face, and I lean in, inhaling his scent.

He smells so good it makes my mouth water. I hear him chuckle and feel the sound rumble through his chest.

Suddenly, I hear Lisa's voice singing out for me, snapping me out of my daze. I step back, confused at my reaction to him, while he stands there with a sly smile. I swear I just saw his eyes darken.

FIVE

Evelyn

"Excuse me," I say, as I step around him and run back inside.

What the fuck just came over me? Lisa is frantically trying to take orders, as I quickly step in and rush past her to the kitchen where I see a heap of orders.

When Lisa is finished, she comes back and helps me cook while we keep an eye on the door. Orion just sits in the corner, watching. Always watching. His presence doesn't bother me as it did the first few days he was here. But these days, he has pretty much become a piece of furniture.

After serving everyone, I grab my tray to clean the tables. I just finish stacking the tray and am about to head out the back when I hear the doorbell chime. Lifting the tray, I turn to see who enters.

Two men enter the cafe, looking around before their eyes fall on me. A loud gasp leaves me, as panic surges through my entire being. My heart rate speeds up until I can hear it pulsating in my ears, and my hands start to tremble. I feel clammy as adrenaline pulses through me, paralyzing me, until I hear Lisa scream and realize I have dropped the tray of plates I was holding as they smash around my feet. The noise makes me flinch as my gaze drops. Lisa rushes out with a towel, and I drop down, scooping the glass up with shaking hands.

"Shit, Evelyn, you, okay?" she asks, but I feel nothing but fear, too scared to answer. "Evelyn, stop. You're cutting your hands," she says, making me look at my hands, which are bleeding from the glass cutting my fingers and palm.

I don't even feel it, but I can hear my breathing coming quickly as I start to hyperventilate. The room and everyone in it are watching with worried eyes as the cafe trembles around me. I realize I am having a panic attack as everything slows down, except for the erratic pumping of my heart.

It is them, the men that killed him in the alleyway. I feel Orion move near me; he takes the tray from my hands. Lisa rushes out the back, but I am frozen in place, paralyzed by fear. I feel Lisa grip my arms, pulling me to my feet and taking me out the back. Orion follows us into the kitchen.

Lisa rummages through my bag as I try to find my grounding place and remember what I need to do to ground myself, yet my mind goes blank. Lisa opens my bloody hand and drops two pills on my palm as she hands me a glass of water. I quickly swallow the pills.

"What are they?" I hear Orion ask her.

"Valium. She has panic attacks sometimes," Lisa explains.

After a few minutes, my heart rate returns to normal, and my body relaxes. Lisa quickly rushes around the kitchen while I gather my bearings and look down at my hand, which has a tea towel wrapped tightly around it. I peel it off as I approach the sink and force my hand under the stream of water. As soon as the water splashes over the cut, I wince at the sting, but ignore it to the best of my ability. Then, I reach for the first aid kit and wrap my hand.

When I go back out, Orion follows, and my eyes fall on the two men, watching me. I close my eyes, willing myself to hold it together.

However, my shock only grows when I open my eyes again and see Orion sitting down at the table with them. I also notice that everyone else is gone.

Lisa comes out behind me. "Where did everyone go?" she asks, placing her hand on my shoulder. I shrug, not able to take my eyes off the three people sitting in the booth. Lisa follows my gaze and then looks back at me. "You okay, Evelyn?" I nod but say nothing. "How about you go home? I can call Miranda and ask if she would come. I know she is looking for work again; the last place she was at shut down. So, go, I will be fine on my own."

I look at her and I can tell it worries her. I haven't had a panic attack in ages, so it is a little out of character for me.

"Go. I will be fine," she says, handing my bag to me.

I nod wordlessly and take off out the door. As I walk home, my mind is stuck in some weird overdrive. I can't help but wonder if they recognized me, wonder how Orion knows them.

When I get home, I flop on my bed and close my eyes. After a few deep breaths, I open them, just in time to hear a knock on the door. I hesitantly peek out the window and find Orion at the door. I groan as I walk over and unlock the door.

"How do you know where I live?"

"Lisa." He shrugs, as he leans against the handrail, watching me. "Are you going to invite me in, or do I need to stand out here and freeze?" he asks, and I step aside, opening the door wider.

Orion walks in but has to duck his head to stop from hitting it on the doorframe. I stand awkwardly, unaware of what to say. To be honest, I have never brought anyone here, let alone had someone show up here out of the blue.

"What do you want?" I ask, folding my arms across my chest.

"I wanted to make sure you're okay," he says, facing me after looking around.

"I'm fine; you can go now," I tell him.

Orion raises an eyebrow and steps closer to me. I, in turn, step back. "I will not do anything," he says, reaching for me and pulling me to him. I feel my heart race at his proximity, so I shove him back, and he looks shocked. I see hurt in his eyes which I find odd - I barely know him.

"How do you know those two men that came into the cafe?"

"They're my mates. Why?"

I shake my head. "You have friends like that?" I ask.

Orion seems gentle, yet I can tell he has a mean streak. "My idea of mates and your idea are two different things. And what do you mean, like that?" he asks defensively, crossing his arm across his chest.

"They…" I can't finish what I should say. The last thing I need or want is to remember that horrid night.

"They what, Evelyn?" Orion asks, stepping closer.

"It doesn't matter; you need to leave," I tell him and open the door.

He looks at me, but he doesn't move. I suddenly hear someone walk up the steps out the front, and my eyes dart outside before I feel my breath catch in my throat. I stumble back, terrified, as I watch the two men from the alley walk up the steps and step inside my trailer. I'm about to run to the back when I feel hands around my waist and realize Orion has grabbed me.

"Calm down, Evelyn; they won't hurt you," he says.

I ignore him, knowing exactly what those monsters are capable of as I struggle against him, but his hold doesn't loosen. I bite into his hand, making him release me, and I run to the bathroom, quickly locking the door as soon as I close it behind me.

Orion's voice calls out on the other side of the door. "Open the door, Evelyn," he says, as I search the bathroom and my eyes focus on the small window.

In a moment of pure panic, the need to get out of here takes over, so I raise the window slowly, ensuring I'm quiet until I lift it enough to climb out. Halfway through the small window, I feel hands on my hips, and I'm ripped back inside.

I open my mouth and belt out the loudest scream I can muster, but someone forces their hand over my mouth to silence me.

"Shh, we won't hurt you," says a voice below my ear. "If I remove my hand, do you promise not to scream?" he asks, and I feel tears burn my eyes. The tears burn my skin as they spill over and run down my cheeks.

They are going to kill me; I should have run and left the city that night. And yet, I nod my head, and he removes his hand. As soon as he does, I scream as loud as I can. A loud growl tears out of him as the stranger clamps his hand back over my mouth.

"Put her in the car," calls a voice from the door, and I see his handsome face as he looks inside the bathroom. His silver eyes are dazzling and hypnotic as he stares at me.

The man walks me out of the bathroom, and I see Orion sitting calmly at the table. "They won't hurt you. I promise. We will explain when we get you home."

Home? What do they mean by home? Where are they going to take me?

I start to thrash against my captor, but he is stronger. My thrashing only annoys him as I feel his breath on my neck.

"We can do this the hard way or the easy way," he says. Panic courses through me as I drop my weight and go limp to try and slip out of his grip. "Hard way it is then," he says as he grips my ankle.

I kick my legs, my foot connects with his face, and he grunts as he rips me toward him and grips my arms. The man pulls me to my feet and wraps his arm around me, holding me in place against his chest. I hit and scratch at whatever I can. He rips my head to the side, and I scream as I feel him bite into my neck. My scream dies in my throat as black dots dance before my vision, and everything around us becomes dull. I try to force my eyes open as I feel them start to droop. What did he just do to me? My last thoughts fade as darkness envelops me.

Evelyn

Groaning, I sit up. My hand instantly goes to my head as I feel a migraine coming on. Man, I had the strangest dream. I rub my eyes and look around my room. Only... it isn't my room. The startling reality of my dream comes back to me, and I realize it wasn't a dream.

"'Bout time you woke up. You have been asleep for hours," says a voice behind me.

I spin around on the bed and come face to face with inhuman black eyes, watching me. Panic grips me as I throw myself off the bed, my heart pounding against my ribs. The man walks around the bed towards me, and the door opens, making my eyes dart to it. In walks the other man from the alleyway.

"Stay away from me," I tell them, trying to find an escape with my hands out.

My neck is searing with pain when I turn my head to look for a window. My hand goes to my neck, and I feel blood staining my fingers. The man with hypnotic green eyes leans against the doorframe, watching, and I suddenly feel trapped and claustrophobic. I back up, only to come in contact with a dresser; the objects on the top rattle and something falls off.

"I am Thaddeus, that is Ryland, and we mean you no harm," says the man leaning on the door.

"You bit me," I say, looking at the man with black eyes. His chest is bare, and I can't stop my eyes from wandering down his chest to his abs and v-line as it escapes into the waistband of his pants. The man clears his throat and I shake my head, snapping myself out of the weird daze that comes over me.

"You done checking me out?" he asks, raising an eyebrow at me.

I feel my face heat as a blush spreads across my cheeks. "I wasn't," I stutter, and he moves toward me.

That very moment, panic seizes me. I have no idea where I am, what to do, or where to run, so I take the most logical route at hand - I run toward the door in the room's corner. As soon as I reach it, I throw it open and run through it. When I realize it is a closet and not a bathroom with a window to use as an escape, I curse under my breath.

I hear a knock on the door and soon after, comes the man's amused voice on the other side of the door.

"Knock, knock," he says, and I feel panic grip me.

Looking around the walk-in, I find nothing useful to aid in my escape. I notice a metal bar with clothes hung on it and yank it, ripping it from its braces. The clothes slide off and land softly on the floor. Backing up, I face the door.

He knocks again, and my heart skips a beat as I watch the door handle twist. I swing the bar when it opens, aiming for his head, but hit his shoulder. He grips the bar, yanking me towards him, and I bring my knee up, hitting him between the legs.

He groans, clutching his now aching balls. I grab the pole and dart past him, only for him to catch my ankle. I fall face-first onto the carpet with a soft thud, knocking the air from my lungs. The other man is watching from the door, amused, which angers me as I roll on my back.

The man's grip on my ankle tightens as he drags me toward him, and I raise my other foot, kicking him in the chest. He reaches out, snaring my other foot in his vice-like grip, holding it to the floor before shoving my legs apart and pressing his body between my thighs.

"Keep fighting. I love it when they struggle," he says, and I feel his erection press into me. Lifting my head, I headbutt him, instantly regretting it as my head throbs, realizing I hurt myself more than him. His lip is bleeding while I feel like I just head-butted a brick wall.

"She is a feisty little one," he mutters, wiping his lip, while I continue to struggle against him.

I see Orion walk in, pushing past the man standing at the door watching the scene in front of him unfold.

"What are you doing? Get off her," he says, shoving his shoulder.

"Well, fucking help, then. Where have you been anyway?" the man asks Orion.

The man hops off me and I scramble to sit up when Orion grabs my face. I feel fog slip over me, but I try to shake it off.

"Don't be scared. We won't hurt you," he says, as I feel a wave of ease rush over me; all fear leaves me as I look at his dazzling eyes, hypnotized by his words. He lets go of my face, and I lean back, his face searching mine.

"This is Ryland, and he is Thaddeus. They won't hurt you, Evelyn," he says, pointing between both men. Thaddeus moves closer, sitting on the end of the bed where I woke up. Ryland stands up, staring down at me.

"Why am I here? And you bit me."

"I didn't bite you; I marked you. Well, I suppose they are actually the same thing," Ryland says in his husky voice, making me shiver.

He smirks and holds his hand to help me up, but I ignore it. Getting up myself, I step away from him.

"Marked me?" I say, trying to process his words. I have heard the term before.

Everyone found out about shifters after the world turned to shit. Dark creatures revealed themselves for the first time. They made the world realize exactly what was lurking in the shadows. That was when the stories people told around campfires suddenly became a reality.

"Yes. You belong to us now," he says, and I shake my head.

"I want to go home. Take me home, Orion," I tell him, and he looks at me with nothing but sadness in his eyes.

"You won't be going home, Evelyn. You belong with us now." He repeats the same words I don't want to hear; the same words I refuse to believe.

"No, I belong at home," I tell him, walking past them, only for Thaddeus to get up from the bed and block my exit. I feel something strange wash over me, and I fight the urge to shiver as dread consumes me.

Something is seriously off about him. Even with Orion saying I shouldn't fear them, something about Thaddeus has me on edge. The negative energy coming off him in waves makes me want to run. My blood turns ice cold in my veins as he looks down at me. He is tall and very broad, I only come up to the center of his chest. There is something really bad about him; something evil, dark, and twisted.

He reaches his hand up, cupping my cheek, and his thumb brushes my lips. I feel a shiver run up my spine and sparks rush over my skin. It is unsettling, and I don't know if I want to cringe away or lean into his hand.

"You're not leaving. I can't let you go now," he says, making me look up at him.

His eyes watch me with a hunger I have never seen before, a cross between wanting to rip me apart and feast on my blood, or something all-consuming. Either way, I don't like the idea. I try to move around him when his hand moves to my arm, gripping it tightly, and fear rushes through me at the tightness of his grip.

"I said you're not leaving. It would be in your best interest not to provoke me," he says, his tone emotionless and cold as I try to walk out of the room.

"Thaddeus?" Orion snaps, making me look at him.

I find both Ryland and Orion looking at Thaddeus with worried expressions. My eyes move to his and I gasp at what I see. His eyes are completely black. It feels like I am staring into the eyes of a demon. Black veins ripple under his eyes and down his cheeks. The air leaves my lungs, and my throat restricts when I notice the fangs protruding from beneath his top and bottom lips. My entire body trembles in fear as he looks down at me, and I take a step back. My stomach turns upside down, and the thought of throwing up becomes a real possibility as I feel fear knot my stomach and goose-bumps raise on my skin. Fear makes me step back away from him. But he steps closer like a predator, ready to pounce. Suddenly, the lights flicker, and my pulse rises.

"Thaddeus, get a grip of yourself," Ryland's voice rings out in the darkness.

"You're him, aren't you?" I whisper, suddenly realizing I'm not just in the presence of shifters, but the Dark Ones. The men responsible for destroying the world, destroying lives.

He chuckles, and I feel my hair stand on end. "And who is that?" His voice is coldly calm.

"The Dark King," I stutter.

Something in me snaps me out of my fear. As adrenaline runs through me, I run, taking off out the door. I am desperately looking for an exit, a way out of this maze of a place. I see a door and run for it, my feet hitting the tiled floor in panic. As I reach for the handle, I find myself spun around and pinned against the door.

Thaddeus' hand wraps around my throat as he presses himself extremely close. His entire body is pressed against mine as his head drops to my neck. He inhales deeply, running his nose from my shoulder to my jaw.

"The things I want to do to you. The things I will do to you," he says with a groan.

Tears brim in my eyes as they start burning. I notice Orion and Ryland behind him, walking toward us. "Orion," I gasp.

Both of them step on either side of him and I watch as Thaddeus reacts to their touch and his eyes go to his shoulder where Ryland's hand rests. I feel a hand press between our bodies, and I feel Orion grab Thaddeus' crotch, and Thaddeus presses himself against me and into his hand.

"Focus on me, Thaddeus; you don't want to hurt her," Orion whispers to him, before pressing his chest into Thaddeus's back. Thaddeus leans back into him as his hand slips from my throat to my chest.

Knowing if I move, he may kill me, I freeze, as his hand cups my breast through my shirt, squeezing and palming it.

"I want her," he growls, but it almost sounds like a purr leaving his lips.

"You will have her, but you need to let her go," Orion tells him. I shiver at his words, and Thaddeus' eyes dart to mine like bottomless pits. I can't tear my eyes from his as they swallow me whole. "She isn't going anywhere, Thaddeus. Focus on me," Orion tells him.

"She is trying to leave me." He groans, as I feel Orion's hand between us, rubbing him harder, and I can feel his enormous length against my stomach. Ryland's hand runs over his chest, and Thaddeus moans at their touch. I can't stop the arousal that spreads through me as I watch them touch him.

"You're not leaving, are you, Evelyn?" My eyes snap to Ryland at his words, and I see he is trying to warn me to agree with him.

"No, I will stay," I gasp out, my heart thumping in my chest erratically at his warning. Thaddeus groans before moving closer, his lips crash against mine hungrily as he devours my lips, forcing his tongue into my mouth. I freeze, letting him have the control he wants as I fight the urge to shove him off and away from me.

His kiss is demanding, and his hand snakes into my hair as he tangles his fingers and yanks my head back. His lips move down my jaw to my neck, and I look to Orion helplessly as Thaddeus assaults my skin with his lips. Ryland tugs his face away from me, kissing him passionately with the same desire Thaddeus has. Thaddeus lets me go and steps away, all but attacking him as Ryland pulls him away from me. Orion tugs me to him, and I follow him; anything to get away from that beast of a man.

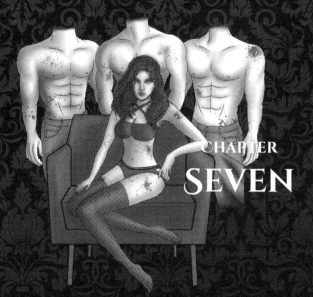

CHAPTER
SEVEN

Evelyn
    Orion leads me through the place and past a lounge room. Then, we enter the kitchen, and he walks me to a sliding door. He slides it open, and I am blasted by the cold, crisp air of the night. Stepping onto the balcony, Orion points to some chairs. I sit on one, peering over the side. I see we are very high up; the lights below look like fairy lights against the snow-covered rooftops.

"Don't ever run from him. Thaddeus is more predator than human," Orion says, making my eyes snap from the view to him. I watch as he lights up a smoke, and my mouth falls open. He lectures me every time he follows me out for a smoke at work. He chuckles softly, "What?"

I raise an eyebrow at him, and he passes the packet to me, and I pull one out. Orion flicks the lighter, cupping the flame so I can light my smoke. "Such a bad habit; you really shouldn't smoke," he says, his lips turning up slightly.

"You smoke," I tell him.

"I'm immortal; it can't kill me," he says. Oddly, he sounds sad. Or at least the way he says those words makes him sound sad.

"What's Thaddeus' deal?" I ask, looking anywhere but at him.

"He hasn't got good control. Don't run from him again like that. I know you're scared, but we really won't hurt you. Not intentionally, anyway." He sounds somewhat distant as he speaks.

"Why am I here?"

Orion looks at me, his eyes softening and twinkling in the light. "You know about shifters?" he asks.

I nod. I kind of do, about as much as anyone else.

"Well, all supernatural creatures have mates; you're ours," he says.

"What does that mean?" I raise an eyebrow. How can I be theirs? I don't want to belong to the Dark Ones.

"You are ours, and we are yours. We are bound together," Orion explains, too calmly for my liking.

I shake my head when something rushes over me, making me gasp. Orion's eyes watch my face, a seductive smile on his full lips.

"You feel that?" he asks, and I nod. A moan escapes my lips, and I clamp my hand over my mouth. Arousal floods into me. "The mark on your neck makes you feel his emotions. It will get stronger. Eventually, you will go into what we call heat."

"Heat?"

"Means you will want to have sex with him." I choke on my smoke, coughing at his words. He chuckles. "Don't panic. Not yet, but once we all mark you. You will still feel what he feels, and he can feel us, so in return, you're picking up on both of them," he says casually.

I just nod, not understanding. I'm not sure how long I sit on the balcony before eventually, I fall asleep, only to be awoken by Orion as he places me on the couch inside. My eyes flutter open to him leaning over me. "Go back to sleep. I will be back soon."

"Don't leave me here with them." I sit up in a panic, looking around. Orion, noticing my panic, stops and sighs. Why does he have to sound so disappointed? They kidnapped me from my home, one of his mates attacked me, of course I'm fucking scared.

"I'm just going to have a shower. They're asleep; they won't hurt you, Evelyn," he says, brushing my cheek with his hand. I nod and watch as he leaves, walking into the bathroom.

I sit there for a few minutes, waiting for him to return, when a thought hits me. If they are asleep and Orion is distracted, this is my chance to escape. I look around for my shoes and find them next to the couch.

My heart is pounding, my body buzzing with adrenaline at the thought of escaping them. Getting up, I walk to the bathroom door and can hear the shower running still. Quietly walking up the hall-way, I find the front door and open it. The door creaks, and my breath hitches, getting caught in my throat. I look down the hall to see if anyone is coming. I pull the door open more, when suddenly, a hand hits the door right beside my face, closing the door.

"Where do you think you're going?" His voice is next to my ear as he leans down, his chest pressing into my back. I gulp, my heart pounding in my chest.

Turning around, I come face to face with Thaddeus. His green eyes watch me as they sparkle brightly, flickering oddly between green and black. "Were you trying to leave me, Evelyn?" he asks. A cold shiver instantly runs up my spine as he presses me against the now-closed door.

I shake my head, words failing me. Thaddeus' hand moves, brushing my cheek softly before gripping my face. "I would hate to see you get hurt because you disobeyed me," he says, watching my face closely. He then straightens up before stepping aside, motioning for me to walk back down the hallway with his hand. He waits for me to move and follows close behind me.

I can feel his eyes roaming over me, and I fight the urge to run. When we get back to the room, I see the bathroom door open. I quickly step inside, preferring to be in Orion's company rather than Thaddeus'.

I lock the door and step back into the bathroom, my eyes don't leave the door as I wonder if he will come in after me. When he doesn't, I turn around and quickly avert my gaze as I see Orion standing in the shower.

"Looking for me, little one? Care to join me?" he asks, making me look at him.

He has a smirk as my eyes roam down his toned body. A blush creeps onto my face as my eyes catch a glimpse of what sits between his legs, making me look away. I shake my head as I sit on the sink basin.

"So why have you invaded my shower if you don't want to join me?"

"Thaddeus," I tell him.

"Argh. Let me guess; you tried to leave." I nod and suddenly, I hear the shower turn off.

Orion opens the glass door, reaches out, and grabs the towel next to me on the sink. He wraps the towel around his waist and stands there for a second, then pushes my legs open to stand between them, making me look at him.

"You're safe here, Evelyn. You don't need to run. Thaddeus isn't so bad once you get to know him," he says.

"He destroyed the world. How can you say that? He has killed innocent people, Orion," I snap back.

Orion sighs. Before he can say anything, the door handle twists and snaps off, landing on the tiled floor with a loud clunking noise. Thaddeus steps in and leans on the door as if he has no worry in the world. I hold my breath as his eyes watch us and the position, we are standing in.

"We will be leaving in the morning. You should get some sleep before sunrise," he says, watching me. He looks at Orion, his eyes roaming over his mate's body, and I can see the lust in his eyes. Is he insatiable? He has spent all night in the room with Ryland. Orion steps back, grabbing my hand, pulling me off the sink. Thaddeus doesn't move from the doorway; he just turns so we can walk past. Orion tugs me toward their room, and I stop. Thaddeus runs into my back, nearly knocking me over.

"What's wrong?" Orion asks when I refuse to go any further.

"I'm not sleeping in there with them." I hear Thaddeus growl. It is a guttural sound, primal. My hair stands on end, and I shiver.

"You will be sleeping in the room, Evelyn. I won't have you trying to run off again," Thaddeus says, pushing me toward the door.

"No, no, please, I won't run," I tell him as he drags me into the room.

Orion puts on a pair of pants. He then walks over to Thaddeus and places his hand on his shoulder. "Let her sleep in the living room. I will watch her," he says, reassuring Thaddeus.

Thaddeus eyes me for a moment and finally lets me go. "If she escapes, I will hold you responsible," he warns, and Orion nods. After the rather tense moment, Orion drags me out of the room.

"What time is it anyway?"

"A little after two. Go hop on the couch; I will get you a blanket and pillow."

I walk over to the couch and flop down on it. Orion walks out, putting a comforter over me and handing me a pillow. I feel a fog roll over me as Orion sits on the couch, flicking the TV on. He scrolls through the channels until he finally sets on some movie in a foreign language.

"Sleep. I won't leave, I promise," he says, placing my feet on his lap and covering them with the blanket. My mind gets foggy and my eyelids heavy as I feel exhaustion wash over me. My eyes close, and I am plunged into the darkness of sleep.

Thaddeus

When the sun rises, I am awoken by Ryland, moving in his sleep, his hand reaching out for me. Sitting up, I rub my eyes. I can hear Orion rustling around in the kitchen. Throwing the blanket off, I open the bedroom door.

Orion puts his finger to his lips, making me look over at the couch. I can see Evelyn still fast asleep with the comforter wrapped around her. Slowly, I approach the couch, bend down, lifting her head to sit down, and remove her pillow.

Her scent is making my mouth water, and longing fills me. I just want to hold her, yet doing that scares me. Evelyn is so fragile, and sometimes I forget she is merely a human. I can practically smell her humanity.

At first, I had my doubts that she was human. Never in history has a human being mated to a supernatural being, yet here she is, living proof that nothing is impossible.

I listen to her breathing and heart rate, brushing her hair from her face, and she turns to roll in her sleep, her face rubbing my crotch. I try to shift, but she continues to move, trying to get comfortable. My dick is hardening as it twitches under her. This delicate little thing does not know the effect she has on me, even while sleeping.

Orion walks over, leaning over the back of the couch to check on her. Looking up, he kisses me softly. "You won't break her. She isn't as fragile as she looks, Thaddeus," he tells me, and I nod, looking back down at her.

Leaning down, I inhale her scent; she shifts, her eyes flutter open, and I find myself lost in her hazel eyes, mesmerized by them. I hear her heart rate rise, the blood pulse through her veins, and practically see the cogs turning in her head.

She sits up, alarm on her face, but she can't pull her eyes from mine, like she is unsure if she should run or freeze. Ryland walks out, snapping her attention to him.

I know he woke up from feeling her fear. She will feel the bond they are forming slightly, while he feels her completely, and I can feel her fear through him.

"I won't hurt you. I just wanted to be near you," I tell her.

She looks at me curiously. I watch as she gets up, instantly missing her contact. She walks over to Orion and I feel jealousy surge through me.

I understand she has been around him more, used to his presence in a way. Yet it doesn't stop me from feeling anger at him. Orion hands me a plate, raising an eyebrow, and I shake my head, shaking off the feeling that comes over me.

Getting up, I sit at the table next to her, and she instantly tries to get up. It angers me how she doesn't want to be near me. I grip her wrist, making Ryland and Orion stare as she sits back down. Orion, watching her, gives her a nod and slides her plate in front of her.

"Eat," I tell her. Evelyn picks up the fork, pushing her food around but not eating it. I can feel darkness clouding me, telling me to force her, feel it licking my skin, urging me to make her submit to my demands.

"If you're not hungry, why don't you have a shower," Orion says, his eyes not leaving mine.

I instinctually go to rip her back down when Ryland reaches over the table, grabbing my wrist. The alarm in her eyes entices me, and I know she can feel my aura giving off a deadly vibe.

Forcing the darkness down, I speak through clenched teeth. "Go," I tell her, and she moves quickly, darting into the room.

Ryland waits a few seconds before letting my wrist go. He sits down and I spear a piece of tomato with my fork, not realizing how much force I use as the plate splits in two. I shove the plate away, get up, and toss the broken pieces in the sink.

"Here, I will make some more," Orion says, about to hand me his plate. I shake my head, walking toward the bedroom.

Ryland stands, making me look at him. "Thaddeus, you will only scare her more," he says.

"I don't care," I tell him, walking off. I just want to touch her, feel her soft skin under my hands.

"Thaddeus," Orion warns me as I open the door.

Walking over to the ensuite, I turn the knob, but it is locked. Just like yesterday, I twist the knob until it falls apart in my hand. The door opens slightly, her scent wafts to my nose. I can't help the growl that escapes my lips, as I push the door open and step inside the bathroom.

Her scream resonates and echoes through the bathroom when she notices me watching her. She turns her back to me, trying to shield herself from my eyes. I notice a large burn on her back that runs from her shoulder to her hip.

"Orion!" she screams, her heart pounding in her chest so hard I worry she might give herself a heart attack. I just need to touch her, just touch her. In a trance, I open the shower door.

Orion steps into the bathroom and leans against the door. "Thaddeus," he growls, and I growl back at him. I feel the darkness creep in as rage bubbles in my veins. How dare he tell me I can't have what's mine?

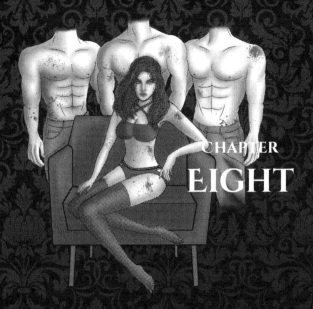

EIGHT

E velyn
    Escaping the dining room, I have only been in the shower for a few minutes when I hear the bathroom door's handle snap and fall to the floor. My heart skips a beat when I look over my shoulder and see Thaddeus standing in the doorway. His sudden appearance makes me scream in fright.

I watch as his chest rises and falls heavily with each breath he takes. A growl escapes his lips, and a look of pure desire graces his face. Fear consumes me as his eyes glaze over, turning pitch black. His fangs protrude, forcing his lips to part. Trying to cover myself as best I can, I keep my back to him. Thaddeus walks in, reaching for the handle on the shower.

"Orion!" I scream out to him, hoping he will make him go away.

Orion steps in, leaning on the doorframe, a bored look on his face. "Thaddeus," he calls to him, and I watch, horrified, as Thaddeus snarls, his face distorting in anger as he turns to Orion.

Orion straightens up just as Thaddeus lunges at him. My scream echoes and bounces off the tiled walls as I frantically turn the water off. I can hear fighting and things getting broken. Grabbing my towel, I wrap it around myself before stepping into the bedroom.

Thaddeus has Orion on the ground, but Orion shoves him off. Ryland walks in and pinches the bridge of his nose. I look to Ryland, but he just shrugs, and I can tell he isn't going to help Orion.

I watch as Thaddeus punches Orion and somehow flings him into the dresser. Orion shakes himself off, getting to his feet when the lights flicker. My heart hammers in my chest and I find it hard to breathe as I watch them fight each other.

Thaddeus kicks Orion, and he smashes through the wall. Orion doesn't even have a chance to get up before Thaddeus stalks toward him. Rushing forward, I grip Thaddeus' arm, trying to stop him when he shoves me away, making me fall onto the carpet at the end of the bed. My body hits the floor with a soft thump.

I gasp and see Ryland move to help me up when Thaddeus' eyes snap to mine. His entire body turns as he reaches down, grabbing my ankle. I kick at him as I try to scramble backward, clutching my towel to me. Thaddeus growls, and I look to Ryland for help, but he just stands there, confusing me. Out of nowhere, Thaddeus lunges at me. I try to shove him off, and he growls low, making my hair stand on end. His face is in the crook of my neck as he inhales.

When he pulls his face back, I see my reflection mirrored in his demonic eyes. Fear floods into me as I see Orion stand. I scoot back on my hands, but Thaddeus just stalks me, following me. He then knocks me flat on my back, his hands clawing at my towel as his lips and tongue move to my neck. I try to shove him off.

Panic consumes me as I watch Orion and Ryland step closer. They do nothing but watch as he pulls me around like a puppet on strings, forcing my hands above my head. I watch as he lifts his head, as his nose runs across my cheek. I feel my breath get caught in my throat when I realize he isn't a man at this moment but the monster lurking beneath the surface. The monster everyone fears, The Dark King.

I can feel my heart pumping blood around my body and hear my pulse in my ears as he leans his weight on me. Tears brim in my eyes as I watch, horrified, as his fangs graze my lips, and I feel my blood trickle down my chin. When he drops his head into my neck, I know he will bite me.

My heart thumps against my chest erratically, and I struggle against his hold on my hands before dropping my face, trying to shield him from my neck when he growls.

"Orion, please," I plead with him to help.

I see how he tries to step forward, but Ryland's hand stops him. "Leave her," he tells him, making my blood run cold. Why won't they help?

I struggle against Thaddeus, but his grip gets stronger as he tugs my towel down until he can palm my breast. His hold is so tight, so rough, it's painful. I cry out when he squeezes it. I feel his fingers bruise my skin. I try to free my hands that are trapped in one of his. Thaddeus' face is leaning closer, his eyes don't leave my neck, and I can tell he wants to feed on me.

He is gone, too far gone; at this moment, everything that makes him part human is gone. His growl is feral, and I see Orion hesitate, but Ryland's hand grips his wrist, tugging him back.

"She needs to learn," Ryland says, making my eyebrows furrow.

Learn what? How to fucking die? I think I am a master at near-death experiences.

Thaddeus watches me curiously, his head tilting to the side as he examines my face like he is trying to remember who I am and what I am to him. His eyes flicker oddly between their hypnotic green and the black orbs.

My eyes dart to his razor-sharp fangs so close to my face, making me wonder if dying will hurt when he sinks them into me. Adrenaline courses through me. I watch as he sniffs the air, closing his eyes and relishing my scent, and I do the only thing I can in the position I am in, completely at his mercy.

I kiss him.

His fangs slice through the skin on my lips. He freezes for a second, and I can practically see the wheels turning in his head, trying to decide if he wants to kill me or take me.

I am about to pull back from him, unsure, when his hand grips my hair tightly, making me scream at his viciousness. His tongue plunges into my mouth, swallowing my scream as he hungrily devours my lips, pushing himself between my legs.

His hand grips my hips, and his nails bite into my flesh painfully as he continues his brutal assault on my lips before finally letting me catch my breath. His lips move to my chin, and I suck in much-needed air. His lips bite and suck on my flesh savagely as he uses his hand to tug my towel down, exposing my breast before he bites into it.

Tears brim in my eyes and fall down my face as I try to get him to loosen his grip, his nails cut into me everywhere he grabs me, his fangs graze my ribs as he hungrily devours my skin.

The pain becomes too much, and I know I am covered in bite marks and am bleeding onto the carpet. I feel his fangs sink into my other breast, and I gasp, choking on air at the searing pain.

"Please stop! You're hurting me, Thaddeus," I choke out, and he freezes again.

My hand shakily touches his face, pulling it away from my chest. He looks at me as if it's the first time he has noticed me. Really noticed what he is doing to me. He sits up on his elbows and looks over my body, and I can see the fear in his eyes at what he has just done. His hand goes to the bite mark on the top of my breast, and I wince when his fingertips brush it, making his eyes dart to mine.

"I'm sorry. I... I..." He doesn't finish, just gets up and looks down at me as I clutch the towel, trying to wrap it around me and cover myself. He then turns on his heel and leaves the room.

Ryland and Orion watch me as I sit up. Orion offers me his hand, and I slap it away. "Why didn't you help me?" I ask, feeling tears run down my cheeks. My skin is stinging, and I can feel blood running down my thigh from my hips as I stand up. Orion looks hurt by my words, but then, he turns and glares at Ryland.

R yland

Helping her will just frighten her and cause more damage. Plus, she could get hurt in the process.

Orion, I can tell, isn't forgiving of what I just did, leaving her at his mercy. She is terrified of him, and she has a good reason. Thaddeus is more a monster than a man. More instinctual and runs purely off of emotions.

Evelyn needs to learn that her fear only entices him and makes him crave her like a drug. She doesn't realize how much her fear perfumes the room; how strong her scent becomes when she is in this state. Some may think what I'm doing is cruel, but she needs to realize that she needs to control her emotions when being around Thaddeus.

We wouldn't let him rape her, I would step in if he tried. We can both see he is hurting her, but I want to see if she can rein him in and bring him back from the darkness that holds him.

Orion and I have tried for decades to help him remain in control, both of us already gave up hope of taming him. I want to help him become a better man, but the lifestyle, I must admit, is addictive, taking what you want when you want it.

Orion never agreed, but to me, it is just easier than putting up with his wrath. I know Thaddeus loves us in his way, as much as the Dark Tribrid can.

However, I can feel him fighting himself more with Evelyn, trying more with her. She just sees him as a monster. If she knew him before we saw her, she would be right in thinking that, but he is always holding himself back with her, even if it doesn't seem like it. Trying to be what she wants so she doesn't fear him.

Anyone else, he would have just fucked them and ripped them to pieces when he was done, or drained them. Humans are mere toys to him, something to fulfill his needs and a food source, but he struggles not to take what he wants with her.

A struggle it is, but at least he is struggling. If she weren't our mate, she would be dead already, and the fact she is ours gives me hope that there is still a part of him clinging to the shred of humanity he has left.

When Evelyn cries out that he is hurting her, I watch his back tense. I can feel him trying to bring himself back at the sound of her voice; he sits up as if a switch has been flipped.

As he looks down at her battered and bruised body, his guilt hits me like a ton of bricks. I watch as he stutters over his words, and in the thirty-seven years I have been with him, I have never seen him try to apologize to someone, let alone ever felt guilt or fear through the bond from his actions.

Even when he hurts us, he never apologizes, just becomes angered. Evelyn has brought back emotions I have never felt from him before. Emotions that I know Thaddeus sees as weakness. The merciless monster feels something that neither Orion nor I could extract from him.

Decades we tried and failed; she has been with us for just over twenty-four hours and got more emotion out of him than we ever have. She may think he is a monster, may fear him, but little does she know, she will have him wrapped around her fingers in no time. She has the power to change him, and witnessing this moment gives me hope. He isn't gone completely, isn't lost to the darkness; maybe he can be saved. Maybe she can be the one that saves him.

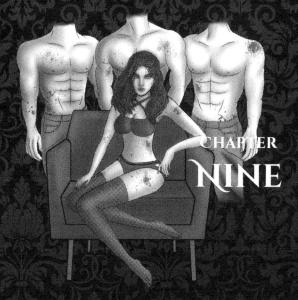

CHAPTER
NINE

E velyn

"Why didn't you help me? You just stood there and watched!" I yell at Orion.

"Stop getting your knickers in a twist, love. You needed to learn," Ryland tells me, making me glare in his direction.

"Learn what? That doesn't make any sense!" I scream at him, and turn my back on him before he can answer the damn question. As fast as my body can move, I walk back into the bathroom and grab my clothes off the counter.

I am about to pull off the towel to get dressed when Orion walks in, handing me some clothes. They still have the tags on them, making me question when he had the time to buy them.

"Get dressed. We will be leaving soon; Thaddeus wants to get on the road."

"I am not going anywhere with any of you," I tell him, taking the clothes from him.

"You keep thinking we are giving you a choice. It's not a choice," Ryland adds, walking into the bathroom. "We need to leave, so we are leaving."

"Whatever. Just get out so I can get dressed," I tell him, shutting the door in his face.

The only problem is that now that the door doesn't have a handle and lock, it remains slightly open. Sorting through the clothes, I find a pair of lace underwear and a bra. Picking up the thin strip of fabric, I groan. Argh, these are going to itch.

I hear Orion from the other side of the door. "What's wrong?"

"Really? Lace? You couldn't have got normal underwear?"

"They looked nice. Don't girls like pretty things?" he asks. His tone sounds amused.

I huff, annoyed as I put them on, trying to pull the lace down that is now riding up my ass. Pulling the bra on, I look in the mirror. They look pretty but so uncomfortable. Now, I brush my fingers over the bite mark to see the damage. His nails are sharp like needle points and have messed up my hip.

Grabbing a cloth, I try to clean the blood off. The cloth makes my skin sting. I am covered in marks; even my lips are bruised. Grabbing the shirt, I tug it over my head before pulling the jeans on. Even when I am dressed, you can still see the bite marks on my breast and collarbone from the V neck top.

Ryland is still in the bedroom. His eyes roam over my body and make me nervous. Suddenly, I hear the familiar ringtone of my phone, ringing loudly, and I walk out of the room, searching for it. I look everywhere but can't find it. I just hear a faint ringing before it stops.

"What are you looking for?" Ryland asks as I pull couch cushions off the couch.

"My phone," I tell him, ignoring his presence.

I continue pulling cushions off when I hear it ring again, only louder, making me look at the glass sliding doors. I see Orion pull it from his pocket, but he just presses a button on it and drops it back in his pocket again.

Annoyed, I slide the door open. Both Thaddeus and Orion lean on the railing overlooking the city, or what is left of it. They both look over when they hear the door. Walking out, I move next to Orion and then reach out to pull on his pants. My phone rings again as I reach my hand into his pocket, pulling my phone out.

Thaddeus shakes his head, turning back to look at the city, and I glare at him as I answer it. Lisa is calling.

"Geez, girl, I have called you about twenty times this morning! Where are you?" she asks.

Thaddeus and Orion are listening in, and I am unsure how to answer that. Do I tell her the truth or lie? Both of them watch to see what I say.

"I'm running late; I will be there soon," I tell her, as my hand reaches into Orion's other pocket, pulling his smokes out and stealing one.

"Anything else you want?" he asks, making me raise an eyebrow at him.

Lisa is chatting away about Miranda coming back to work. Thaddeus is glaring at me for some unknown reason. Thankfully, Lisa's voice pulls my attention away from him. "Evelyn, are you there?"

"Yes, I am still here," I quickly answer her.

"Are you sure you're, okay? You are being really quiet."

"I'm fine. I will see you soon," I tell her.

Orion turns to face me, crossing his arms over his chest. "We are leaving. You will not work, Evelyn."

"No, *you* are leaving. *I* am going to work, then home," I tell him. Thaddeus growls, making my attention go back to him. Thaddeus leans forward and snatches my phone from me. "What are you doing? Give it back," I tell him when he suddenly crushes it in his hand, effectively destroying it.

Thaddeus moves forward, stepping in front of me, and I step back. "We are leaving, and I won't be leaving without you. You are mine. Now stop being a brat and do as you're told."

"I am not going anywhere with any of you," I tell him.

Thaddeus grabs my arm, pulling me to him. His eyes burn brightly and turn obsidian again. His fangs protrude, and a devilish look transforms his face. I watch as he pinches the bridge of his nose, frustrated, the hand gripping my arm tightens its vice-like grip, and my heart pounds in my chest. I expect the worst, but he suddenly lets go and walks away.

Orion stares at his back, and after a brief moment of shock, he pulls himself together and escorts me inside. Once back in the confines of the apartment, I watch as Thaddeus leaves, slamming the door behind him.

"Where is Mr. Cranky Pants going?" I ask, instantly regretting it when I hear Ryland answer.

"To find someone to eat," he says with a smirk on his face. A shiver runs up my spine and I feel the blood drain from my face.

"He won't be long. Wait here while I take some things down to the car," Orion says. I nod, not knowing where they're going, but I definitely won't be going with them.

Ryland wanders into the room, and I follow him. "What's wrong?" he asks, looking at me.

"Have you got a smoke?" I ask. I know for a fact that I saw a fire escape running alongside the balcony.

Ryland eyes me before going over to a jacket, draped over the back of a chair. He puts his hand in the pocket, pulls out a packet, and hands it to me. "You really shouldn't smoke, you know that?"

I nod and take them from him. When I am leaving the room, he speaks again. "Don't be too long out there. Thaddeus won't be long." I nod, not bothering to say anything.

Quickly, opening the sliding door, I step onto the balcony, closing the curtain that hangs in the doorway. Walking over to the barrier in the balcony's corner, I climb onto the railing and manage to reach the ladder. My shaky hands grip it tightly. I gulp when I look down and see how high up I am. My hands feel clammy as I grip the ladder even tighter.

I just need to get down the ladder and drop to the fire escape. Only, it isn't easy. My heart pounds so hard I think I will have a heart attack and fall to my death. I pray silently that if I fall, the heart attack will kill me so I don't feel myself hitting the concrete.

Once I get to the bottom rung of the ladder, there is a six-foot drop. I gulp while hanging a foot off and nearly pull myself up, fearing the drop when my fingers slip from the rung, and I drop. My stomach plummets somewhere deep from the rush of falling.

Hitting the stairs with a metallic-sounding thud, I land on my side. Looking up, I shake my head. I can't believe I did it. Well, to be fair, I chickened out and fell the rest of the way, but still, I did it.

Racing down the stairs, I hear Ryland curse, making me look up, and I run down the stairs skipping some in my haste as adrenaline kicks in, making me move quicker. Getting to the bottom, I jump onto a trash bin, and then jump onto the ground in the alleyway, still shocked I escaped.

Running onto the street, I look in both directions but do not know where I am. Shit, now what? I keep running, not wanting to risk stopping, until I see a taxi pull up down the road. I wave it down just before it takes off. I all but jump in the car and quickly duck down. The taxi driver must think I am a lunatic.

"Drive! Go! Please!" I yell at him.

Startled, he takes off. Once he turns around the corner, I sit up. The Indian man stares at me in the mirror with wide eyes. "Where to?" he asks, looking in all his mirrors like he is paranoid that someone is following, which I suppose is a good assumption with the way I jumped in his taxi and hid.

"The Pit Stop Cafe," I tell him, and he drives toward my work.

Reaching into my pocket, I realize I don't have my wallet. Damn it. The trip takes about fifteen minutes with the traffic. When I pull up, I tell the driver to wait, and I dart into the cafe.

Walking over to the tips jar, I grab twenty dollars out of it and run back to the driver. When I go back in, Lisa is waiting at a table. She nods to me, and I dart into the back to grab my apron. I wait tables for about an hour and then put my tips back into the jar to pay back the twenty dollars I borrowed. When things calm down, Lisa pulls me out of the back with Miranda.

"So, what happened the other day? And what happened to your neck?" she asks, pushing my hair aside to look at the bite mark.

I am about to tell her when I hear the bell above the door Bing. Looking out, I see Thaddeus, Orion, and Ryland enter. I drop to the floor, so they don't see me. Lisa looks down at me and mouths to me. "What are you doing?" I place a finger to my lips to keep them both quiet.

As soon as Miranda sees my alarm, she walks out. "Hi, what can I get you?" she asks in her best customer service voice. I can almost see the fake smile plastered on her face. And then, just as my heart calms a little, Lisa screams.

CHAPTER
TEN

E velyn

"I know she is here."

I can hear Miranda choking, and Lisa nudges me with her foot.

"You have three seconds to come out, Evelyn, or I kill your friend," Thaddeus growls out.

I instantly hear the sound of chairs moving and the bell going off as people run from the cafe. Standing up, I walk out of the kitchen, Thaddeus has Miranda by the throat. As soon as he notices me walking out, he releases her. My eyes catch her stumbling back, clutching her throat, her red hair half pulled from its bun. She has tears on her cheeks.

I feel so guilty. I shouldn't have run, or at least shouldn't have come here. But where else do I have to go? I was hoping they wouldn't make a scene here, seeing as it is a pretty popular cafe on this side of town.

Thaddeus moves around the counter, reaches for me, and rips me towards him, making me stumble into his chest. His hand goes into my hair as he yanks my head back, making me cry out. "You're going to regret running," he growls below my ear, then quickly tugs me and shoves me toward Orion.

"Now, all their deaths will be on your hands," Thaddeus bellows, as his eyes go black.

The air thickens, the lights flicker and at first, I am confused, until the windows start bursting. Orion shoves me to the ground, and Ryland also ducks down, dropping over me. Gunfire sounds from every direction, and I watch, horrified, as Thaddeus gets hit in the chest and shoulder.

He growls loudly, walks through the door, and heads outside. I cover my ears. The noise is deafening, and I can only make out Lisa's hysterical screams. Suddenly, the ground moves like a wave, I hear metal on metal and the sound of buildings exploding before everything goes silent. Eerily so.

Smoke and dust fill the cafe, and I can hear electricity zap loudly. I hear a crash and look up just in time to see the roof in the kitchen collapse in on itself. Lisa screams for Miranda, sobbing loudly. I try to see where she is, but can't see her through the dust and smoke. Alarms are going off in neighboring shops. Car alarms are blaring outside, and people are screaming. I try to get up when Ryland shoves me back down before rolling me onto my back.

His eyes are pitch black orbs, and his canines protrude. "You shouldn't have run," he says so calmly I shiver at the coldness of his voice.

I hear the crunching of glass, making me squint into the dust. Thaddeus' boots stop next to my face. Ryland hops off me, and Thaddeus grips the collar of my shirt, yanking me to my feet. I cough on the dust when the shrill sound of Lisa screaming hysterically hits my ears, making me look in her direction. I can't see her, but I recognize Miranda's blue shoes and legs behind the counter.

Getting out of Thaddeus' grip, I run over to them and see that Miranda has been shot in the stomach. Lisa's hands pressure the wound as she bleeds out on the floor.

"No, no, no!" I scream, dropping to the floor. This is my fault.

Orion comes over, trying to pull me to my feet, but I grip onto Miranda, refusing to let go.

"No! Please help her," I tell him, but he continues to try to pry my finger from her arm. Thaddeus growls loudly as he walks over and grips me, ripping me away from her. I try to fight him off as he drags me away, kicking and screaming. "Please, please help her!"

"No. You did this. I warned you not to run. Ryland and Orion warned you not to run!" Thaddeus screams in my face.

"Please, Thaddeus! Help her. I will do what you want, but please don't let my friend die because of me."

Thaddeus growls, and is about to pull me away when Ryland speaks. "He helps her, you let him mark you."

"What?" I say, looking over my shoulder.

"Your friend is about to die; choose, Evelyn," he says, and Thaddeus shakes me, making me look at him.

"What's it going to be? Choose."

"Evelyn, please," Lisa cries out to me.

I nod. "Please help her," I beg, and Thaddeus lets me go. He turns around and walks over to her. Following him over, I see Lisa jump back, moving out of his way. I watch as he bites into his wrist and places it over her mouth.

Thaddeus pulls his hand away, then shoves his finger into the bullet hole, and I scream, rushing over. "You're killing her!" Miranda groans in pain.

"Move. I am helping her. She won't heal with the bullet still in her," he growls, right as Orion pulls me back.

He drops the bullet to the ground and lifts her shirt. The bullet hole closes before my eyes, and Miranda takes a deep breath like she has been underwater for a while. Her eyes snap open, and she crawls away from him in fear, though he just saved her. Thaddeus growls at her, stands up, and yanks me from Orion.

"Wait! Stop!" I call out to him as he pulls me toward the door. Thaddeus growls again, tosses me over his shoulder, and completely ignores my screams and attempts to kick him.

I won't stop fighting him. I need to go back to my friends. Then, I feel his hand come down on my ass. The slap is stinging, and I feel his handprint bruising.

"Enough, Evelyn, we need to leave," he growls, as he finally places me back on the ground and grabs my wrist.

Looking around, I gasp.

The entire street is in ruins; a car is even impaled on a light pole. Bodies are strewn everywhere; the road is split down the middle, and buildings are on fire and torn to pieces. It looks like a hurricane has swept through the city, destroying everything in its path.

Then suddenly, I see Orion grab me. The sound of wind rushes around me, and I struggle to breathe from the pressure. Everything moves by in a blur of destruction. I feel myself becoming dizzy from the motion and am on the verge of passing out when he suddenly stops, knocking what little air was in my lungs out of me. Orion places me on my feet, and I collapse, the ground rushing towards me as my body goes limp.

"Shit," Orion yells, scooping me up in his arms.

He places me on something soft, and as soon as my body touches it, I lurch forward, throwing up. Orion jumps back, and I barely miss him. He pulls my hair from my face. My ears ring loudly. Something cold touches my face, and my eyes snap open as I flop back onto what they placed me on. When the dizziness subsides, I find we are back in the apartment. Ryland is cleaning the floor beside me with a towel.

Thaddeus comes into my line of vision and glares down at me. "Grab her. Ryland, grab the bags in the room with me." Orion scoops me up and starts walking. The motion makes my stomach turn, and the dizziness returns before I am placed on leather, and I realize I am in a car. Orion then leaves, and I slide onto my side before I feel hands grip my shoulders, making my eyes open, and I see Thaddeus sit beside me, placing my head on his lap. Hearing car doors close, I feel the car start. Thaddeus brushes my hair out of my face, and I feel myself slipping into the darkness of unconsciousness.

ELEVEN

E **velyn**

Waking up, I feel fingers run down my spine, making me shiver, and my eyes fly open. Sitting up, I find I am in a room, and the person touching me is Thaddeus. He watches me as I look around at the unfamiliar surroundings.

The room I am in is huge and has arched windows looking out into the darkness. Shaking my head, I try to remember the last thing that happened. All I remember is Miranda getting shot and the sensation of moving fast. I feel a draft brush across my skin from the open window, making me look down to see I only have my jeans and a bra on.

"Where is my shirt?" I ask, my voice trembling as confusion sets in.

"You threw up at the apartment," Thaddeus tells me, and I vaguely remember. I tug the surrounding blanket, covering myself from his watchful eyes.

"How did you get the burn on your back?" he asks, looking at my exposed shoulder.

I often forget it is there, and looking down, I can make out the charred edges of flesh that wrap over my shoulder to the back of my neck. "Where am I?" I ask, ignoring his question.

Thaddeus doesn't answer, and when the door suddenly opens, Ryland and Orion walk in.

"Sleeping beauty awakes," Ryland mocks. I roll my eyes at him as I tug the blanket over my shoulder, covering myself completely. Their eyes watch every move I make.

Orion sits on the end of the bed, kicks off his shoes, and lies down. As I get out of bed, I scoot to the edge of it and look around. I can see a bathroom through the door near the windows. Ryland and Orion stepped in through this door, so I guess that leads to the rest of the place. There are antique-looking wardrobes along one wall and a huge four-poster bed that can easily fit five or six people.

"Can I borrow a shirt, please?" I ask, looking at them.

Ryland pulls his off, handing it to me. I scrunch my nose up but take it from him.

"Now you will have my scent all over you," he states as he leans against Thaddeus.

My eyes trail down his bare chest. His abs look like an artist sculpted them, his tanned skin glows under the lights. Turning my gaze away when I realize I am gawking, I pull the shirt over my head and remove the sheet I wrapped myself in. It is very warm here. Even the draft doesn't have the frosty bite I am so used to, making me wonder where we are.

I walk to the window and look out; it is dark, but the moon is full and the sky so clear I can see stars instead of smog. All I can make out are trees, hills and more hills and nothing, just darkness. I feel my heart rate pick up. I know instantly we have to be hundreds of miles from home.

Turning around, I look at them. All three of them watch me, and I break out in a cold sweat as fear consumes me. My mind goes to a crime show I watched once. The narrator said never let your killers take you to a second destination because that means they will kill you. Well, technically, this is the third destination, but that doesn't make me any less uneasy.

"Where are we?" I ask, looking back out the window.

"At our home," Thaddeus answers.

"And where is that?" I ask.

"Where you don't need to know, but I can tell you it's in the middle of nowhere," Thaddeus answers vaguely.

"Why won't you tell me?" I ask.

"Because you don't need to know. We won't be leaving. At least, not until the heat dies down," Ryland tells me.

"Heat?"

"Yes. Because of your little runaway attempt, hunters have found us and tracked us, and frankly, I am tired of running, so we will remain here."

"The people with the guns, were they hunters?" I ask.

"Precisely. And because of you, Thaddeus had to kill them, and God knows how many other people were caught in the crossfire," Ryland says.

"I never asked you to follow me, and I certainly didn't ask you to kill anyone," I snap back at him.

Ryland's eyes turn dark, and he growls a deep throaty growl that spreads goosebumps over my body.

"Watch your tone, little one. I would hate to see it get you in trouble," Thaddeus warns. Orion glares at him, and I wonder what sort of trouble he means from the look Orion gives him.

"Whatever," I tell him, turning away and walking to the window, sitting on the ledge. I can't imagine being in any more trouble than I am in already. Orion gets up and walks over, brushing my hair over my shoulder. "Don't touch me," I tell him, swatting his hand away. I get up and walk out of the room, Thaddeus' voice calling after me.

"Where are you going?"

"Away from you," I call back as I walk down the hall.

I come to some landing. Looking over the side, I can see another floor below. The house seems to be some sort of log home. Exposed beams run across the roof, which I notice is an A-frame house by its high pointed ceiling. Skylights run down the sides of the roof.

It feels smooth, running my hand along the wooden banister, and I follow it downstairs, which has an onyx stone floor. They look glittery under the lights that hang randomly from the beams. It is a pleasant house and has a modern country feel to it.

Once on the bottom floor, I see a fireplace that I can easily fit inside. I wouldn't be surprised if the four of us could stand in it; it seems to take up most of the wall. Underneath the stairs is another door. I walk through it and find a kitchen with stainless steel appliances, marble countertops, and a matching backsplash. There is also a huge island set in the middle with stools along one side. Walking out of the kitchen through another door, I find a laundry and another door with a window beside it.

Peering out the window, I can see outside. I twist the handle intending to open the door, when a hand falls on my shoulder, tugging me backward. "You aren't leaving, Evelyn," Ryland says, yanking me against him.

His chest presses into my back, and I feel the heat radiating off his body, seeping into me. I can feel his chest move with each breath he takes, his nose running from my ear, down my neck and shoulder, making me shiver.

Everywhere he touches, delightful sparks move over my skin. My body reacts to his touch as his arms wrap around my waist, and I feel his hand travel up my side until he squeezes my breast. My body reacts to him, and I don't like it. How can he have this effect on me?

I force myself away from him, only for him to pull me back against him. When I turn around, I am about to shove him, but the look on his face makes me gasp. His eyes are pitch black orbs. The eyes of a demon, staring back at me, and I gulp.

Spinning around, I grip the door handle, throwing the door open, and it crashes into the wall with a loud bang, and I dart out of it. Adrenaline makes me run faster as my heart pounds painfully against my chest.

Chuckling on my way out when I am around a hundred yards away from the house in some field. My hair stands on end, and a shiver runs up my spine, my breathing becomes short and fast, and I can hear my heart pounding in my ears. I can't see anything in the long grass, but I can feel eyes on me, observing me. Hearing a noise behind me, I spin on my heel, trying to catch a glimpse of it, only to spin the other way when I hear the noise behind me again.

My entire body goes tense as I hear growling, and my stomach drops somewhere deep inside me. I can feel the blood drain from my face. My skin feels ice-cold, and I am becoming paralyzed by fear.

"Ryland," I whisper into the darkness, and I hear the rustling of grass before hearing movement behind me again. Just as I turn, I see something lunge at me, knocking me over. A scream leaves my lips as I am knocked to the ground. My eyes open to see the white, gleaming teeth of a beast above me. It is huge as it snaps its jaw near my face, its huge paws on either side of my head.

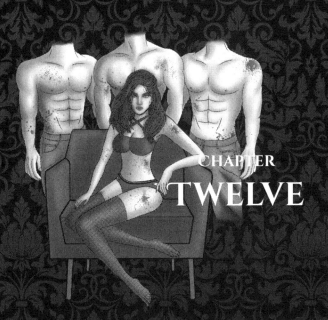

CHAPTER
TWELVE

Evelyn

Sitting up, it growls menacingly, and I scramble backward on my hands, trying to get away from it, when suddenly, my hands hit boots, making me look away from the beast.

Thaddeus has his arms folded across his chest and an amused expression on his face. "It's Ryland; he won't hurt you," Thaddeus says, looking down at me.

Looking back at the dog beast, it licks a long line from my chin to my hairline. I push its face away, and gag as drool covers my face. The dog makes a weird noise, and it almost sounds like it is laughing at me.

"Gross! Why would you do that?"

Thaddeus grips me under the arms, pulling me to my feet. Suddenly, I hear the sound of bones cracking, and Ryland grabs my hand, making me look at him. He is naked. My mouth falls open, and I quickly avert my eyes.

"What? You expect my clothes to remain?" he asks, laughing.

I pull my hand from his and walk ahead. I hear them sigh and follow. Heading inside, Orion is sitting in the lounge room. Looking at the grandfather clock beside the fireplace, I see it is midnight. My hair has grass in it, and I am feeling itchy.

When Thaddeus walks in with Ryland, Orion raises a brow at him being naked. Yet, I can also see lust behind his glowing eyes.

"So, if all of you are gay, why am I here?" I ask, looking at each of them.

"Because you're our mate," Thaddeus says, confused.

"But you're gay?" I say, and they shake their heads.

"We aren't anything; not gay, not straight, not Bi," Ryland answers, confusing me further.

"Sexuality isn't a thing when it comes to mates. You could be a unicorn and we would still be attracted to you, still want you. That's how mate bonds work; once you find your mates, that's all you care about."

"So, you have been with other women?"

"Yes, but not like you; they were merely toys and dinner," Thaddeus adds coldly.

"Right, still makes no sense to me, but can I go shower?" I ask.

"Orion will bring you a towel," Thaddeus says, and I watch Orion get up off the recliner and walk upstairs.

Waiting for Orion to come into the room, I sit on the end of the bed. Orion walks in a few minutes later with a towel and some clothes. Taking them from him, I walk into the bathroom. Orion sits next to the sink, and I stare at him.

"What are you doing? Get out," I tell him, but he doesn't budge; just pulls his phone out, playing Candy Crush.

Ignoring him, I keep my back to him as I step into the shower and turn it on. The shower has a frosted glass door, so I feel a little better that I know he can't see me, though Orion doesn't bother me; he always seems calm and has a carefree personality that I find relaxing.

Rinsing my hair, I hear the shower door open. I try to wash the soap that is now burning my eyes from my hair, only to open my eyes and see Orion, standing next to me. He reaches past me, grabbing the soap, yet his eyes never wander down, in fact, they don't leave mine.

"Chill, Evelyn. I am just showering with you. Not a big deal; we are all adults," he says as he washes himself.

My eyes trail over the lines of his chest and lower to his ass when he suddenly turns, giving me an eyeful of himself.

"God, you act like you've never seen a man before." He sighs, and my cheeks heat. "What, you've never seen a man naked?" he asks, shocked.

"No, I have seen men naked. Just not this close to me, just standing there, and not where I can see them." Orion's brows furrow in confusion, and I turn away, looking anywhere but at him.

"So, you aren't a virgin then?" he questions.

I don't answer. What do you class as a virgin anyway, does rape count as losing your virginity? I like to think it doesn't; I think of virginity as something you willingly give, not something one takes. I have come across my fair share of scumbags in my twenty years of life. Saw and witnessed more than any person should have at my age.

Foster care is supposed to be a safe place for children to grow up until they are returned to their families or adopted. Unfortunately, many people see being a foster carer as an opportunity to torture their victims before being shipped off to the next house.

Not all are bad, but I seemed to be a magnet for the horrid ones. Nothing worse than growing up, never catching a full night's sleep for fear of who may be trying to creep into your room or fear of the monster that sleeps in the room next to yours.

Orion, realizing I won't answer, changes the topic as he hands me the soap. "The burn on your back, how did that happen?"

Thaddeus asked the same question earlier. However, Orion's question doesn't irritate me as much.

"Why? Does it bother you?" I ask.

Orion shakes his head. "No, just curious. It looks like it would have hurt," he replies.

"Yeah, it did. Doesn't anymore, I often forget it's there," I tell him truthfully.

"So, what happened?"

"Does it matter? It was years ago; not a pleasant memory."

"How old were you?"

"Sixteen," I answer.

"So a house fire?" he asks, and I can tell by the look on his face it is eating at him, not knowing.

"Did you do something to Vick?" I ask, changing the subject.

Ever since they first kidnapped me, I had this nagging feeling Orion did something to Vick. It is unusual that he randomly went on vacation when I have never known the man to leave, even for a weekend.

Orion's eyes darken for a second.

"You killed him, didn't you?"

"Do you really want to know?"

I shrug, not sure if I do. I hate Vick. He is slimy and sleazy, but that doesn't mean I necessarily want him dead. But from the look on Orion's face, I know nothing good came of him.

"Come on, let's hop out. You must be hungry," he says, opening the shower, grabbing a towel, and handing it to me.

He then wraps another around his waist and steps out. I wrap the towel around myself and follow him into the room, quickly putting on a shirt and a pair of shorts that Orion gave me.

"Thaddeus is making pancakes," Orion says when we finish getting dressed. Orion grabs my hand, pulling me from the room, taking me downstairs.

As we walk into the kitchen, Thaddeus is indeed making pancakes. My belly rumbles loudly from the aromatic smell of melted butter and golden syrup.

"I did not picture you being one to cook," I tell him, sitting at the island next to Orion.

Thaddeus looks back at me, turns around, and places a plate of pancakes on the center of the island. Orion hands me a plate and dumps a heap of pancakes on my plate. I slide a couple off; fully aware I can't possibly eat that many. Cutting off a piece, I pop it into my mouth and nearly moan at the taste; so fluffy, and it melts in my mouth.

"Good?" Thaddeus asks, a smirk on his face.

"Very," I tell him.

"So, how long have you guys lived here for?"

"Can't remember. A while."

"Where were you before here, then?" I inquire, hoping that one of them will inadvertently reveal our location.

"Everywhere. I traveled before that, and mainly with my parents," Thaddeus answers.

"You have parents?"

"Everyone has parents, Evelyn," Thaddeus says.

He is right. Sort of. Yes, biologically, but I have learned that blood doesn't make a parent. As far as I am concerned, I don't have any. "You know what I mean."

Thaddeus nods. "Yes, I know what you mean, Evelyn, and yes, my parents are still alive. I also have a sister," he says, making me look up at him.

He stares off into space for a second, shakes his head, and snaps himself out of whatever trance he was stuck in. I wonder where his mind took him at that moment.

"What about you?" I ask, looking at Ryland.

"Mine are dead, killed by the council."

"Council?" I ask.

"Just think of it as supernatural law enforcement," Ryland says.

As I look at Orion, I don't even have to ask; he just answers. "No family; they died before I was changed. This here is all the family I have and need," he answers. I nod.

"What about you? What are your parents like?" Ryland asks.

"Don't know, never met them," I answer and quickly pop more pancakes in my mouth to busy it with chewing.

They seem to think for a second until Orion breaks the silence to ask another question. "What about other families?"

"No idea; I grew up in foster care."

"And the foster carers never had any information on them?" Orion raises an eyebrow.

"Nope, I was dropped out in front of a church when I was a few days old; a nun found me." I shrug.

"That explains the newspaper clipping we found," Ryland says, looking at Thaddeus.

"Newspaper clipping?" I raise an eyebrow at him.

"Yeah, the box we found under your bed."

I nod, not really knowing what to think about knowing they snooped through my stuff. Not like I have much or anything valuable.

"You're not upset we went through your stuff?" Thaddeus asks.

Shrugging, I pick up my plate and wash it in the sink. "Not really; I doubt you would have found much. Besides, everyone has skeletons in the closet," I tell him.

"And what are yours, then?" Thaddeus asks curiously.

"You tell me yours, and I will tell you mine," I challenge. He shakes his head. "That's what I thought." I chuckle, for once feeling better that I might have won a battle with him.

"Like the burn on your back?" Thaddeus adds.

"Yes, exactly like that," I tell him.

CHAPTER
THIRTEEN

Evelyn

After having breakfast for dinner, I head into the living room. Orion follows me out of the kitchen and sits right next to me the moment I take a seat on the couch.

"We should head to bed soon," Orion tells me. Thaddeus and Ryland walk out and head upstairs, and I see Orion watch them go. "Come on. You should sleep," he says, and I shake my head, not wanting to go to bed.

I don't want to sleep in a bed with Thaddeus and Ryland. I have spent most of the day and night asleep. "I'm not tired. You go to bed," I tell him. Orion chuckles to himself, making me look at him. "What?" I ask, wondering what he thinks is so funny.

"Nothing. I don't sleep. I wish I could; I miss sleeping," he says.

I furrow my eyebrows. "You don't sleep?" Orion shakes his head. "At all?"

"I'm not human, Evelyn. I don't require sleep. Not like Ryland and humans," he says.

"But Thaddeus sleeps?" The statement comes out more like a question and Orion nods in agreement.

"Yes, but he is a Tribrid, so like Ryland, he needs sleep. He can go weeks without it, but he becomes manic without sleeping," Orion explains.

Manic? Great, not only do I have a psychopath for a mate, but he is fucking bonkers. I have heard so many rumors about the Dark King, and I know that most of them are correct, but how can someone be more than one thing? Probably a stupid thought, considering the world just found out that there is an entirely different world from the one I grew up in.

"So exactly what is Thaddeus?"

"It's complicated. He is a vampire and Lycan, but his mother is a witch hybrid, so it's too hard to explain. Just be careful, Evelyn. I don't mean to scare you, but Thaddeus is the first tribrid, and not even he understands it completely. He's..." Orion thinks, trying to find the right word when Thaddeus answers for him.

"A monster," Thaddeus says, making Orion look up. I didn't even hear him sneak up on us or notice him walk down the stairs. Knowing he heard us makes me a little uneasy.

"I wasn't going to say that. Don't put words in my mouth, Thaddeus," Orion tells him.

"Not like you weren't thinking it," Thaddeus replies.

Orion shakes his head, disagreeing, but Thaddeus doesn't even glance in his direction; his eyes don't leave mine.

"What about your sister?" I ask, wondering if she is the same as Thaddeus.

"Amara is the same, but the darkness doesn't affect her. Her magic is purer; mine is old magic, tainted and dark and not of this realm," Thaddeus answers, making me more confused. "Enough with the questions. Now get up and come to bed," Thaddeus says, stepping closer to the couch.

"I'm not tired, and I am not sleeping in any room you are in," I tell him. Thaddeus growls, and his eyes darken. It is like a switch just goes off in his head, or an alter ego takes over. Walking over, he rips me off the couch. "Ow! Thaddeus, you're hurting me," I tell him, trying to pry his fingers from my wrist.

"That's nothing compared to what I will do if you don't get upstairs now," he growls, causing goosebumps to spread over me and a shiver to run up my spine.

"What the fuck is your problem? You don't just force people to do what you want," I tell him, trying to pull my hand away.

"And who is going to stop me, little one? Not Orion, not Ryland. No one can do anything; no one can save you from me. You are weak and human, no match for me."

"Thaddeus, please let her sleep down here until she is ready," Orion insists.

Yeah, that will most likely never happen. The first chance I get, I am out of here and will happily live my life on the run if it means never seeing Thaddeus again.

Thaddeus glares at Orion. "Clearly, you're forgetting the deal we made, Evelyn. For your friend's life," Thaddeus says, his eyes darting to mine.

I watch as veins run down his face and his fangs protrude. Orion stands up, moving to my side, and I feel his hand on my lower back. My breath becomes stuck in my throat, and I begin to panic.

"You know you can't, especially when you are like this, Thaddeus. You could kill her."

"I don't care," Thaddeus says, shoving him away from me.

"That's exactly my point. I won't let you mark her while you're surrounded by darkness. Ryland!" Orion yells, and I hear footsteps. Soon, I see him coming up behind Thaddeus as he runs down the stairs. Ryland grips his arm, but Thaddeus backhands him, not letting my arm go. Thaddeus pulls me towards himself, pressing me against his chest.

Orion reaches for me when I hear a menacing growl escape Thaddeus, and the lights suddenly flicker, the air around us becomes dense. I can hear the sound of static.

"Thaddeus!" Orion yells when I feel my arms burning.

My skin burns so hot that I think it is melting off. I scream, his grip sears into my flesh, and Orion tackles him, forcing him to let go, while I am thrown violently onto the floor. My head smacks the floor with so much force, I see black, and my vision turns blurry.

Sitting up, I clutch my head, feeling blood trickle down the side of my face. As I pull my hand back, I see it's coated in blood, and I feel my eyes roll into the back of my head.

Orion's voice reaches my ears, but I have no idea what he is saying. All I can think about is the throbbing in my head as the darkness descends. I feel weightless and cold, and then nothing.

Orion

I knew I shouldn't have tackled him the moment I did. His grip on her was too tight, and the force threw her like a rag doll; her head smacked into the edge of the fireplace.

She sits up, swaying slightly, and then clutches her head. As she pulls her hand back, I see blood running down her face, bleeding everywhere onto the floor.

"Evelyn!" I gasp, making Thaddeus's eyes snap to her.

I feel panic run through him. He moves so quickly I think he will attack her at first; I know he needs to feed, and she is bleeding everywhere. I could feel his bloodlust through the bond when he burnt her.

Thaddeus grabs her, pulling her onto his lap. He is quick to bite his wrist, but Evelyn is floppy and limp as her eyes roll into her head, and she slumps against him. Ryland rushes to his side, and all I can do is watch, completely paralyzed by fear at seeing her in that state.

Thaddeus bites into his wrist again, and Ryland opens her mouth, letting his blood run down her throat. Her skin is turning so pale she looks like she is dead, her skin turning blue.

Thaddeus rocks her in his arms, her head falls backward, and I can hear her heart rate getting slower. It didn't work; she is going to die. He killed our mate.

I knew we should never have pursued her. I knew she would never survive him, and all I can feel now is anger. Her breathing becomes shallow, her heart rate slows down.

Ryland rips her from him and blows air into her lungs as his hands perform CPR.

"There's no point. She is gone," I tell him.

Ryland growls, his eyes snapping to mine. "She isn't, I can feel her. We just need to keep her alive long enough for his blood to work," Ryland snaps at me.

Thaddeus has his head in his hands, and I can feel darkness wrapping around him, consuming him like never before. I know if she dies, he will kill us all when he releases it.

When Ryland notices the darkness in him, he looks panicked, and I finally move, going to her side and trying to help. Biting into my wrist, I hold it over her mouth while Ryland keeps pumping her chest.

A minute feels like hours as we wait to see if our blood helps her. Suddenly, she chokes on our blood, and Ryland stops. He falls backward in relief. Evelyn is trying to spit out the blood as she gasps for air, the long gash on her head escaping into her hairline starts healing, and she rolls on her side, retching, spewing our blood onto the floor.

"I'm so sick of puking," she gasps.

Thaddeus grips her, crushing her against his chest. Relief floods the bond as he cups her face, and I feel the darkness leave him, feel him relax with her in his arms.

"Get off me, asshole," she says, smacking his chest, making me chuckle. Yep, there she is, our feisty little mate. She nearly died and doesn't even realize it; she is pissed off because she woke up in his arms. Thaddeus loosens his grip, letting her move, and she looks around, confused. Then, her eyes snap to the floor where her blood has pooled. "What happened?" she asks, shocked, and I realize she can't remember.

"I'm sorry, I didn't mean to," Thaddeus tells her, guilt flooding into me through the bond, mixed with fear of her rejecting him over what he has done to her.

"You're fine. You will be fine, Evelyn," I tell her.

I see her look up at Thaddeus as she realizes he has done something, yet she doesn't understand what. I hold my hands out for her, and she moves off his lap, coming toward me warily before gripping onto me like I am her lifeline.

Ryland stands up. I watch him as he bends down, kisses her head, and turns around to walk into the kitchen. Thaddeus is staring at her like she is about to vanish in front of him, and I can feel his longing and jealousy that I am holding her, that she always seems to gravitate towards me.

Yet, he needs to understand every time she has been in his presence, he has hurt her or scared her. I have done neither. Humans tend to go where they feel safest, and at the moment, that is me.

"She is fine, Thaddeus. Go get some sleep and calm down," I tell him, and he growls at me. Ryland touches his shoulder, making him look up. After a brief moment, he stands reluctantly and leaves me with her.

"What happened?" she asks.

"You hit your head. Ryland's quick thinking just saved your life. You will be fine, Evelyn."

"And Thaddeus?" she asks, turning her face into my neck.

"Thaddeus didn't mean it; he just wants you. He isn't particularly good at being gentle. He had no intentions of hurting you. I am partly to blame; I shouldn't have tackled him."

"Why can't I remember?" she asks, pulling back and looking at me.

"Might be best you don't," I tell her.

As I stand up, I place her on the couch and grab a wet cloth and a blanket. Putting the blanket over her, I clean the blood off her face and peel her shirt off. Evelyn eventually falls asleep just as the sun rises, and I carry her upstairs, laying her on the bed next to Thaddeus and Ryland.

Going downstairs, I pull the mop bucket and mop out to clean up the mess left from last night, praying that she never remembers what happened. For this to work, Thaddeus needs to learn control, and she needs to accept him. After tonight though, I feel the shock of almost losing her might be enough to make him realize she is only human and can't be mistreated like Ryland and myself.

I know Ryland is holding himself back. He feels the pull to her the most because he has marked her, feels what she feels. Somehow, he has pushed the parts of him that remind me of Thaddeus aside for her.

Thaddeus, however, struggles with who he is and with his own identity. I have lived among humans for centuries and have grown to like their humanity. I like the way they perceive the world, and understand emotion better than they do. I just hope Thaddeus can find his humanity in her. Because if it comes down to choosing, I will choose her over him, and I know Ryland feels the same way.

FOURTEEN

E velyn

When I wake up, I roll and squeal as I feel myself fall-ing, my eyes snapping open. However, before I hit the floor, an arm snakes around my waist and pulls me back and onto their chest.

My heart races at the sudden shock of nearly falling off, and then races harder when I realize I am now lying on top of the devil himself. My eyes open to see Thaddeus with eyes half-open, watching me. He yawns, and I can tell I woke him. What I don't remember is getting in bed with him.

I can feel Thaddeus' breathing change as he wakes up completely. With a smile on his lips, he almost looks human in this moment. All traces of the monster I know are gone. Just hypnotic green eyes I could get lost in and full lips only inches away from mine.

"Good morning, Evelyn," he whispers, watching me closely. His hand on my back rubs my skin softly, sending sparks everywhere he touches. His hands are warm, different from the cold hands of Orion.

Thaddeus moves his other hand, brushing my hair behind my

ear, his hand cupping my face and his thumb brushing my cheek gently. I involuntarily lean into his touch and find it soothing. I don't understand why, but now all fear I have for him is gone; maybe because he isn't killing people, he isn't being rough. He is almost normal at this moment.

"Morning," I tell him, wanting to move off him, yet my body seems quite relaxed in his arms and doesn't want to move.

"I'm sorry I hurt you. That was never my intention, I never want to hurt you," he says, his breath fanning my face, and I inhale his intoxicating scent.

He smells nice; they all do in a weird sort of way, addictively sweet and intoxicating, erotic. I have never been turned on so much by the way someone smells.

Thaddeus moves underneath me slightly, and then rolls onto his side. One of his hands is under my head, the other rests on my hip. He pulls me closer, crushing me against his chest. I place my hand on his chest, and he shivers under my touch, making me chuckle.

"What?" he asks.

"Nothing. You're just being nice for once," I tell him, and he pulls back, looking down at me.

"Never heard someone describe me as nice." He chuckles, as he pulls me closer once again. I feel his hand run down my side to my hip and sparks move across my skin, tickling me and making me squirm.

"Are you ticklish, little one?" he asks, doing it again and getting the same reaction.

"Yes, but it doesn't tickle. It's a weird sensation," I tell him, not knowing how to describe it.

"Tingling?" he says. I nod against his chest. "The mate bond is working then; I feel that every time you touch me."

"Does it stop?" I ask.

"No. Been years, and I still feel it every time Ryland and Orion touch me. If anything, it gets stronger," he says, and I feel the bed dip behind me. More sparks run up my shoulder, and someone rests their chin on me. Looking over my shoulder, I see Ryland.

He kisses my nose. "What are you two doing?" he asks, a devious glint in his eyes.

"Nothing. We just woke up," Thaddeus tells him. I feel Ryland lay behind me, making my heart race when I feel his hand move my hair off my shoulder. His warm hands brush my skin, making me shiver.

Ryland chuckles softly behind me, his lips next to my ear. "She can feel the mate bond," he states. He starts running his finger along my shoulder, making me gasp as sparks move everywhere he touches. Thaddeus' grip on my hip tightens. I feel Ryland's breath on my neck where he bit me.

Then, I feel his tongue move over it, and my eyes close as pleasure makes my toes curl, and I moan softly. Thaddeus' hand moves over my hip to my waist, and Ryland sucks on my mark. Feeling pleasure erupt through me, sparks rush down from my neck to between my legs, making me moan loudly and forget who they are as I become lost in the feeling of arousal washing over me. I have never felt pleasure before, and it is mind-blowing. I don't want it to stop.

Ryland's hand moves down my body and brushes over my stomach. His lips don't leave my neck as I feel his hands slip into my pants, rubbing my slit through my panties. I feel his lips move from my neck, and he nips at my shoulder. Thaddeus' hand pulls my leg over his hip, and I roll my hips against Ryland's fingers. I can feel my panties become wet with arousal.

"She is so wet," Ryland growls next to my ear, making me wetter.

"Do you want him to stop, Evelyn?" Thaddeus asks, making my eyes snap open, and I realize I am lost in their touch, yet it feels right. Nothing feels righter than this right here. But yet, I know it isn't. They are killers, and I am human.

Ryland's fingers slip beneath my panties, his finger rubbing between my wet lips before I feel him rub my clit, making me moan loudly.

"Evelyn, do you want him to stop?" Thaddeus asks.

I don't want him to stop. I have never felt like this before, almost high on the feeling of him touching me.

"It's okay to want us, Evelyn," Ryland says. His fingers stop moving, and I know he can feel my unease through the bond, my mind and body at war with themselves.

"Don't stop," I gasp, moving my hips against his fingers.

Ryland moves his fingers again, rubbing my clit in a circular motion. I feel my juices spill onto my thighs as I moan at his touch. Thaddeus' lips brush mine, and I feel his tongue brush my bottom lip, wanting access. I part my lips, and he plunges his tongue into my mouth. His tongue tastes every inch, and I moan into his mouth when I feel Ryland slide a finger in me, making me flinch and my mind becomes flooded with memories; memories I keep in the back of my mind; memories that I try my best to detach myself from.

I feel my entire body tense, and I squeeze my eyes shut tightly, trying to fight them off. I feel Ryland pull his hand from my pants.

Thaddeus growls at me, making my eyes snap open. I try to breathe, find my grounding place, try to remember the mantra that always saves me. My breathing is coming harder as I try to shove the memory aside, to remember it's not happening and that I am not in that monster's den.

I feel his greasy hands on my body, the bourbon on his breath, the pale-yellow color of his skin. I try to get up and remove myself, and I feel hands grip me as I stumble off the bed. My vision is becoming tunneled, and I try to force myself to take a breath, to force the air into my lungs as my heart beats erratically in my chest.

My hands reach for the nightstand where I know my handbag is. Muttering my mantra, trying to ground myself, I grab the bottle of pills, only for it to slip from my shaking hands, and the tunnel vision worsens as dark spots take over my vision.

I welcome the darkness; it's where I feel safest because it makes it go away. Makes the feelings go away, the shame, weakness, the dirty feeling of being used. Darkness wraps around me, and I take a breath of air as it sucks me under.

Thaddeus

She is fine. I can feel her through Ryland. She feels safe and likes what he is doing to her. She is a little shocked and uneasy at her reaction to us but I can tell she is new to pleasure. She wants to know what it feels like. Her inexperience shows in how she doesn't know what she is feeling, just that she likes it.

That's why I ask; why I ask if she wants him to stop. I can still feel her fear of us, but our hands override it, touching her. I can smell her arousal perfuming the air; she is so lost in the feeling of us that she hasn't noticed Orion, watching from the armchair. He wants her not to fear us, so he gives us this moment with her.

Then, she freezes, her entire body locks up when Ryland pushes his finger inside her. I pull back slightly, and the look on her face is like she is somewhere else, trapped wherever her mind has taken her. Her face becomes flushed like she can't breathe, and I feel her struggle to take a breath. It reminds me of when she first saw us when we stepped into the cafe.

The feelings from Ryland are pure panic and fear, and they take my breath away. She clutches my skin, her nails dig into me, breaking the skin on my shoulders as she thrashes, tears roll down her cheeks and off her chin.

I growl. I don't mean to scare her. Her eyes snap to mine, but it is like she is looking straight through me, that vacant look in her eyes as they dart around the room. Getting off the bed, she gets up, and she gasps for air, her hands tremble, and she nearly falls off the bed.

I grab her arm to steady her, trying to figure out what she wants when Orion calls out.

"Her bag, her pills," he says, and I watch her digging through it, trying to find them, muttering to herself.

"See, feel, touch. See, feel, touch."

I have no idea what she is talking about.

When she finds the pills, she drops them onto the floor. I watch her eyes roll into her head, and her face goes slack as she plummets to the floor. Catching her, I scoop her up, cradling her to my chest. Her breathing is going back to normal. Ryland looks pale and his hands tremble. His canines protrude from his lips, and I can feel guilt run through him. Orion, noticing it too, stands up, rubbing his arm.

Ryland must have felt her emotions ten times worse than us because of his mark on her neck. What I felt makes me sick to my stomach, so whatever he feels must be crippling. Ryland's skin returns to normal, and his breathing slows. He closes his eyes, fighting against every emotion running through him, replacing it with a rage so strong, it nearly knocks me over.

"I don't understand; she was fine. What did I do?" he asks, questioning himself, questioning everything he did, guilt and anger flooding into me.

"You did nothing. Something must have triggered something," Orion tells him as he looks over at Evelyn in my arms. I inhale her scent and can no longer smell fear radiating off her, and her body relaxes in my arms as she stirs. "We can ask her when she wakes up," Orion says, staring at her as she stirs in my arms.

Walking downstairs, I sit with her on my lap, her head on my shoulder. Orion hands me the bottle of pills and places a glass of water on the lamp table next to me.

"She will wake soon; I can feel her consciousness fighting to come back," Ryland says, watching her worriedly.

Orion sits next to me, and I open the bottle of pills, finding two left. "How many?" I ask, looking at Orion.

"Lisa gave her two," he says, a little unsure.

"Were there more in her bag?" I ask. Orion shakes his head. "One of us might have to head to the city."

"I will go; I am faster," Orion says.

"Shouldn't you be here when she wakes? I can go."

"Why?" he asks while putting on his jacket.

"You know why; she likes you more," I tell him, though it pains me to say it.

"You will be fine; just don't yell at her or force her to do anything. Ryland will be here, and I will only be gone for an hour, max. If you go, or Ryland, you won't be back till tonight," he says, and I nod, knowing he is right. Orion is way quicker and knows his way around the city better.

"Maybe when she wakes up, phone Amara," Orion says, making my eyes snap to him. I haven't spoken to my sister in years. "If she won't tell us what happened, maybe Amara may know."

"Amara would need a photo or something of hers to pick her up," I tell him.

"Just see what she says when she wakes up. She might tell us, if she feels comfortable enough," Orion says.

"Maybe I should go?" Ryland offers.

Orion shakes his head. "You can feel her emotions, know what they are. You should stay. I won't be long. By the way, what she was muttering was her trying to ground herself. I read a book on it once. Panic attacks can lessen or stop if they ground themselves. Something they can see, something they can feel, and something they can touch and taste," Orion tells us.

I raise an eyebrow at what he just told us. "Makes no sense to me," I tell him.

"No, but obviously it does to her."

I nod and watch as he bolts out the door. Ryland gets up, shutting it behind him. Slowly, he comes back and sits next to me, brushing her hair out of her face.

We sit in silence, waiting for her to wake up. Twenty minutes pass, and I see Ryland straighten up and glance at her. Evelyn sits upright suddenly, and I hear her heart rate rise as she looks around frantically until she spots us; and she takes a deep breath.

Ryland grabs the glass of water, hands it to her, and she clutches it, her hands only trembling slightly as she takes a sip. I open my hand, revealing the two pills, and she pinches them with her fingers before popping them in her mouth and downing the rest of the glass.

She then leans against me, and I rub my hand up her back. Ryland and I are unsure what to do. I suddenly wish Orion stayed; he is better with humans than us.

The silence is becoming deafening. I don't know what to say. Is there a right or wrong thing to say? Suddenly she gets up, walking into the kitchen. Her movements are a little sluggish as she fills up her glass, drinks it and refills it again. Ryland and I follow her. She seems fine, like nothing has happened, and then I realize we aren't getting answers from her. She is just going to pretend like nothing happened; push whatever it is away like it doesn't exist.

FIFTEEN

Evelyn

It's been four years since I escaped that house of horrors, yet the memories come back to plague me, hanging over my head like a dark cloud. I shoved it to the back of my mind for four years, but it has returned with a vengeance, making me relive every minute.

Is it because of that night in the alleyway? Did that undo everything I worked so hard to suppress? I have always suffered from anxiety, and always found my way back from it; but now, my walls are crumbling, and I am killing myself trying to rebuild them back to the way they were.

Everything I worked so hard to leave behind is now resurfacing in the worst way possible, haunting not only my mind but my body. Panic attacks, something that becomes crippling, the feeling of complete dread threatening to consume you, make you believe it is the end, and sometimes, I wish it were. At least I wouldn't have to suffer through another, and I wouldn't have to relive my past.

I wouldn't have to remember again if it all ended. The nightmares that haunt my sleep and the memories that haunt me when I'm awake are a never-ending cycle. It scares me to sleep, scares me to hear him creeping into my room, scares me to sense the doom that comes when he does. The dreams feel real, feel like it is happening. It doesn't matter that I am safe away from him; he might as well have been doing it all over again in those moments.

For three days now, I have been awake. I feel like a zombie. My body is on autopilot, yet my mind is reliving a nightmare. I am tired, so tired. I just want to rest, but I know even in my sleep, there is no rest.

I have been staring at this TV for three days, too scared to move. Orion just sits watching with me. Yawning, I stretch. My muscles ache from sitting, my back and neck crack from sitting in this cramped position. I feel Orion watch me as I walk into the kitchen, feel his eyes on my back, boring holes into me. I am nearly out of pills again, only four left in the bottle, and the panicked feeling of knowing I will run out creeps over me.

They help me relax and numb everything around me. Feeling his presence behind me, I look over my shoulder and see him leaning on the counter.

"You need to sleep. If you just sleep, you will feel better."

Easy for him to say, he doesn't suffer through the nightmares. Rolling my eyes at him, I bring the pill bottle to my lips, dropping the four pills in my mouth. Maybe he is right; maybe if I could sleep even for an hour, I would feel better. My body is exhausted, and I feel sick and uneasy. Orion snatches the pill bottle from my hand, but he is too late. I have already swallowed them.

"They won't hurt me. They aren't strong enough to kill me," I tell him, but he eyes me carefully.

I have been on these pills for three years now. I know what I can handle and have taken more than the prescribed dose before. They just make me sleepy and numb. I may be many things but never suicidal. Although I have considered it, I would never do it because it will imply that he still has control after all these years. Even though he is dead, I will never give him the satisfaction of knowing that he destroyed me.

Walking up the stairs, I head for the bathroom, wanting to shower. Orion is following me up as he always does. He usually sits on the sink watching me, or sometimes he hops in. I am comfortable in his presence and find him being near relaxing. I can't explain it.

Orion tries saying it is the bond. I feel comfortable around Thaddeus and Ryland now, but with Orion, I feel safest. Stripping off, I turn the water on and hop in. Only instead of Orion, Thaddeus, and Ryland step into the shower. I look at them, worried. I know they won't hurt me, yet Thaddeus always makes me feel uneasy, and Ryland's eyes always roam, making me feel uncomfortable.

"Where is Orion?" I ask. My voice sounds slurred, and they both stare at me for a few seconds.

"He went to get your medication," Ryland answers, studying me as I lean heavily on the wall.

The pills are kicking in; my muscles are relaxing, and I feel like melting jelly. I shower quickly, knowing I need to get downstairs before I can barely walk. Stepping out, I wrap my towel around me and walk into the bedroom, but now even dressing feels like a major task that I am not up for.

Forcing my limbs to move, I grab one of their shirts, slip it on, and walk out. Heading for the stairs, I have to grip the banister tightly as I feel myself stumble. Only the grip keeps me upright.

Ryland moves closer to me.

"Don't touch me," I tell him, and he puts his hands up in surrender, but lingers as I descend the stairs.

I flop heavily on the couch. A giggle escapes my lips at the rush of falling. I must look mad, but I don't care. My face and limbs are numb, but my mind is awake and alert as I roll on my side, facing the TV. I'm not really watching, but the pictures help, the voices, that sound like a soft murmur, barely reach my ears as I zone out, staring blankly at the TV. Time is slipping by.

I don't know how much time passes, but Thaddeus eventually

leaves me, and I finally relax, knowing he is gone. Minutes tick by slowly as I lose track of time.

My eyes become heavy as I fight sleep. Panic sets in, and I realize I shouldn't have taken the pills. I need sleep, but the thought scares me. Panic seizes me as I stumble to the kitchen. My mouth feels so dry it leaves an unpleasant taste. I drop the glass into the sink when I try to fill it. Picking it up again, I clutch it with both hands only to drop again. My fingers are still numb, and I resort to just drinking straight from the faucet.

Walking back to the couch, I flop down, wondering when Orion will be back. Ryland wakes as I sit down, his eyes snap open. I can see how tired he is.

"Go to bed," I yawn while speaking.

"I will when you do," he says, yawning, causing me to yawn. Is it true that yawning is contagious?

Thaddeus walks downstairs, sitting next to me before retrieving the remote. He flicks through the channels until a growl leaves him when he realizes the only thing on is infomercials. He drops his back on the couch, and I watch him. He seems tired, too, and his aura feels electrified. Even Ryland looks at him worriedly, feeling the vibe he is giving off.

"Go get some sleep; I will wait with her till Orion comes back," he says, rubbing Thaddeus' thigh.

Thaddeus shakes his head. "I can't, the bed feels empty," he murmurs, pinching the bridge of his nose in frustration. He growls and turns to me, a glare on his face. "You need to sleep; why do you keep fighting it?"

I ignore him, for days they have asked the same question. At least when Orion is here, he doesn't ask, he just leaves me be.

"I want to go home. I was fine until I came here," I tell him, and he growls louder, making my heart rate pick up and thump erratically in my chest.

"Come, I will lay with you till you fall asleep," Ryland says to him.

Thaddeus sighs and gets up, and I feel bad knowing I am the

reason they remain awake. Yet, if they dreamed the things I did, they wouldn't want to sleep either. But I can't tell them that, can't let them find out what I have done. I will only relive what he did, what I did. I'm not proud of it. I did what I had to, but at what cost? Am I any better than the monsters I now live with?

Ryland and Thaddeus head upstairs, and I find myself staring off blankly for a while before I try to rest my eyes. They feel dry and sore so I close them for a few seconds. I let myself drift.

My mind slips into unconsciousness. The dream starts the way it always does. The creak of stairs. The top step was always loudest and creaked under any weight. I tug the blanket around myself, praying he walks past my door, letting out a breath when I hear his steps move past to his bedroom. Relief floods me.

He always touched me, from the first night I moved in with them. Fear paralyzes me each time, and I blame myself for being weak and not fighting back. After that first night, he would always sneak in but never do more than grope me, touch me. But that night, I heard him walk past the door, and relief flooded into me, thinking I would finally get rest.

Only, I heard him stop. Not hearing his door click shut made me hold my breath. His footsteps returned, getting louder. The twist of my doorknob as it turned is forever engraved in my head.

The smell of bourbon filled the room, and I felt like I couldn't breathe. I know he is standing next to my bed, and I feel dread creep into me, feel his eyes roam over every inch of my covered body. Only this time, he doesn't touch me. This time, he does something way worse, something so painful that I feel my heart break into a thousand pieces. My soul is shattered; fear paralyzes me for a second until I feel him remove everything.

I struggle, but he is so heavy, and I am small and trapped beneath him. My fear consumes me when I hear his voice next to my ear. "Struggle and Lana is next. You don't want me to hurt little Lana, now do you?"

My mind goes to her in the room a few doors down, she got here a week after me. She was ten; I was nearly sixteen. As far as I knew, he never touched her. Lana assured me he never did when we escaped, but that night, what he said paralyzed me instantly. I remember her innocent face, her blonde ringlets that hung to the middle of her back, and her blue, doe eyes. We had become close, having both grown up in foster care. We shared the same struggles and knew how lonely a place it was.

The thought of her made me freeze, and I watched, praying I would pass out from the pain, praying his wife would come home and stop him. Neither happened, and I was forced to endure and watch the terrible things he did, silent tears running down my face. Minutes felt like hours but when he was done, he walked out, leaving me there. My sheets turned red with the blood of my innocence; my soul bled out of me. I was used goods, nothing but filth, and I felt so dirty, pathetic. The shame that came with what he did kept me silent. Shame was what stopped me from speaking out. Shame made me endure for an entire year after that, shame and fear of what he would do if I tried to stop him.

And right now, my dreams are forcing me to relive it. I struggle to force myself to wake. I subconsciously know I am dreaming and not there, but the dream is sucking me in. My heart pounds in my chest when I suddenly break out of it, sitting upright. I gasp for air, drenched in sweat; my skin feels cold, and my lungs are restricted. The TV has gone into sleep mode and switched off; the place is completely dark and silent except for the erratic sound of my breathing.

Looking around, I notice Orion still isn't back. I do not know how long I was asleep, but it was probably minutes, as my eyes still feel like sandpaper. Getting up, I hunt for my pills until I remember I have none left. My entire body is trembling, and the dark makes me feel claustrophobic. I flick on the lights, illuminating the house. Sitting on the couch, I try to calm myself and ground myself.

I can hear movement upstairs before hearing footsteps on the stairs. Ryland must have felt my panic as he suddenly appears at the bottom of the stairs, looking alarmed and looking for danger. His eyes fall on me, and he sits on the couch furthest from me.

"You, okay?" he asks. I can see something flicker in his eyes, something I can't decipher. I nod. "You know he can take it away?" he says, making my eyes snap to his.

"What?" I ask, confused.

"Whatever happened that haunts you, Thaddeus can make it stop, make you forget," he says.

I want to forget...What I would do to forget, to erase that year from my memory. "How?" I ask.

"By telling him what happened, he can erase it all," Ryland says.

I shake my head; I can't do that. I can't let anyone know. The thought alone disgusts me and makes bile rise in my throat.

Ryland stands up, his entire body radiates anger, and his eyes darken. His canines protrude, and I feel fear creep in. "You're not the only one affected by it; you realize that, don't you? You need to either deal with it or let him remove it. Evelyn, I can't keep feeling what you feel with no fucking answers. Every emotion you feel, I feel. Your fear, sadness, shame, and guilt, your fucking exhaustion. I feel it all, and it is infuriating that I can feel everything and not know what is causing it. They can feel it too, through me. You are turning our fucking bond into a curse!" he yells at me.

I stay silent and eventually, he storms upstairs. "You think feeling it is bad? Try fucking reliving it!" I scream back at him as anger bubbles through me.

Ryland freezes. A menacing growl escapes him before he suddenly stands in front of me.

"I didn't ask for this. You all brought me here; you brought it back. I was fine until you fucking walked into my life!" I scream at him.

I hear movement upstairs again. Thaddeus' growl makes my eyes snap to the stairs. Ryland is breathing heavily, and I can feel the rage inside him.

Thaddeus appears behind me, making me jump. The intensity of his gaze makes me flinch away from him. His eyes are like storm clouds, his fangs protrude as he steps toward me. "We can't help you if we don't know what's wrong," he says, his voice emotionless and cold.

I suddenly wish Orion was back. Fear consumes me as the lights flicker, something I know as his anger before he erupts. No sooner than I think it, Orion walks in, and I instantly run to him; anything to get away from Thaddeus. Orion grips me tightly, worried for a second as he takes in the room. I notice he is saturated, his clothes dripping wet, making me step away from him as I feel the coldness seep into me, making me shiver.

"What's going on?" he asks, looking at them.

Thaddeus calms slightly and pinches the bridge of his nose in frustration. "Ask her; you can deal with her. I am going to bed to try to sleep," he says.

I watch as he walks upstairs. Ryland follows, but he stops next to me. His eyes soften as he looks down at me and quickly pulls me to him. "I'm sorry," he whispers, and I can feel Orion's eyes on us.

Tingles spread all over my body, and I relax against him. I place my hand on his chest. He feels warm, and as much as I hate to admit it, he feels safe. They all do, yet touching leads to memories, and I reluctantly pull away. Ryland sighs and walks upstairs. I walk back to the couch and flick the TV on.

"You were gone a while," I tell Orion, and he nods. He then drops a bag on the counter. He looks tired, even though I know he doesn't sleep.

"I know you're hiding something. Whatever it is, we won't judge you for it, Evelyn. They only want to help, and you keep shoving us out," he says, as he rummages through the bag. He walks over, placing a bottle of pills in my hand. "I need to shower, and you need sleep. These aren't helping you." Orion states, then turns his back on me and walks up the stairs, leaving me with my thoughts.

I look at the bottle, get up, and place it back on the counter. I can't take any more, not without the risk of an overdose. My clothes are wet from Orion, so I decided to change. I walk up the stairs, rummaging through the closet until I find another shirt and slip it on.

Hearing the shower running, I notice light coming from under the bedroom door, casting shadows throughout the room. I open the door, step inside, and sit on the sink. Orion has his back to me, but I know he heard me come in, because he speaks.

"Go lay down, Evelyn. Please."

I feel tears brim at his words. He sounds annoyed with me, making me feel annoyed at myself for being weak. Opening the door, I step out, intending to go back downstairs.

Thaddeus rolls over, his hypnotic green eyes glow as he watches me, making me freeze. He tosses the blanket back, and I think he will get up until I realize he wants me to hop in with him. I look toward the door and turn toward it, about to go downstairs, but then I stop and look back. He is still watching, waiting to see what I will do, and for some reason, I feel drawn to him like a moth to a flame.

"Please, just sleep. We won't let anyone hurt you," he whispers.

He says that, but how safe am I sleeping in a bed with two monsters? Yet, they feel safer than my mind does. Walking over, I climb in and feel him pull the blanket up. He rolls on his back and closes his eyes. His bare side touches my arm, sending sparks to my neck, making me relax slightly.

I sit there for a few minutes and hear the shower turn off, making me sit up on my elbow, looking at the door. Thaddeus shifts slightly, making my eyes look down, and I see he is watching me closely. I lay back down and put my head on his chest. He takes a breath in, and I feel him relax. Then, I feel his hand rubbing my back and finally, my eyes get heavier as I fall asleep.

O rion

Walking out of the bathroom, I slip into the walk-in. Evelyn's scent is strong in the room, and I quickly put on some clothes. When I walk out, I notice something move out of the corner of my eye on the bed. Walking over, I feel relief flood into me when I see Evelyn is asleep. Thaddeus' green eyes stare up at me, and he shrugs, shocked himself.

He moves over, pulling her with him and makes room for me. I lay next to her, feeling relaxed. Her racing heartbeat and frantic emotions have had all of us on edge. Thaddeus the most because he hasn't fed, and I can tell he wants to mark her. Evelyn has relaxed, and I know it's because she allowed him to be close to her.

Thaddeus is usually a man of few words. He usually takes what he wants without question or permission. The last few days, he has been on edge, wanting to force her to tell us, but Ryland and I have held him back each time.

He doesn't want to scare her, but it's killing him not knowing. Once they fall asleep, I walk downstairs and head to the library. I sit for a few hours reading, trying to consume my mind with anything other than Evelyn and my mates.

Hours tick by, and the sun comes up. I stay quiet as I walk upstairs, not wanting to wake them. Evelyn moves, and Thaddeus' grip on her tightens. She snuggles into him, and I drape my arm over her and Thaddeus. Nothing feels righter than having them all in the same bed, yet I also know it won't last.

Evelyn will wake, and everything will come back. Whatever it is will make her plummet. We have a rough idea based on her feelings, but we can't understand her guilt. I pray that sleep finally helps her, helps her mind clear of whatever it is.

When I was in the city, I sent a message to Amara. Thaddeus will be angry when he finds out, but he will forgive me. He always does.

Amara is one of his weaknesses. His little sister brings out a protective side of him, just like Evelyn does. Only, she knows what he is like, and usually, he distances himself from her, going years without speaking to her.

Sometimes, I feel his jealousy over her, jealous that she is the good one. Thaddeus tries to be good, but everything he touches turns to dust by the time he is done with it. He destroys everything and implodes on himself.

He never feels guilty for his actions, never sees the repercussions of his destruction, and continues to destroy everything he comes across. He doesn't even know what he is looking for, but I feel the urge to find it and leave him with Evelyn by his side. This is the longest we have stayed home. Usually, we last two days max before he has us searching and moving from city to city and country to country, leaving destruction everywhere he goes.

Two broken people found each other. This will either be the best thing that happens to them or the worst and most dangerous thing. Unfortunately, not all things broken can be fixed. No one can go back and change the past, but maybe the future?

I hope they can change the future; Amara always says nothing good will come of Thaddeus if he can't find his way back, and that our future is uncertain. She once said that he will be our downfall, but she never saw Evelyn in that future. I am curious to know if she could see her now, see her a part of our world, or will her demise be at his hands.

I am pulled from my troubled thoughts when I feel her waking, Ryland is stirring, and a feeling of unease settles over him. Thaddeus' eyes open as he peers down at her with a frown on his face. Her eyelids move as she watches her dreams play out. Ryland sits up and looks over Thaddeus, his eyes resting on Evelyn. He brushes her hair from her face, and I feel her relax under his touch.

One word slips from her lips in her sleep.

"Lana."

CHAPTER
SIXTEEN

Evelyn

Waking up, I am pressed against Thaddeus, his hand in the center of my back. I feel wide awake, like I had the best sleep and am completely rested. Sitting up, I find Thaddeus is the only person left in the room. He is watching me, and he looks like he has been awake for a while.

His arm tightens around me as I try to get away from him. "I didn't want to wake you," he says, and I notice a book beside him, proving he has been trapped under me for a while.

"What time is it?" I ask.

"Little after lunchtime," Thaddeus answers.

"I should let you get up," I tell him, trying to shift off him.

"I would rather you stay," he says, and my eyes dart back to his.

He taps his chest with his other hand, wanting me to lay back down. Looking around, I notice Ryland and Orion aren't in the room. Being around Thaddeus usually makes me nervous. He can be so intense sometimes. His aura makes me feel uncomfortable, yet he looks pretty relaxed right now, so I lay back down. Thaddeus absentmindedly plays with my hair while I listen to the sound of his heartbeat thumping softly in his chest.

A few minutes pass, and I don't mind his company.

"Can I ask you something?" Thaddeus speaks softly, and I turn my head to look at him. I prop my head on my hand on his chest, facing him. I feel a fog slip over me, and I instantly relax, my breathing evens out.

"What did you do?" I ask, knowing he is doing something that is calming. His eyes glow hypnotically, while my mind is becoming foggy.

"It's a form of mental compulsion or glamor. I can control your emotions and what I want you to do or say with it."

"Are you going to make me answer your questions?" I ask. I know I should be worried, but I feel light and foggy.

"Not if you don't want to. Do you want me to stop?" he asks, watching me. Thaddeus is always watching, and yet I have trouble reading him. He is so cold and calm, despite his anger. That is the only emotion I can ever feel coming off him, mainly because the entire atmosphere shifts. Now, he seems calm, but the monster lurking behind his eyes doesn't go unnoticed by me. "Who is Lana?"

My mind reels: I am sure I have never mentioned her name. Sitting up, I feel the fog get stronger as it slips over me. "You said you wouldn't." I panic.

He brushes my hair from my face. "I'm not; stop running. You don't need to run from us; you don't need to hide," he says, pulling me back down. I relax against him, giving in. I don't want to answer his questions, but I don't want to risk him forcing me to answer.

"So, who is Lana?" he asks again, making my heart race just at the mention of her name.

"Where did you hear it?" I ask, trying to wrack my brain, wondering if I ever mentioned her.

"You said her name in your sleep."

"She was one of the foster children I lived with," I answer, turning away from him so I don't have to see his face. Hearing her name makes me sick to my stomach. It reminds me of what I did, what he did.

"Did she do something to you?" Thaddeus asks, and I can hear the curiosity behind his words.

"No, Lana was ten; we lived with the same family for a year." I feel Thaddeus nod before I feel his hand in my hair again. I shiver when his skin comes in contact with the back of my neck.

"Was she there when you got that burn on your back?"

"No," I tell him. As soon as the answer leaves my lips, I hop up. I don't like where this conversation is going.

Walking into the bathroom, I shut the door, hearing him sigh loudly in frustration. I turn the shower on and quickly strip off. The door opens just as I open the shower. Thaddeus walks in and I just roll my eyes at him as I step into the shower.

"Well, I am fine talking to you in the bedroom, but if you want to chat in here, I am all for that too," he says.

I feel the shower open, and he steps in. I turn my back to him so he can only see my ass and back. I hear him move behind me, and then I feel his chest against my back, making my heartbeat erratically. The fog slips over me again, but I try to shake it off this time.

"You're safe with me, Evelyn. Well, not safe from me, but I won't let anyone do anything to you," he says right behind me.

"If that was supposed to make me feel better, it didn't," I tell him, grabbing the soap, trying to ignore his presence behind me, which only lasts a second before I feel his hand run down my shoulder to my side. I freeze, wondering what he is doing, and he seems to freeze as well. A moment after, he removes his hand.

"Sorry. Your scent is a little overwhelming here, and I haven't fed since we left the city," he says, I feel him move away from me. Looking over my shoulder, I see he has moved closer to the shower door.

"It's fine," I tell him until I see his face and notice the veins spread across his face, his fangs piercing out through his top and bottom lip.

I step back, frightened, but there is nowhere to go. Thaddeus notices my movement, and something flips inside him, and I am pinned against the wall with his arms on either side of my head, his body impossibly close, his fangs mere inches from my face. Fight or flight kicks in, but I have nowhere to go and no way to fight him off. His fingertips trail down my neck, and his inhuman eyes watch my face.

Ryland comes busting through the door, and Thaddeus growls, warning him.

"Thaddeus," Ryland says, and I can hear the alarm in his voice, making me more scared.

"Get out," he growls, his head whips in Ryland's direction.

Orion walks in behind him. "Let him try," Orion says, grabbing his arm. My heart races as they walk out, leaving me with Thaddeus.

"You have no idea how intoxicating your scent is when you're scared, Evelyn," Thaddeus whispers.

My heart is thumping loudly in my chest at his words as he leans in, inhaling my scent. I feel his fangs brush against my skin, making me shiver.

"Thaddeus, please stop," I stutter out of fear.

Thaddeus moves closer, pressing his entire body against me, and I feel him lick my neck, his fangs grazing my skin. I put my hand on his chest, trying to push him back.

"Just give me a minute. Don't shove me away," he whispers, and I can hear the desperation in his voice. The hunger makes me feel guilty, knowing he has been trapped in the house because of me.

I want to help him, and I don't know if that makes me just stupid or suicidal. I move my head to the side, offering him my neck. He stops, stepping away from me, his eyes not leaving my neck.

"You don't understand what you are offering, little one. I bite you; I will mark you," he says as I watch his entire body shake as he fights for control.

"Will it hurt?" I ask, wondering if it will feel like Ryland's bite.

Thaddeus' eyes snap to mine, his fangs stop him from being able to close his mouth. His eyes flicker dangerously, and I feel the air thicken.

"Only if I make it hurt," he says. The door is suddenly opening, and Orion and Ryland walk in. Thaddeus looks relieved.

"Thaddeus has trouble stopping. He just wanted to see if he could control himself," Orion says, I can make them out through the frosted glass.

"Thaddeus, do you need help or not?" Orion asks. Thaddeus looks toward the door.

"He's fine; he just wants to feed on me, right?" I ask, looking at Thaddeus.

I see his eyes dart to my neck, and a growl rips from him loudly, sounding louder from the tiled walls and the confined shower.

"I will open the door for you, Thaddeus," Ryland says, but I move closer, all fear gone when I realize he doesn't want to hurt me. As I move closer to him, blocking the door, his eyes never leave mine.

"Do it. They will rip me away if you go overboard, right?" I ask, as the door opens behind me, and I see Orion before he nods at me, reassuring me.

"Evelyn, you don't have to do this. I can take him to town," Orion says behind me.

"Does he kill them?" I ask, stuttering over the words.

They don't say anything, and I feel my heartbeat pick up, knowing I am right. Ryland grips my arm, and Thaddeus growls, making goosebumps rise on my skin. This side of him is animalistic, and at the moment, I am prey. Thaddeus' hand goes to my hip, tugging me to him and away from Ryland. I feel Ryland step into the shower behind me. Thaddeus' eyes don't leave me.

"Don't make it hurt," I tell him, and Thaddeus cocks his head to the side, observing me.

"You know once I bite you, I mark you, like Ryland did?" he asks.

"So do you plan on letting me go?" I ask.

"Never," Thaddeus growls, and I shrug, stepping closer.

"Well, it will happen eventually then," I tell him. His eyes darken, and he growls, ripping me to him.

I whimper when I feel his teeth sink into my neck, but then a different feeling wraps around me. I don't know if Thaddeus or Orion is using that weird fog as I relax against him and feel his tongue lapping at my neck. Arousal washes over me as I feel the bond snap in place stronger, feel Ryland stronger, and feel Orion, but not as much. A moan escapes my lips, and my core pulsates, the feeling foreign, but I don't push it away.

Thaddeus' grip on me becomes tighter before he pushes me away at arm's length, holding me there, his grip tight as he fights with himself. Reaching up, I place my hand on his face, and he leans into it. His grip loosens, and I watch as his fangs go away and his face goes back to normal, the black veins leave, and he no longer looks like the devil incarnate.

CHAPTER
SEVENTEEN

Evelyn

My head feels foggy from his bite, and I have a strong desire to sleep. As I sway on my feet, my eyes flutter closed. The last thing I remember is tingles spreading all over me as someone tries to steady me on my feet before I feel strong, warm arms wrap around me as I plunge into the darkness, my body succumbing to exhaustion.

I know I am dreaming because I have been here before and know what happens next, yet I can't pull myself out of the dream as I follow him toward the basement. I have three weeks, and I am officially free of this hell. They will age me out of the system. I can go out on my own, but the uneasy feeling of leaving Lana with this monster has been haunting me.

I tried twice to go to the police station, each time standing out the front, looking at the building that was supposed to offer protection, but would they offer protection from one of their own? He was a well-respected officer, the man with the perfect wife, perfect house, and perfect life.

I am a throw-away child, the broken foster kid he took in. The voice in my head told me they wouldn't believe me, that what happened is my fault. The thought of having to go through the courts and tell a bunch of strangers what happened for an entire year, have them question every detail and scrutinize everything about my childhood, about me; the victim becomes the accused.

The term innocent until proven guilty irks me. Why must I be questioned as if I am the guilty one before being proven innocent? So, each time I turn around, not able to go through with it, not able to mention my biggest shame.

That is what plays on my mind when he tells me to come to the basement. I know he doesn't need help to sort things; he only wants me to go down there so he can torture what is left of my soul, to make sure I am destroyed beyond repair.

That sickening feeling fills my gut as my feet touch the cold basement floor. His wife is a nurse and always works the night shift, leaving us with this monster. I often wonder how many before me. How many more girls has he destroyed?

I'm not sure, but I know his next target will be Lana. I couldn't live with myself knowing I left her with him, left her to this house of horrors. I watch as he undoes his belt and points to the dusty couch in the corner. Bile rises in my throat as I walk over to it. I can hear the TV upstairs above us, Lana watching cartoons, completely unaware of what is happening below her. He places his belt and gun on the mini fridge before roughly grabbing me. I tune out while he has his way with me, only coming back to reality as he pulls my pants back up. Tears roll down my cheeks, I hear the TV click off, knowing it is nearly bedtime.

I can hear him talking to me, but I don't understand what he says. All I can focus on is her footsteps as they go up the stairs to her bedroom. I can't abandon her like that, leave her with him to do as he pleases. Before I realize what, I have done, I pick up his gun. My hands tremble as I point it at him. He cocks an eyebrow at me before swigging from his bottle of bourbon. He laughs.

"Hand it over. We both know you won't do it," he says, laughing as he moves toward me.

My hands shake as I turn the safety off. His eyes widen before he tries ripping it from my hands. We struggle, he backhands me, my head whips to the side and the gun falls from my hands on the floor. He bends down, picks it up and puts the safety back on before walking up the stairs like nothing happened. Hours, I sit down there until I get the courage to go back up the stairs. My dream feels like it is only minutes. Everything moves quickly, and next, I am sneaking upstairs.

Walking to his room, I find him passed out drunk. Running down the stairs, I grab a bottle of liquor. He always smokes in bed, so it will look like an accident. It is no secret the officer is an alcoholic. Apparently, he suffers from some form of PTSD. I pour the liquor onto his bed, careful not to wake him. The smell is pungent and burns my nose. Grabbing one of his smokes from the bedside table, I light it, smoking half of it before grabbing the bottle again and tipping it on him. He wakes immediately, looking up at me, half asleep. He has a cruel smile on his lips as he reaches for me before realizing what I tipped on him. Anger blazes as I draw back on the cigarette, trying to calm my nerves.

"Burn in hell," I tell him as I flick it.

I watch as it lands on the bed.

The covers catch fire before his clothes do, he screams. I watch, horrified at what I have done until my brain kicks into function. He tries getting up, but flames engulf him; I can smell his burning hair as he climbs off the bed, trying to put out the flames frantically. I step back, watching as everything catches fire before I run for the door. His screams will forever haunt my memory.

I run from that room, bolting down the stairs only to remember

Lana is in the room next door to his, making me run back up, but the hallway is already on fire. The wallpaper is burning and peeling off the walls as I run past and into her room, shaking her. She wakes up just as the fire alarms blare.

I rip her from her bed in her Harry Potter pajamas. Her eyes widen when we step into the hall, and she sees the flames. I shove her toward the stairs, and she runs down when I feel something fall on me, shoving me down the stairs, and I thrash. Burning pain moves up my back, making me scream in agony, and all I can focus on is the pain as Lana screams. I writhe in agony, trying to get whatever is on me off.

I hear voices; they sound familiar to me, getting louder and louder.

"Evelyn, wake up, wake up." Someone is shaking me from my dream, and my eyes fly open.

My heart is pounding against my chest painfully. Sweat coats my skin, and my eyes try to adjust to the light. I scream, trying to get away from the hands shaking me, thrashing to get him off.

"Evelyn, it's me. Stop." That voice, that familiar voice rings through my head again, and my eyes focus as they land on Thaddeus.

I stop, looking around the room, and I am not in the house of my nightmares but my bed with my mates. Tears roll down my cheeks as I realize I am awake, no longer burning, and the searing pain dissipates.

Thaddeus's hands clutch my face. "You're okay. You're okay, little one. It was just a dream," he says as he pulls me towards him and into his lap.

Ryland moves closer, placing his head in my lap, and I feel my breathing even out as reality comes back to me. I then notice Orion watching me from the end of the bed, an indecipherable expression on his face. Looking down at Ryland, I notice claw marks across his back and angry red lines that are nearly healed.

"What happened to your back?" I whisper. My voice sounds hoarse, like I have been screaming and my throat hurts just speaking.

"Everything you feel, we feel. That's what woke us, I thought I was on fire," Ryland says as he rolls his head and looks up at me. I lean back against Thaddeus; his hand strokes my damp hair from my face. Guilt floods me as I stare down at Ryland. They can feel it, feel everything, and the thought sickens me.

"How long have I been asleep?"

"A few days," Thaddeus answers, making my head whip to the side to look at him.

"Thaddeus, marking you knocked you out. His mark did the same to us as well. Think it's because he is a Tribrid," Orion answers the question I am about to ask.

I nod, not knowing what else to say. Guilt is eating at me as I stare at Orion. His curious gaze is watching me.

"What happened? If we are going to burn every time, you're asleep, I need to know why," he asks.

"Please, Evelyn, just tell us so Thaddeus can take it away. I can't live like this, not knowing. At least tell us, so we understand," Ryland says, reaching his hand up and cupping my face.

I feel a lump form in my throat, and I try to swallow it down, but my mouth is so dry.

"You have been reliving it for days now; we haven't been able to wake you until now. What's once more," Thaddeus says, kissing the side of my face.

"Nothing will make us leave you, Evelyn. You can trust us," Orion says, moving onto the bed.

"You may just change your mind about that if you know," I tell him.

His eyebrows furrow in confusion.

"What do you mean?" Thaddeus asks as he grips my chin, forcing me to meet his eyes.

"You're not the only monsters. What I did made me just as bad as him. But I couldn't leave her with him," I whisper, looking away toward the window.

"Leave who?" he asks.

"Lana."

Chapter
EIGHTEEN

Evelyn

"I thought you said Lana wasn't there," Thaddeus asks over my shoulder.

"She was there. She tried to put me out; she burnt her hands terribly," I answer. My heart pounds in my chest as I remember the smell of my burning flesh and hair, so pungent I can almost taste it in my throat, making me want to gag. "I don't want you to take it away."

Orion watches me, confused. I thought I wanted that, but I don't want to forget Lana. Why I did it, makes it easier to live with what I have done.

"I don't understand?" Orion says, moving closer, his head lying next to Thaddeus' leg as he lays down.

"I don't want to forget her; I need to know I did it for a reason," I tell him.

"What do you mean?" Thaddeus asks, pulling my face to his, his eyes searching my face.

"I... I..." I can't bring myself to say it.

"You what, Evelyn?" Thaddeus asks again, and I can feel all their eyes on me.

"Anything you have done cannot be compared to what we have done, Evelyn. We won't judge you," Ryland tells me, looking up at me.

"He wouldn't have stopped, so I killed him. I set the fire; I set him on fire."

They look shocked, and I can feel their shock through the bond before confusion sets in again. I have carried that for so long, and saying it feels like a relief, like someone has lifted the weight off me. I killed somebody. He may have been a monster, but I still killed someone.

"He would have raped her, too. I couldn't leave her with him, so I killed him. I was going to age out of the system, but she would have had to put up with it for another six, or more years. A year was bad enough for me; I couldn't imagine leaving her with him. I couldn't let him destroy her, too." I whisper, looking away back toward the window.

Thaddeus growls loudly, and I jump, anger radiates through the bond. I knew they would hate me for what I have done and should have kept it to myself. Getting off the bed, I move away. Ryland sits up, watching me.

"See? This is why I didn't tell anyone; no one would believe me," I tell them, tears brimming in my eyes.

"We aren't angry at you, Evelyn. He deserved it, you did nothing wrong," Orion says, but Thaddeus is glaring at me.

I step back as the lights flicker. My eyes dart to Orion, who is watching me, and I don't understand the look he is giving me. Disbelief, shock, I am unsure, but I can tell Thaddeus is angry at me. Is it because I am used goods or not as innocent as he thought?

When I hear Thaddeus growl and the lights go out, I turn on my heel and run for the door. Running into something hard, I nearly fall over as I feel a hand reach out and grab me. The flickering of the lights stops, and I find Thaddeus standing in front of me, blocking the door. My heart is beating in my chest so hard I can hear it, feel it jolting against my chest painfully.

He clamps his hands on the sides of my face. I brace myself, knowing this is how I die. This is my karma for what I did. Then suddenly, I feel his hands heat before they go ice cold, and I scream as my mind is consumed. I feel what feels like fingers sifting through the files of my mind.

It's the weirdest sensation, like I can feel him picking through memories before I am suddenly plunged back into my fifteen-year-old self, seeing the moment I am dropped off at their house by my caseworker.

I feel my breath hitch when she knocks, and I am excited to be, with what I thought, was a friendly couple. I feel tears brim and fall as I sob.

The entire year I am with them, every waking memory of that year flashes before my eyes so fast I can't catch my breath. Thaddeus growls loudly, and I can feel his hands shake as the movie of my life suddenly stops, and I am staring into Thaddeus' hypnotic green eyes, dazzled by them. His words echo in my head, and it's all I can think of.

"It's over. It happened, but it doesn't hurt. You did what you had to do. You are safe now. Let it go." I try to shake off what he says, when I find it slipping deeper into my mind, the memories become foggy and distant, the surrounding feeling slips away with them. I find myself repeating after him. The words leave my lips, and I feel like I am in a trance.

"It's over, it happened, but it doesn't hurt. I did what I had to do. I am safe; I can let it go." The moment the last words leave my lips, I feel the weight lift, feel everything holding me back, lift, and I feel light, like I can breathe for the first time.

I feel free. Free of the guilt, free of the pain, and free to move on. Thaddeus' eyes are searching my face, and I feel tears run down my cheeks; not tears of sadness but tears of relief. I am finally free. I run into his arms as he lets go, hitting his chest hard. I am safe. They are safe.

"Thank you," I whisper, as I sob into his chest, his arms wrap around me, holding me to him before I feel him grip my waist, and I wrap my legs around him, hugging him tightly, his hands rub my back soothingly.

R yland

She panics, thinking our anger is at her and bolts for the door. Our anger isn't directed at her but at what happened.

Thaddeus growls, the lights flicker out before flicking on, and he is directly in front of her. She freezes, her entire body tense as he grips her face and sifts through her mind, digging through every memory.

His eyes turn black once he finds what he is looking for, his grip tightens on her as he watches every memory. Every emotion she feels in that year hits him and me, and I feel sick to my stomach.

Running for the bathroom, I throw up, feeling everything that piece of shit did to her. I have never been sick, so this is a fresh experience for me. My throat burns as I throw up the contents of my stomach. I can feel him still sifting through her memories and feel what she endured as I wash my face before walking out.

Orion is sitting there with wide eyes, and I know he is in Thaddeus's head, watching along with him. I am glad I don't have that gift for once because curiosity probably would have made me snoop. Thaddeus' words pull my eyes back to him as I feel the ill-feeling coiling in my stomach leave.

"It's over, it happened, but it doesn't hurt. You did what you had to do. You are safe now. Let it go," he says. Her eyes glaze over as she tries fighting against it.

I am shocked he doesn't just completely erase it. He lets her keep the memories because of the girl she doesn't want to forget. Thaddeus' hands glow green as I watch him pull the darkness from her, absorbing it and taking it from her.

A range of emotions flood the bond as he repeats his words, and she repeats after him. Relief is all I can feel from her as the heavy burden of what she carries is lifted. She runs to him, her little arms wrap around him as he picks her up, hugging her close like they are each other's lifeline.

Thaddeus' green eyes go to ours, and Orion and I watch as he closes his eyes, tears run down his cheeks at what he saw, what she went through.

It is the first time we have ever seen him cry.

I didn't think he was even capable of tears. Orion, I can feel, is just as upset, and I promise myself never to ask what they saw. Orion moves to her, wrapping his arms around them, and Evelyn turns her head on Thaddeus' shoulder. She looks completely relaxed and at home in their arms.

I let out the breath I am holding, watching them in awe. Thaddeus kisses her head, and she lifts her face from his shoulder to kiss him. Thaddeus' shock hits me as he kisses her back softly. His hand goes into her hair, gently holding her in place. I chuckle at the sight as she pulls back, resting her forehead on his.

Evelyn

We spend the rest of the day watching movies. Thaddeus, though, I can tell is slightly off, and Orion and Ryland keep sending him nervous glances, which I can't understand.

You can feel the negative energy in the air. When we finish dinner, his entire body is shaking, and his eyes flicker between black and green frighteningly. Orion abruptly stands up, giving me a nervous glance as he grips Thaddeus and tugs him outside.

Grabbing everyone's dishes, I walk into the kitchen and start stacking the dishwasher. Ryland follows behind me and helps me.

"What's wrong with Thaddeus?" I ask while rinsing a plate.

"He will be fine. Sometimes, the darkness becomes too much," he answers, not adding anything else. We walk out once we're finished, and I notice Orion and Thaddeus haven't returned.

"Where did they go?" I ask, confused.

"To blow off steam. Thaddeus isn't safe to be around when he is like that. It's not worth the risk to you," Ryland answers. As I walk upstairs, Ryland sits on the couch. "Where are you going?" he asks, looking up at me.

"To go shower. You can join me if you want," I tell him, and he jumps up and rushes up the stairs.

Ryland grabs me before I make it through the bedroom door, spinning me around and slamming me into the wall. My legs wrap tightly around his waist as he knocks the air out of me, making me cough as I smile at him.

He's breathing hard as he presses closer, his nose goes into the crook of my neck as he inhales my scent. Ryland sucks on my mark, and I moan loudly without realizing I do. Ryland chuckles softly and pulls back to kiss me gently. I can feel his erection pressing against me, yet the old, frightened feelings no longer affect me. For the first time, my mind is completely mine. I can feel his shock as I kiss him back, but he quickly deepens the kiss and growls.

"We should shower before I piss off our mates by taking you first." He chuckles and kisses me again, as he lets me stand.

Going to the bathroom, I strip my clothes off and turn the shower on. Ryland's intense gaze makes my skin heat. My eyes roam over his muscled arms as he moves closer and cages me against the wall with his arms on either side of my head. His black eyes look down at me. Lifting my hand, I trace it down his chest to his abs. His body tenses under my touch.

Standing on my toes, I kiss him softly, feeling his tongue run over my bottom lip as he sucks it into his mouth. Then, Thaddeus' voice echoes through me.

"Hands off, Ryland!" Thaddeus growls, and I pull back, looking toward the door, only no one is there.

"I'm not using my hands," Ryland growls back. I furrow my eyebrows, confused.

"I heard that," Thaddeus says, making my eyes snap back to the door. I could have sworn he said that aloud in the bathroom, his voice is echoing around us.

"Thaddeus has marked you now. He can get in your head no matter how far away you are," Ryland tells me.

"So, he isn't here?" I ask.

Ryland shakes his head. "No, and I am not sure when he will be back."

"What do you mean?" I ask, worried.

"It doesn't matter. Come on, let's shower, get dressed, and see what's on TV before we piss him off more," Ryland says, turning back around and grabbing the soap.

We wash quickly, jump out, and I grab one of their shirts, pulling it over my head. We walk downstairs and flick the TV on. I scroll through the channels, past a news report, then go back to it when I hear the news anchor talking about breaking news and a recent development on the Dark Ones. My heart skips a beat. My blood runs cold when a street view comes on, and I can see Thaddeus' blurred figure move onto the screen, another figure chasing him and tackling him, and I know it has to be Orion.

Suddenly, the entire street is plunged into darkness as everything explodes, and one can only see the flicker of lights and the explosion. Then, the screen goes blank, and the news lady's voice comes across the air. "Main street has been destroyed. Anyone in the vicinity is urged to take shelter and remain indoors."

Suddenly, the remote is snatched out of my hand, and the TV is turned off. I turn to face Ryland. "You weren't meant to see that," he says, sighing in frustration.

"Is that where he is? Is that where he went?" I yell at him. Ryland looks away.

"You know who he is, what he is, Evelyn," Ryland says.

I shake my head; I won't be a part of them destroying the world. "No, I won't accept this. You expect me to be okay with that?" I scream angrily.

Ryland shrugs. He sits down and places his head in his hands. "He can't help it. The darkness takes over, and there is no controlling him. Believe me; we have tried."

"That's no excuse! You don't just go around killing people! He has been fine for days, and now this?"

"Yes, before he took it away, Evelyn. Everything has a price. The more he uses his magic, the worse it becomes. He absorbed your memories and turned them into his own. He did it for you so you wouldn't have to deal with it. Now he is paying the price for it, and the only way to do so is to release it."

I stumble back at his words, horrified. "So, this was my fault? I did this?"

"Shit, I didn't mean it to come out like that," Ryland says.

"No, don't touch me! What, he couldn't destroy an empty field or something? Why an entire city?" I scream as tears start rolling down my face.

"He would have gone running, trying to get rid of it, but sometimes it doesn't work, and he explodes, okay? He doesn't mean to destroy things; it just happens. Besides, he rarely kills anyone, just destroys the buildings. Sometimes people get caught in the crossfire. And sometimes..." he hesitates, not wanting to answer.

"Sometimes what, Ryland?"

"Hunger takes over."

"No. Fucking, no. I won't deal with this shit! Make him come back!" I yell at him.

Ryland's eyes go completely black, and I feel his anger rising.

"Fine! If this is how it will be, I am done!" I tell him as I walk up the stairs. Grabbing some pants, I slip them on and grab my wallet, walking out of the room. Ryland growls at me, blocking me on the stairs.

"You're not leaving."

"Yes, I am," I say, shoving him, but he doesn't budge. "Fucking move, Ryland. I will not stay here knowing you are all killing innocent people," I tell him, trying to walk past him. Every step I make, he blocks me again. "I reject you then," I tell him, and his eyes go dark as a smirk graces his face.

"That's not how you reject someone. Nice try, though."

"Whatever," I tell him, ducking under his arm on the banister and bolting down the stairs only for his arms to wrap around me as I reach the bottom step. He growls loudly, tossing me over his shoulder and marching back up the stairs.

"Fucking put me down!" I scream, smacking his head with my palm.

It has no effect as I squirm in his arms. I give up on hitting him and sink my teeth into his back, letting go when I feel his hand come down on my ass. I hit his back and feel him laugh. My hand stings from smacking him when he smacks my ass again, harder, making me forget my hand. I feel tears brim at the sudden intense pain, feel his handprint bruising. Suddenly, I am dumped on the bed, and I glare at him as I try to hop off the bed.

"I wouldn't, Evelyn. You try to leave, and I will spank your ass until it bleeds," Ryland warns me, as he pushes me over and lies down next to me.

"So, what? I am supposed to wait here until the psychopath returns from his killing spree?" I ask, glaring at him and defiantly fold my arms over my chest.

"You look so cute when you're angry. And yes, that is exactly what I expect you to do. Take it up with Thaddeus when he returns. For now, lay down," he says, tugging me down.

Groaning, I flop down on the bed. Ryland rolls on his side, trying to pull me against him. I throw his arm off and hear him sigh. "No point being angry about it, Evelyn. What's done is done."

"If I had known, I never would have let him meddle in my head," I tell him.

"He would have done it anyway; Thaddeus isn't a patient man. You will come to see that. You leaving when he's gone will only make things worse. After all, he's on his way home, so you wouldn't get very far."

"How do you know?" I ask.

"I feel him getting closer, feel his mood has shifted, and he is calmer," Ryland answers. We sit in silence for God knows how long, waiting until the silence becomes too much.

"So, how does one reject someone?"

"I can't believe you expect me to tell you. You are ours; whether or not you reject us, you aren't leaving," Ryland says.

"Well, if it means he won't kill anyone, I will reject him."

Suddenly, his hand is clamped over my mouth. "Shh, someone is in the house," he whispers, making my heartbeat pick up. Ryland rolls off me and gets up. "Get in the closet," he growls. I dart off the bed, doing as he says, feeling his alarm through the bond. Closing the door, I hear him walk downstairs. A growl leaves his lips.

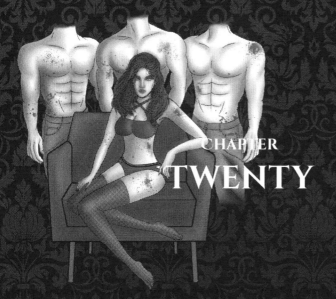

CHAPTER
TWENTY

E velyn
My heart is pounding hard in my chest as I hear a loud growl that makes me jump. Then, I hear a woman's voice. "You want to explain why my son is currently destroying the city north of here, Ryland?" The woman sounds young, but the authority behind her voice intimidates me. This woman isn't to be messed around with.

"Evelyn, you may come down!" Ryland yells out.

I hesitantly get up from my hiding spot as I hear another woman's voice. Her voice is softer but easily heard. "Evelyn? Who is Evelyn?" the person asks, just as I get to the top step.

I see two women standing at the bottom of the stairs. Both look to be in their mid-twenties and are strikingly similar. Both have long blonde hair to their waist, the younger-looking one has hers tied in a braid, and she has green eyes like Thaddeus. The older woman has blue eyes, and her hair is hanging loose down her back. I walk down the stairs, watching them stare up at me, shocked.

"This is Evelyn, our mate," Ryland says, putting his hand out for me to grab. I grip it tightly, letting him pull me to him. The older woman, whom I would guess is around twenty-five, steps forward, a shocked look on her face as she looks at Ryland, confused. "Evelyn, this is Imogen, Thaddeus' mother, and that one over there is Amara, Thaddeus' sister."

"Hi," I tell them, giving them a brief wave.

It shocks me that the woman standing in front of me is his mother. She looks younger than Thaddeus, and the girl, that I reckon looks around my age, just stares at me. Her hypnotic green eyes are watching me.

"She is human?" Amara whispers, not even hiding her shock.

"I'm more shocked she is female," Imogen says, looking me up and down. "Nice to meet you, hun. I wish it was under better circumstances, and that my son had told me. It has been twelve years since I laid eyes on him, besides seeing him on a goddamn TV screen, Ryland," she says, turning to glare at him.

Ryland shrinks back under her gaze, and I chuckle softly. This woman is small, but man, she is fierce.

"Call your brother; he answers your calls. Get him back here now," she says to her daughter. Amara pulls a phone from her pocket and dials a number. She places the phone to her ear, but no answer. Ryland pulls his phone from his pocket and hands it over to her.

Thaddeus answers after a few rings, but I can only hear one side of the conversation.

"Hey, brother, about time you answered." She goes quiet for a few seconds and speaks again.

"You have thirty minutes to get home, or I am taking your mate," she says, and hangs up on him. I step back away from her and Amara puts her hands up. "I won't. I just said it to get him moving faster. Come, let's make coffee," she says, wandering off to the kitchen.

Imogen and Amara enter the kitchen and sit, while Ryland makes the coffee. I sit across from them, unsure what to do or say.

"Orion called a week ago and said you were all home. Thought I would stop in and see him; try to talk some sense into him," Imogen tells us.

Ryland nods and hands her a coffee. Amara watches me, her head turning from side to side occasionally, like she is examining some science experiment. Her green eyes pierce into mine as I stare back, uneasy. She then blinks, shaking her head and looking away.

"She was trying to get a reading on you," Imogen tells me. I nod, wondering if she saw anything.

"So, I see two of them have marked you already. Orion hasn't?" Imogen asks, as she sniffs the air, and I pull my hair over my shoulder, covering my mark.

"Don't worry, hun, nothing to be worried about. I have two mates myself. Just wasn't expecting you to be female, honestly. Been decades since these two dragged Orion into this mess. Didn't think they would drag a human girl into it."

"She is fated, mom. Not like we had a choice," Ryland says, shaking his head.

"So, you gave her a choice? She came willingly?" Imogen asks, raising an eyebrow at him. Ryland looks away. "Like I thought," she says, turning back to me.

"So, you're Thaddeus' mother?" I ask, to change the topic of conversation.

"Yes. I know it must be a bit of a shock, considering technically, I am younger than him in human years."

I nod. "So why are you shocked I am their mate?" I ask curiously.

"Because I thought he was gay. He never showed much interest in women besides killing them."

"You know how mate bonds work, mom," Amara says, and Imogen shrugs.

"Still a bit of a shock."

She says something else when the front door bursts open, and Thaddeus runs in, grabbing me and pulling me from the chair I am sitting on. "Don't fucking threaten to take my mate again, Amara. Sister or not, I will kick your ass," he says, glaring at her.

"Is that any way to greet your mother?" Imogen growls at him, and he suddenly realizes she is there.

"Mom?" he says, stepping back.

"Don't you dare run, boy; you aren't too old for me to spank!" she says, rising from her chair. His shoulders slump as he walks over, letting me go, and hugs her.

Orion leans against the doorframe, a grin on his face. Ryland gives him a look and Orion shrugs as he walks over to me and wraps his arms around my waist. Imogen sits back down, letting her son go.

"Mom," Orion nods to her. The poor woman is the universal mother. It surprises me she isn't gray, having to put up with their antics.

Thaddeus walks over, pulling me from Orion. He sits down and pulls me on his lap. Orion frowns but walks over to the kettle. "Don't think I don't know it was you who rang them, Orion," Thaddeus says.

Orion says nothing, and it makes me wonder why Thaddeus hasn't spoken to or seen his mother in years. She seems nice. Amara is watching me again, and Thaddeus.

"So, is there a reason you destroyed that city?" Imogen asks, but before he can answer, Amara does.

"Because he stole the darkness from his mate," she says, watching me again. She doesn't seem mad, but from the feeling coming through the bond I can tell Thaddeus is. Looking up at him, he kisses the side of my face.

"That's enough, Amara. Stop snooping. Okay, well, it was great seeing you; now time to leave," Thaddeus announces, and his mom glares at him.

"You're going to kick me out?" she asks. I can see the hurt behind her eyes.

Amara stands up abruptly. Her eyes go to me, then she glares at Thaddeus before turning back to me. "You know your mark isn't completed until Orion marks you, did you know?"

Thaddeus jumps to his feet and grabs her. Imogen screams, as Amara is ripped over the table towards him. Ryland yanks me out of the way. Thaddeus growls low at her.

"Don't fucking tempt me, Amara," he says, his voice deadly calm as the lights start flickering. Amara smiles at him as her eyes glow brighter, and suddenly, the lights are burning so bright, I have to squint to stop the light from hurting my eyes.

"Oh, for God's sake, you two, stop fighting," Imogen calls out as they glare at each other. The power is flickering on and off, and my heart is racing in my chest as the lights burst, the house goes dark, and I hear things being slammed around.

"That's it!" Imogen yells, and claps her hands.

The bang is so loud my ears ring, and I feel a force that makes me stumble back into Ryland. The only light is coming from the fireplace in the lounge room, just enough to see but not clearly. I find both Amara and Thaddeus frozen in place. Thaddeus growls loudly, as he breaks whatever spell she put on him and shoves his sister away. Thaddeus rips me toward him and away from Ryland.

"Leave, now!" Thaddeus bellows.

I feel goosebumps rise on my skin. Imogen throws up her hands and walks over to me.

Amara smiles deviously. "Fine, we will leave, but I will be back, Thaddeus. Don't try to run. I will always be able to find her now that I know what she looks like and have met her," Amara says, as she looks at her mother. Imogen sighs, accepting that they are being made to leave. I just don't understand why.

Imogen gets up and walks over to hug me. "Please make him visit; he may listen to you," she tells me.

I look up at Thaddeus. He is looking away, not meeting her gaze. Imogen touches his cheek gently as he turns away from her. She has tears brimming in her eyes, and I feel terrible for her.

"You need to come back to us, son," she says softly.

"Your son died a long time ago, mother. Now leave; I won't have you putting nonsense in my mate's head."

Amara shakes her head at him. Imogen rushes out the door, but Amara lingers for a few more moments. "Mom has only ever wanted what was best for you. We all want you to come home. Dad has forgiven you; we all have. But you keep pushing us away. Soon it will be too late, and you will destroy your only chance at happiness," she says, her eyes darting towards me.

She then turns around to leave, but Thaddeus grabs her arm, tugging her back. "What did you see?"

"Come home, and I will tell you," she taunts, shaking his arm off and following after her mother.

Orion comes back into the kitchen with another lightbulb. He silently removes the old one and replaces it. "You can never sit civilly and just chat, Thaddeus; always take things too far," he says, as the kitchen light suddenly flicks on.

"You shouldn't have interfered, Orion, so keep quiet."

Orion sighs loudly.

"What did your sister mean about my mark?" I ask.

"It was nothing. It won't matter anyway once Orion marks you," Thaddeus says.

"But I want to know."

"And I will tell you once Orion marks you," Thaddeus growls.

I cross my arms over my chest, annoyed. There's no point in trying to get the information he refuses to give, so I just storm off into the living room. To my displeasure, Thaddeus is fast on my heels.

"Just leave me, Thaddeus. I am angry with you right now," I tell him, but I can feel his rage building at me walking away from him.

Ryland suddenly appears at the bottom of the steps and slumps on the couch. I sit on his lap, and he wraps his arms around me.

Thaddeus stops in front of me, looks down, and I shrink back against Ryland. "You think he will save you from me, little one?" he asks, raising an eyebrow. I don't answer, knowing no one can save me from him. Thaddeus sits next to us, running his fingers through his hair.

"How many?" I ask, glaring at him. Thaddeus sits back, putting his head on the back of the couch.

"None, Evelyn. I didn't kill anybody, okay?" He sighs, but I don't believe him. "Don't believe me. I don't care," he says, replying to my thoughts. Thaddeus turns slightly. "You can be mad at me, but please come here," he says, tapping his chest.

Ryland nudges me. "You won't be able to stay mad at him long. Believe me; we have tried. The mate pull won't allow it," Ryland tells me.

I turn my face away from them, ignoring them when Ryland grips my hips, dumping me on Thaddeus' lap. Thaddeus chuckles and wraps his arms around me, his face goes to the crook of my neck, inhaling my scent. I melt against him, loving the feeling of his warmth. Thaddeus grips my chin, turning my face to him as his lips find mine. His tongue brushes my bottom lip, wanting me to kiss him back, and I cave.

My lip's part, and he plunges his tongue into my mouth, making me moan. I hear Ryland laugh beside me as I turn on Thaddeus' lap, so my legs straddle him. Thaddeus' hands go to my ass, and he squeezes it, his lips move to my neck as he nips at my skin and sucks on my mark, making me moan.

My moans are swallowed when Ryland grips my face and kisses me. His tongue plays with mine as I feel cold hands on my sides, making me pull away as a shiver runs up my spine. I look over my shoulder and see Orion. He grips my shirt, tugging it off over my head, and Thaddeus attacks my chest, his lips biting my breast. I whimper as he runs his tongue runs over it, then growls softly and pulls back. "Sorry," he whispers, kissing my chin.

"Just not so hard it hurts. Your teeth are sharp," I tell him, and he chuckles, nipping the skin of my neck. Orion moves behind me, stepping closer, making me look up at him. He bends down, kissing me while Thaddeus attacks my breasts again. I feel Ryland squeeze my other breast that Thaddeus isn't attacking with his teeth.

TWENTY-ONE

Evelyn

Thaddeus stands and starts walking to the stairs. His lips never leave my skin until I suddenly feel the mattress under my back and realize we are back in the bedroom. Thaddeus growls and his kisses become fiercer as he devours my skin.

"Not so hard," I scold him when he bites into my shoulder, breaking the skin. Feeling the bed dip, I look up and see Orion watching us with a worried look on his face. Ryland moves behind Thaddeus, and I can feel his worry coming through the bond.

"Ow, Thaddeus," I tell him, pushing his face away as his teeth sink into the top of my breast. I feel my blood run down the side of my boob and my eyes water from the sting. Gripping his face, I pull it up, my hands on either side. Thaddeus' eyes are pitch-black orbs; the demonic look on his face makes my heart skip a beat. Veins run under his eyes, rippling under his skin.

Thaddeus growls and sinks his teeth into my neck, making me scream. I see Ryland grip his shoulder as I feel the fog slip over me, washing away the pain of his bite. I can feel Thaddeus' tongue lapping at my skin. His hand moves to my hip, and I feel him trying to push my leggings down.

Lifting my hips, he growls softly, pulls his teeth from my neck, and pulls my leggings down, leaving me naked under him as dizziness washes over me. Thaddeus sits up, looking down at me.

"Thaddeus, she is nearly unconscious; leave her be," Ryland warns, and I hear Thaddeus growl. I am fighting to remain conscious against the blood loss when I feel shock hit me through the bond. My eyes open to see Thaddeus, hovering over me. "What have I done?" I hear him gasp, before my eyes flutter shut.

Thaddeus

Evelyn is unconscious once again because of me. Guilt hits me hard when I realize I have fed on her enough for her to pass out from blood loss.

"She won't be out long, Thaddeus. You just need to be gentler," Ryland tells me.

"You say that like I know how," I snap back at him.

"She is human; you'll have to learn," Orion snarls as he scoops her onto his lap. Her body is floppy and limp, but her heartbeat is strong as it pounds in her chest.

"Go get some juice," Orion tells Ryland, and he rushes downstairs. A moment later, he returns just as she wakes up. She groans, holding her head, and I can feel she has a headache.

"What happened?" she asks, clutching her head in her hands.

"You passed out. Thaddeus fed on you," Orion tells her, and I can feel his anger through the bond.

Ryland hands her the juice and some Tylenol. She quickly pops the tablets in her mouth and drinks the entire glass. Once it's empty, she hands it back to Ryland. "Better?" he asks.

"I will be once this headache goes away," she mutters, clenching her eyes shut from the light. Moving on the bed, I lean over her, and Orion flicks the lamp off on the bedside table. The only light remaining in the room is coming from the bathroom.

"Thanks," she mutters, as I lay beside her.

"What did Amara mean when she said your father forgave you?" she asks, draping her arm over her face. I can tell she is just trying to distract me from what I have done, though she is also curious.

I wonder if I tell her, will it just make her hate me more, but somehow, I still find myself opening up to her, answering the question. "I hurt my father by accident," I tell her, but I don't add anything else.

Evelyn rolls to lay in between Orion's legs, placing her head on his thigh. Orion brushes her hair from her face, and she leans into his touch. Jealousy runs through me with how effortlessly Orion gets her affections.

"What did you do?" she asks, watching me.

Ryland climbs on the bed beside me, propping his back against the headboard. I place my hand on his leg, which doesn't go unnoticed by Evelyn. I watch her lips tug up slightly as she stares at my hand on Ryland's thigh.

"I nearly killed him when I took my magic back from my mother."

"Weren't you born with magic, though?" she asks.

"Yes, but my mother and some coven of witches decided when I was a baby that my magic was dangerous and took it from me, trapping it in a talisman. I didn't know about it until my sixteenth birthday when I had a fight with my father. My magic could feel me, and the talisman broke. My magic escaped, and that's how I got it back."

"You didn't know about having magic till your birthday?"

I nod, looking over at her. "I heard my mother telling the oracle – she was my godmother; her name was Astral– that her bracelet needed to be reinforced. I was curious; I knew I was different because my sister had magic, and I didn't understand why I differed from her. So, I asked my father about it, and he told me, which pissed me off. I didn't know the bracelet reacted to my emotions, so when I snapped, it escaped and came back to me."

"So, you hurt your father because of that?" she asks, looking at me. I can see her trying to understand what I am saying but can feel that she has more questions to every answer I give.

"No. When it escaped, Astral and my mother tried to take it back from me. I lost control and attacked my mother. My father got in the way, and I didn't know how to control it. I watched my mother teach my sister how to use her magic but didn't understand how to control my own or use it. When I released it in a rage, it exploded out of me. I knocked my sister unconscious and accidentally killed my godmother and the few coven witches that came to help. My father thought I did it deliberately because of them hiding it from me; he attacked me when I hurt my sister and mother. I set him on fire. He is alright, though. One of his arms was severely burnt, and his torso. Most of the scars healed because he is Lycan, but some remained."

"You set your father on fire?" she asks incredulously.

"I didn't mean to, and after that, I left. I came back a few times, but every time I did, my mother wanted me to hand my magic over to her, so because of that I would leave. After a while, I stopped going back. I didn't need them, I had Ryland," I tell her, and avert my gaze to look up at Ryland.

Ryland bends his head down, kissing my lips softly, and I squeeze his thigh.

"Your mom seems nice," she murmurs, and I turn back to her.

"She is, but she can be a little controlling," I tell her. I can't resist the urge to be closer when she looks at me like that, so I don't bother to fight against the need. I lean forward and kiss her as softly as I can. She reacts almost instantly as she kisses me back.

"Thaddeus," Orion growls down at me, making me pull back.

"I'm fine, Orion," she tells him, looking up at him. I smirk as I move closer and push her legs open, climbing between them.

CHAPTER
TWENTY-TWO

Evelyn

"I'm fine, Orion," I tell him, looking up at him.

Orion stares down at me for a second, nods, and I look back at Thaddeus, who has a devious smirk on his face, making me smile back at him. He kisses me softly as he pushes my legs open and rests between them.

"No biting," I warn him, and he chuckles against my lips, deepening the kiss.

His tongue plays with mine, fighting for dominance, and I let him take control, knowing I wouldn't win anyway. Thaddeus grips my hips, and I feel his nails dig into my skin. I push his hand away, making him growl softly before he moves lower, kissing my breast and sucking my nipple in his mouth, making me moan.

Orion leans down, seizing my lips and swallowing my moans as Thaddeus moves lower, nipping at my hip until he settles between my legs. I feel his teeth graze the inside of my thigh and soon, I feel his breath on my core, making me pull away from Orion.

"I swear, Thaddeus, if you bite me there, I will kick you in the face," I tell him, making him smile at me.

I feel a fog slip over me, tingles move over my body, and I see Ryland move closer to me on the bed. My eyes set on him right when Ryland is close enough to kiss me. His tongue plunges into my mouth, tasting every inch as I feel Thaddeus sink his teeth into my thigh next to my throbbing core, making me jump as sparks move over my skin straight to my clit. Thaddeus removes his teeth and replaces it with his tongue, which runs across my slit. I instantly moan into Ryland's mouth.

I try to close my legs, but Thaddeus grips my thighs, pulling my legs further apart and holding them in place. His tongue runs a straight line from my ass to my clit before he sucks it into his mouth, making me move my hips against his face.

Ryland pulls back and his lips go to my mark, sucking on it hard, intensifying the sparks, making me shiver. Orion's icy hands grip my face, making me look up at him and he kisses me while Ryland moves his face lower, sucking my nipple into his mouth, teasing it with his teeth.

I feel Thaddeus slide a finger inside me and then, he stops. Freezes. I can feel him through the bond, waiting for my reaction, which never comes. I move my hips against his finger, and he slides it out to add another.

"Good girl," he growls against my slit, sending vibrations straight to my clit as he sucks it into his mouth again, swirling his tongue around my sensitive bundle of nerves.

I feel my stomach tighten, arousal floods me, and I can no longer tell if it is mine or theirs. My walls clamp down on his fingers, and I feel my skin flush as pleasure washes over me, moaning against Orion's lips.

Thaddeus speeds up his movements, and I move my hips against his face while he devours me. Orion pulls back to brush my hair over my shoulder where my mark is.

I feel him kiss it until he speaks up right next to my ear. "Can I mark you?"

I nod; words fail me.

I am quite sure I would have agreed to anything at that moment. Anything they asked for, wanted, needed, all they had to do was keep doing what they are and ask.

I feel his fangs brush my neck. My toes curl as my stomach tightens; I am thrown over the edge. My pussy pulsates around Thaddeus' fingers, making me moan loudly as I come. Wave after wave of pleasure rolls over me, just as Orion sinks his fangs into my neck, only intensifying my orgasm as I come apart at the seams. My juices spill into Thaddeus' mouth as he licks me clean, leaving me panting, when I feel Orion's fangs leave my neck, feel the tether snap into place, and his emotions rush into me.

Thaddeus crawls up my body and plunges his tongue into my mouth. I can taste myself on his tongue. Orion pulls his face away and kisses him. I am hit with their arousal, and mine springs back to life at seeing them kiss. Feeling Thaddeus' erection press against me, I move my hips against him sleepily, trying to keep my eyes open.

Ryland kisses me and talks against my lips. "Sleep, Evelyn. We will take care of Thaddeus." He chuckles, as exhaustion from being marked again creeps over me, knocking me unconscious.

Waking up, I find it is dark. Thaddeus, Ryland, and Orion are asleep, naked next to me. Hopping off of the bed, I quietly duck into the bathroom to pee. After using the bathroom, I head downstairs to get a drink. The fireplace is still burning brightly, illuminating the living room. As I walk to the kitchen, I turn on the light and grab a glass from the cabinet, filling it with water from the faucet.

Turning around and leaning on the counter, I nearly choke on my water when I realize I am not alone in the kitchen. Amara is standing in the kitchen doorway, silently watching me. I cough and sputter on my water from nearly being scared to death.

She raises her finger to her lips, motioning for me to be quiet as she walks over to me. "Hi Evelyn," she whispers.

"What are you doing here?" I ask, looking nervously toward the door. She laughs softly and hands me a shirt. I look down, remembering I am still naked, and I feel my cheeks heat while I stand naked in front of her. I take the shirt from her and quickly tug it over my head.

Amara cocks her head to the side and flicks my hair over my shoulder. "Damn it, you let him mark you?" she asks.

I furrow my eyebrows, confused. "They're my mates," I whisper.

She nods, appearing deep in thought. But then, all of a sudden, she startles me by gripping my arms, her eyes focused on mine as she speaks. "Nothing can be done for it now. I'm sorry to have to do this to you."

I try to step away from her when I hear movement upstairs, my eyes snap to the roof. "What do you mean? Do what?" I ask, worried.

Her eyes glow hypnotically as a smile lights up her face. "I'm kidnapping you," she says, her eyes sparkling as her grip on me tightens.

I'm about to scream when she bursts out laughing. I blink as a strange sensation rolls over me, like a ripple in the water. Opening my eyes, I am no longer at home, my surroundings no longer familiar, and I have no idea where I am.

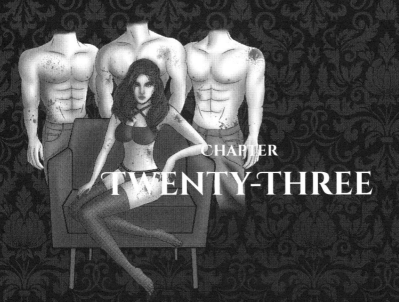

CHAPTER
TWENTY-THREE

Evelyn

Based on my observations, we are in what appears to be a small studio. The smell of incense hangs strong in the air. Beaded curtains cover a door leading somewhere with a tie-dyed bedspread and rugs; it is a very artsy-looking room.

"What did you do?" I ask, wondering how we appeared out of thin air, from one place to another.

"We misted, or as you humans like to say, teleported," Amara says, like it is no big deal. She walks over to a dresser, pulls some clothes out, and hands them to me. After removing my shirt, I quickly put on the sweatpants and clean shirt. Amara watches me the entire time I'm changing, making me feel self-conscious.

"You have lovely breasts," she comments, making me feel awkward.

"Thanks," I say, looking away from her and her awkward remark. "Where are we?"

"My parent's house. They turned the back room of the shed into a studio for me," she answers, as she sits on her bed. I sit on the chair at the desk. "On the plus side, they won't leave you long, especially now they have marked you," Amara tells me.

"What do you mean?" I ask, curious.

"Now that they have marked you, you will go into heat, and to answer your next question, I brought you here hoping to lure my brother home," she tells me the answer to my next question.

"So, you can see the future?" I ask, and she nods as she starts chewing her nails. "Can you see mine?" I ask, and I watch her eyes glow brightly. It looks like she is looking straight through me and then, she looks away.

"The future isn't so clear. Things change. Decisions change. I get glimpses or memories of things, like the burn on your back and how you got it. I don't like looking into the future because it can change its path; not something to be meddled with," she says, not adding anything further on the subject.

"So, your parents know I am here?" I ask, and she shakes her head.

"No, but they will in 3... 2... 1..."

The door suddenly opens, and a blonde woman walks in; one I haven't seen before.

"Hey, Aunty B."

"Amara?" she asks. Her eyes dart to me, widen, and she starts sniffing the air. "You didn't?" she says, not even hiding her shock at me being kidnapped.

"I did, and I regret nothing. It will work. I have seen it," Amara tells her.

"And ends with whose funeral?" the woman asks.

"No one. Evelyn, this is my aunty, Bianca. She also stays here. Well, until she can't handle the noise inside the house."

I watch as Bianca sniffs the air. "She is marked, Amara. He is going to go ballistic."

Amara shrugs. "He won't hurt me, and I will kick his ass if he tries."

Bianca watches me carefully, cocking her head to the side. "Your scent smells familiar for some reason; I just can't put my finger on it," she says, walking over to me. She dips her face in the crook of my neck and sniffs me. "Hmm. Odd," she says, pulling back while I eye her like she is crazy. Who walks up sniffing people?

"So why are you here in my studio?" Amara asks her.

"You really need to ask? They have been going at it like rabbits, and there are some things I don't want to hear my sister do," Bianca says, as a visible shudder runs through her body.

Amara snorts and breaks out in laughter. "Exactly why I live out here," she says, a silly grin on her face.

"Oops, sounds like they stopped. Let's go say hi," Bianca says, tugging my arm, pulling me out the door leading to a garage with some luxury cars.

Walking out, I see an enormous house with stone walls and a massive veranda, fields, and gardens surround the entire property. Bianca pulls me up some stairs, opens the door, and sings out.

"Hope you are decent; we have a guest," she says as she pulls me into a living room with a fireplace and couches. I look around; it is very homey, with many pictures on the walls.

Walking over to one, I see Amara and Thaddeus when they were younger, playing in a puddle of water, drenched, and wearing yellow raincoats and rain boots. They look to be about 8 to 10 years old. Hearing movement upstairs, I look up while Amara walks in the front door.

"Coffee?" she asks.

I nod and follow her and Bianca into a kitchen much like the one back home. In fact, a lot is similar on the inside to what is at his home, making me wonder if Thaddeus designed it because he misses being home.

Amara sits on a stool at the island and makes coffee, setting 6 mugs out. Grabbing mine, I take a sip just as Imogen and two men walk in, both with a startling resemblance to Thaddeus. The men freeze, but Imogen walks over and hugs me.

"Mom, gross. You were doing God knows what with my fathers, and now you come over and hug her, leaving your sex scent all over her? I have to share a room with her," Amara scolds her mother, making Imogen chuckle.

"Your brother will love knowing you're sharing a room with his mate," Imogen tells her, making me confused. Doesn't Thaddeus like his sister?

"Evelyn, these two are my mates and Thaddeus' fathers: Tobias and Theo. Or you can call them dad, whichever you prefer."

"Hi," I say, giving them a brief wave.

They are both handsome and look the same age as their son. I don't know how I will get used to people looking the same age as Thaddeus yet refer to them as his parents. I do notice, though, Tobias doesn't take his eyes off me, watching me, cocking his head to the side.

"Does Thaddeus know she is here?" he asks, turning to his daughter.

"He will soon," she says, and his father pinches the bridge of his nose.

"Amara, you can't just kidnap people, especially since she is marked and unmated. Your brother will go on a rampage!" he scolds her.

"I doubt it; he won't want to risk her getting hurt," Imogen tells him. I see his other father sniff the air and suddenly, his mouth falls open.

"She is human," he states, looking at me like I am the strangest thing he had come across.

"Why does everyone keep saying that? You are aware half the earth is human, right?" I ask, making Imogen chuckle.

"Yes, dear, we know that. You're probably the first human ever to be fated to a supernatural," she says, making me look just as confused as I feel.

"Is that a bad thing?" I ask.

143

"No, just means Thaddeus has to be careful, is all. He could easily kill or hurt you. Not that I want to scare you," she answers.

Yeah... that definitely doesn't make me regret asking in the first place.

"God, she smells familiar," Tobias says, making me look at him as he walks over to sit on the stool next to me. I can see burns on his arm and chest now that he is closer. "My burns gross you out?" he asks.

I shake my head. "No, I have my own," I tell him, flicking my hair over my shoulder and showing him. He smiles, realizing we have something in common.

"Yeah, she killed someone. Not so innocent looking now, is she, dad?" Amara says, making my mouth fall open. "Don't worry, he deserved it," she adds.

"Don't snoop into people's pasts, Amara. It is rude," Imogen tells her.

Amara rolls her eyes at her mother, and her mother's lips twitch as she presses them in a thin line, annoyed.

Note to self: don't roll my eyes at his mother.

I notice Bianca staring at me again strangely, like she is trying to figure something out. "Where are you from?" she asks curiously.

"What do you mean? I am from Parse City."

She looks thoughtful for a second. "She smells familiar. I just can't put my finger on it," says Bianca, and I see Tobias agrees with her.

"So, Amara, what is your grand scheme?" Theo, Thaddeus' other father, asks, eyeing me worriedly.

"No scheme. Mom wanted him home, so I thought, what better way than to kidnap his mate?" she says cockily, walking over to me and wrapping her arms over my shoulders like we are best buddies.

"Yeah, go on, Amara. You're really going to be pushing his buttons, leaving your scent all over her," Bianca warns her, making me confused.

"So, tell us a bit about yourself, Evelyn," Tobias says, his eyes darting to Bianca for a second, which I think is odd. It's like they are having a secret conversation.

"Not much to tell. I grew up all over Parse, worked at a café, then Thaddeus and Ryland stumbled across me," I answer, not wanting to share all my secrets.

"So, you lived nowhere else?" Tobias asks.

"Nope, grew up in foster care, shipped from one house to another," I answer honestly without giving many details.

"Foster care? What happened to your parents?" Bianca asks, and I find everyone staring at me like I just grew a second head.

"No idea; I was dropped at a church when I was a baby."

"A church?" she asks. Her eyes go wide.

"Yep, an old convent just outside the city," I tell them, and Bianca shoots a look at Tobias. "Is something wrong?" I ask, wondering why they keep eyeing each other every time I answer their questions.

"No, nothing. Just curious," Bianca answers. I have a sneaking suspicion she is lying, though. Tobias gets up, walking out a few minutes later; so, does Bianca. Theo and Imogen watch them go, then Imogen turns to me.

"Well, why don't you get cleaned up and get some sleep, and we can all chat in the morning? That is if my son hasn't destroyed my house by then," she states, shooting Amara a death glare.

Amara chuckles as she grabs my hand. "You can sleep in my room, like a slumber party but without the party," she tells me, pulling me into the living room.

I see Bianca and Tobias talking on the stairs. They stop, both looking at me.

"Good night, Evelyn," Tobias says, and I see Imogen come out and eye them, giving them a look, I can't decipher.

I follow Amara back to her little studio. "Your parents seem nice."

"They are. They worry too much, though; worry Thaddeus will attack me when he realizes I took you."

"And you're not worried?" I ask.

She shakes her head. "No, he knows I wouldn't let harm come to one of his mates," she says as she shuts the door. She walks into her room and opens a door I didn't see before, which is a small bathroom. She hands me a towel. "You can shower if you want. I will find you some pajamas," she tells me, and I turn the shower on and close the door.

CHAPTER
TWENTY-FOUR

E velyn

    I shower quickly, hop out, and open the door to find Amara on the phone. She raises an eyebrow at me, a devious smile on her lips as she puts the phone on the loudspeaker so I can hear. Instantly, I recognize the voice to be Thaddeus.

"You want to explain why your scent is throughout my house, and my mate is missing?" he yells through the phone.

"Thought it was time she met the rest of the family. No need to get your knickers in a twist," she taunts.

"Bring her back now, Amara. I am done playing your games."

"No. You will have to come get her yourself if you want her. Besides, she just got out of the shower. She looks quite delicious if I do say so myself." The phone goes silent for a second, and I stand there awkwardly in my towel until Amara motions with her hand toward some clothes on the bed.

"I swear to God, Amara, if you put your hands on her, I will bloody kill you."

"Chill, brother, nothing to worry about here. Besides, I know you're just jealous; she may like me more if I do." This makes me raise an eyebrow at her, wondering what she means.

"Do you want to speak to her? She can hear you," Amara asks, holding the phone out toward me. I take it from her as I pull a shirt over my head and slip on some brand-new underwear.

"Hello?" I ask, concerned when he says nothing.

"You're okay?"

"Yep," I answer awkwardly with Amara's eyes roaming over my bare legs, making me self-conscious.

"I will come to get you soon. And stay away from my sister," Thaddeus snaps.

Amara grabs the phone from my hand. "She is fine. I promise to take good care of her," Amara purrs at him. I can feel his rage hit me through the bond.

"Amara, I am warning you. Hang on; I have another call coming through." He is silent for a second and then he speaks again. "Why is Bianca calling?"

"You better take that; I know it is important."

I hear him sigh.

"Fine. Hands-off, Amara, and I am sending Orion to get her," he tells her and hangs up the phone.

The thought of Orion coming to get me makes me queasy because that means we will be running. Amara puts her phone on the charger, hops in her bed and taps the space beside her. I climb in, a little worried after Thaddeus said I should stay away from her.

"Why does your aunt think my scent is familiar?" I ask her.

"Because supernaturals only have to smell a scent once and they won't forget it, like how humans get Deja vu; that's what your scent did to her and my father," she answers.

"So, do you know why?" I ask, wondering if she has the answer, seeing as she can see the past and future.

"Yes, but it is best left alone for now. Thaddeus can answer that when he comes here."

"But Orion is coming to get me," I tell her.

"That doesn't mean I will let him leave with you, Evelyn. If Thaddeus wants you, he will have to come to get you. It's about time our family reunites," she tells me.

Letting her words sink in, I ask another question that has been eating at me ever since Thaddeus said it. It makes me worry about exactly how safe I am with his sister. "Why did Thaddeus say to stay away from you?" I ask, getting comfy.

"He worries for no reason. If I wanted you, I would have you," she says, not adding anything else as she flicks the lamp off. The room is plunged into darkness. I find the aromatic smell of lavender in the air quite relaxing, and it doesn't take long to fall asleep.

Thaddeus

As soon as I hang up on Amara, I call out to Orion. He walks over, looking bored.

"Go get Evelyn. She is at mom and dad's," I tell him, and he nods wordlessly, already turning around to get his coat. Ryland walks over to me where I am leaning against the kitchen counter. He presses his body against mine, and I instantly relax as his scent overwhelms my senses.

"You know Amara won't hurt her," he tells me as he kisses my collarbone.

I groan and grip his chin to kiss him. His tongue instantly darts into my mouth, making me moan. One thing about Evelyn is that she is making me sexually frustrated. Holding myself back and being gentle is an unnatural experience for me. I want to mate with her, but at the same time, I know she will give in when she goes into heat.

"I know, but that doesn't mean I want Amara around her when she goes into heat," I tell him.

Orion walks out to join us. He kisses Ryland on the cheek and when he is about to give the same kiss to me, I rip him towards me, forcing my tongue in his mouth. He kisses me back just as forcefully and passionately until he pulls away from me.

"You better call Bianca back," he says, right as he walks out the door to retrieve our mate.

Sighing, I pull the phone back out of my pocket. My eyes scan the screen until I find Bianca's number and hit the dial. I place the phone to my ear, and she answers after the first ring.

"Finally, Thaddeus. Why didn't you answer?" she asks, and I can hear the concern in her voice.

"Sorry, I am dealing with Amara kidnapping my mate," I snap back.

"She is fine; she is asleep with Amara," Bianca tells me, worrying me even more. I don't like the idea of them sleeping in the same bed.

"What did you call for?" I ask, already tired and wanting to get this conversation over with.

"I actually called about Evelyn."

"What about her?"

"I recognized her scent, and so did your father."

"So, what's bad about that?" I ask, growing confused.

"How old is Evelyn?" Bianca asks me, making me wonder where she is going with this.

"Twenty-one, why?"

"Where were you twenty-one years ago, Thaddeus?"

"Geez, Bianca, I don't know. I don't keep track of every place I go," I tell her. As much as I love and respect Bianca, she's starting to annoy me with the stupid questions.

"Well, I will answer that for you, then. I couldn't recognize where I had got her scent, before your father recognized her as well."

"And?" I ask when she goes quiet.

"You destroyed the town just outside of Parse. Your father and I were tracking you. We were trying to catch up to you as you decimated that town."

"Your point, Bianca? I ain't got all night."

"Fine. We heard a baby crying amongst the rubble when we came through that town. Your father and I dug through it and came across a man and a woman - dead. It was some old house on the outskirts of the town. We only stopped when we heard the cries. Since the man and woman were both dead, we took the baby. We took her to a convent and left her in a basket in front of the small cathedral."

My blood runs cold as her words set in. What are the chances of coming across a baby, and not just any baby, but my mate?

"I am certain that baby is Evelyn, Thaddeus. You killed her parents, and that is how she ended up in the foster system. We didn't find any information on her parents, not even ID. We are pretty sure they were squatting in the house because there were no belongings, and she was naked, in a towel like she had just been born a couple of days before. How she survived is beyond me because her parents were crushed to death. The only thing that wasn't destroyed was the crate we found her in."

"You're saying I killed her parents?" I ask. The realization slowly sinks in. I am responsible for my mate's life, everything that has happened to her leads back to me and my doings.

"Yes, Thaddeus. We haven't told her, but she may be suspicious. When talking to her, your father and I asked her a few questions, and I think she knows something is up. But I thought it would be best coming from you."

I shake my head before I realize she can't see me. "No, she doesn't need to know. Nothing good will come of her knowing."

"Thaddeus?"

"No, Bianca. I won't lose my mate because of something I didn't realize I did!" I snap at her and hang up the phone. I can't listen to more, can't let her talk me into this madness.

As I turn my gaze, I see that Ryland is watching me. The feeling in my gut sinks as I meet his eyes. He has heard everything.

"You can't keep that from her. She has a right to know what happened to her parents," Ryland growls at me.

"No, she doesn't need to know. She survived just fine without them," I tell him.

"I can't believe you can even say that. Look what happened to her, all because you threw a tantrum twenty-one years ago," he snaps at me. I growl, warning him. "You tell her, or I will. I can't live knowing we are lying to her," he snaps and turns his back on me, walking out of the room.

"Where are you going?" I shout after him.

"To get our mate," he snaps back, and I follow after him.

I am responsible for everything. Is this my karma? Give me a mate that is going to hate me? Will she still want me after knowing the truth? I follow Ryland upstairs and watch him pack a bag. "Why are you packing?"

"Because you know your parents will make us stay for a bit," he mutters matter-of-factly.

"No, we are getting her and coming home," I tell him.

"And what if she doesn't want to go?" he asks, facing me.

"And why wouldn't she want to come back?"

"Because you have to tell her. I am not keeping this a secret from her to come out in the future and break the little trust we have gained from her, Thaddeus. If you don't tell her, I will."

My anger is bubbling dangerously close to the edge at his words. She doesn't need to know. I can feel my energy shifting within me.

My family has always been out to get me because I'm not perfect like Amara, and now, they are determined to ruin my mate. This is making my blood boil. They have turned my mates against me before and I won't allow them to do it again.

CHAPTER
TWENTY-FIVE

Evelyn

I wake up just as the sun rises to someone climbing in bed next to me. Opening my eyes, I find Orion, looking down at me.

"You're here," I mumble, half asleep.

As I place my head in his lap, Orion tucks in the surrounding blanket, trying to keep me warm against his cold skin. Amara moves behind me and his eyes snap to her. A smirk appears on his face as she puts her leg and arm over me, rolling into me.

She is the worst person to sleep next to, hogging the bed. I was woken a few times by her randomly putting her hand or leg on me, and I was even smacked in the face with her elbow.

Just as Orion is about to say something, Theo walks in. He smiles down at us as he walks over and shakes his head at his daughter who is half on top of me, snoring like a chainsaw.

"Can I speak to you inside for a minute?" he asks Orion, who nods and instantly hops off the bed.

"I will be back soon," he whispers, leans down to kiss my head, and follows his father-in-law.

I close my eyes, trying to go back to the slumber I was awoken from. Amara tugs me against her, snuggling into me like I am her teddy bear. Sighing, I give up trying to get out of her grasp. Closing my eyes, I drift off, but not for long; it must have been only a couple of hours because my eyes feel like sandpaper as a loud growl awakes me.

Stretching, I find Amara's head on my boob, her arm over my waist, and we are tangled in the blanket. But that isn't what woke me up. Thaddeus, standing next to the bed, his eyes on his sister, lets out another menacing growl.

"I thought Orion was the only one coming," I say, looking up at him. I notice his teeth protruding. His eyes snap to his sister as she sits up slightly, looking down at me.

"I drooled on you," she says, not realizing her brother is in the room with us.

As I look down, I realize she indeed has drooled on me. She smiles and brushes my hair over my ear. A moment after, she sniffs the air and turns her face to see Thaddeus glaring at her.

"Brother, finally, you're here. See? Perfectly safe snuggled with me," she says, a smirk on her lips.

"Get off, my mate," he spits at her, and she rolls on her back, yawning.

"You are far too angry for this early in the morning," she mutters, stretching as Thaddeus picks me up out of bed, crushing me against his chest.

I inhale his scent, wrapping my legs around him, loving the warmth of his skin and his closeness. "Where is Ryland?" I ask.

"Inside, with my parents," he says, hugging me close. "You smell like my sister," he growls, clearly annoyed.

I shrug, not seeing that as a problem. "So, you saw your parents?"

He shakes his head, and I pull back, looking at him. His eyes are searching mine. He places me down on my feet. "I have to go meet my aunty in town. Ryland and Orion will stay with you for the day," he tells me, making me a bit confused.

"You're not going in to say hello?" I ask, arching an eyebrow at him.

"No, Evelyn, I am not. I will see them when I get back. I need to verify something."

I nod, wondering what he needs to verify but let it go. I can tell he is angry through the bond, and it is way too early to put up with his wrath this morning.

"Sounds good to me. I want to take her shopping. She has no clothes," Amara tells him, and he glares at her.

"No, you're not taking her anywhere, Amara. Ryland and Orion can take her," he snaps at her, and she rolls her eyes at him, making me smirk. Thaddeus then walks out, slamming the door behind him, causing the floor to vibrate.

"Come on, let's get breakfast and head to the city," she tells me, swinging her arm over me and tugging me toward the door.

"Ah! Amara, I only have panties and a shirt on!" I screech as she tries to take me through the shed.

"Oh right, hang on." She walks back into her room and gives me a pair of shorts.

I slip them on, following her to the main house. Her mother rushes out and suddenly come to a stop. A frown appears on her face, so I guess she was hoping Thaddeus would come in. I shake my head sadly at her, and she looks a little disappointed. Walking into the kitchen, I find Ryland and Orion talking with Thaddeus' fathers; when we walk in, they all look up. Orion instantly grabs me, crushing me against him as he sits me on his lap on a stool. Ryland comes over, gripping my chin so I look up at him right when his lips press against mine. He forces his tongue between my lips, so I push on his chest, embarrassed that we are in a room full of people, but he doesn't seem to care.

"Ryland," I scold, pulling away from him.

His eyes darken, but he steps away. My face heats up with embarrassment, but no one cares except me. Imogen hands me a coffee, and Tobias is cooking what smells like bacon. Amara steals a piece from the frying pan as her father smacks her hand with the tongs, but she still manages to pinch a piece with a silly smirk on her face.

"I am kidnapping your mate again," she tells Orion, who looks to Ryland.

"Why?" he asks, not even hiding his disapproval.

"Geez, what is your problem? It is shopping; I am not taking her to some whore house," she snaps.

"Did Thaddeus approve this?" he asks.

Amara crosses her arms over her chest, pouting, making me giggle.

"Didn't think so. Orion and I will take her," Ryland tells her. Amara glares at him but adds nothing, and I suspect Amara is used to getting her way.

"Let Amara take her. I don't see it being a problem," Imogen tells him, but Ryland shakes his head.

"I agree with Ryland, love. If she goes into heat, what good will Amara be to her?" Tobias says while removing the frying pan from the stove.

"Ryland is just worried I may satisfy his mate more than him," Amara taunts, making me confused until it finally clicks.

"You're lesbian?" I ask.

Amara nods, a cheeky grin on her face. Now I know why Thaddeus was so upset that I was in bed with his sister.

"Yep. She has amazing tits, by the way. Perfect little button nipples," Amara says to Ryland, and he throws a tea towel at her, which she catches and throws back. "I wonder if she tastes as good as she smells," Amara says, licking her lips as she jumps off the stool and runs for the back door, just as Ryland lunges at her. I hear her laugh as she runs outside. Theo and Tobias laugh at the pair of them and a moment later, Tobias rushes to the door.

"Oi, don't ruin my garden, Amara!" he yells after her, making me chuckle.

"Never a dull day when Amara is around," Imogen says. Tobias hands me a plate of food, and my stomach growls, making me blush with how loud it sounds. I can't even remember the last time I ate.

"Don't you boys feed her?" Imogen scolds.

"We do, but sometimes we forget she is human," Orion says apologetically. I lean against him, and he rubs his chin across my shoulder.

"Food is ready!" Tobias yells out the back door. I can hear Amara and Ryland still running outside, and it sounds like Amara is winning with the way she keeps teasing him.

"Amara, my fucking roses, you brat!" Tobias yells and darts out the back. I watch as he drags his daughter inside, covered in grass, and a very ticked-off Ryland walking in behind her.

"She killed my rose bush!" Tobias says angrily, walking over and sitting next to his wife. Imogen shakes her head and glares at her daughter.

"What? Ryland landed on it, not me."

"You shouldn't have riled him up," Imogen snaps at her.

Ryland grabs a plate and sits next to me. We eat our breakfast, and afterwards Tobias walks outside to fix the mess his daughter and Ryland made, muttering under his breath.

Imogen walks upstairs to retrieve some clothes and shows me where the bathroom is. Ryland and Orion walk in a few seconds after me. Pulling my clothes off, I hop in only to be slammed against the shower wall by Ryland.

I wrap my legs around his waist while he devours my lips, his tongue playing with mine, and I can feel his erection pressing between my folds, making me moan into his mouth. I kiss him back, and he presses himself closer, his hands squeezing my ass right as Orion steps in. Orion moves off to the side of me and his hand moves between us. He rubs my clit, my hips move against his fingers, making me moan. Ryland kisses my neck and sucks on my mark as I throw my head back at the pleasure rolling over me, only to nearly knock myself out from the force.

"Ow," I squeak, making Orion chuckle. Ryland steps away, and I pout until Orion kisses me gently. I feel his fangs graze my lip, making me pull back.

"I'm fine, Evelyn; I have more control than Thaddeus," he says, kissing me again, but I shake my head, pulling away and moving my hair. "Are you sure?" he asks, gripping my chin, making me look at him. I kiss him, sucking his bottom lip into my mouth, and he groans right when I pull away. Ryland watches us with hungry eyes.

"I'm sure," I tell him, offering him my neck. I feel his fangs sink into me, making me loudly moan the very moment Ryland kisses me, swallowing my moans. Orion only feeds for a few seconds, and I actually miss the feeling of his teeth on my neck.

"We should hurry, or we may not leave," Orion tells me, and I grab the soap.

Ryland doesn't look like he wants to leave at all, quite content remaining in the shower. Once we are dressed, Ryland tells Imogen we are leaving but will be back. As I walk outside, I notice Ryland's car and realize he and Thaddeus must have driven here.

Hopping in, I sit in the front with Ryland. We drive to a vast city that is in perfect condition; not like Parse, which is half destroyed.

"Thaddeus hasn't been here?" I ask.

"No, this is the first time he has been back here in decades," Ryland answers.

Driving down the main street, I look out the windows, wondering where they are taking me, when I see her. I haven't seen her in four years, but I instantly recognize her. I can't believe that she is still with April, my old foster mother.

"Stop! Stop the car!" I yell to Ryland, and he pulls the car over. Hopping out, I call out to her. "Lana!"

She turns around, and I know I am right, that it is indeed her. I feel tears brim in my eyes when I see her. She drops her bags and runs to me, and I grab her, hugging her close.

"Evelyn!" she cries. I kiss her now-straight blonde hair. She must be fourteen now. April walks over warily, watching our exchange. A moment later, she recognizes me.

"Evelyn?" she says, looking a little taken aback. I hear car doors, making me look over my shoulder. Orion and Ryland hop out of the car, but they stay back, just watching instead of approaching.

April's eyes dart to them nervously, making me wonder if she recognizes them. If she does, she says nothing. I chat with her and Lana for a bit until April says they need to leave, and I have a feeling it is because of Ryland and Orion.

Lana gives me her phone number, which I put in Ryland's phone. Ryland and Orion hop back in the car while I say goodbye and hug Lana. April comes over and wraps her arms around me, shocking me.

I never told her what her husband did, or even Lana. I only asked Lana if Derrick ever hurt her, which she denied. After that, I left and never looked back. I left before the police arrived, so I never heard of them again. I knew with him gone; she was safe.

April grips me tightly, a little too tight. Her words, however, make my blood run cold. "I know what you did, whore. You will pay for what you did to my husband," she whispers, let's go of me, and steps back. My heart rate rises, and I feel a little sick as I swallow back the bile rising in my throat. I feel Orion behind me when I stumble back. April grabs Lana's hand, tugging her away.

"Call me, Evie," Lana sings out, using her nickname for me, and I nod.

"You okay? What did she say to you?"

"Nothing, it doesn't matter," I say, turning back around and getting in the car. I can feel Orion's eyes on me, watching me carefully. I know they must be able to feel my emotions through the bond.

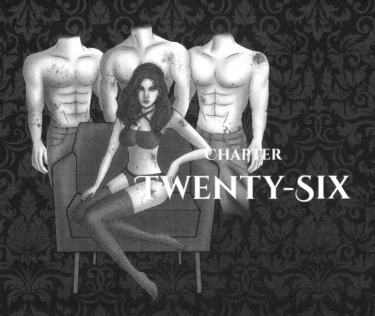

CHAPTER
TWENTY-SIX

E velyn

I can feel Orion watching me as we pull up. April's words replay in my head. How does she know? Did she know what he did? Did she know all that time and never bothered to help?

"Evelyn, what did April say to you?" Orion asks, leaning between the seats.

"It doesn't matter, Orion. I just want to go home," I tell him. Ryland looks over at me. At this point, I can feel both of their worries through the bond.

"Evelyn," Ryland says, but I cut him off.

"Please, can we just go home? I want to go back," I tell him.

Ryland turns the car around, going back the way we came. I lean against the window, wondering what April meant. It scares me knowing she knows what I did. Ryland suddenly pulls over, making me look up at him.

"What are you doing?" I ask, but he says nothing, just hops out and walks into a store and a moment later, comes out with a bag. He dumps it on my lap, and I place it on the floor between my feet.

Ryland starts the car and drives back to Thaddeus' parents' house. I get out of the car and walk toward the front door as another car pulls up in front of me. I can see Bianca and Thaddeus sitting in the silver BMW. Thaddeus looks up at his parents' house, shaking his head, and he doesn't look like he wants to get out.

Walking over, I open his door. Ryland and Orion get out and close their car doors, making me look back. Thaddeus still sits in the car.

"Come on, are you going to sit in there all day?" I ask, holding out my hand.

He grabs my hand, hopping out. As soon as he's at his full height, he scratches the back of his neck. I can feel his nervousness through the bond, but before I can question him, the front door opens. Imogen walks out, her face lighting up when she sees him. She runs down the steps and hugs him, relieved he has come back. Theo and Tobias walk out, and I suddenly feel nervous. The feelings through the bond hits me hard as I am consumed with Thaddeus' guilt.

Theo walks off of the porch first. He walks over and rips Thaddeus towards him, hugging him tightly and smacks him on the back. "Son," he says, and steps back.

Thaddeus looks towards his other father. Tobias walks down, stopping in front of his son, and I watch Thaddeus' eyes go straight to the burns on his father's skin. He swallows, and I can feel his sadness at what he did, but his guilt is the worst. His father is alive, so I don't understand the overwhelming guilt he is feeling. Surely it can't be over his father's scars.

"Come on, let's go inside," Tobias tells him, clapping his hand on his son's back.

Thaddeus nods, following them in, his mother clinging to him. I see Amara walking out of her little home as she skips over and leaps on Thaddeus' back. Orion grabs my hand, tugging me toward the house. I laugh as I watch Amara cling to his back like a monkey, until he tosses her off, wraps his arm across her shoulders, and puts her in a headlock, messing her hair. She squeals as he drags her up the stairs and finally lets her go. Ryland walks up behind and then shoves her off the side, making her growl at him as she lands in the garden.

"Mutt!" she screeches at him, just as Tobias spins around and glares at her.

"Get out of my garden, Amara!" he snaps at her.

She dusts herself off and stomps inside the house. We walk into the kitchen, and I help Imogen make coffee. Thaddeus sits at the island counter next to Bianca. They seem close, as he seems more comfortable in her presence than his parents.

Ryland walks over to Thaddeus. He wraps his arms over Thaddeus' shoulder and kisses his neck. I smile at them and turn back to the coffees. No one says anything, and it actually feels awkward as I place coffees in front of everyone and sit next to Thaddeus.

He instantly pulls me on his lap. His face goes into my neck as he inhales my scent. "I missed you," he mumbles against my neck. Amara makes kissing faces at us, and I roll my eyes at her. Bianca tosses a napkin at her, making her stop.

"So, well, this is awkward," Amara states. I see Ryland glare at her for stating the obvious. Amara stands up. "Well, I will start, then, shall I? Some of you may know me as Amara, my favorite color is yellow, and I am a Gemini, and I have a coffee addiction." Her father yanks her down, and I can't help but giggle at her strange attempt to start a conversation.

Thaddeus snickers at his sister while Imogen just shakes her head.

"Well, how about I start dinner?" Imogen suggests, and everyone except me screams no, making me look around, confused. They all burst out laughing. Imogen looks pissed off, her face flushes red in anger. "My cooking isn't that bad!" she snaps at everyone.

"You would think after a hundred years she would have learned how to cook; the woman can't even make toast properly," Tobias says, looking at me.

I try not to laugh as Imogen folds her arms across her chest. "Fine, then you cook," Imogen snarls at him.

"I vote for pizza," says Amara. Bianca nods her head. "I will go with Amara; you want to come, Evelyn?"

I'm about to agree when Thaddeus tells her no, tugging me against him. She sighs, hops up, and Amara follows her out. Tobias gets up to grab a beer from the fridge. He offers one to Thaddeus and tosses it once Thaddeus nods.

"Can werewolves even get drunk?" I ask, curious.

Imogen nods. "Yes, I can. So can Amara and Thaddeus. Them not so much, they just like the taste. It takes a lot for them," she states. Tobias tosses one to Ryland, but Orion shakes his head when offered one.

Imogen grabs a bottle of wine from the cupboard pouring two glasses and handing me one. Tobias eyes her, but she shrugs, handing me a glass, and Thaddeus takes it from me.

"Leave her be she can't get in any trouble with all of us here, Thaddeus," Imogen scolds, and he reluctantly hands it back to me. I sniff it and take a sip. I scrounge my face up, it tastes dry and sour.

Imogen chuckles at the reaction. "It won't taste like anything after a few more glasses," she says. "Come on, let's go watch a movie and let the boys chat. " She pulls me from Thaddeus.

"Mom?" Thaddeus says, grabbing my hand.

"You need to speak to your fathers, Thaddeus. We are only going out in the living room," she says, and he lets go.

I follow Imogen as she grabs the bottle of wine off the counter. Walking into the living room, I sit beside her on the couch. "Do you like horror movies?" she asks.

"As long as they aren't ghost movies."

"Excellent, let's watch paranormal activity," she says and flicks the TV on. She scrolls through the movies until she finds one and puts it on.

"I hate ghost movies," I tell her, and she grins.

"More reason to watch them. No point watching horror if it doesn't scare you," she says.

She looks to the kitchen door. I raise an eyebrow as she grabs my wine glass and fills it to the brim, making me have to take a sip, so it doesn't spill out. Only she places her hand underneath mine when I do. I shake my head and have to drink the entire glass. She chuckles lightly.

"Are you trying to get me drunk?" I ask, chuckling.

She fills my glass again and laughs. "You're young and should be able to enjoy yourself. Besides, best get it in you before the fun police come out," she says with a wink.

My face feels like it is getting hot, and I have a feeling my cheeks are bright red. We sit huddled on the couch, and half an hour later, Amara walks in with pizza. Bianca takes a couple of boxes out to the boys, before Amara opens three on the coffee table. Reaching over, I grab a slice and almost moan at the taste. Bianca chuckles at my reaction until she spots the bottle of wine. Amara walks out and comes back in with another bottle, but it isn't red but a pink color. She refills everyone's glasses, and we watch the movie.

About halfway through, I feel drunk and can barely move when Orion comes out, leaning over the back of the couch. I start laughing when his face comes so close, but he just smiles.

"How much has she had to drink?" he asks, eyeing them. They all smile, and I can tell Amara is drunk as she sways on her feet, trying to stand.

She reveals five bottles of wine beside the fireplace and makes me giggle. I didn't even realize we drank that much. Bianca looks normal, or maybe that's because of my beer goggles.

"Ladies, she is human; you should know better," he says, eyeing me.

"Leave her be; she is fine," Imogen scolds him.

Orion walks out the front door when I call out to him. "Where are you going?"

"For a smoke."

I hold my arms out to him, wanting to go too. He shakes his head but turns around and comes over. He lifts me over the back of the couch and stands me on my feet. My head spins, and I feel the sudden urge to throw up, but I hold it back.

Orion growls, and Thaddeus walks out with Tobias. I stumble forward when I try to take a step and go into a fit of giggles when I try to right myself. Orion grabs my arms, holding me steady.

"Yeah, maybe we gave her too much," Amara says, swaying on her feet, or maybe I am swaying.

"You think?" Thaddeus says, walking over.

"She seems fine. You're fine, aren't you, dear?" Imogen asks.

"Peachy," I tell her, and she chuckles.

Tobias shakes his head as he grabs all the bottles and walks out. Thaddeus walks me outside with Orion and sits on the step, pulling me on his lap. Orion lights his smoke, but I pinch it from him.

I lean back against Thaddeus heavily, his arms snake around my waist. "Did you sort things out with your fathers?" I ask, my words slurring slightly.

"Yeah. They may forgive, but I don't know if I can," he says.

Ryland sits beside him, and I place my feet across his lap as I lay across all their legs on my back, looking up at the sky. My head is in Orion's lap.

"What do you mean?" I ask Thaddeus, and he rubs his hand underneath my shirt and across my belly.

"Because I hurt my mother worse than my father," he tells me, and I look at him, wondering what he means. Thaddeus looks away.

When I look up at Orion, he answers. "Thaddeus didn't just burn his father; he made his mother infertile when he hit her with lightning. That's why he and his fathers haven't spoken," Orion says, brushing my hair from my face.

I nod in understanding and look at Thaddeus, which is a bad idea as I topple off their laps. Thaddeus is quick to grab me before I roll down the stairs. "What are we going to do with you?" he says, shaking his head at my drunken state.

"I feel great; a little woozy, but great."

"I bet you do; your face is so red," he says, kissing my nose and pulling me against him. I place my head on his shoulder, close my eyes and yawn. Thaddeus gets up and starts walking toward Amara's place.

"Where are we going?" I ask, clinging to him.

"Amara is sleeping inside; we are taking her room," Thaddeus says, and I nod. Thaddeus places me on the bed, and I feel heavy.

"Evelyn?" Orion says, making my eyes open as I roll on my side. "Evelyn, what did April say to you?" he asks. I try to answer, but my words sound like a mumble.

"April? Who is April?" I hear Thaddeus ask him, but I am suddenly overtaken by sleep.

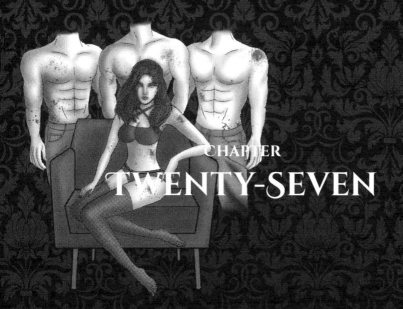

CHAPTER
TWENTY-SEVEN

Thaddeus

Looking down at my passed-out mate, I watch Ryland climb in beside her. "So, who will tell me who this April is?"

"When we went into the city, we ran into Lana and the foster mother. Everything was fine, but as soon as Ryland and I got in the car, April, the foster mother, whispered something too low for us to hear. Evelyn won't tell us what she said. I know it was bad because Evelyn's fear hit us through the bond," Orion tells me.

"And you let her live?" I ask, shocked that they let her just leave and didn't demand an explanation.

"Yes, Thaddeus, we can't just kill everyone. I don't think Evelyn would like that. Besides, Lana still lives with her," Orion tells me, and I pull my jeans off, climbing into the bed next to Ryland.

"Fine, we can make her tell us tomorrow."

"What did you find out with Bianca?" asks Ryland.

"Nothing much, but we did find out the name of the people Evelyn was found with."

"What do you mean?" asks Orion, propping himself up on his elbow and looking at me before looking down at Evelyn.

"Just that they were her parents. Autopsy reports proved the woman had given birth recently. Their names were Michael and Sarah Carter, other than that, nothing else. Dental records identified them. Nothing special about them, and they were both human. Also, her father had a criminal record, and so did her mother. Just petty crimes and a couple of drug charges," I tell them.

Evelyn stirs in her sleep, and I watch her over Ryland's shoulder. "She would have to be one of the unluckiest and luckiest people to be alive from that town. Everything was flattened except the fireplace, which she was next to. Bianca believes that saved her because when they dug her out, the crate she was in was completely intact, and the roof leaning against the fireplace directly above her."

"Are you going to tell her?" Ryland asks, looking at me over his shoulder.

I nod, and he kisses me softly. Just as he is about to pull away, I pull him towards me, making him roll on his back and kiss him harder. He groans into my mouth, and I am hit with his arousal and apparently, so is Evelyn as she moans in her sleep, making me chuckle and pull away to stare at her. She pouts in her sleep.

Orion watches her with a silly smirk on his face. "We should head home soon; her scent is changing. I don't think it will be long before she goes into heat," Orion says, running his nose across her neck. She instantly turns her face seeking him out. I love how responsive she is to us, even when she refuses to be.

"Yeah, mom will be upset, but maybe I will tell her they can visit. It isn't that far from here," Orion agrees, as he pulls the blanket higher, but she kicks it off again.

"So, are you done?" Orion asks, making my eyes snap to his.

"What do you mean?"

"This entire destroy-the-world shit you've been doing. Evelyn won't stick around and watch you do that shit, Thaddeus."

"I know, okay? I know, but I can't control it."

"Maybe it is time to give it up, Thaddeus."

"Fuck you, Orion. You sound like my bloody parents," I growl at him.

"That's because they are right," he says, annoyed. I get up. "Where are you going, Thaddeus?" Orion asks, following me.

"Why do you have to piss me off? I was fine until you brought that up. I swear half the time you are looking to start a fight with me," I snap, pulling my jeans on. Orion walks over, grabbing my arm, but I shake him off.

"It's not like that. It is just different now that we have her. I don't want her to get hurt," he tries to reason.

"Neither do I, Orion," I tell him, picking up my belt.

"I know," he says, and grabs my belt from me.

I growl, annoyed, but he loops his finger through my belt loop and tugs me against him. His lips crash into mine and I groan into his mouth as I kiss him back. Orion reaches into my pants and wraps his hand around my cock. I thrust into his hand and push him toward the bed, careful not to wake Evelyn.

We know Evelyn doesn't care, but still, it might shock her if we woke her. Ryland moves her over as Orion sits on the bed, tugs my jeans down and wraps his lips around my knob, making me grip his hair, wanting nothing more than to ram it in his mouth. I feel his tongue run along my shaft, and I moan as I feel his lips part as he takes me in his mouth.

I thrust into his mouth, making him take more of me. Ryland watches but doesn't move, not wanting to wake Evelyn as she wriggles in her sleep, feeling our arousal. Orion moves faster, gripping my hip, I grip his hair when Evelyn moans loudly, making Ryland chuckle beside her. I watch as his hand skims across her exposed belly, the shirt having ridden up from her squirming. I feel my balls tighten, and Orion sucks harder, using his hand to rub what he can't fit in his mouth. My hand in his hair tightens, and I feel my eyes bleed black, turning to onyx.

My fangs protrude, and I groan loudly, spilling my seed into his mouth. Orion swallows as my cock twitches in his mouth. He slowly pulls away and I rip him to his feet, kissing him. He groans when my fangs break the skin of his lip from my savage kiss. He knows my sex drive makes the hunger worse, the darkness worse. After a while, Orion pulls away, and I pull my briefs up.

"Go to bed, Thaddeus. And don't eat her, please," Orion says, his hand on my cheek.

The familiar sparks of the mate bond soothe me, and I feel my fangs retract. Yawning, I hop in bed beside her and Evelyn rolls into me, looking for my warmth. She smells different; her scent is over-whelmingly strong, and I have to force down the need to feed on her. Ryland moves closer, pressing his chest against her back, warming her, and she melts against us, plunging into a deeper sleep.

I hear Orion rustle around in a bag, making me look over my shoulder at him. "What are you doing?" I ask as he pulls a box out of a plastic bag.

"Ryland got her a phone, so I am going to set it up. Lana gave Evelyn her number."

I nod, rolling over onto my back. Evelyn places her head on my chest, and I hear Ryland groan, making me look at him. A smirk spreads on my face when I realize her ass is pressing against his cock, which I know is hard from the arousal of her movement flooding through the bond.

"So, what is this Lana like? Evelyn seems protective of her?" I ask as I look over at Orion tapping the screen with his fingers.

"She seems sweet, maybe fourteen. She called Evelyn Evie; it must be a nickname. Argh, I don't know Evelyn's email to set this up."

"Just use mine; you can change it later," Ryland tells him. Orion nods and types away.

"Are you coming to bed?" I ask him, making him look up.

"I will wait until you two fall asleep, then I will probably go inside and see Theo, seeing as he doesn't sleep either. It might kill the boredom of watching you two snore; might also go buy her some clothes. Amara is right; she has none," he says, his lips tugging up into a small smile.

Pulling Evelyn onto my chest, I move over for him, and Orion sits next to me. Evelyn moves, draping her legs over either side of me, making herself comfortable.

"Your parents really like her," Orion states.

"Wouldn't care if they didn't; she is ours," I tell him.

"I know, but it is good she gets along with them. Amara fancies her," Orion chuckles softly.

"What do you mean?" I ask, wondering if I need to give my sister a beat down.

"She knows Evelyn is ours, and she would never do that to you. Your sister loves you, Thaddeus." Orion is quick to point that out.

I sigh. "I know. I just worry someone will take her away from us."

"I don't think that will happen; the bond is pretty strong, Thaddeus. And not only that, where would she go? She may hate the way we control her, but I don't think she wants to leave; she feels safe with us," Ryland says, and I nod.

"You think she will after she finds out I am the reason her parents are dead, and she ended up in foster care?"

Nervousness comes through the bond.

"She might surprise us. Probably be hurt if anything. She didn't know them, so she didn't have an attachment. Besides, what kind of life would she have had with drug addict parents anyway?"

"Yeah, but they probably wouldn't have raped her," I mutter to myself. I can't stop the growl that leaves me, as her memories are still fresh in my mind. The things she had to endure sickens me. And it's all my fault. It is because of me she ended up in that monster's home.

"We will deal with it when it comes. Sleep, Thaddeus. You don't need to be agitated when you tell her," Ryland tells me, and I nod, closing my eyes.

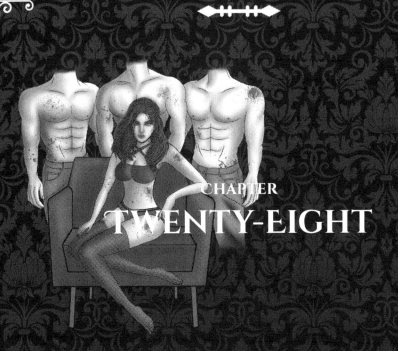

CHAPTER
TWENTY-EIGHT

Evelyn

The next morning, my head is pounding to its own beat. My hand instantly moves to my head, trying to lessen its throbbing. Thaddeus and Ryland are both in bed, asleep still. Crawling over Thaddeus, I walk into the bathroom. I am so thirsty I drink from the tap; I gulp the water running into my mouth like an animal. My mouth feels dry, and I feel so dehydrated.

Hearing someone clear their throat behind me, I spin around and notice Orion, leaning against the door. I didn't see him when I got up, so he must have just come back from wherever he came from.

He holds up a bottle of juice. Clutching my head, I take it from him. I twist off the cap and chug down the entire bottle as if I hadn't just had a drink. The juice is cold, refreshing, and somehow rids me of the foul taste of the wine in my mouth.

"A little hungover?" Orion teases.

His voice makes my head pound at the noise. "Argh," I groan, as my head pounds against my skull. Orion walks in, handing me a box of Tylenol. I pop four out of the foil and swallow them down with more water from the sink.

"Why does it hurt so much?" I whine. My head is killing me and all I want to do is go back to bed.

Making my way back out to the bed, I flop down on it, not even caring that I just flopped on top of Thaddeus. He grunts from the impact and his eyes snap open as I roll back to the center of the bed, pulling the pillow over my head to block out the horrendous light coming in through the window.

I hear Orion laugh and feel Thaddeus roll over to face me. Thaddeus tugs the pillow, and I grip it tighter. "Let me sleep; my head is pounding," I whine, thinking of anything other than the pain and thirst.

"You know you could just ask?" Thaddeus says.

"No? Let me sleep," I tell him, confused. My brain feels like mush.

Thaddeus chuckles, yanking my pillow off. "I have something stronger than Tylenol," he says, making me look up at him. Thaddeus bites into his wrist, offering it to me, and I don't hesitate. Grabbing his wrist, I bring it to my lips and drink his blood. My headache instantly soothes.

"Now, why do that? You should have let her suffer the consequences of drinking that much."

Ignoring the scolding, I climb on top of Thaddeus and slump on top of him.

"Now, she will know you will just heal her every time she gets a hangover," Orion scolds him. He then walks over and looks down at me.

"Just proves he likes me more," I tell Orion teasingly.

"Is that so?" he says, rolling me off Thaddeus, climbing over him and on top of me. His legs straddled my hips.

"Yep," I tell him, and his lips tug up in a grin. His eyes sparkle with mischief before he leans down to kiss me. I kiss him back, wrapping my arms around his neck pulling him closer. Orion moves to push his leg between mine and then settles between them.

His lips move to my neck as he sucks on my mark, making me moan loudly. His hand slips into my pants, and his cold fingers move to my clit as he starts rubbing them against me. I move my hips against his fingers, moaning at his touch before he slides a finger in me, making me gasp. His teeth graze my skin as he nips and sucks on my mark. I move my hips against his finger as he slides in another, making me moan loudly. Then, he suddenly pulls them from me, making me pout.

He sits up, popping his fingers in his mouth and sucking on them. I buck my hips against him, and he chuckles. "Nope. Apparently, I love you less," he taunts.

Thaddeus chuckles. I purse my lips together at his teasing and huff at him in annoyance.

"Do you take it back?" he asks, raising his eyebrow at me.

I move my hand and grab his cock through his pants. I feel it twitch against my palm, and he groans, instantly leaning down to kiss me. However, I turn my face away, not allowing him to kiss me. He pulls back, and I squeeze his cock, feeling it strain against his pants.

Thaddeus laughs, making me and Orion look at him. "Give up, Orion. You won't win; everyone knows she has you wrapped around her little finger," he says, holding up his pinkie.

"Don't pretend you're not wrapped around it too, Thaddeus," he retorts.

Thaddeus' smile doesn't waiver as he shrugs.

"Can you two stop bitching? We all know I am her favorite, right Evelyn?" Ryland says, rolling onto his side, facing us.

"Really? Fine, Evelyn, who is your favorite?" Orion teases.

I roll my eyes at them. "None. I hate you all equally," I tell them.

"You don't hate us," Ryland huffs.

Orion leans down, pressing himself against me, and I moan, feeling the bulge in his pants press against my pulsating core. "She definitely doesn't hate me," Orion mutters. He doesn't give me a chance to snap back anything as his lips assault mine and he grinds his hips into me.

I wrap my legs around his waist, tugging him closer, moaning into his mouth. My panties are dampening as arousal floods me.

"You guys are not fucking in my bed!" Amara shrieks. Orion stops, looking over his shoulder, and I look too. Amara is standing in the doorway. "My eyes! You have scarred me for life. I cannot unsee what I have just witnessed."

"We are not doing anything," Orion chuckles at her as she fakes injury like she has been blinded.

"I can smell her arousal over here; you were definitely doing something," Amara states.

"Why, jealous, Amara?" Thaddeus taunts his sister, and I slap his chest.

"You better change the fucking sheets, Thaddeus," Amara warns him, pointing a finger at him like a scolding parent.

"I will; I don't want you sniffing the sheets," Ryland says. Amara growls at him, a dangerous look in her eye as she glares at him.

"We are heading home today anyway," Thaddeus answers.

My head snaps towards his. "Already?" I ask. I like it here, but I do miss home.

"Yes, Evelyn, you will go into heat soon. Besides, I miss home," he says, and I nod.

"Mom will be upset," Amara states, walking over and laying at the foot of the bed.

"I know, but it isn't that far away and-" Thaddeus says and stops himself mid-sentence.

"And what?" Amara asks, raising an eyebrow at her brother.

"And I will tell her she can visit."

"You're not leaving?" Amara says, sitting up on her elbows and staring at him.

"No, not while-" he pauses again, looking at me. I can feel something through the bond but can't understand the feeling; the only thing I know is he doesn't want me to know what it was.

"Argh, don't worry. I see. And by the way, that discussion will not go down well; just a heads up."

"Amara," Thaddeus growls.

She puts her hands up. "Looks like you will be discussing that earlier than planned now," she says, jumping off the bed and laughing.

"Discuss what?" I ask, curious at what Amara has seen.

"Not here; at home," Ryland says.

Orion hops off me, and Thaddeus gets up, putting a shirt on. Ryland, however, pulls me on top of him. I sit up and look down at him, his hands on my hips.

"When are we leaving?" I ask, looking over my shoulder at Thaddeus, knowing he will be the one deciding.

"After breakfast."

I hop off Ryland, grab one of Ryland's shirts and pull it on. When Orion hands me a bag, I open it and find some new clothes and underwear. Orion kisses my cheek as I pull them out and start putting them on. "You should have enough clothes now; I went shopping this morning and the trunk is full. Oh, and Ryland got you this," he says, tossing me something. I catch it before realizing it is a phone.

"Thank you," I tell them.

"I didn't know your email, so you're using Ryland's, but you can change it," Orion tells me, and I nod.

"I bought it yesterday so you could call Lana," he tells me.

Orion starts stripping the bed, and I am forced to move. Getting up, I flick to the contacts and see all their numbers, and Lana's has already been put in it along with Amara's and Thaddeus' parents and Lisa's. "How did you get Lisa's number?"

"She gave it to me," Orion smirks. I shake my head; of course, she did.

I send her a text to let her know it is from me. I don't know if she will reply after what happened, but I will wait and see. I also send one to Lana, letting her know I have a phone now and she can call me.

"Can I ask you a question?" says Thaddeus, making me look up at him. Orion has placed fresh sheets on the bed and picked up Amara's room, which I am sure is most of her normal mess. "What did April say to you yesterday? Ryland and Orion said she said something that upset you."

"It was nothing," I tell him. My heart rate spikes up as I remember what she said.

"By your reaction, it was something," Thaddeus says, walking over and gripping my chin, making me look up at him.

"It doesn't matter, Thaddeus. I am fine," I tell him, and he examines me carefully.

"Then you won't mind telling me then," he states, and I shake my head.

"Evelyn," Ryland warns, making my eyes snap to his, and I roll my eyes at his tone.

"It's fine, and I don't want you stopping me from seeing Lana because of something she said," I tell him, getting up, but Thaddeus grips my arms, and I feel fog wash over me.

"What did April say to you?" Thaddeus asks again, his eyes sparkling brightly, and I can't help but answer from his mind control.

"I know what you did whore; and you will pay for what you did to my husband," I find myself saying.

Thaddeus growls loudly, letting me go, and his eyes go pitch black, the fog lifts off me, and I gasp at what he just forced me to do.

"You said you wouldn't use that on me," I tell him.

"I had no choice; you wouldn't tell us. And you're right; you won't be going near her again," Thaddeus growls, his hands clenched into fists by his side.

"You can't do that! You can't keep me away from Lana, Thaddeus!"

The ground shakes violently, and the air becomes electrified as Thaddeus' anger increases. Ryland tugs me away from him. The movement doesn't go unnoticed by Thaddeus as his eyes snap to him, and Thaddeus snatches me back off him. Orion and Ryland are moving simultaneously, and I can sense their fear of him in this state, especially with me so close to him.

Thaddeus growls and dips his face into my neck. The floor stops shaking; his anger fades as he inhales my scent. I wrap my arms around his waist, and he calms down just as Imogen and Theo burst through the door.

Thaddeus calms down completely, hugging me back. He then kisses the top of my head, and Ryland and Orion relax, stepping away. Imogen lets out a breath seeing him calm.

"I'm fine, mom," Thaddeus says, cupping my face with his hand.

Imogen nods and her eyes dart to me, "You're okay, Evelyn?"

"I'm fine; he just got upset at something I said," I tell her.

My hand moves to Thaddeus' face; he leans into it, relaxing more, and I can feel Imogen and Theo's eyes watching us, watching their son's reaction to me. Theo smiles softly when Thaddeus kisses my palm. Orion and Ryland both step away from me and go back to cleaning the room.

"Orion, you don't need to clean her room; Amara can do it herself," Theo tells him, but Orion just shrugs, picking up some dirty laundry and throwing it in the basket.

"Come inside; your father has made breakfast. Amara said you are leaving already," Thaddeus nods.

"Yes, mom, but you can visit," Thaddeus tells her, and her eyes light up.

"Meet us inside," Theo tells us, and we agree as they walk back to the main house.

"Come on, we should head inside," Thaddeus says, grabbing my hand. Ryland and Orion follow us.

CHAPTER
TWENTY-NINE

E **velyn**

We have breakfast before Thaddeus rushes our good-byes, wanting to head home as quickly as possible. Orion is driving, and Thaddeus is in the back with Ryland, who is asleep. Thaddeus is staring blankly ahead. My phone rings so loudly it makes me jump, as I retrieve it from the center console. Turning the screen on, I see Lana has sent a message asking if I can meet her.

"Who is it?" Thaddeus asks, leaning forward and peering over my shoulder.

He growls softly when he sees her name pop up. "You aren't going anywhere without us, Evelyn. Tell her no."

"You can't blame her for something April said," I tell him, but he leans forward and steals my phone, which he puts in his pocket.

I cross my arms across my chest and lean against the window, annoyed. Orion places his hand on my thigh, but I ignore his attempt to comfort me. The drive feels like it is dragging on, and the silence is becoming deafening as everyone is either asleep or off in their little world inside their heads.

Orion pulls down a hidden driveway amongst the trees. The trees create a canopy above it as he continues to drive for another half an hour until he finally pulls up at the front of the house.

As I get out of the car and close the door, Thaddeus wraps his arm around my waist, lifting me off the ground and crushing me against his chest. "I'm not blaming her, love. I just don't want you to get hurt," he says as he maneuvers me and carries me bridal style into the house.

Stepping over the threshold, he places me on my feet, and I run upstairs and flop on their bed. Their bed is huge and so comfy. Orion walks in, lying next to me, looking at the ceiling. He reaches into his pocket and pulls out my phone. I glance at him right as he puts a finger to his lips and gives me a wink. He hands it to me, and I put it on silent, placing it in Orion's sock drawer beside the bed.

"He will notice, though," I tell him, and Orion shrugs, pulling me on his chest.

"Got to find it first," he whispers, sitting up with me on his lap so I am straddling him.

Orion pulls my shirt off and unclasps my bra. His mouth goes to my breast, and he sucks my nipple in his mouth. I moan loudly before I feel hands in my hair tugging my head back, and as I look up, I see Ryland. He leans down, slipping his tongue between my lips, tasting every inch of my mouth. Orion is nipping and sucking on my skin as he devours my flesh. Sparks dance across my skin wherever they touch. Arousal floods me, and I roll my hips against Orion and feel the bulge in his pants. He groans, biting down on my nipple, making me hiss at the sudden pain. Thankfully, he instantly moves his tongue over the bite and soothes the sting.

Thaddeus walks in, Ryland lets my lips go as Thaddeus grips my chin, pulling my face toward his and the next moment, his lips come crashing down on mine.

His kiss is urgent and rough, and I feel his fangs scrape across my lip, making it bleed. He sucks on my lip, my core pulsates, and my stomach tightens. Thaddeus pulls away but walks over to the chair at the end of the bed and sits down, making me pout. I feel blood trickle down my chin. Then, I feel Orion lick my neck and chin; his tongue dances over my skin until he reaches my lips and sucks on my bottom lip.

I feel the bed dip and turn to see Ryland climb on the bed. He rests against the headboard. Orion moves and he places me on my back, hovering between my legs. His lips devour my skin as he presses himself against me. I tug on his shirt, and he pulls it off over his head while I run my fingers down his chest and over his abs, his muscles contracting under my touch.

Orion hooks his fingers inside the waistband of my pants and kneels to pull them down my legs. Sitting up, I tug on his belt, but he grips my hand, stopping me from removing it. Orion's eyes focus on Ryland and Thaddeus, making me look between the two of them. Nervousness is eating at me, and I feel a little rejected.

Orion looks down at me, and I tug on his belt again. As I do, I feel the bed dip behind me and then, I feel hands grip my shoulders, forcing me back on the bed. Thaddeus hovers above me for a brief moment until he steals a quick kiss and then looks down at me.

"What's wrong?" I ask, confused by their sudden change of behavior.

I feel Orion's hands push my legs higher and I don't get enough time to glance down as I feel his breath on my core. Without a warning, he sucks on the inside of my thigh, making me moan loudly.

Thaddeus chuckles and kisses me again. "Orion is worried about hurting you," he whispers against my lips just as I feel Orion's tongue move between my moist lips. It's enough to make me buck against his face. My back arches off the bed as he sucks my clit into his mouth.

Ryland moves to bite down on my nipple, making me shudder as arousal floods me, and I can feel my juices spilling into Orion's mouth while he devours me. His tongue licks and sucks me, making me a moaning mess until he stops all too soon. I prop myself up on my elbows to watch him stand up and undo his pants, letting them fall to the floor.

I gulp when I see his hard, intimidating length. It's fully erect and suddenly, the view alone makes me nervous.

Ryland's hand moves between my legs and as he slides two fingers in me, I throw my head back. He slides his fingers in, and I can feel my juices coat his fingers as they slide in and out of me.

"Ah, she is so wet," Ryland growls, wriggling his fingers, making me moan. His thumb rubs my clit, and I move my hips against them. Thaddeus kisses me, and I feel the bed dip again. Orion climbs on and settles between my legs. He pushes my knees up and carefully positions himself.

His arms go to either side of my head and lips assault mine. I can feel his erection slide between my wet folds, making me move my hips as I moan into his mouth. Thaddeus moves away and sits back on the chair away from us.

Orion's kisses become harsher, and I kiss him back with equal amount of passion as I wrap my legs around his waist, tugging him closer. His cock moves between my folds and rubs against my clit. Orion's hand moves between us as he positions himself at my entrance. He kisses me and pushes the tip in, waiting to see how I react.

Orion pushes his length in more, and I grip his arms on either side of my head, moving away from him. He stops kissing me and pulls back. "We can stop Evelyn," he says, but I shake my head.

"It just burns," I whimper.

Orion is huge; they all are. I knew that, but I wasn't expecting it to hurt like this. I'm not a virgin, but this is an entirely different pain; I am willing, yet it still hurts.

Orion moves, and I hiss at the pain. Orion kisses me, trying to distract me from it, but my entire body has locked up, predicting the pain. I feel fog slip over me and know it is Thaddeus. My body relaxes and my grip on his arms loosens.

"Orion, just do it," Ryland tells him.

Orion shakes his head. "I don't want to hurt her," he growls, and I wiggle my hips, trying to get my body to adjust to his size.

"If she can't handle you, she won't handle us," Thaddeus says.

His words make me look up at him. I feel the fog slip over me harder, fiercer, so I start to slowly move my hips against Orion. My walls stretch around him and once again, I feel the arousal flood me.

"Good girl," Orion says, kissing my lips, holding still while I move under him as my juices coat his cock. Finally, Orion moves and thrusts into me. I tense again, for a moment, forgetting how to breathe as tears spring in my eyes.

"Breathe, Evelyn, it won't hurt for long, I promise," he mutters and starts sucking on my mark.

As if on cue, I instantly feel relaxed. Orion moves his hips, and I moan loudly as tingles spread throughout my body. Soon enough, I move my hips against him, making him groan. Orion pushes my knee up higher, holding it with his arm as he slides out and thrusts back in. His lips seize mine and he starts moving a little faster. His cock slips in and out of me easily. My walls clench around him at the friction, and I move my hips to meet his thrusts. My stomach tightens, and I can feel my orgasm building, my core pulsating. My juices are spilling onto my thighs as I am left moaning underneath him.

Orion speeds up his movements; my nails dig into his arms as I feel my skin flush. A new sensation washes over me; it's different, more powerful. My stomach tightens, and I feel like I am about to combust.

"Come for me," he growls, biting my bottom lip, and I explode.

An insanely loud moan leaves my lips as my walls flutter around his length, clenching around him. Orion's movements become changeable as he thrusts in harder until he stills inside me. I feel his cock twitch inside me, and as he groans, I feel his hot seed spill into me. Orion kisses me, and we are both left panting, trying to catch our breaths. Orion's now flaccid cock pulls out of me as he sits up.

The next moment, Ryland leans over me, kissing me. His tongue is playing with mine, his hand goes to my breast as he pinches my nipple between his fingers.

I moan, surprised by my own willingness to continue. Ryland

moves between my legs, kissing me harder, his tongue fighting mine for dominance. My hand is on his hip as I tug on him. He thrusts against me, making me moan. Ryland chuckles as he hops up, which in turn makes me wrap my legs around him to tug him back.

He kisses me and uses his arms to push off so he can sit up. Orion walks out of the bathroom with a wet cloth. He has a silly grin on his lips as his hand moves between my legs, cleaning me. Thaddeus gets up and grabs a pair of panties, handing them to me, and I slip them on without question. Thaddeus lays on the bed and I instantly climb on top of him, placing my chin on my hands on his chest. He kisses my forehead and brushes my hair from my face.

"We will make dinner," Ryland says while Orion slips some shorts on.

I try to get up to follow them, but Thaddeus tugs me back down on him. "Stay. I need to tell you something."

I settle myself, laying back down on top of him and yawning rather loudly. "Is this about what Amara was talking about?" I ask, but Thaddeus shakes his head.

"No, we can discuss that later. Right now, I need to tell you something I did." My eyebrows furrow and I feel guilt flood me from Thaddeus, making me wonder what he has done. For some reason, my heart rate spikes up and fear settles in.

CHAPTER
THIRTY

Evelyn

"What did you do?" I ask, wondering if he has destroyed another city or hurt someone. I know the possibilities of what he could have done are endless, and the suspense is worse than if he would just spit it out.

"I am the reason you ended up in the foster care system," he says, making me confused.

How can he possibly be the reason I ended up in the foster care system? He didn't abandon me there. Oh, that would be so gross and nasty if he turned out to be my father; well, technically, he is old enough to be my great grandfather, I think. I will have to remember to ask how old they are.

"What do you mean? You're not my father, are you? Because that would be just plain nasty," I ask.

Thaddeus chuckles. "Definitely not any relation, but I am the reason you ended up in the church."

"How so?"

"Well, remember how my aunty said you smelled familiar?" he

starts, and I nod, remembering his aunty and father stating the same thing.

"My aunt and father were following me and stumbled across you just outside of Parse; your parents were killed when I destroyed the town they were living in. So, my father and aunty heard you crying and dug you out of the rubble. They didn't know what to do with you, so they dropped you off at the old convent," he says, watching me carefully.

I sit up, trying to make sense of his words. "What are their names? Do you know?"

Thaddeus nods his head, running his hands up my thighs, making me look down at him. I don't know how I feel; shocked if anything.

"Yes, Michael and Sara Carter," he tells me, which means my parents were married. I nod.

"Anything else about them?"

"Just that by the autopsy reports, your mother has recently given birth and that they both had drug and petty crime charges on their records."

Evelyn Carter, I think to myself. Hmm, I think I prefer my made-up last name - Harper.

"I like Harper better," I tell him. He looks confused, and I can feel confusion through the bond.

"You're not mad?"

I shake my head; how can I be mad at something he did before he met me? Not only that, if my parents were drug addicts and crimi-nals, chances are, I would have ended up in foster care anyway.

"No, chances are I still would have ended up in foster care anyway," I tell him.

"You're not mad at all?" he asks again, shocked by my reaction.

"No. I'm a little shocked, but I didn't know them to miss them. And besides, I have been on my own all my life. I have no family, never had one, so it's a bit hard to miss something I never had, right?" I tell him.

"We are your family, and you can share mine if you want them," Thaddeus chuckles, pulling me back down on him and kissing the top of my head.

"Dinner is ready," Orion sings out from downstairs.

I sit up again. "Good, I am starving," I tell Thaddeus, peck his lips and hop off of him.

Thaddeus and I walk downstairs and discover Orion and Ryland have made tacos. Sitting at the table, I help myself, and Orion hands me a glass of Coke. As I bite into the taco, my belly starts rumbling embarrassingly loud.

"Good?" Ryland asks, and I nod.

"You need to remind us if you're hungry, Evelyn. Thaddeus, and I don't eat as much as you do. And Ryland hunts when he shifts, so forgets to eat real food." Orion explains, but I just nod again, enjoying my food.

Thaddeus is still watching me when I remember I wanted to ask how old they are. I quickly take a sip of my drink to drown the bite of food and ask. "How old are you?"

Orion chuckles, "I am surprised you haven't asked already. Honestly, I wonder if it will weird you out," he says, biting into his taco. I shake my head, not really caring, but also curious.

"I am a hundred and one, but I stopped aging at thirty," Thaddeus answers, which isn't as old as I thought he would say.

Then, I look at Ryland and he answers without me asking. "A hundred and seventy-two."

I snicker; that is old, considering he looks older than Thaddeus.

"What age did you stop aging?"

"Thirty-five," he answers, and I nod.

As I look at Orion, he snickers and shakes his head. "What?" I ask.

"Nothing. I can't remember exactly; I only know the century."

"Century?" I squeak. Exactly how old is he if he can't remember?

"Time wasn't as easy to mark back then. I was born in the fourteen hundreds and changed when I was... I think, twenty-seven."

I choke on my taco at his answer. "So, you're like 700 years old?" My eyes widen as the words leave me.

"I think so; maybe a little less," he says, and I sip my Coke, trying to wash down the taco that nearly choked me to death.

"What was that like?"

Orion chuckles. "Definitely different than now: no electricity, everything by horse and carriage, kings and queens." I nod, trying to imagine what it would have been like back then to live. "Do our ages bother you?"

"No, but it would have been handy to know you in school. I sucked at history and geography; you would have been handy back then." I laugh, and Orion nods.

"That's one way to look at it," he states.

I finish my taco when Thaddeus passes me one of his. "Does food taste the same to you guys?"

"Yes and no. Some things taste the same, but everything tastes bland to me except blood," Orion responds.

"Tastes the same to me, but I was born, not changed, and same for Ryland, so I can't really compare," Thaddeus answers.

When we finish eating, we end up watching TV. Everything is fine until Ryland suddenly gets up. "Where are you going?" I ask, as he walks past the couch where I am lying with Orion.

"To go for a run," he says, bending over and kissing me. When I instantly hop up, he raises a suspicious eyebrow at me. "What are you doing? It's a little chilly outside."

"I want to see you turn into a fluffy poodle."

My answer makes Ryland huff. "I am no poodle," he states, but holds his hand out for me and I grab it. Thaddeus and Orion follow behind us. We walk out back, and I sit on the step. Ryland starts removing his clothes and dumps them on my lap.

"Does it hurt?" I ask as he stretches, wearing nothing but his briefs.

He shakes his head. "Not anymore; used to, but now I can shift fast. It doesn't hurt, just a strange sensation."

"Do you have to worry about fleas?" I ask, curious exactly how much like a dog werewolves are. Orion laughs and snorts at my question. "What? I actually want to know," I tell him.

"No, Evelyn, I don't get fleas," Ryland states dryly.

"What about..."

"Do you want to watch me shift or ask a million questions?" he asks, cutting me off.

"Both," I state. The silly grin on my face fades as a breeze picks up and makes me shiver. Thaddeus grabs me, pulling me onto his lap and wrapping his arms around me, trying to keep me warm from the breeze. It is chilly here tonight. Kind of odd, considering it is usually warm even at night.

I watch as Ryland crouches on the ground and then, the sound of bones snapping and moving fills the air around us. For some reason, I can't watch anymore so I clench my eyes shut. The sound alone is horrendous. When I hear no more snapping, I open my eyes and see a black wolf, but his fur looks blue under the moonlight. I jump out of Thaddeus' lap and walk over to him to run my fingers through his fur. He rubs himself against me like a cat, making me laugh and nearly knocking me over. Even in this form, he is nearly bigger than me.

"So, the whole tale about werewolves and the moon is a load of shit?" I ask, looking at Thaddeus. He shakes his head. "But it's not a full moon?" I tell him and look up at the sky to make sure I'm not mistaken.

"No, but full moons make werewolves stronger; they harness the moon's energy, making them faster and a little crazed if they're not careful."

"What about you? You're part werewolf, right? Can you shift?" I ask him, raising an eyebrow.

Ryland takes off and heads for the trees. I walk back and sit on the step between Thaddeus' legs.

"I can, but a little differently than Ryland; for one, I remain on two feet, not four, and I get fur, but my face doesn't really change, and I also don't like shifting. I prefer this form," he explains.

"Why?"

"I don't know, I just never liked shifting. I have more vampire DNA than Lycan, so it feels a little unnatural, if that makes sense."

After a few minutes of silence, Thaddeus gets up and walks back inside. Orion and I follow him; no one knows if Ryland will be back anytime soon or if he wants us to wait for him outside.

"When will he be back?" I ask, yawning. To be honest, it is getting pretty late, and I want to go to bed soon.

"Probably not till morning. Come, you should sleep," Orion says, following Thaddeus upstairs.

Sleep comes easily. Driving has really taken a toll on me; I am exhausted. When I wake up the next morning, I dash to the bathroom because I need to pee. Only when I do, I freeze. No, no, no. Why are women cursed with periods, and how awkward is it, being in a house full of men and vampires?

Washing my hands, I duck out, looking for my handbag only to find one measly pad. I grab it and duck back into the bathroom. Now, I need to get more. What a topic to bring up in this house. The idea of bringing this up horrifies me.

"Evelyn, are you okay in there?" Orion asks when he notices I don't leave the bathroom. Shit, I'm too embarrassed. I wonder if they can already tell what's up with me?

"Ah, yeah," I call out.

"That doesn't sound like a good 'yeah'," Orion retorts.

My face is flaming red. "Could you, um..." God, I have never had to ask someone to go to the store for me. This is humiliating, and I usually keep a good track of these sorts of things, but being here with them, I forgot about the monthlies.

As I open the door, I see Orion standing there with a concerned look.

"What's wrong?" he asks, and I know he can feel my embarrassment through the bond.

"I... ah, need feminine products," I tell him looking anywhere but at him.

"Ah, yeah, we don't have those here."

"Well, duh, I need to go to the store," I tell him. Orion scratches the back of his neck, and I can tell he is a little uncomfortable with this topic.

"I might be best off going. It's over three hours by car, just tell me what you need, and I will go get them," he offers.

"Pads and tampons?" I tell him, wondering how he doesn't know. Like, he is as old as dirt, so surely, he has been around women. But now, he is making this more awkward than it needs to be.

"Okay, I will go get those. Need anything else?" I shake my head at his question, more than ready to be done and over with the exchange.

My eyes follow him as Orion grabs his jacket and walks downstairs. I follow him and at the right moment, Thaddeus walks out of the kitchen with a glass of juice.

"Where are you going?" he asks, looking toward Orion, who is putting his shoes on.

"To the store for Evelyn," he says.

"What's wrong?" Thaddeus instantly questions him.

I can feel the concern, hear it in his voice, but come on. Kill me now; how fucking awkward.

"She's on her period," Orion says, and Thaddeus makes a face.

"Don't make faces; I am already embarrassed enough. Besides, you have a sister and a mother," I snap at him.

"I'm not," he says with a shrug, just when Ryland walks in naked. I assume he just got home from his run, but this whole thing about my period and all of them being around me at the same time isn't cool.

"Where are you going?" he asks Orion.

For fuck's sake! That's exactly why it isn't cool to have all of them around me now.

"We got a bleeder," Thaddeus chuckles.

"A what?" Ryland asks as I shake my head, pinching the bridge of my nose. Men! Fucking men! Enough said.

"Evelyn," Thaddeus states.

Ryland looks over at me, raising an eyebrow before it suddenly clicks, and he makes the same face Thaddeus did a moment ago. "How long does that last for?"

"A couple of days, now stop being a creep. It's a natural bodily function," I tell him, growing a little more annoyed with every word that leaves any of them.

"To you maybe, not to us," Ryland states, and turns his back on me to walk upstairs. He glances at my red face and starts laughing at me.

"I will be back in about thirty minutes," Orion says, and I nod.

While waiting, I make some toast and coffee. Then, I sit down on the couch to watch some morning shows. Ryland has a shower, and Thaddeus is busy hanging out the laundry. Then, when he is done, he vacuums. It is so freakishly weird to watch him do simple things and everyday chores, that I can't put it in words.

Once I finish my breakfast, I wash my plate and tidy the kitchen. Soon, the front door opens, and Orion walks in with a huge duffle bag. Thaddeus turns the vacuum off as Orion walks over to the dining table. He empties the bag on the table, making me gasp. "Did you buy the whole store?"

"There are so many, I didn't know which ones to get," he states.

"Least you won't run out for a while," Thaddeus laughs, picking up a packet and quickly dropping it.

"More like a lifetime. These aren't even pads; they are Depends, for like, old people who need diapers," I say.

"It is in the aisle. I thought they were period pants," Orion states, and I feel my face heat up.

"Well, looks like I have enough here to last until I have incontinence issues when I am an old lady," I state, shaking my head. Thaddeus and Orion look at each other, giving each other a strange look.

"What?" I ask, confused.

"Nothing, it doesn't matter right now," Thaddeus says, just as Ryland walks out.

"You need that many for a couple of days? And what is that? Looks like a diaper," he says, picking up the packet of depends.

"That's because it is, and no, I don't need all these, just this packet," I state, holding up a small packet. While the morons watch me, I chuck everything else back inside the duffle bag.

Ryland opens one of the packets. "Looks like a surfboard," he states, and I snatch it off him.

"Well, if you're done embarrassing me, you can go away," I tell them, taking the packet, marching upstairs. I can hear them laughing amongst themselves. Man, the next couple of days are going to be long. I will need to remember to get the depo shot so I don't have this discomfort again. Damn man-babies.

The next week passed by slowly, but when Thaddeus leaves for the city to get supplies with Orion and Ryland, I use that opportunity to reply to Lana.

I expect more texts, but she ends up calling me.

"Hey," I answer my phone, happy to hear her voice.

"Can you come see me today?" she asks.

"No, I am not in the city anymore. I can try to meet you in a couple of days. Can you get to Leven? It's halfway to where I am," I tell her.

I can hear her ask April if she can and then, Lana's voice rings through the speaker again. "April said she can drive me to meet you."

I really don't like the idea of having to see April but know it will be the only way to see Lana, so I agree. "Okay, how about the park near the train station at around lunchtime on Monday?" I ask, and she asks April. I hear April tell her that my offer sounds fine.

We chat for a little while and hang up. Now, I just have to try to convince one of them to take me to either meet her or wait for a chance to sneak out and find a way to get there alone. Hopefully, they will agree, or I might have to take Thaddeus' mustang from the garage that he never uses. I know how to drive, but the problem would be getting the keys.

CHAPTER
THIRTY-ONE

Evelyn
I slide the phone in my pocket and focus on doing some laundry. When I hang the last piece on the clothesline, I feel cold hands touch my shoulders and jump with fright. "Geez, don't sneak up on people." I turn around and glare at Orion.

He runs his hands down my arms and picks up the already empty basket. "What did you do today?" Orion asks as we walk back inside the house.

"Nothing much: some laundry, and I had a call with Lana," I tell him, not realizing Ryland and Thaddeus are on the back porch listening.

"How did you speak to Lana, Evelyn?" Thaddeus growls out as I reach the top step.

I roll my eyes at his angry tone, but that doesn't go unnoticed. Thaddeus grips my chin, forcing me to look up at him. He presses his lips together, expecting an answer from me.

"There is this thing called a phone. You know, it sends signals to a satellite in the sky, allowing you to speak to people," I tell him, and he growls at my sarcasm.

Thaddeus grips my chin tighter, a little too tight, making me smack his hand away from my face. As I push past him, he grips my arm above my elbow. "Hand it over," he says, holding his other hand out.

"No, Thaddeus, I won't stop talking to her just because of April!" I snap at him, ripping my arm away from him.

And again, my attempt results in nothing as Thaddeus yanks me back. He sneaks an arm around my waist and pulls me against his chest. His voice is deadly calm, yet I can feel his anger surging through the bond. "I am not in the mood today to put up with your tantrums. Now, give me the phone."

"Thaddeus, leave her alone; she isn't doing anything wrong," Ryland tells him, stepping forward, but Thaddeus refuses to let go.

Instead, he starts rummaging through my shorts' pockets until he finds it. He lets me go, flicks through my phone and hands it back to me. As I inspect it, I see he has deleted and blocked her number. I try to undo it, but I need to put in the password that he has added.

I hand it back to him, and he takes it. "Keep it," I tell him as I turn my back on him and walk away. He has no idea how pissed I am with him right now.

"It's for your own good, Evelyn!" Thaddeus yells from behind, but I ignore his words. Instead, I walk into the laundry room to throw the basket in the corner. Then, I walk upstairs and lock myself in the bedroom.

I don't see what the problem is. Lana is fourteen and no threat to me. Now I know that none of them will take me to see her, so that leaves only option two - find Thaddeus' keys. But I also fear his wrath if I go against him.

Just as I lay down on the bed, there's a knock on the door, followed by Orion's voice. "It is only me," he says, and I get out of the bed to unlock the door for him. As Orion enters, he closes the door and lays next to me. "He just worries about you," Orion states, rolling on his side and propping his head upon his elbow.

"Doesn't mean he had to be a jerk," I tell him.

"He is just on edge; the magic is tainting him."

"But he hasn't been using it," I try to argue.

Orion brushes my hair behind my ear and kisses my forehead. "He doesn't have to; it's magic in general. Using it makes it worse. He feels destructive and therefore, wants to destroy things himself."

"Did he destroy anything while you were gone?" I ask.

"No, because he knows you would have heard about it on the news or radio. He doesn't know what to do with it but bottle it up, which will make it worse," Orion tells me, and I look away and sigh. How are you supposed to help someone who needs the destruction that gets him in trouble? "Don't think too much about it; Ryland and I will figure something out to help him," Orion says, and I nod.

"Did he kill anybody?"

Orion shakes his head. "No, but he needs to feed; his bloodlust is making him worse."

"Fine then," I tell him, getting up.

"No, not you, Evelyn. Not when he is like this. Ryland will let him," Orion says, grabbing my arm.

"Can he feed off Ryland?" I ask, wondering how that works with him being Lycan.

"Yes, but..."

"But what?"

"He is just rough with him. Thaddeus nearly killed him when he marked him, put his hand through his chest," Orion explains.

As the words leave him, I feel intense fear hit me. "But he has fed off me?" I tell him, raising an eyebrow.

"He held himself back, and he wasn't tainted like he is now, Evelyn. Not only that, but your scent is also stronger now. It's not a good idea," Orion shakes his head as he warns me.

I know I should listen, but I ignore the warning and walk downstairs as he chases after me. I find Thaddeus sitting at the dining table with his chair turned, watching Ryland make something in the kitchen. He looks up when we walk in, and I walk over to him. I don't speak as I sit on his lap, facing him, and move my hair off my shoulder.

Ryland instantly tries to rip me away from him. I know because I feel hot hands on my arms and insane panic hits me though the bond we share.

Thaddeus' arms wrap around my waist, tugging me to him. I place my hands on his shoulders just as his eyes turn pitch black and he lets out a menacing growl. The sound makes goosebumps spread all over me and my stomach does a backflip with fear, but I force myself to stay calm. My fear only entices him more, so I have to push it away. I have to do anything to stop fearing him.

Thaddeus' eyes, focusing on my neck, making me wonder if I have just made a mistake. Orion and Ryland step closer, and Thaddeus growls so loud, I fight the urge to shiver as it vibrates from his chest like he is a predator, about to attack.

Thaddeus' grip on my hips tightens, and his nails dig into me, making my heartbeat pick up. Leaning forward, I kiss him, trying to distract him. Thaddeus instantly reacts and kisses me back. His tongue tastes every inch of my mouth hungrily until I pull back and offer him my neck.

A scream escapes my lips as his fangs puncture my skin. As his grip tightens, I feel the fog slip over me, rushing over me in a cold wave. His bite is no longer painful, and I feel arousal coil within my belly. My core pulsates, and I roll my hips against him. His tongue moves over my neck, lapping at my blood, making me moan at the sensation. I feel his teeth leave my skin and then, they're replaced with his tongue that runs over his bite mark.

A shiver runs through me as I slowly pull away from him, to find Thaddeus just watching me. His hand moves to my face, and I lean into his touch, loving the smell of his skin.

"You shouldn't have done that," he whispers, pulling my face toward his and kissing me as softly as ever.

I feel Ryland's hands move over my waist, making me look up. He smiles down at me and quickly pecks my lips. Thaddeus' lips move to my neck, but he seems more interested in running his nose across my shoulder than the actual kissing.

"You smell divine," he says, making me laugh when I feel his stubble run over my skin, tickling me.

Ryland bends down, pushing his face into the crook of my neck, inhaling my scent. "That she does," he whispers, as I feel his hand move over my stomach to the front of my pants. Ryland slips his hand under the waistband and cups it over my pussy, his fingers tracing my slit. I throw my head back against him, moaning at his skillful fingers teasing me. He pulls his hand away from me all too soon, and I instantly miss his touch.

Thaddeus chuckles, kissing my lips. "Have you eaten today?" he mumbles against my lips while still kissing me. I shake my head, and Thaddeus pulls back. His eyes observe me for a bit, and he leans closer to kiss my cheek and tap my butt. "What do you want to eat?" he asks, and slowly sets me on the chair next to his. My eyes follow him as he looks in the pantry.

"Ramen noodles," I answer, and Thaddeus nods.

He grabs them and fills a pot with some water. When they are done, I get up and start cutting the sachets of seasoning open while he drains the water out and mixes it through the noodles. He hands me a bowl and then hands Orion and Ryland theirs. I sit on Ryland's lap, stuffing my face while Thaddeus picks at his. I can tell he isn't very hungry after feeding on me.

I get up to get some milk, since my tongue is burning from the noodles. I used to leave the chili out when I made them; now, I remember why, I think to myself, as I gulp down the glass.

"They're not even spicy," Orion says.

"To me, they are," I tell him, and he just shakes his head, finishing the rest of his bowl. When we finish, I wash the bowls. In the meantime, Ryland walks out and soon returns with a pair of boots.

"Want to come hiking with me?" he asks.

"Hiking? Where?" I ask, wondering where there is to hike beside the huge-ass mountains surrounding the place.

"The mountains," he states, confirming what I thought he might say.

Looking out the kitchen window, I look up at the mountain; it is covered in thick trees and so goddamn high. "That will take me all year to walk up," I tell him, and he chuckles.

"Probably longer than that, shorty."

"I am not short; you're all just freakishly tall," I tell them.

"Nope, you're short," Thaddeus tells me as he walks over and places his elbow on my head. I am only up to the middle of their chests.

"This is the average height; I will have you know. Not everyone can be giants," I tell him, pushing his arm off me.

Ryland shrugs and reaches for me, pulling me over to him. I stand between his legs as he wraps his arms around my waist and stands up, making my feet leave the ground. "See? Short," he chuckles, kissing the top of my head. I smack his chest and slide down.

Orion comes out with my shoes, and I put them on, but groan when he pulls me to my feet. Then, we head outside, walking across the field towards the forest.

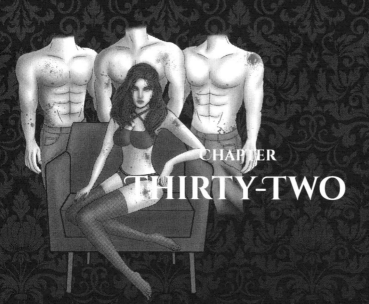

THIRTY-TWO

Evelyn

We trek through the thick brush for what feels like forever, going up, and I am starting to get a cramp from walking. Grabbing a skinny tree trunk, I use it to pull myself up. Thaddeus pinches my ass, which is in his face, making me yelp. I look over my shoulder and glare down at him.

"What? You put it in my face! I will bite that sweet ass of yours next time. Now get moving; we are falling behind," he tells me.

Orion and Ryland are way higher up already, while Thaddeus is staying behind to help me. When we reach the flat, I almost squeal in joy, only to see another mountain. "Argh, that's it. I'm done," I tell him, collapsing on the ground with a huff.

Thaddeus walks over and looks down at me. He hasn't even broken a sweat, while my shirt is so wet with sweat, it sticks to me like a second skin. Thaddeus reaches into his backpack and hands me a water bottle. I pop the lid off, drink down the entire bottle, and fall back, laying down.

"If you get up now, we may just make it to the next peak by summer next year," Thaddeus says, smiling down at me.

"I'm good; I will be here when you get back," I tell him, too sore to move.

Whoever said hiking is fun is insane; every muscle hurts, I am sweating where I shouldn't be sweating, I feel dirty and sticky, and there are bugs; it is horrible. Thaddeus laughs as he rips me upside down, holding me by my ankle, and dangles me in the air. The blood instantly rushes to my face.

"Thaddeus, put me down!" I scream to him, but instead, he jiggles me like a teabag, still laughing. I can feel the noodles coming back up. "Thaddeus, you're making me feel sick," I screech. Thaddeus chuckles and tosses me in the air. Somehow, he manages to catch me, which does nothing but make my stomach drop.

He wraps my legs around his waist and places his hands on my butt." Hold on," he warns.

"No, no running," I tell him, shaking my head. I don't think my stomach can handle it.

But alas, he doesn't listen. Instead, Thaddeus takes off, and I tuck my face in his neck, already waiting for it to be over. The wind whips past so fast it is stinging my bare legs. When he stops, I feel dizzy and cling on to him. I can feel him laughing at me, and then, cold hands run up my back.

It's Orion, I can tell him apart from anyone. Maybe someone is on my side here.

"Shorty couldn't hack it," Ryland laughs and smacks my butt.

I lift my face from Thaddeus.

"God, Thaddeus, how fast were you going? She is white as a ghost," Orion says, making Thaddeus grip my face and look at me.

"You okay?" he asks and I just nod.

I don't trust myself to speak without puking. My legs are wrapped so tightly around his waist, I am surprised it doesn't hurt him.

"Give her here," Orion says, reaching for me. I lean back, gladly allowing him to pull me away from Thaddeus. The moment Orion's hands are on me, I grab him, welcoming the coldness of his skin. Orion takes his shirt off, and I melt against him. My body cools down instantly, and the urge to throw up leaves me. "Better?"

"Yes," I whisper, kissing his shoulder.

"Come, have a look at the view," Orion says.

I look around to see no more mountains and that we are up the top. A few humongous trees are up here, but it is pretty clear. Orion walks to the edge and sets me on my feet. I look out and can see everything, and nothing, because we're definitely in the middle of nowhere. Only trees and fields. Looking down, I gulp as I step back against Orion. My stomach plummets when I see how high up the mountain actually is. Looking straight out isn't so bad, but looking down makes me queasy.

"I won't let you fall, love," Orion whispers near my ear, as he wraps his arm around my waist. He then sits down, pulling me on his lap.

"We are going to run down, aren't we?" I ask, already dreading the moment we have to leave.

Orion nods and starts laughing at the desperation in my voice. "You hate running that much?"

"Yes, it makes me feel sick," I admit.

"I will take you and go slower," he says, not that his words make me feel any less anxious.

Ryland and Thaddeus come over to sit with us. Ryland is lying on his back next to me, and I run my hand underneath the hem of his shirt. He raises an eyebrow at me as I move my hand over the hard muscles of his abdomen. He shifts a little closer and grabs my hand, pushing it lower to his crotch, and I can feel his cock beneath my hand. I squeeze it through his pants and pull my hand away.

"Tease," he mutters.

"You put my hand there; you teased yourself," I correct him.

We watch the sunset until Orion gets up, pulling me with him. The temperature is dropping, and it is even colder up here. Orion moves quickly, but not fast enough to make me sick. We get back to the house to find Ryland and Thaddeus in the shower. Ryland is pressed against the wall and Thaddeus is pressed against him. Arousal floods me at seeing them together, and Thaddeus freezes; clearly he had been too distracted by Ryland to notice us standing in the bathroom.

Thaddeus spins so quickly I barely notice the movement. He rips me into the shower and slams me against Ryland; his lips devour mine. I try to push him away.

"I still have my clothes on," I mumble around his lips.

My clothes become drenched; nothing worse than wet denim shorts. I feel hands on my hips, and Ryland pushes my shorts down while Thaddeus' lips move to my neck. As Orion steps into the shower, I give him a worried look. Their hands grab and touch me hungrily, my heart rate increases with how rough they are.

"Stop," I tell them, and Ryland instantly freezes. He glances at me and places his hand on Thaddeus' shoulder. Ryland manages to push him back a little, enough for me to notice he isn't my Thaddeus, but the Dark King.

He growls, yanks my body to his, and sinks his teeth into my neck. My scream echoes off the walls loudly. At first, I think he's done with me as he pulls his teeth from my neck, but I couldn't be more wrong because he bites into it again.

I see black dots dance before my eyes and tears roll down my cheeks from the intense pain. Thaddeus is ripped back by Orion almost instantly and I stagger forward only for him to lunge at me again. Ryland maneuvers me behind him, and Thaddeus' fangs sink into Ryland's neck. Ryland grunts and I sink to the floor, feeling equally lightheaded and terrified of him.

Ryland and Orion manage to pull him from the bathroom, and all I can see is my blood, running down my body and spilling onto the shower floor. I touch my neck and immediately pull my hand back - it is dripping with my blood.

I can hear them fighting and things being broken as Thaddeus loses control. I'm trying to get up, only for a wave of dizziness to wash over me and all I want to do is sleep. I hear glass breaking, and it sounds like a window. My head falls heavily against the tiles with a thud I can only hear, not feel anymore.

"Evelyn!" I hear Orion scream as he rushes into the bathroom, Ryland hot on his heels. I try to force my eyes to remain open but it's getting harder with each second. Orion taps my face every time they close and soon, he presses his bleeding wrist to my lips.

I open my lips and drink his blood, focusing on remembering how to swallow because it seems like a mammoth task. After a few seconds, I am able to move and grip his wrist, drinking from him more. I let go of him on my own and Ryland helps me up, while Orion washes the blood from my hair as I lean against him.

"Where did Thaddeus go?"

"Don't know, and right now, I don't care," Ryland snaps, making me look up at him. He brushes my cheek with his thumb.

I don't pay much attention to anything that is happening until I have to get out of the shower and get dressed. I pull on some cotton shorts and a shirt.

"Come. You need to eat," Ryland says, scooping me up off the bed. He carries me downstairs and places me on the couch. Worry makes me wonder what Thaddeus is doing, and who he is killing. I know I shouldn't worry, but I can't help it.

"I will go find him, okay?" Orion asks as soon as he feels my unease through the bond. He quickly kisses me and walks out, shutting the door behind him.

Ryland comes out of the kitchen with grilled cheese and tomato on toast on a plate. As he places the plate in my lap, he throws me a worried glance, but I dismiss it. I eat, but can't finish, too worried about what Thaddeus is doing. Ryland takes my plate, places it aside, and lies down on the couch. He doesn't say a word as he pulls me onto his chest, not even a single word about the food I haven't finished.

"Don't worry. Orion will find him," he breaks the silence. I nod;

just nod. When the news turns on, Ryland flicks the TV off. I look at him. "Just in case, you're better off not knowing," he explains, and stands up to carry me back upstairs.

We lay in bed for a bit, and just as my eyes begin to close, I hear the door open downstairs. Ryland instantly tugs me against him. "They're back, see? No need to worry," he whispers.

Soon after, Thaddeus walks in with Orion. He is covered in mud, and so is Orion, like they had a mud fight. Thaddeus stops next to the bed, looks down at us, and leans down to kiss Ryland, and then me.

"Sorry, I didn't mean to. You know that, right?" he asks, looking at me.

"I know," I breathe.

He takes a breath, runs a hand through his hair, and walks into the bathroom. Ryland gets up from the bed and walks downstairs. I wonder why, until he returns with a large board he uses to cover the broken window. My eyes flutter shut as I give into exhaustion; now I know they are home, and I can finally sleep.

However, the issue is that I wake up halfway through the night because of a strange sensation rolling over me. Ryland stirs in his sleep, and I kick the blankets off, feeling hot. Ryland moves to throw his arm over me, and I moan loudly at his touch, my entire body tingles, and burns. Feeling cold hands touch my forehead, sending sparks over my skin, I open my eyes and see Orion leaning over Thaddeus.

"You are burning up," he mutters, and sniffs the air around us.

His hand freezes just as Ryland's eyes snap open and he tugs me to him. My skin feels electrified, as sparks move over my body to my core, pulsating with anticipation. As he runs his hand down my side, pressing his face into the crook of my neck, my toes curl. He growls softly. "Ah, she smells so good."

"Yes, she does Ryland, and she is human," Orion warns, when suddenly, I feel Thaddeus stir beside me. I moan as his hands move under my shirt, and he squeezes my breast hard. But it doesn't hurt, it has the opposite effect. Instead, it makes me wrap my leg around Ryland, tugging him closer. I feel strange; I want them to touch me. Want isn't a strong enough word. No, I need them to. My body is calling out for their touch.

THIRTY-THREE

Evelyn

My entire body is flooded with arousal, every piece of me aching to be touched, caressed. I rip Ryland to me, and my lips crash down on his hungrily as desire fills me.

I moan into his mouth, loving his skin's warmth on mine. Thaddeus' hands run up my side from my thigh to my ribs; his touch leaves a trail of goosebumps everywhere his fingers graze.

Ryland pushes my shoulder, forcing me onto my back to climb between my legs. He tugs my shirt, pulling it off my head. His lips land on mine as he hungrily kisses me, his tongue tasting every inch of my mouth, and I wrap my legs around his waist, pulling him to me. Feeling his hard length pressed against the thin cotton of my shorts, I roll my hips against him, needing the friction.

Ryland's claws slip from his fingers and into my hips, making my skin burn even more for his touch.

"Ryland!" Orion snaps, and I am suddenly ripped from under him, pulled against Orion, and placed between his legs. "You're hurting her," he hisses, as I melt against him.

The cold skin of his chest is soothing the burning heat that runs through me. Ryland growls but doesn't try to take me from Orion. Instead, he looks down at my hips where his claws dug in.

Thaddeus suddenly sits up. I watch his claws come out, and he runs them down my thigh to my knee, drawing blood. While most people would have most likely screamed –I should probably scream– all his action does is entice me even more. It draws out a moan I didn't know I was capable of making.

"She doesn't seem to mind, Orion," Thaddeus whispers. His eyes darken as he grips my pants, pulling them down my legs and pushing my knees apart. His claws sink into my thighs and as the sting of the cut slowly fades, I feel his breath on my core. The mere feeling makes me arch my back. Thaddeus' tongue runs over my slit, and he groans. The vibration moves straight to my clit, and I grip his hair tightly, bucking my hips against his face. His tongue flicks over my clit, making me moan while his claws dig deeper into my thighs, forcing them apart.

Reaching up, I grab Ryland and bring his face closer to mine and force my tongue into his mouth. I feel him chuckle against my lips as he kisses me back. His hand goes to my breast. First, he cups it, and then, he pinches my nipple between his fingers, forcing another moan from me. Pain and pleasure, what a strange mix, yet I feel like I am on the verge of combusting when Thaddeus shoves his fingers in me roughly, making me break the kiss.

His fingers move inside me, slick with my juices as he slides them in and out of me. But it isn't enough; I need more. I want his cock, buried deep inside me. Want to feel the fullness only his hardened length can offer.

When I grip Thaddeus' hair, he growls and instantly moves between my legs, crawling up my body. I can feel his erection pressed against my wet folds, so I move my hips, needing the friction, with a newfound sense of desperation. He can feel how much I need it, so the next moment, I feel him grab his cock and run it between my wet lips to my clit. Thaddeus' voice alone is nearly enough to send me over the edge.

"You want this?" he purrs below my ear, as he grinds his hips against me.

"Yes," I breathe.

I want nothing more than for him to sink himself into me. Thaddeus chuckles and sits on his knees. He grabs my hands, hauling me toward him, and crushes me against his chest, my legs straddling him as he holds me close. I can feel his cock beneath me, rubbing my slit. I move my hips against it, moaning, wanting to sink onto it, but his grip on my ass prevents me from going any lower.

"You are sure, Evelyn? I won't be able to stop," he asks, and I move my hips against him, my answer sounds more like a moan.

"Please, Thaddeus," I beg, desperate for the release.

Thaddeus' grip loosens a little, and I feel the tip of his cock push between my wet lips, making me gasp. Without another word, he slams me down on his hard length. I shudder and grip his shoulders tightly as my body adjusts to his large size, stretching and filling me. He is still waiting for me to move, so I roll my hips against him, making him groan.

Thaddeus rolls onto his back, letting me remain on top. My nails dig into the skin of his chest, and I feel possessed as I move my hips against him. Orion moves in closer, grabbing the back of my neck, pulling my face toward his and kissing me. His tongue brushes mine as Thaddeus' hands go to my hips, slamming me down on his cock, making me moan into Orion's mouth.

Feeling the bed dip behind me, I break the kiss and look over my shoulder to see Ryland. He grips my neck and pulls me against him, forcing my hands to go onto Thaddeus' thighs behind me to stop from falling backward.

Ryland's teeth skim my shoulder as he nips and sucks on my skin. I feel Orion's cold tongue latch onto my nipple, and Ryland lets go. I suck in a breath of air as I feel his hand run across my backside, making me jump when I feel his fingers move between my cheeks and press against the tight muscles of my ass. Thaddeus speeds up his movements, slamming my hips down on him, his cock smashing against my cervix painfully good.

My skin is heating more as I feel my orgasm building, my juices spilling onto him. Ryland shoves me forward, and Orion grips my hands, placing them on the headboard as I feel something cold and wet move between my cheeks. Then, I feel his fingers press against my ass.

Orion's fingers instantly move to my clit, and I move my hips against them. My entire body trembles when I feel Ryland push a finger inside me, making me groan. Ryland moves closer, sliding his finger out and adds another, making me moan loudly as my walls clench around Thaddeus' cock.

Ryland's fingers slip in and out of my ass while Thaddeus slams me down on his cock; I feel my orgasm build all over again. My arms give way as I lean forward, hovering over the top of him, my hands on his shoulders. All of a sudden, I get a strange urge to roll over as I am shoved over the edge violently. My entire body tenses, my walls flutter around Thaddeus' cock, and I feel his claws sink into my thighs as he grips me, making me come harder. I bite into Thaddeus' neck; his blood floods into my mouth as I ride out my orgasm. I hear Thaddeus groan as he stills inside me.

My entire body is trembling, and I feel the heat die down, finally getting a release as I let go of Thaddeus' neck. Ryland pulls his fingers from me as he leans over to kiss my cheek and moves my damp hair from my face.

"I bit you," I gasp, trying to move, but my body feels too weak as exhaustion slowly takes over, trying to suck me under.

Thaddeus rolls, and I feel his now flaccid cock leave my body. He is careful as he kisses my lips softly and chuckles. "You marked me," he mumbles against my lips.

My eyes feel heavy, sleep takes over and I am sucked into the darkness.

When I wake up the next morning, my entire body feels relaxed; I feel like I had the best sleep. Sitting up, I find I am lying on Ryland's chest. "Sorry," I mumble as I slump against him again, unwilling to move off him.

"I put you there. I like how soft your skin is, and the smell of your scent," Ryland says, kissing my head.

"Hmm," is the only response I make, also loving the feeling of his hot skin against mine and the mouth-watering smell of his skin. Ryland sits up, making me groan. He carries me, one of his arms under my ass, holding me up, and I wrap my arms around his neck.

"Someone is clingy this morning," he chuckles.

"I like being close to all of you; it feels right," I tell him, and I hear him turn on the shower. He steps under the spray of water but even that doesn't encourage me to let go. Unfortunately, Ryland has another plan. He places me on my feet, and I reluctantly let go of him to step away and under the water.

Opening my eyes, I see Ryland watching me. My eyes scan over his muscled body and stop at his erection. Ryland smirks, stepping closer, and I reach my hand between his legs, grabbing his hard length in my hand. He groans and I run my hand up to his shaft. He closes his eyes, leaning against the shower wall. I move my hand a few times and then, drop to my knees, looking up at him. His eyes are still closed, not a care in the world. My gaze travels to the doorway, where I notice Thaddeus standing, watching me.

I wrap my lips around his knob, and I hear him gasp; my eyes instantly shoot up. Ryland's eyes are now open, watching me, his cock twitching as I take more of him in my mouth. I don't know what I am doing, but he doesn't stop me, so I continue sucking and moving my head along his cock, using my hand in rhythm with my mouth for the part of him I can't fit in my mouth. My other hand is resting on his thigh to help me remain upright. I hear Thaddeus growl a second before Ryland's body tenses. His hand goes into my hair and grabs it as he thrusts into my mouth. Arousal floods me when I realize the effect I have on him.

As he starts to move faster, I feel his grip on my hair tighten. A few thrusts and Ryland is ramming his cock in my mouth. I hear him groan seconds before his hot seed spills into my mouth.

I quickly swallow it; his grip on my hair loosens. Ryland rips me to my feet and pulls me into a mind blowing kiss. His tongue plunges into my mouth as he tastes me and pulls back. "You didn't have to do that," he whispers.

"She wanted to," Thaddeus answers behind him, making Ryland look over his shoulder at him. Thaddeus pulls his shirt off and steps into the shower. My eyes focus on his neck where I bit him. I reach my hand up, running my fingertips over it, and he shivers, his eyes darkening.

"How is that even possible? I am human," I ask, confused.

"It doesn't matter if you're human; you only have to bite us to mark us because you are our mate. It wouldn't have worked if you weren't," Thaddeus tells me, and he pulls my hand away from the mark kissing my knuckles.

Thaddeus' hand drops to my hip as he pulls me against him. I can feel his emotions running a bit rampant and feel his hunger, but I am mostly more aware of him, which is hard to explain. Like I have a strange sense, an overwhelming sense of him. I felt him walk into the bathroom before I noticed him in the doorway. Like now, everything he does, even his emotions, feel more heightened.

Pushing my hair over my shoulder, I offer him my neck. Thaddeus smirks, leans forward, and runs his tongue over my neck, making me shiver before he sinks his fangs into me and makes me moan loudly. His bite is no longer painful; it actually arouses me, which makes me wonder if Orion's will feel the same now.

I don't have to wait long to find out because just as the thought crosses my mind, I see him step into the shower.

Thaddeus pulls his teeth from my neck, and I offer the other side to Orion. He kisses my shoulder, pulling me against him. His chest is against my back as he kisses my shoulder, and I feel the familiar fog slip over me again. Then, his teeth penetrate my skin. Orion drinks from me for a few seconds and pulls back. Thaddeus grabs the back of Orion's neck and pulls him in for a passionate kiss. My stomach tightens and arousal floods me, seeing them kiss.

"God, she tastes good," Orion says when Thaddeus lets his lips go.

I step under the water, rinsing the blood off of my neck. Thaddeus and Orion turn to wash themselves, and I hop out when Ryland does, grabbing a towel. Walking into the bedroom, Ryland hands me one of his shirts and one of my pairs of cotton shorts from the drawer. I slip them on and walk downstairs. Ryland follows me to the kitchen, and I grab the toaster, putting some bread in.

I can still hear the shower running upstairs, so I turn to face Ryland. "Ryland?" I ask, and he turns to look at me from making coffee. "Can we go to Leven on Monday?"

"Leven? Why?" he asks, stepping closer and gripping my chin, forcing me to look up at him. "Please tell me you didn't make plans with Lana?" he asks, searching my face. I look away, and he pinches the bridge of his nose. "Don't tell Thaddeus; if he finds out, he will make us leave," Ryland says. I can tell he is annoyed with me.

"What did you say to her?" he asks, and I can tell he is trying to keep the anger from his voice.

"Just that it is halfway between here and where she is."

Ryland sighs. "So, you didn't tell her where we are?" I shake my head. "No, you won't be going to Leven, and secondly, you can't tell anyone where we are, understood? Thaddeus will make us move; and don't bring this up with him, okay. It will piss him off, and I don't want to see you get in trouble," he says, kissing my forehead and hugging me close.

I just nod and wrap my arms around his waist, just as Thaddeus and Ryland walk in. "Are you planning on burning the house down?" Thaddeus asks, and I realize the toaster is smoking. I quickly pop the toast out and nearly burn my fingers as I try to pull it out and quickly toss the piece in the sink.

"Move, I will do it," Thaddeus says, grabbing the other burning piece. "Sit. I will cook something for you," Thaddeus adds, and I sit at the table and watch. Ryland comes over and puts a cup of coffee in front of me, giving me a wink as he sits down next to me.

Orion is helping Thaddeus. I take a sip of my coffee, trying to figure out how I will get to Leven now. I have no way of telling her I'm not going, so I have to figure out a way to get there without them finding out and get back without them catching me.

CHAPTER
THIRTY-FOUR

E velyn

It is finally Monday.

Orion, Thaddeus, and Ryland left Sunday night to go God knows where and I didn't even ask, knowing their absence gives me a gate to leave for a few hours. Thaddeus said they would be back Tuesday from wherever they are going.

Getting up early, I quickly get dressed and head to the garage. I manage to find Thaddeus' car keys in his car. Like seriously, that's just asking for it to be stolen. Not that anyone would find this place anyway; I only know which direction to drive. I rely on the fact that eventually, I will come across a sign indicating which way to go. I know, for a fact, Leven is halfway because we stopped there on the way here from his parents' house for gas.

Getting in the car, I carefully reverse it out, groaning when I see the tire marks. I will have to rake the grass when I get home; I know they won't miss that with their eagle eyes.

It takes me over an hour and a half to arrive at the first gas station and I put gas in the car. It takes me ten minutes to figure out

216

how to pop the fuel cap, but eventually, I figure it out, fill up, and head to the park.

When I get there, I am early, and I can't help but watch the time on my phone.

As soon as I spot April's Volkswagen pull in, I walk over to her car and open Lana's passenger door. Lana squeals excitedly, wrapping her arms around me, hugging me tight, and I hug her back.

April gets out. She looks tired, but smiles softly at me, which I think is odd considering her parting words the last time I spoke to her. She walks over, wraps an arm around my shoulder, and I figure she is just playing nice because Lana is present.

"I'm sorry about last time, Evelyn. I shouldn't have said what I said. I am tired and haven't been sleeping well. I know the fire wasn't your fault," she says, and I nod as Lana starts pulling me toward the swings.

We both sit on the swings, and April sits over at the table and chairs, reading a book while keeping a close eye on us. We speak about her new school, her grades; Lana has even got an after-school job at the local deli for a few hours a day.

Around lunchtime, I am about to suggest we go to a café I drove past on the way to the park when April tells me she has made a picnic basket. We sit on the grass on a rug and eat.

"So, where are you living now, Evelyn?" asks April.

"Not far from here; I don't know the suburb's name," I answer vaguely, remembering what Ryland said about not telling anyone.

April nods, realizing I'm not going to answer. To distract her, I ask a question of my own. "How is work? Obviously, you're not working at Parse hospital anymore?"

"Yeah, we moved for work. I work at a doctor's surgical office now," she answers. "You will have to visit the new house; you will love it. Right near a reserve, so peaceful out there," she states, giving me a warm smile.

"So those men you were with, who are they? They look familiar," Lana suddenly asks.

To be honest, I don't like this line of questioning, but I don't get a chance to answer when their eyes dart behind me.

"Her mates," his deep voice sounds directly behind me, and I feel the blood drain from my face. His words sound normal, yet I can hear the anger they are laced with, having grown accustomed to their different tones. "Hi, I am Ryland," he says, holding his hand for April to shake.

She nervously shakes his hand, and I can see the terror in her eyes. Ryland is a very intimidating man. Even if they weren't my mates, I would run at the first sight of them. April looks at Lana and smiles, but I notice the tremble of her bottom lip.

"Well, we better be off; you will have to come to visit soon, Evelyn. I have an early shift, and need to get back before dark," she says.

I help her pack everything up, delaying when I have to deal with Ryland's wrath that I can feel festering through the bond. Walking Lana to the car, I can feel Ryland's eyes, watching my every move. Dread fills me. How did they know where I went, and why are they home early?

"Oh, Evelyn, I tried calling you earlier. Is something wrong with your phone?" Lana asks when she winds the window down.

"Sometimes I don't get reception," I tell her.

April leans across Lana to speak to me. "We can come to see you next Friday if you like. We can meet here again. I have next Friday off," she tells me, and I nod.

"Okay, sounds good."

"I will call you," Lana states as she eyes Ryland behind me.

"Nice to meet you," he says, waving to her, and she smiles nervously and waves back.

I watch as they pull out and drive off. Nausea rolls over me as I turn to face Ryland. His expression alone makes me want to run. "You're back early?" I announce.

He glares at me, taking a step forward, and I take two back, about to run, but he pounces on me as soon as I turn to run. His arms wrap around my waist, and he rips me toward him. "Do you have any idea how much trouble you are in when we get home?" he growls; his voice sends goosebumps all over me.

Ryland reaches into my back pocket, pulls out Thaddeus' keys and lets me go. "Get in the fucking car, Evelyn!" he yells at me, making me flinch.

"No. I am not going anywhere with you when you are this angry," I stutter out, stepping away from him.

His eyes turn pitch black as he steps forward and grabs my arm roughly, walking me to the passenger side. He rips the door open and pushes me in, slamming the door. Then, he walks around to the driver's side. Ryland starts the car and tears out of the parking spot, driving alarmingly fast; so fast he is passing other cars like they are standing still.

"I can't believe you would be so stupid to leave without telling us. And you thought you would get away with it?" he says, taking his eyes off the road and looking at me.

"I didn't tell them where you lived, okay? Geez, I don't see the big deal, and April is nice," I tell him.

He growls loudly, and I can feel it vibrate through every cell in my body. "You are lucky I was able to talk Thaddeus out of coming to get you; this would have ended badly if he came," Ryland says, speeding up even more.

"Please, slow down," I tell him when he hits a bump, and I nearly smack my head on the roof.

Ryland chuckles darkly and does the complete opposite by going faster.

"Please, Ryland, you're scaring me!" I tell him, gripping the seat, petrified as he zips between cars on the highway.

"Scaring you? I am scaring you? Now you know how we felt when we returned to find you gone!" he says, not even bothering to slow down.

With Ryland driving, the trip takes less than half the time. I am getting car sick when I notice the hidden turn-off. Ryland, not even slowing down as he turns the car sharply, makes it skid along the driveway and makes me slam into the door. His hand reaches over, grips the front of my shirt, and pulls me back onto the seat. He slams the brakes as he pulls up, and I put my hands out to avoid hitting the dash, jarring my hands before being thrown backwards in the seat, my hands tingling painfully. I manage to get my seatbelt off, my hands shaking violently as I open the car door before I puke everywhere, narrowly missing the side of the car.

When I hear the front door slam open against the outside of the house, I look up and see Thaddeus. His glare sends shivers up my spine and chills my blood. I panic and head toward the forest surrounding the property.

I know they warned me about running from him, warned me so many times, but I'm not thinking straight. Fear makes adrenaline pump through me, and flight or fight takes over. I know I can never fight them off, and I also know I will never be able to outrun them, but that doesn't stop my body from acting as any sane person would, by running for their life.

I hear a feral growl rip through the air, birds take off from the trees as it echoes and bounces off them. I don't even get ten meters before I feel my feet leave the ground and I'm being slammed onto the grass, knocking the air out of my lungs. Thaddeus' black eyes stare down at me as he pins me down. I hear Orion scream out to him, when suddenly, the grass catches on fire, forming a circle around us. I watch the flames get closer and move in around us.

His entire body is shaking in rage; I feel it through the bond. His anger makes my blood run cold as ice. Thaddeus rips my arms above my head and leans down. His nose goes to the crook of my neck as he inhales my scent. "You're scared," he states. His words are cold, and I feel tears start to brim. "You should be," he says, and I struggle against his grip, feel the flames move in closer, licking at my fingers, and cry out in pain.

The next second, I feel his fangs sink into my neck, making me scream. Pain radiates everywhere before I finally pass out.

CHAPTER
THIRTY-FIVE

Evelyn

My eyes are opening, and the first thing I see is the canopy over the bed. Sitting up, I hear growling, which makes my head snap toward the chair by the door. Thaddeus' hypnotic green eyes are staring back at me. His glare chills me to the bone, making me want to shrink under his intense gaze. His hands are clenched so tight I can see his knuckles pressed tightly against his skin. I gulp as I force myself to look away, as terror runs through me.

Now, I understand what it means to be scared of the Dark King. His anger fills the room like a thick cloud; it is almost hard to breathe. My skin feels like it is crawling, making me itchy as he stands up, making me jump off the bed and move toward the window.

It is a high drop, but I would rather that than his wrath. My hands shake as I grip the windowsill behind me as he approaches, stalking me, and I suddenly feel tiny in front of this monster of a man; never in my life had I felt so small and breakable.

Just as he is about to say something, the door opens, and I let out the breath I am holding as I watch Orion walk into the room. My relief is short-lived when I see the look on his face, mirroring Thaddeus'. He is livid, and I made him that way. His usually calm demeanor is now frightening as he walks over, his eyes blood red and his fangs protruding.

"Do you have any idea what you have done?" Thaddeus spits through gritted teeth, his hands shaking at his sides. Yet, the rational part of my brain isn't working, and I instantly regret the words that leave my lips.

"You act like I whored myself out. I left; I came back. No harm done," I tell him.

Thaddeus' fist slams through the wall next to my face, making me jump. "You think you did nothing wrong?" he asks, and I don't bother answering. "You disobeyed us!" he screams, making me cower away from him. Tears brim and spill onto my cheeks, my body trembles in fear.

Thaddeus grips my face, forcing me to look at him. His fingers dig into my jaw as his hands shake; he wants to kill me. I can see it in his eyes, he wants to hurt me, and I know if Orion wasn't standing next to him, he would have.

"I'm sorry," I stutter and burst into tears, which only seem to anger him more. Like seriously, what more does he want from me?

"You're sorry? Will sorry save the people of that town when I burn it to the ground?" he asks, making my tear-filled eyes dart to his before going to Orion, begging him to tell me he is only joking. "Or should I go visit Lana? Is that what you want?" he asks, gripping my face tighter, making me cry out as his nails dig in. The lights are flickering above, casting shadows on the walls, and I can tell he is losing control.

"No, please! I won't leave again!" I blurt out in panic.

"You're right; you won't be leaving again. You will not be leaving this house ever again," he says through gritted teeth and grabs my face with both hands as he jerks me towards him. I see Orion grab his arm, trying to calm him, but he suddenly let's go and steps back.

"You did this to yourself," Orion says, turns his back on me, and walks out, abandoning me with my monster of a mate. I feel fog slipping over me; it feels cold. As cold as his anger. It makes me shudder as it rushes through every cell in my body, making my stomach drop somewhere deep within me. It isn't relaxing like it usually is when they use the fogginess on me. No, this raises goosebumps on my skin, and fear paralyzes me where I stand, nearly making me wet myself in fear; it is cold and demeaning.

"You will not leave this house unless I say, and you will obey my every command."

I feel tears burn my eyes. My mouth speaks even though I know this is wrong. I want to scream at him, yet the force of his command smashes against me like waves, hitting rocks on the beach, violent and relentless, and I know whatever he asks of me, I will not be able to deny him. My entire body shakes as the words leave my lips hypnotically, and I feel like I am placed on auto pilot as I say them, not even recognizing my own voice.

"I will not leave the house unless you say so; I will obey your every command." As soon as the words leave my lips, I feel my free will leave me in a rush, and my shoulders sag, defeated. How ridiculously easy it is for him to take my freedom from me; not that I had much to begin with. I suppose I should be used to being someone's toy; I am his puppet on strings he gets to pull.

Thaddeus, seeming satisfied, lets my face go. "Now sit here until I say you can come out," he tells me and turns on his heel to walk away, leaving me shaken. I feel betrayed by Orion for just walking away, allowing this, and where is Ryland? Does he agree too?

My legs buckle underneath me, and I hit the floor, not even feeling the impact. I feel nothing but hollow. I don't know how long I am stuck on the floor. I want to get up, but I can't because he told me to sit here; my body fails to do anything I need it to do. I need to pee, my bladder is screaming at me, and I am starting to worry he will leave me here to wet myself and degrade me even more.

I let out a breath of relief when I see him walk into the bedroom. His eyes dart to me on the floor.

"Get up and come downstairs," he tells me.

My legs and back are killing me, and I hop up, glancing toward the bathroom, but he has already turned and left. I chase after him, calling out to him, but he ignores me, and I can't stop following his order. I follow him all the way to the living room. I stand there awkwardly, moving from one foot to the other.

"What's wrong with you?"

"I need to pee," I tell him, and he smiles. Orion and Ryland walk out of the kitchen.

"Then go," Thaddeus says. and I let out a breath. However, as I turn around, his voice stops me. "Did I say you could go anywhere?" I turn back around, confused by what he means. A cruel smile slips on his face.

"Thaddeus, that is cruel; don't you dare," Orion snaps at him.

"She will learn not to disobey us."

"Thaddeus, she is our mate. Just let her go to the bathroom; she can't leave the house," Ryland growls at him.

He won't, will he? Nobody should be so cruel to deny someone to use the bathroom.

"Evelyn needs to learn there are consequences to her actions. What a perfect way to make sure she never forgets." His words make my face fall, and I try to turn around to head to the bathroom just to be met with the same end as previously. "Stay where you are!" Thaddeus snaps, and I freeze, my blood runs cold and my entire body tenses at his command.

"What?" I squeak, horrified; my bladder is on the verge of bursting. I shouldn't have drunk so much water at the park, but it was hot.

"Thaddeus!" Orion screams, marching toward him, but he is too late.

Thaddeus' words compel me to do as I am told. "Wet yourself."

CHAPTER
THIRTY-SIX

Evelyn

Orion freezes at his words, and I can't stop myself. I can't do anything but what he tells me. Ryland's angry growl echoes through the entire place.

My pants become saturated, and never have I ever been so humiliated. It is worse than when I got my first period at school in front of the entire class when I was thirteen when I stood up and the boy next to me pointed out that I had blood on the back of my pants. I thought that was humiliating and considered it at the time to be the most embarrassing thing to ever happen to me.

This is worse because I have never wet myself in front of anyone. I was a kid then, not an adult. This is worse because I am grown, and he is doing this to shame me, showing exactly how much control he has over me. This is worse because he is my mate and put me on display to hurt me.

This is no accident; this is shame as I feel my legs become wet and my face burns red with embarrassment. I can't watch his evil smirk or the pity in Ryland and Orion's eyes; I place my hands over my face to shield myself from embarrassment. This isn't punishment; this is cruel.

I hear Ryland gasp, and I burst into tears, sobs wrack my entire body, and all I want to do is run away from their watchful eyes. Yet, I can't move my feet like they are rooted to the floor. I can't believe he just made me do that.

"You sadistic prick!" Ryland growls at him.

Orion comes over, I know it is him by the cold hands, trying to pry my hands away from my face.

"Please don't touch me," I sob, pulling away from his touch.

As soon as Orion moves his hands away, I hear Thaddeus' voice. "You can go," he says so calmly, with no hint of remorse in his voice.

I take off running upstairs to the bathroom, not even looking back. Tears are still flowing as I peel my clothes off and hop in the shower, scrubbing myself with the soap. I can hear them fighting downstairs, hear their raised voices, when the whole place goes eerily silent, and I hear a door slam.

A few minutes later, Orion walks into the bathroom. "He shouldn't have done that to you," he says, reaching down to pick up my clothes from the floor.

"Leave them!" I scream at him.

"Evelyn, I..."

"Get out! Just get out, Orion!" I scream at him.

He allowed this; he allowed Thaddeus to compel me, knew what he would do, and just walked away from me. Orion hesitates until I hear him mutter something under his breath and he finally walks out. Building up some courage, I quickly get dressed and scoop up my clothes with the towel.

Taking a deep breath before opening the door and walking past them without even looking in their direction, I head straight to the laundry and dump my clothes in the washer. My eyes feel like sandpaper from crying, and I have a headache.

Ryland walks in behind me, leaning on the door frame. "Are you okay?"

'What do you think?" I spit back at him. All this over visiting Lana. What's next? "Where did he go?" I ask, as I put the laundry detergent in.

"For a walk," Ryland says, pulling his packet of smokes from his pocket and offering me one.

"I can't go outside," I tell him, looking back at the washing machine screen and turning it on.

Ryland walks past me, opening the laundry door leading outside and sits on the step. "You just can't go past the door," he says, tapping the spot next to him.

I sit down, lean against the door behind him, and take one of his smokes. "Did you know he was going to compel me?" I ask, and Ryland shakes his head.

"No, I wouldn't have agreed to that," he says, as he hands me his lighter.

I light my smoke, and Ryland turns, leaning against the door-frame, facing me, but I look outside, unable to meet his gaze. "Can't Orion compel me not to listen?" I ask him.

"It doesn't work like that. Only the person who compelled you can break it," Orion says from the door leading into the living room.

Great, I am screwed. I know he won't lift it anytime soon; I know he will use it against me. We sit in silence while I finish my smoke. I get up and head upstairs just as I hear the front door open. I walk faster, not wanting him to call me back down, not wanting to see him. I close the door into the spare room, climb on the bed and pull the covers back. I am trying to sleep, and the house is so silent that I can't hear them downstairs or the TV.

I fall asleep for a while until I am jostled awake by Thaddeus. "Why are you in here?"

"To get away from you," I tell him, rolling back over, wanting to go back to sleep.

"Get up; dinner is ready," Thaddeus says, and I am forced to haul myself out of bed and follow after him. Walking into the kitchen, Thaddeus points to the stool, and I sit down, resting my head on the counter. Orion puts some pasta dish in front of me, making me look up, the smell alone makes my belly rumble.

Thaddeus places a fork in my hand. "Eat," he says, and Ryland and Orion sit on either side of me, eating their dinner. I pick at mine, not really hungry. When I am full, I place my fork down and go to get up when Thaddeus' voice hits me again. "All of it."

"I'm full," I tell him.

"I said eat all of it." My hand shakes as I am forced to pick up the fork. There is more on my plate than Ryland's, and he eats more than us. There is no possible way to eat all this without being sick, and I already didn't want to eat to begin with.

"Thaddeus, she can't possibly eat that much. I can't even finish mine," Ryland tells him, but Thaddeus shakes his head, ignoring him and instead, watching me.

By the time I am halfway through it, I have started feeling sick. Literally forcing myself to chew. I have been sitting at the counter for over an hour, trying to force it down. I feel heavy; even chewing is becoming harder and harder, and I have to use my arm to keep my head upright as I lean on it.

"You're going to make her sick. This isn't punishment; this is torture. Enough already," Orion says, and I can feel sweat run down the back of my neck. Who would have thought eating could cause this much discomfort?

"Fuck off, Orion, or I will make her eat what's left in the pot as well," he says, turning his glare on him.

I look at Orion, pleading with him not to add anything else. Orion walks past me, his hand touching my face, and I lean into the coolness his skin offers. I feel hot and bloated and on the verge of throwing up.

"Go, Orion. She won't die," Thaddeus spits at him, and I look up.

Orion looks like he is on the verge of saying something, when he presses his lips into a line, and I sigh, relieved that he holds his tongue. If he said anything, it would have just been worse for me.

Thaddeus sits there, watching, his arms folded across his chest, glaring at me. His anger has no end. How long is he going to make me suffer? It takes another half an hour for me to finish everything on my plate. I drop my fork, resting my head on the counter. The cool surface offers relief from how hot I feel. Thaddeus grabs my plate, and I almost cry when I see him walk over to the other counter, thinking he will put more on the plate, letting out a breath when I see him place the plate in the sink.

"Do you want a drink?" he asks, and I shake my head. I am thirsty, incredibly so, but I won't drink anything after what happened earlier. I don't want a repeat of it. "You can go then," he says, and I get up, walking up the stairs, when I hear him call out. "Our room, Evelyn!"

I groan but walk into the room and lay on the bed, which is a mistake; as soon as I lay on my belly, I jump up, rushing toward the bathroom and throwing up into the toilet. When I am done, I quickly brush my teeth. I feel better now; my stomach isn't so full, but I know I will be hungry again later.

Laying on the bed, I feel the bed dip. Warm hands touch me and pull me against them, and I know it is Ryland. I fall asleep easily after the overwhelming day I just had.

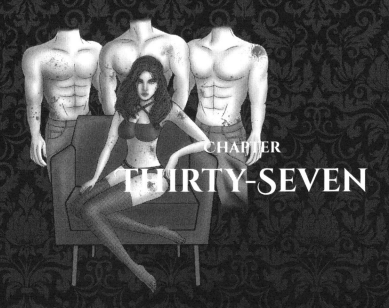

CHAPTER
THIRTY-SEVEN

Evelyn

I wake up because of the heat. Of all the times to wake up in heat when I want nothing to do with them is torture. My skin is coated in sweat, my hair damp and sticking to my face, and my stomach tightens as arousal washes over me.

Sitting upright in the bed, I toss the blanket off. My skin is burning, and my core is pulsating. Ryland pulls me against him when Orion walks in from downstairs. His eyes darken as I struggle to get out of Ryland's hold.

Thaddeus is tossing and turning next to me. Arousal floods the bond as I hear Thaddeus growl, but hasn't woken yet.

Desire courses through me, but I force it away. No way am I letting them touch me. I push against them, wanting their hands off me. Their touch makes me react to them, and I can't help but moan at the feeling of their skin on mine as they reach for me in their sleep.

Orion approaches and places his hand on my head, and I have to fight the urge to lean into his touch. "You're burning up; you're in heat again," he says, a concerned look on his face as his eyes dart to

Thaddeus next to me. I don't even remember them coming to bed; I only remember Ryland being in bed with me before I fell asleep.

"I know; help me get off the bed!" I snap at him.

I need to get out of this bed before they wake up, but it is too late. Ryland's head whips to the side, his eyes open and he grabs me and pushes me on my back. "Get off me!" I scream.

His arousal makes it so much harder to fight my own. He reluctantly moves to allow me up, and I crawl over the top of him. He grips my hips as I straddle him, but I force his hands away and run to the bathroom.

Orion follows me, and I don't even get undressed; I just turn the shower on to jump under the cold water just as pain washes over me, making me double over. Orion and Ryland walk in and open the shower screen door.

"Get away from me!" I snap at them, slamming the door shut as I try to breathe through the pain washing over me. Everything in me tells me to go to them, but my mind is clear for once. I will rather drop dead than give in to the mate bond.

No matter how cold the water is, it doesn't ease the heat rushing through me. The pain is all I can focus on, yet the antidote sits on the other side of the shower. But I won't give in; that's what they want: some submissive plaything to order around. I just hope Thaddeus doesn't wake up, but that hope is short-lived when I hear him growl, and I notice Ryland spin around, blocking the door.

Thaddeus shoves past him and he stops, opening the shower screen wider, right as I am forced to my knees when pain rolls over me again. Why is this so painful yet arousing at the same time? Longing fills me, and Thaddeus reaches down, gripping my shoulder. A moan leaves my lips at his touch.

"She is in heat; why is she here?" he asks.

"Because I don't want you touching me," I spit at him through gritted teeth.

Thaddeus growls, and I can feel his arousal through the bond only getting stronger as he takes a deep breath in. "You would rather be in pain than let us help you?" he asks curiously.

Is he mentally challenged? Who, in their right mind, would want anything to do with him after what he has done to me?

"Not like pain isn't something I am not used to, Thaddeus. Now get out, all of you!" I scream as I feel stabbing pain move between my legs. It becomes worse as another scream leaves me and I force myself to breathe through it.

"Evelyn," Thaddeus says, growing angrier, but he's cut off by Orion.

"You can't force her, Thaddeus."

"I will, if I have to," Thaddeus snaps at him. "Evelyn," Thaddeus goes, but this time, I cut him off.

"You are no better than Derrick if you do," I tell him.

I find myself lifted and slammed against the wall of the shower. His hands on my skin make me tremble, and as they burn into my skin, desire flows through me. I want to touch him, want him to touch me, yet I hate him.

"I am nothing like that piece of shit. How could you say that?" he growls next to my ear.

"Derrick?" Orion questions.

"The man who raped her," Thaddeus growls back at him, his grip tightening on me.

"You're right, nothing like him. You have never forced me to do anything against my will, right? How dare I compare you to the monster that tortured me for a year? You're nothing alike, right? What are you, my mate? That's you, right? You're entitled to do what you please with me?" I ask.

Thaddeus lets go, and I crumble to the floor. Pain hits me as soon as he lets go. I am almost tempted to grab him just to ease it as it rolls back over me.

"I am not like him; I wouldn't do that," Thaddeus says, taking a step back. His clothes are drenched from the shower, and I can feel his hurt through the bond at being compared to him.

How can't he see they aren't much different? What he is doing is taking my control, just like Derrick did, forcing me to do what he pleases. The only difference is this is worse because Thaddeus is supposed to be my mate, love and protect me, but all he has done for the last day is torture me because I did something he didn't like. How is that any different?

Thaddeus storms out of the bathroom, and I let out a breath of relief. My body shudders as another wave washes over me, making my toes curl in pleasure and scream in pain at the same time. Such a strange sensation is agony, a form of torment on its own. He is not the only one brutalizing me, but myself, for not giving in; but this is my choice, the choice I want, and I can bear it because it is my choice not to give in. Ryland steps into the shower, making my eyes snap to his.

"I'm not going to do anything, I promise," he says through gritted teeth as he sits on the shower floor, becoming drenched by the cold water. "You don't need to be in pain, though," he says, removing his shirt and dumping it on the floor as he opens his arms up. I glare at him, but he puts his hands up in surrender. "I know you don't want us touching you, Evelyn, but it will ease the pain. I have control, I promise," he says, reaching for me.

He grips my arms but waits for me to move, not forcing me. His hands instantly give me relief, letting me let out the breath I was holding, and my body relaxes slightly. I crawl onto him, resting my head against his chest. Orion tugs on my shirt, and I slap his hand away.

"It will help, Evelyn, skin to skin," he says, and I let him tug it off over my head. It does help, Ryland's warm chest against mine helps. I wiggle my hips as arousal floods through me, and I can feel the bulge in his pants underneath me.

Ryland growls, and I try to get off when he pulls me against him. "I am fine; I can keep my pants on," he says. I can feel through the bond he wants nothing more than to remove them and sink himself into my throbbing heat.

My heat lasts hours, longer than before because I refuse to ease it. Ryland remains rigid underneath me, keeping his word and not touching me. I can hear Thaddeus pace in the bedroom, feel his hunger and desire through the bond, but he never steps foot back in the bathroom, fighting with himself. My words cut him deeply, and I can feel guilt through the bond, but he is too stubborn to admit to it.

I can tell they are all in pain and just as uncomfortable as me. I'm not sure how I survive it, it is torture, especially knowing they can stop it, but they respect my wishes and don't push me. Instead, they just watch me, Ryland, still as a statue beneath me, his hands clenched tight at his side.

Eventually, the pain becomes too much, and I pass out. Welcoming the darkness as it consumes me, I survive the heat, but I'm unsure for how long until it comes back. One thing I am aware of is that I am stronger at resisting the bond than I thought, because the entire time, I wanted to give in, wanted it to end, but I didn't break; the heat didn't break me.

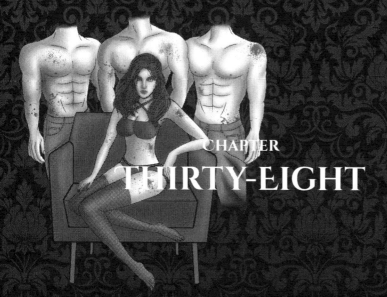

CHAPTER
THIRTY-EIGHT

Evelyn

When I wake up, my body is killing me, every muscle aching like I have run a marathon. Stretching, I roll and come nose to nose with Thaddeus. His eyes are wide open, staring back at me, and I can't help the squeal of fright, opening my eyes to his green ones so close.

He says nothing, just watches me, sending a shiver up my spine with how hollow he looks, empty and emotionless. My heart is pounding in my chest before palpitating.

Fear is something I have grown used to, but it never gets any more welcoming; you can never get used to the feeling. And even though fear is something I feel regularly, it never becomes familiar or comfortable, just there, waiting to flood me when I least expect it.

I feel a knot form in my stomach and wriggle away from him.

"Do I scare you?" he asks, his eyebrows furrowing.

"Sometimes," I answer honestly.

He does most of the time, but I can usually get rid of the fear or push it aside and look past it. This feels different, though. The fear feels different; it isn't what he can do to me but what he can make me do to myself. That is a different level of fear, knowing he has that sort of control, that level of power over me. It's one thing influencing someone's actions, another when they are vulnerable and unable to help themselves, like the puppet on the strings. And right now, I am his puppet; he gets to choose what happens next. The ultimate control, and knowing he has control over me scares me. He can ask me to kill myself, and I won't be able to stop myself from doing it.

"Am I scaring you now?" he asks, rolling on his back.

"Yes," I tell him.

He seems to think, and I try to sit up and get off the bed when his hand grabs my wrist. "Lay back down," he says, his voice leaving no room for argument, and I do as I am told. "Why do I scare you?" he asks, letting go of my wrist. How can he ask that? How does he not see anything wrong with his actions?

"Because I am your puppet, your little breakable toy you can do what you want with."

"You don't trust the decisions I make for you?" he asks, still looking up at the roof.

"No, why would I? You made me wet myself," I tell him, my cheeks burn just at its thought.

"But did it work? Will you run again?" he asks.

"You mean did you succeed in humiliating me? Yes, you succeeded. Nothing more degrading than being deprived of something so basic," I tell him, and his head snaps to the side, looking at me.

"But will you run?" he asks again, putting his demand behind it, but I don't even fight against it.

"First chance I fucking get," I spit at him.

Thaddeus growls and jumps on me, pinning me beneath him. I try to kick him off, but he just presses between my legs, his face barely an inch off mine. "You will never leave my side, Evelyn, and even if you somehow manage it, you will come back. The mate bond will see to that," he tells me.

I shake my head. His hands grip my wrists tighter, pushing them into the mattress. "I hate you," I tell him, and he smiles sadistically. I can feel the darkness within him, consuming him.

"And I love you," he says, his eyes glowing hypnotically back at me.

"You have a funny way of showing it. Do you treat everyone you love like this, or is that part of you reserved for me only?" I ask him.

Thaddeus growls; his nose runs along my jaw to my neck. "They know their place is beside me, they know I would never do anything to harm them intentionally, yet you disobey me. I didn't think you would be stupid enough to go alone after that woman threatened you and put yourself in unnecessary danger."

I know I shouldn't play with fire but fuck it; I have already been burned before. "The only time I find myself in danger is when I am around you," I tell him.

His grip tightens and he pushes off his arms, sitting up. His hands shake as he clenches them at his side, and for a second, I think he is going to punch me. The darkness inside him eats away the good parts and turns them dark.

All this talk about me being his puppet, makes me realize that he is also a puppet to the darkness, a puppet to his own mind. Cruel and unforgiving, just as he is to me.

It doesn't change anything, though; he still did what he did. Thaddeus' breathing becomes heavy, the lights flicker as he fights against himself. He wants to hurt me, and I know he will enjoy it when he does because a part of him enjoys other people's pain and fear.

When was the last time he fed? I mentally question myself. The darkness is always worse when he hasn't fed for a while, but he fed off me the other day; surely his bloodlust isn't that bad? His entire body is trembling, and I gulp, my mouth suddenly feeling like I am trying to swallow down the sand. His eyes turn to pitch-black orbs as they snap toward me. The lights flicker and the entire house starts shaking like an earthquake.

"Run," he says, and I stare, stunned. Then, he screams, "Fucking run!" He bellows, and I jump off the bed but not quick enough before he lunges at me. His hands are gripping my ankle, ripping me to the ground.

"Orion! Ryland" I scream, petrified. Where are they? Did they leave?

Turning on my side, I use my other leg to kick him as hard as I can in the face. He lets go, and I scramble to my feet before being tackled and thrown violently through the railing, plummeting to the ground below.

Everything is moving in slow motion, and I think I will die when I feel him grab me, ripping me toward him as he turns so he is underneath me as we hit the floor below. Landing on his chest knocks the wind out of me. For a second, his grip is gentle, his eyes their vibrant hypnotic green until something inside him flips, going to the monster; his grip tightens around my waist, and I feel the air leave my lungs.

"Thaddeus," I choke out.

His head turns to the side, this isn't him. This is something demonic, like looking into the eyes of the devil, his bottomless eyes pits of darkness that threaten to suck me into their void.

"Thaddeus," I gasp, and I can feel my ribs cracking as the last bits of air leave my lungs.

I scratch his face, needing air as it is being squeezed out of me. My hand drops as I become weaker and weaker. I feel my eyes rolling into the back of my head. And suddenly, he lets go, his arms are unraveling around me, and I gasp for air. My eyes flutter open to see Ryland and Orion, gripping his arms and prying them off me.

"Run, Evelyn!" Orion yells to me, and I force myself to move, running for the front door.

I swing it open and freeze. I can't take another step, physically can't do it. I try everything, but all I do is give myself a worse headache and coat myself in sweat. I can hear things crashing around until I hear Ryland's voice which makes my eyes dart to him.

"Shit," he says when he realizes I can't leave the house.

"You're going to have to run with her," Orion grunts to Ryland. My eyes watch him being flung into the fireplace as they try and hold him back.

"It could kill her," Ryland yells to him, just as Thaddeus grips Ryland's throat, making me scream.

Thaddeus' eyes snap toward me near the door. His eyes flash like he is trying to remember who I am, fighting with himself. His head snaps towards Ryland, and his grip lets go as he gains control slightly before I feel the darkness consume him again. That split-second distraction is enough to get Orion back on his feet as he tackles Thaddeus to the ground.

What the fuck is going on? I just don't get it; I don't understand how he can get this bad. How he can just switch personalities like this, one second calm, the next like a hurricane.

THIRTY-NINE

Evelyn

I don't know what to do; Thaddeus is throwing them around like rag dolls. Ryland is drenched in his own blood; Orion is fairing a little better but not much when suddenly, Ryland is knocked unconscious.

Orion's eyes snap to me and he starts running toward me in panic. If Orion goes out, I am next, and there is nothing I can do. I can't even run. I know I am as good as dead.

Orion is ripped back by Thaddeus. Orion turns around and punches him, knocking him backward for a second before he is ripped back toward him. Thaddeus sinks his teeth into his neck, and it is the strangest thing I have ever witnessed, almost cannibalistic. He is feeding off his own kind. Orion struggles against him until Thaddeus tosses him like he weighs nothing.

Thaddeus' clothes start tearing and his entire body grows bigger. Black fur sprouts along his arms and chest, and claws slip from his fingers. The house is suddenly plunged into darkness, and I squint into the darkness, waiting for my eyes to adjust, but seeing nothing.

My body's hair stands on end when I hear him growl. My heart pounds so hard I can hear it. My breathing becomes harder as I fight to stay conscious and not faint out of fear.

"Orion," I whisper into the darkness but get nothing in return, only a menacing growl from Thaddeus. Then, I feel his hot breath fan the side of my face. I whip my head to the side, coming face to face with sharp white teeth, and I scream, running for the stairs and only making it up one or two steps before I am yanked backward.

Thaddeus' claws rip the back of my shirt, and I drop my weight, slipping through his hands. I crawl up the stairs as fast as I can, only to get halfway when I feel his breath on my neck, so I flip onto my back and crawl backward. All I can see are sharp teeth and his reflecting eyes hovering above me as he stalks me.

As I am crawling backward up the stairs using my hands, every step, he follows, his arms on either side of mine until they go above my shoulders, stopping me from going any higher up the stairs. As I feel fur touch them, I freeze, flattening myself beneath him. The stairs dig into my back painfully.

His face drops into my neck, and he inhales. I will myself not to be afraid, but it is impossible when I literally have a furry monster about to rip me to shreds. "Thaddeus, you don't want to hurt me," I whisper, and he growls against my throat. My entire body shakes in fear when I hear Ryland's voice, softly speaking.

"Evelyn, don't move," he says, and I hear the bottom step creak.

Thaddeus' head whips towards the noise. A growl escapes him, and I hear the movement stop. Thaddeus turns back to me, and I feel his tongue run across my neck before I feel him sniff where my mark is. He then licks it, and I curse myself inwardly when I moan at the sensation.

Thaddeus seems startled by my reaction, and I see his eyes flicker for a second going green so quickly I think I might have imagined it. His nose goes to the crook of my neck, and I move my hand. He growls when I place it on the side of his face, but then, he suddenly purrs deep in the back of his throat.

His stubble prickles my skin. I feel his tongue on my neck again and he bites me, making me whimper. He pulls his head back, my hand still on the side of his face, and shakes his head. I can feel my hand shaking in fear; I'm still worried he will bite it off. His eyes flicker again, and I know he is still in there; there is some piece of him, holding on, refusing to give in, though I feel nothing of him through the bond, which I think is odd.

Taking a chance that will either kill me or save me, I grab his face, catching him off guard, and smash my lips against his. His teeth go through my bottom lip, but I ignore the pain and blood running down my face, shoving my tongue in his mouth. He growls as his claws dig into my side above my hip.

I think I am done for good when I suddenly feel him kiss me back. His claws retract along with his fangs. His tongue plunges into my mouth hungrily, and I feel his hand go to the back of my neck, pulling me closer. I feel his body shudder, and the fur covering his arms and chest disappears.

The lights flicker and turn on, hurting my eyes when they open as I feel him take a shaky breath. Thaddeus suddenly tears up as he pulls away, but I pull him against me, holding him there. He grips me like I am his lifeline, pressing against me, and I don't know what to do other than hold him and hope he doesn't turn homicidal again.

Ryland walks up the stairs slowly, his eyes make contact with mine; I see relief flood him when he sees I am okay underneath him. Both mine and Ryland's heads turn when we hear Orion groan on the floor below us.

I can feel blood dribble down my chin and spill onto my neck from my lip. Thaddeus finally stops crying, and my shirt –well, what's left of it– is wet with his tears. Thaddeus suddenly gets up.

He looks down at me, clutches my face with both hands and gazes into my eyes. "I love you," he says, then lets go of me and walks upstairs.

I hop up off the stairs, and I find Orion sitting on the floor, Ryland by his side rubbing his back. Walking down the stairs, I rush over to them. Ryland's head wounds have healed, but he is still covered in blood.

Orion's clothes are torn to shreds. Ryland pulls me toward him, hugging me, and I wrap my arms around his waist when I hear movement on the floor above us. The entire railing on the stairs is smashed above our heads from where I fell. My stomach turns when I see Thaddeus walk down the stairs with a bag. He drops it at the foot of the stairs and walks into the kitchen. Ryland and Orion look at each other as confused as I feel. He returns with his car keys.

"Where are you going?" I ask, and his eyes snap at me. The anguish behind them nearly knocks me over, and I step back as he walks toward me. Orion and Ryland jump to their feet.

"I'm not going anywhere; you are." I feel my stomach drop; what does he mean?

"Thaddeus, what are you doing?" Ryland says, grabbing his arm, and I can see the fear in Ryland's eyes, feel it hit me through the bond.

"What's right. We never should have let her get involved with us," he answers, shaking off his arm.

Thaddeus reaches for me; grabs my face and I feel the fog rush over me. "No," I gasp, but he doesn't listen.

"You will take my keys and the bag and leave. Go live your life away from me. You are free to go where you want; just don't come back here," he says, and his words suddenly sound very reasonable. But if so, why do they hurt so badly?

He lets go of my face, and I stumble back. Tears fill my eyes. He is letting me go, but why does it feel so hollow inside me? Why does it feel so wrong?

"You can't decide that for all of us, Thaddeus. I won't, I can't be without her," Ryland growls, grabbing my arm and stopping me from leaving.

"She is right; I only hurt her, all of you. You're free to go with her," he says, and turns on his heel to walk up the stairs.

I feel destroyed; they look torn on what to do. My choice is taken, and the longer Ryland grips my arm, the worse the nausea gets from not leaving the house and following his order. I grit my teeth as nausea washes over me. Then, I am suddenly pulled toward the door. Ryland bends down, grabbing the bag.

"What's going on?" I ask, confused. Ryland walks me outside, and the nausea instantly stops. Orion steps out behind us. Ryland walks to the garage, opens it, and gets in the car to reverse it. Cold arms wrap around my own, and Orion turns me around to kiss me. His tongue traces my bottom lip, and my lip's part, his tongue playing with mine as I feel him pull me closer. He pulls back and grips my face. "I love you, Evelyn. I will see you soon," he says and kisses my forehead.

"You're not coming?" I ask as tears fill my eyes.

He shakes his head. "No, I will talk some sense into him." I look toward the upstairs window and see Thaddeus, standing at the window watching us. It hurts when he turns around and walks out of view.

Ryland places his hand on my lower back, making me look up at him. "Come. We need to go before you end up in pain," he says, kissing the side of my face.

"You're coming with me?" He nods and looks at Orion. Orion grips the back of his neck, tugs him closer and kisses him. They look reluctant to pull apart, but Ryland grabs my hand and walks me to the car. I sit in the seat, my stomach churning at leaving them. Ryland leans over me, plugging my seat belt in.

"You will see them again, I promise," he says, and kisses my head.

I watch him walk around to the other side. Ryland starts the car, turns it around and drives down the driveway. The house disappears behind us.

"Where are we going?" I ask.

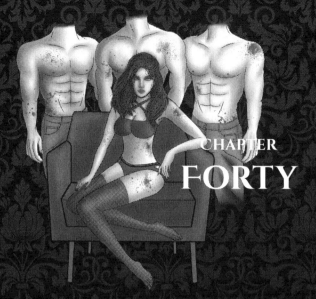

FORTY

Evelyn

Ryland drives us to a motel since we have no idea where to go. We know I can't go back, so that doesn't leave many options. The motel is one of those you find on the highway, in the middle of nowhere, that looks like something a serial killer has used to stalk their victims.

The man behind the counter looks like he doesn't get much human interaction; he is awkward and makes me feel uncomfortable. Even after we are inside, I check the locks and the windows; Ryland shakes his head at my paranoia.

"What are you doing?" he asks, as I check the door again.

"Checking the door. He gave me the creeps," I tell him, and Ryland shakes his head again, chuckling.

"You're in a motel room with a Lycan, but that puny human gives you the creeps?" he scoffs.

"You don't scare me. You're mine; I trust you not to murder me in my sleep and stuff me as a house ornament," I tell him, looking out the window.

"You need to stop watching Bates Motel," Ryland says, pulling me away from the window.

"Do you think Orion and Thaddeus are okay?"

"We would feel it if they weren't stop worrying. Come, let's shower, then get some sleep," he offers.

"You shower; I will watch to make sure no one comes in," I tell him.

I have watched too many horror movies, and know shit always goes down when you're showering.

"Evelyn, I promise, anyone who comes in won't be leaving alive. Come. Have a shower with me," he says, as he grabs the bag and unzips it. Rylands pulls out some clothes for me, placing them on the bed. "I need to get clothes tomorrow. All he packed is one set of clothes for you; the rest is cash," Ryland says, shaking his head.

He starts stripping off his clothes as he walks into the bathroom, but I just watch. "Evelyn, shower," he sings out, and I look toward the door, then follow him in and lock the bathroom door as well.

I know it's irrational, but I have an irrational fear of motels, and spiders, so I know I am not going to be getting much sleep if we continue to stay in motels. I actually miss home; I would rather be with Thaddeus. At least I know he is psychotic. People tend to hide their true intentions well. Thaddeus doesn't care if you don't like him; you know what you're going to get with him. Well, most of the time, but he can be sweet. A little bipolar, but sweet when he wants to be.

Ryland rips me into the shower as soon as I strip my clothes off. While washing my hair, I hear a knock on the door. My heart is beating rapidly. Ryland groans and steps out, not even grabbing a towel, just walks out and answers the door. I hear nothing but silence until the door unexpectedly swings open, and I hide behind the shower curtain.

"Why are you hiding?" Orion asks, pulling the curtain back, and I jump on him, wrapping my arms around him.

"Where is Thaddeus?" I ask, looking to see if he is in the room.

When I don't see him, I pull back. Orion shakes his head. "I don't know, we had an argument, and he took off. When he didn't return after a few hours; I came looking for you," he says.

I don't remember him calling, or Ryland telling him where we are. "How did you find us?" I ask, confused.

Orion smiles and presses a kiss to my mark. He sucks on it, and I moan loudly as sparks run straight to the apex of my thighs. "Your mark pulls us in your general direction; that's how Ryland found you when you left. We can feel direction, just not the exact place, and as long as you're conscious, we can find you no matter where you go," he says.

Ryland steps past, and I move over, letting him in. Orion can't fit in the shower because it is too small, so he sits on the sink and watches us.

"Don't suppose you brought any clothes?" Ryland asks him as he steps out, wrapping a towel around his waist.

Orion nods and walks out to grab a bag. He tosses some loose-fitting pants to Ryland, and I grab my sweatpants and shirt. Drying myself, I slip them on.

"Where do you think he went?" I ask Orion.

"Don't know. Evelyn, this isn't the first time he has gone off the radar. He can mask himself, so we can't feel him. Last time we didn't find him until he came looking for us, which was about three months."

"Three months?" I gasp. I can't imagine being without them for more than a couple of days, no matter how much I deny it. The mate bond is in full swing; it is like losing a piece of yourself without them.

"He will come back, but for now, we just need to think of what to do next," Orion says.

"What did you do last time?" I ask.

"Well, I went to mom and dad's," Orion says.

"And I went searching for him," Ryland adds.

"So, you two didn't see each other either?" I ask, and they both nod.

"No, but we still communicated."

"Why didn't you look for him with Ryland?" I ask curiously.

Orion doesn't answer, but Ryland does. "Because Thaddeus was in a dark place. He enjoyed hurting us. Orion couldn't take it and tried to leave."

"Hurting you?" I furrow my eyebrows at his words.

"Yeah, you think what he did to you is bad? He locked Orion up for two years in a cell under the house and drained him of his blood, so he was weak."

His answer just led me to more questions. "Why?"

"Because I left him. I didn't want to be a part of his effort to destroy the world," Orion answers.

"Amara and Bianca got him out; finally made Thaddeus see what he was doing was wrong."

"Why didn't you?" I ask, wondering how he could let his mate suffer at the hands of his other mate.

"Because he scared me, and I wasn't a good person, Evelyn. I enjoyed being with Thaddeus, doing what he was doing." His answer floors me; I am gobsmacked. He enjoyed killing people with Thaddeus.

"So, what changed?" I ask, wondering when he suddenly stopped going along with everything Thaddeus did.

"I met you," he answers, and I look at Orion who just shrugs.

"But you aren't like them?" I ask Orion.

"No. I like humans, Evelyn; like their humanity; like their simple minds and energy. I have never agreed with Ryland and Thaddeus' ways."

"Then why did you stay?" I press the matter more.

"The mate bond. You can't escape it. Three months without him is torture, kills your soul, and you become a shell of yourself without them," he says.

His answer scares me. What if he doesn't come back? Will I become like Orion and Ryland, a vacant shell of a person?

"We should get some sleep. We might go to mom and dad's tomorrow; at least you might be more comfortable there with Amara and Imogen," Ryland says. I agree; I don't know how I will handle going from motel to motel.

Evelyn

It has been a month since we left. We have been staying at Thaddeus' parents' house. Orion is right; without Thaddeus, I feel his absence deeply, even though I still have them. I miss him; the first week was fine, the second was harder, and now it is agony.

Orion and Ryland try to cheer me up. They have even been letting me see Lana every week. We meet in the city every Friday. Tomorrow, I will see her again, and I look forward to it. It is my favorite day of the week because I get to see her.

April hasn't said anything since the first day I saw her, and we have been getting along fine. Though, I sometimes catch her staring, and the look on her face is a little off sometimes when I catch her watching. Ryland and Orion don't trust her and say there is something off about her that makes them not trust her. She has given me no reason to distrust her, so I just put it down to the fact they don't like her because of what she said that one time.

Amara lets us have her room, and she stays inside with her parents. His parents are always welcoming and nice, but I often catch his fathers watching me. Not in a bad way, but like they want to ask me something but don't know how, or maybe they blame me for their son taking off; I'm not sure.

Walking into the kitchen, I see Ryland talking to Tobias at the counter. Amara is talking to her other father while making coffee. I'm about to see if they want help, but Imogen pulls me toward her, pulling a stool out. I sit down, and Tobias has that look on his face again, like he wants me to answer something.

Imogen nudges him with her elbow. "Don't stare; you scare her when you do that," she tells him, and he looks away. "Don't mind him, dear. Guilt is eating at him," she says, making me furrow my eyebrows.

"I don't understand," I tell her. Theo places a coffee in front of me, messing my hair as he goes and retrieves another. Tobias says nothing, but Theo answers.

"Amara told us what happened to you. Tobias, and even Bianca, blame themselves for what happened. They think they should have just kept you," Theo says.

Well, that's not what I thought he was going to say.

I shake my head. "You told them?" I ask, shocked; I haven't even told her, but I know she snooped into my past.

"I know I shouldn't have shown them, but dad kept pestering me, thinking he destroyed your life," Amara says, and my face flushes with humiliation.

It is one thing for Thaddeus and Orion to know exactly what had happened down to the last detail, and quite another to know that it is now public knowledge.

"Don't be ashamed; you did nothing wrong. Evelyn, you were a child," Imogen tells me.

"So, do you hate me?" Amara asks,

I shake my head. "Please don't do that again; some things I like to keep to myself," I tell her, and she nods.

"It was never your responsibility, and like I said to Thaddeus, chances are I would have ended up in foster care anyway. Thaddeus said my parents didn't exactly have the best lifestyle." Tobias looks relieved, letting out a breath. "You really thought I would blame you and Bianca?"

"Yes. Can I ask you something else?" he asks, but Amara stops him, waving her arms and shaking her head.

"What's wrong?" I ask her.

"Nothing, but I know that conversation is best between you and your mates," she answers, and I look at them. They both shrug, not understanding what she is talking about.

"Believe me, when Thaddeus comes back, you will have that discussion."

"Thaddeus will come back?" I ask; even Ryland and Orion look up at her.

"Yes, my idiot brother will come back soon; he won't stay away, but I am not sure when."

"You can't dig into the future?" I ask, wanting to know.

"No, I can't. I let things come to me. Me, peeking can change things and manipulate the future, which is never a good idea, so I try not to pry. The past has already been, so I can snoop as much as I want into people's past, but the future, if I slip up and tell you the wrong thing, could alter it," she explains.

Kind of makes sense, although I really want to see him.

The rest of the day is spent with Imogen. She shows me where she works, which is Kane and Madden enterprises. She is Tobias and Theo's secretary, and I go with her today to kill the boredom. She shows me around the building and explains the different departments. It all goes over my head. She also introduces me to one of her best friends, Merida. Orion and Ryland stay at home and figure I am safe enough with Imogen. It feels good being out of the house without their lingering, concerned eyes all the time.

I am never alone; one of them is always by my side because my heat has been more frequent. Amara says it is because Thaddeus is gone, that my soul is calling out to him in a way, the body's natural reaction to missing their mate. I don't understand and gave up trying. To be honest, their world, which is my world now, is strange, and I just can't wrap my head around some things.

After a few hours of helping Imogen with the new file system, Theo walks out, telling us it is time for lunch. I lost track of time, engrossed in the headache task Imogen and I were trying to complete.

"I have a few more to do still. Evelyn can go down for us, can't you, Evelyn?"

Theo gives her a worried look, glancing at me.

"Are you sure that's a good idea? Thaddeus will have our heads if something happens to her," Theo questions.

"Well, if he wants her watched 24/7, he should be watching her. She is quite capable of going to the café, Theo. She isn't a child, and I am sure she is sick of being babysat," Imogen tells him, leaving no room for argument.

Theo sighs but nods as he hands me his card. Imogen gives me their coffee and lunch orders, and I take the elevator down to the ground floor before walking to the café at the end of the street.

After putting in the order and paying, I wait outside. I suddenly feel eyes on me. Looking across the street, I see nothing out of place, no one is anywhere near me, yet I have this strange sensation like I am being watched, and can feel their gaze.

Feeling creeped out, I am about to walk back into the café when I notice him. Thaddeus is leaning against the wall near the alleyway. I stare at him, shocked, thinking I have lost my mind and started imagining him. Yet ,when he moves off the wall towards me, I have no doubt it is actually him.

Just the sight of him makes my heart beat faster and I suddenly get nervous. Thaddeus walks over and stops in front of me.

"Hello, little one," he says as he reaches his hand out and cups my face with his warm hand, his thumb rubbing along my cheek-bone. I lean into his touch, sparks moving against my skin.

"I missed you," I tell him. Thaddeus drops his hand, stepping back, and I reach out for him, but he steps away from me. My heart clenches at his rejection.

"Why are you alone?" he asks, looking up the street.

Instead of answering his question, I ask my own. "Are you coming back with me?" I ask, hoping he is going to say yes. Thaddeus says nothing.

"I will walk you back," he says when the woman behind the counter calls my name.

"I don't need a sitter. Are you coming home or not?" I ask, as she places the order on the counter for me.

"You're better off without me. I won't be coming back, Evelyn."

"Then why are you here? Don't bother if you plan to disappear for months and then pop up out of the blue. Just choose to be with us," I tell him.

"I just needed to see you; I didn't want to disturb you."

"You thinking you can just pop in and out is disturbing. Either come home or don't come back, Thaddeus," I tell him, turning to grab the coffee and bag off of the counter.

When I turn back around, he is gone. I look up the street in both directions but can't see him anywhere. I guess he has made his choice, then. I felt his leave deeply; he didn't say anything, just poof and he is gone, like a figment of my imagination. Swallowing the lump in my throat, I walk back to the office.

Imogen looks up as I enter and darts over to me. "What happened?" she asks.

"Nothing." I smile, but I feel it falter as my eyes burn with unshed tears.

"You look on the verge of tears, dear. You smell like..." she shakes her head.

"Thaddeus," I answer, and she nods.

Tobias rushes out the door. "Thaddeus, did you see him?" he asks. I press my lips in a line, trying to fight the overwhelming feelings seeing him has conjured up.

"Where is he?" Tobias asks, looking around the foyer just as Theo rushes out of his office.

I shake my head. "He's not coming back," I tell him. His eyes move to Imogen, and I can see the hurt on her face. She longs for her son, just as much as I long for my mate.

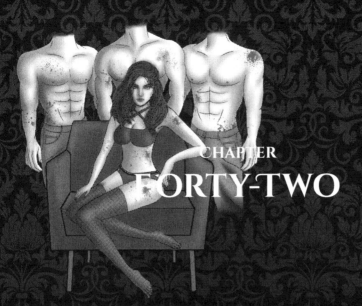

CHAPTER
FORTY-TWO

Evelyn

Orion comes to pick me up; Imogen must have called him because I know I didn't. As I get in the car, he looks at me.

"Are you okay?" he asks, but I can tell he misses Thaddeus just as much as I do. He is simply better at hiding it, yet I can feel how badly he wants him through the bond.

"Where is Ryland?" I ask instead of answering. I know he already knows I don't feel okay.

"Went looking for him," Orion answers, and I turn to the window.

Ryland doesn't come home till late that night, waking me as he climbs into bed. As I feel the warmth of his skin pressed against mine, I roll over and nestle into his chest, inhaling his scent as he wraps his arms around me, pulling me closer.

"You didn't find anything?" I ask.

He says nothing, just pulls me closer, resting his chin on my head. Orion hops out of the shower. I didn't even realize he was gone from the bed; his side always feels colder. Pulling the covers back, he hops in, his cold hands make me shiver. Not even the heat from the shower makes him warm. He props himself up on his elbow, looking at Ryland.

"Nothing?"

I feel Ryland nod. Orion sighs as he rolls away and I feel Ryland's hand move. He grabs Orion's chin, pulls him towards him, and kisses him. I love seeing them together; I love the feeling through the bond.

"I will find him," Ryland tells him, and Orion nods as he lies down.

"We should go to bed. You still want to see Lana in the morning?" Orion asks.

"Yes, I promised I would meet her," I tell him, and he leans over, turning off the lamp as he lays back down and snuggles against me.

All night I toss and turn. I even hear Ryland grunt when I kick him in my sleep, and he sits up.

"Do I need to restrain you?" he asks, and I yawn, fighting to stay awake. I hear Orion chuckle behind me but he just climbs over me to hop in the middle.

Then, Ryland's phone rings on the nightstand. He hops out of the bed, muttering something. Sitting up, I rub my eyes and yawn. He answers the call and walks out of the room.

"Where did he go?" I yawn and drop my head in Orion's lap, wrapping my arms around his waist.

"He will be back; he just went inside to see Amara," Orion says.

"Did something happen?" I ask.

"Go back to sleep, Evelyn," Orion tells me, and I feel the fog creep over me, but I am too tired to fight it, so instead, I give in and go to sleep.

Waking up early, I get dressed. Ryland and Orion must have gotten up early because neither of them is in bed. When I get inside, they aren't there either. Imogen is the only one home.

"You're up?" she asks, and I nod.

"Where is everyone?" The last thing I remember is Ryland's

phone ringing and him walking out, leaving me with Orion, but even he was gone when I woke up this morning.

"Work and Ryland and Orion got a lead on Thaddeus, so they went to check it out," she explains.

My eyes snap to the clock and I realize that I am supposed to meet Lana in half an hour. "What sort of lead?" I mutter the question.

"It's probably nothing; I am sure they will tell you when they get back," Imogen says, but I can tell she is hiding something; something she isn't sure she is allowed to tell me. Knowing I won't get answers from her, I give up. I don't want her to get in trouble for telling me, and I know she is right; they will tell me if they find anything.

"Can you give me a lift to town?" I ask, and she turns around from doing dishes.

"Where do you want to go?" she asks.

"To see Lana. I am supposed to meet her at the park," I tell her, and she nods.

"I can give you my keys, if you want to go by yourself."

I nod, wondering if I should message Ryland and Orion to let them know. Deciding I should, I quickly pull my phone out. "I will just message Ryland and see if I can go by myself; don't feel like arguing if he says no."

Imogen nods, and I quickly message Ryland. His reply is quick, telling me to call if I need them. "He said it's fine," I tell her, and she walks over to the microwave, grabs the keys from the bowl, and tosses them to me.

It doesn't take long to get into the city. However, when I arrive, I receive a message from Lana inviting me to meet her at her house. I try calling her, but she doesn't answer. Checking Facebook, I can see she hasn't been online for a few hours, but remember she sent her address on Messenger. She probably put her phone down.

Typing the address into Google Maps, I see her house is only ten minutes away, just outside the city. Driving toward the address, I have to cross a bridge over a river; she wasn't wrong when she said it is peaceful out here. I haven't driven past a single house, and most of the road is dirt. In fact, it isn't that far from Imogen's house. Instead of turning at the intersection, you just keep going straight. After driving for another twenty minutes, I finally pull up to a house. It looks more like a cabin. It has a porch out the front, and gardens; April loves gardening, so I'm not surprised to see it has cottage-style gardens everywhere, though it would wreak havoc on my hay fever.

The place is secluded, and from the road, you wouldn't even be able to see the property because trees surround it. There's even a tire swing hanging from the tree beside the house. Getting out of the car, all I can smell is plants and fertilizer.

Closing the car door, I walk toward the house, and April walks out. "Hey Evie, she is inside," she tells me with a bright smile.

"Sorry it took me a while to find the place," I tell her, and she nods.

"Yes, I like the privacy out here; Lana is a bit under the weather today, so I thought it would be best if she stayed inside. She is in the living room down the hall," she says, pointing in the direction.

The house is nicely decorated, but as I move further into the house, my stomach drops; there are pictures of Derrick all over the walls and furniture. There isn't a single wall or surface that doesn't have a picture of that vile man.

I thought I would never have to see his face again, yet the house looks like a shrine; photos of their wedding, photos of them together looking like the perfect couple, and I feel sick when I see a huge photo of the day Lana and I came to live with them.

Stopping, I look at the photo. That was the happiest day. I finally thought I found somewhere we could call home. Little did we know when we took that photo with Derrick's arms draped over both our shoulders, that it was the beginning of the worst year of my life.

"That is Lana's favorite. Thank God for Google Photos; I thought we lost all our memories," April says. I nod, feeling bile rise in my throat. I follow the hallway to the end but don't see her.

Stepping in, I find the room dark; the curtains are closed, and the

TV is off. The house is eerily quiet and cold, considering the temperature outside. Something feels off. Really off, and I feel goosebumps rise on my arms and legs.

"Where is she? She isn't in here," I call out to April as I turn towards the hall when I feel a pinch in my neck. My hand goes to my neck as I feel a needle stuck in my skin. I pull it out and look up just in time to see her swing a wooden object at me, my head snaps to the side by its force when she cracks me in the head. My vision is turning blurry, and I feel blood trickle down my face from my temple. I see the ground rush toward my face and see darkness; my head starts pounding, and my ears ring.

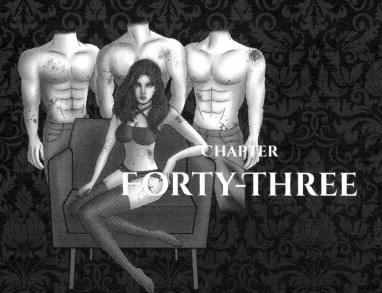

FORTY-THREE

Evelyn

    My head is pounding, and I can't figure out why. The last thing I remember is turning to see April. The look on her face... I remember the look she gave me. Disgust and burning hatred.

Why is she angry? I think to myself as I open my eyes; sweat coats my skin, the fluorescent light blares down on me, making my eyes hurt.

I can smell a strong coppery smell, feel something trickling down the side of my face. I try to reach up before panic kicks in. Why are my hands zipped tied to a chair? I pull on my restraints, trying to put the pieces together, trying to remember but coming up blank. I know I was going to see Lana. I know I saw April, but why is she so mad? My wrists start bleeding; the zip ties cutting into my flesh.

As I look around, I don't recognize anything, and I have no idea where I am or how I got here. The floor is concrete and cold under my bare feet; my ankles are also zip-tied to the wooden chair. The room smells damp and cold, and I am facing a wall. Craning my neck, I try to figure out where I am. Is this a nightmare I am yet to wake up from? Nothing makes sense; how did I get into this situation?

Argh, I wish my head would stop hurting; it is pounding to its own beat. The more I move, the more I can feel the warm trickling of blood, hear it dripping off me onto the ground, my shirt drenched.

Hearing a noise, I try to crane my neck to see who has entered. They are behind me in my blind spot; I can see their shadow on the wall ahead, just standing there. Goosebumps rise on my skin, and shivers run up my spine.

Suddenly the chair is turned; the wood creaks on the floor as I come face to face with April. "April?"

"Don't look so shocked, Evelyn; what did you expect to happen?" she asks, and my eyes fall to what is clutched in her hand, a baseball bat, coated in blood.

"Where is Lana?" I ask, trying to remember why I am down here. Is she here?

"Lana is at the hospital."

"Hospital? What did you do to her?" I ask, and I can see an evil glint in her eye. She looks deranged, not at all the well-together woman she usually is.

"I did nothing to her. You are the one that did something, you slut. You ruined my family. You are nothing but a home-wrecking whore, seducing my husband," she spits at me. I mean literally spits on me.

"I did not seduce your husband!"

She slaps me. The force whips my head to the side, my skin stings, and my ears ring.

"Two fucking years, I watched him lay in a coma for what you did, because he wouldn't leave me for you. You spiteful bitch, you burned our home down and nearly killed him!" she screams, grabbing my throat with her hands. The bat falls to the ground with a thump.

Her grip tightens as she crushes my windpipe. I struggle, trying to loosen my hands. She is full of burning rage, her nails dig into my skin, tearing through the flesh as I try to breathe around her grip. She suddenly lets go and moves her hair out of her face, wiping her hands on her jeans. I gasp for air, sucking in each breath to fill my lungs.

"You thought you could have him, and when you couldn't, you tried to kill him and take him from me."

I shake my head at her words. "He is alive? Is that what he told you?" I breathe, trying to catch my breath.

"You really thought you could kill him? A man as strong as him? He suffered from what you did. Burns to seventy percent of his body. Two years he spent in a coma, another two years and he still can't leave the hospital. You ruined him; you ruined me!" she screams, and I flinch at her anger, her hands outstretched like she is about to strangle me again. She laughs at my reaction. She is enjoying my fear, enjoying what she is doing to me.

"He lied. I never seduced him."

"Whore! You think I will believe you over my husband? No wonder no one wanted you, always the throw-away child." She chuckles, pacing. Nothing I say is going to make her believe me; make her see him for what he is. She continues pacing, muttering under her breath, pulling at her hair in frustration.

"April, just let me leave. Untie me. You will never have to see me again," I tell her, and she shakes her head.

"I tried. I tried to forgive you. I really did, but it is too late now; I have to do this. I need to do this. You must die for what you did. But first, you need to suffer," she says, stopping her pacing and looking around the room.

My eyes follow her, and my heart skips a beat when she stops in front of a wall full of different tools. What is she looking for? What happened to the woman who was kind and willing to help anyone? I struggle to understand how someone, who used to be sweet, loving, and understanding could now be so manic and cruel.

April grabs a hammer off the shelf, turning it in her hand as she walks toward me. I struggle against my restraints as she kneels in front of me.

"What are you doing, April? You don't need to do this. I can explain if you would just listen," I beg her as she brings the hammer down on my foot, my toes breaking.

I scream, but she doesn't stop. She repeatedly hits my foot till every toe is broken, and I am fairly sure it's the end of my foot; I can feel my foot swelling painfully. My screams echo against the wall, and my voice becomes hoarse as tears stream down my face. She stands up, looking down at what she did, then rushes to the sink in the corner to throw up. All I can do is try and breathe, breathe through the pain, and sob.

April washes her face and grabs the hammer off the sink basin. Panic courses through me. "He raped me. Derrick raped me. I didn't seduce your husband, April!" I try to tell her.

But she just steps forward and punches me in the face. My head snaps back, and I hear the crunch as my nose breaks. Blood spurts from my nose like a tap has been turned on.

"Liar! He told me you would say that. Said you would try to tarnish his name to save yourself from what you did! Was I not a good mother to you that you would hurt me so?"

"I am not lying; every goddamn night for a year, I had to endure him. Every night I wished you would walk through that door, wished that you would realize and save me from him, to make it stop," I scream at her, which only angers her more.

April's face distorts in anger. "You're lying, or you would have told me. Why didn't you speak up then, Evelyn, huh?"

"Because he threatened Lana; because of who he is. I tried, April. No one would believe me; why would they? You couldn't even see what was right under your nose the entire time."

Her hands grip my throat; my words die out as I try to breathe and the chair suddenly tips, and she comes down on top of me. "Liar! Fucking liar!" she keeps screaming, and I can feel the darkness take over my vision just as she lets go, stands up and kicks my side.

I start choking on the breath I try to take, as she struggles to lift the chair back up under my weight. When she finally has me upright again, she strides over to the shelf with tools again, and I groan.

"Please, no more, no more April, just let me go," I cry.

"No, I will make you suffer the way he did." My stomach drops when she turns around. "No one will recognize you when I am done," she says, walking toward me with a blow torch, a sadistic look on her face. One of pure insanity.

FORTY-FOUR

Thaddeus

I fucked up; I know I fucked up. I let my walls down. I fell asleep, and as soon as I opened my eyes, I knew they would find me. I shouldn't have gone home or closed my eyes for those few seconds, which turned into hours.

I can feel them getting nearer. Looking at the clock, I see that it is 10 AM. I have to get moving; they won't be far out. My mates will convince me to come back, and I can't risk her safety. She is safest away from me.

My life has been hell without them. I haven't slept in a month, sitting down and resting is my mistake. I should have kept moving, stayed awake, and then they wouldn't have found me. Putting my clothes on, I head for the door. I know I don't have long before they get here. Time slipped away from me, and I'm not even sure how long I slept, but I can feel how close they are.

Moving quickly, I start running. No direction in particular, just away from them catching up. I can feel Orion getting closer, feel his emotion creep into me, flooding me, forcing me to stop. I usually block them out. I can't handle their suffering. I know it is hell for them, as much as it is for me, but this is the right choice, or so I thought, until I feel her, feel them suffering along with me.

First, it is unease creeping in from her. What is she doing that is making her unsure? Then it is fear, then pounding pain, ripping through my skull, forcing me to clutch my head.

Something is wrong; something has happened. Then suddenly, I can't feel her at all; she is gone. Looking around, I have no idea where I am; stopping at a sign, I read: Town of Forse.

Ryland and Orion are just as far away as I am. They are 6 hours away from her. Turning on my heel, I take off, heading back the way I came. My surroundings blur into a sea of color; I am moving that fast. My heart is pounding, and dread consumes me. Why can't I feel her? Is she unconscious? Ryland and Orion would have left her in safe hands. I know them; they love her just as much as I do. So why is she hurt? Why isn't she safe?

Running, I dig my phone out slowly, as I ring my mother.

"Hello?" her excited voice comes through to me.

"Ma, where is Evelyn? Put her on."

"I can't hear you. Are you running?" she asks.

I slowly come to a stop so she can hear. I can feel Ryland and Orion moving away, heading toward her. They must know where she is. "Ma put Evelyn on the phone," I tell her.

"Evelyn, she went into the city to meet Lana," my mother says.

My blood runs cold. "By herself?"

"Yes, Ryland said it was okay." I hang up to dial Evelyn's number.

"Hi, you've reached Evelyn. Leave your number, and I will get back to you." Her voicemail. Either it is off, or she has no reception. Running, I can feel myself catching up to Ryland, feel the pull of the mate bond pulling me towards his direction.

That's when I feel her wake, her panic courses through me. My wrists are hurting. I can feel everything she feels. My mate is in trouble; she is hurt. Finally catching up to Ryland at Leven, I see him in wolf form and then, he drops. So do I when the pain starts radiating throughout my left foot. My foot is throbbing, and Ryland groans, the pain forcing him to shift back.

Grabbing him, I slam him to the ground as anger takes over me. "Where is she?"

"She went to the park to visit Lana. Go, Thaddeus, find her," he says and starts screaming in agony. I can feel her pain but push it aside; her mind is consumed in pain. Letting him go, I start running. Just hang on, Evelyn. I am not far now.

E velyn

Watching, horrified as she walks towards me with the blow torch, I feel bile rise in my throat, nausea swirls within me at what she is about to do. She has lost her mind.

"Look, your foot is bleeding. How about I cauterize it for you?" she mocks and holds the blue flame to my broken foot. I scream.

At first, it feels cold, but then it is melting my skin off. I thrash, trying to get her to stop as she starts with my toes. My screams fall on deaf ears as she ignores me. I have never felt pain like it; not even catching fire hurt this badly. This is torture in every sense of the word. My skin is literally melting under the intense heat.

She stops, checking out her handy work. I can smell my burning flesh. It fills the room. The stench is horrendous. She then stands up and walks upstairs; relief floods me that she is leaving. I am drenched in blood and sweat, drenched in my own tears.

"No, no, no," I scream when I hear the door open and realize she is coming back.

She walks down the stairs, a cruel smile on her face. She is carrying a knife. "Burns are terrible, aren't they? So painful," she tells me. "I was planning on burning you to death, but I can't handle the smell. It is atrocious." She grabs a medical mask from her pocket and puts it on. She then ties her hair up, getting it off her face and picks up the knife.

She runs the back of the blade across my shoulder to the middle of my throat, pushing the point in slightly. "You are a pretty little thing. Let's change that, shall we?" she says, her words muffled by the mask.

She turns the blade and runs it down my chest. I scream as it slices through my chest and across my breasts. She starts yanking on my shirt, tearing it away, jerking me forward, the zip ties cutting into my wrist painfully. I feel one snap from the pressure of my wrist, being in a weird angle from her tugging.

She rips my shirt down the middle; the knife cuts into my skin as she continues yanking on me, trying to remove my bra while holding it. This woman is sick; she is going to mutilate me.

Once my bra is undone, she grabs the knife, and just as she is about to slice my breast, I grab the blade. I can feel it slicing through my palm and fingers; she seems shocked as she yanks the knife away. Like it's the most casual thing to do, she walks over to the table and grabs another zip tie.

I frantically start yanking on my other wrist, trying to free it, when she comes back, grabbing my hand and prying it away, trying to restrain it. I can't let her do that, so I use the only thing I have, my head. I headbutt her, and she stumbles back. Gold flecks dance before my vision from the impact of our heads colliding. Pain shoots through my skull, and she gets up.

She screams, and I can see her eyebrow is bleeding, blood runs down the side of her face as it twists in anger, and she screams again, tackling me. I can't do anything as the chair falls backward. My head smacks the concrete with a loud crack, making me see black for a few seconds. The air is knocked from my lungs as she comes down on top of me.

I don't even register the first few blows as she rains down punches on my face. I have lost feeling for a few seconds, and I fear that I am going to die; I am pretty certain any more knocks to the head, I am going to be out. Suddenly, I hear a loud noise upstairs; she stops, looking at the ceiling, and I scream, hoping she can hear me; Lana must be home.

April instantly clamps her hand down on my mouth. I bite her hand, letting out a scream when she jerks her hand away and she punches me in the mouth. My lips swell and I can taste my own blood. I watch her raise her fist again, when suddenly she is gone. Just vanishes as I hear a loud crash, and her body bounces off the wall. She lands next to me, unconscious on the floor when suddenly I see him.

His fangs protrude, and never have I been so thankful to see someone. Orion is coming into my line of vision. Then suddenly, I heard another violent crash; I think the roof is about to cave in.

"Down here!" Orion yells out to them, and I hear fast-moving footsteps, followed by a terrifying growl. Orion picks me up in the chair, placing it upright and snapping the cable ties. Looking over his shoulder, I see Thaddeus, a murderous look on his face, his eyes trained on the unconscious April on the floor.

"You're okay now; we got you," Orion says, grabbing my face and making me look at him.

Everything is becoming fuzzy around the edges. My vision is becoming tunneled. Everything hurts, yet all I can focus on is that they are here. Orion bites into his wrist, and I don't even think about it, just wrap my lips around his bite mark, knowing his blood will offer relief and stop the pain. I can feel his hand, rubbing the back of my head.

"Get her out of here!" Thaddeus yells at him as he stalks toward April.

Orion grabs me, lifting me, and I can feel my body healing, the pain slows as I wrap my legs around his waist, and Orion heads for the stairs. I see Thaddeus grab April and toss her in the chair; he has to catch it to steady it from the force he uses.

He is going to kill her, and even after what she did, I don't want her to die. Does she deserve death? Probably, but that isn't for me to decide. She was still my mother for a year, still Lana's mother.

"Please don't kill her," I whisper, and Orion stops, pulling back and staring at me as if I have lost my mind. Thaddeus' head whips in my direction, a look of anger on his face, directed at me.

"Get her out of here, Orion! I will deal with her and Ryland later," he growls, and I see April stir when suddenly, I feel a rush of air and smell fresh air. Opening my eyes, I see we are outside.

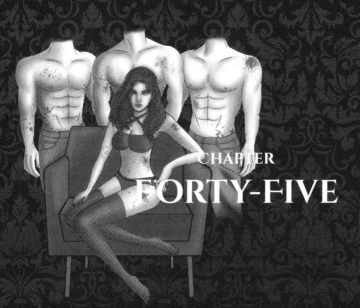

FORTY-FIVE

Thaddeus

There are worse ways to die than death. Worse ways to torture someone other than physical pain. Looking down at this weak, pathetic woman, I want to inflict the same pain Evelyn endured.

Yet, Evelyn, for some strange reason, wants me to leave her alive. If it were me, I would want to torture her slowly. I will still enjoy this, though. Evelyn doesn't need to know as long as she remains silent.

"Get her out of here, Orion! I will deal with her and Ryland later." I watch as they go, and the woman stirs.

How could she inflict what she has done on another woman? But I can see this one is tainted with madness and jealousy; she honestly thinks Evelyn was having an affair with her husband.

The thought of touching this woman disgusts me, but I have no choice. Grabbing her face, I force her to look up at me. She whimpers, cowering back in fear.

"You will not make a sound; you will not cry; you will only suffer internally," I tell her, watching her eyes glaze over. She doesn't even put up a fight. Evelyn is tiny, and even she can sometimes fight off my compulsion; however, this woman doesn't put up any fight. "Now you will suffer what Evelyn did."

Grabbing her head, I rifle through her thoughts, her body shakes in my hands as I flick through the files of her mind; what I'm not expecting is to find out that the man who tortured my love has survived. Evelyn was so sure he died, and so was I by her memories.

Seeing his burnt face in her memories angers me further. Twisting her memories is easy; I ruin the memories she has with him, twist them into something dark and painful when another thought comes over me. What better revenge than to make Evelyn's memories hers?

I shove Evelyn's first horrid encounter with that man into her, letting it flood her mind. April gasps and starts shaking her head, but I hold her tighter. Letting Evelyn's memories flood her and the emotion she felt during that encounter: her helplessness, fear, shame, repulsion. I give her Evelyn's every emotion that ever registered within her. Letting go, I look at this vile woman. She has tears rolling down her face, guilt evident on her face. She truly didn't know what a monster her husband was.

"Speak," I tell her.

"I didn't know. Please, no more," she whispers.

I arch an eyebrow at her begging. "No more?" I ask. There will be more; that is her first memory. If she can't handle one memory, how will this woman endure what he took from my mate, memories which almost destroyed her? One memory, and Evelyn has a year of them.

"Please, no more," she begs again.

"That's what Evelyn begged every time. That is only one; we haven't even got to the best part. You haven't seen how much of a monster he truly is. Now be quiet," I tell her as I grab her face, kneeling in front of her.

She grabs my wrist, not wanting to endure any more, but she will see everything —every goddamn thing— and I will make sure she feels it.

Her face twists in pain; her mouth opens in a silent scream as I shove every memory in her mind, every thought, every emotion. April's face is tortured; I actually feel bad seeing the look on her face. What that man has done makes me sick; to do that to a child, to abuse his power and trust.

Standing up, I look down at her. She is shaking, but not a word comes out of her, her eyes hollow as she is now forever haunted by what Evelyn endured, just like Orion and me. I am thankful Ryland didn't see. Orion and I, we swore to each other we will never let him. I felt everything along with her, felt every emotion of Evelyn's when I took them, like I was with her the entire time; how she didn't kill herself is beyond me.

Looking at April, though, she isn't as strong as Evelyn; she just might. There are worse things than death. The mind can make you wish for it; make you want it. The mind is a form of torture on its own, nothing worse than toxic thoughts. Nothing worse than losing your will to live.

E velyn

Waiting is torture in itself. Thaddeus has been down there for ages, and I haven't heard a sound from the house. My hands are trembling as we wait, when suddenly, Ryland comes tearing through the trees surrounding the property.

Trampling over the gardens as he rushes over, shifting mid-stride, his feet skid on the grass as he stops next to us in front of the porch. "Thank God," he breathes, hands on his knees as he drops to the ground, exhausted.

Orion growls at him when Ryland reaches for me, pulling me away from Ryland, which confuses me. Didn't Ryland tell him that he said I could go? I reach out for him, and Ryland grasps my finger-tips. Orion's anger hits me along with Ryland's guilt.

Yet, Thaddeus, I can't quite feel him. He's calm? It feels like when you hit the eye of a storm, and everything goes silent and peaceful before the hurricane hits again. That is the vibe I am getting.

I try to move off Orion's lap, but he grips my hips and pulls me down on his lap. "Don't," is all he says to me, but that simple word's venom makes me freeze. Suddenly, the front door opens, hitting the wall and splintering everywhere from the force.

Thaddeus growls, so menacing that birds flee the trees, and I cringe away from him. His eyes are on Ryland as he stalks toward him, and fear and guilt consume me. Thaddeus is one minute behind me, and within a blink of an eye, he has Ryland by the throat.

"It's not his fault! I didn't go where I said I was going!" I blurt out, just as he raises his fist.

Thaddeus freezes, his fist still raised as he looks over his shoulder at me. I shrink back under his gaze, leaning into Orion. "I didn't know, I thought...." I can't finish; they tried to warn me there was something wrong with her, something off, and I stupidly fell into her trap.

"Did Ryland say you could leave the house without him?" Thaddeus asks. I look frantically at Ryland, worried, and he just nods. Thaddeus growls and turns back to him.

"He said I could meet Lana at the park; I got a message telling me to come here. I didn't tell him," I confess, worried Thaddeus will seriously hurt him.

Ryland instantly shakes his head, telling me to stop speaking. I bite my tongue, wondering how much trouble I am in; he wants to kill me by the look on his face.

"She could have fucking died!" he screams, and Ryland hangs his head as Thaddeus shoves him away, ripping me to my feet and crushing me against his chest. His bunched muscles instantly relax as he inhales my scent. "You are in so much trouble when we get home," he hums below my ear, making me shiver.

"What did you do to April?" I whisper, worried because she hasn't come out of the house.

"She is alive. For now," he says as he grips my chin, forcing me to look up and meet his stormy gaze. "Derrick is alive," he states, and I nod.

A cruel smile spreads across his lips, and I feel a sadistic feeling come through the bond. Thaddeus rummages through my back pocket, pulls out his mother's car keys, and unlocks the car. His grip on my arm tightens as he drags me to the car, opening the back door and shoving me in. Orion remains silent, and I can feel he is seething through the bond between Ryland and me; he says nothing the entire drive back to Thaddeus' parents' house.

I don't dare say a word, not wanting to get in any more trouble, and I am still trying to wrap my head around what happened and the fact I am still alive.

Shock hits me now that I have time to think. My mind is racing, and I see Thaddeus glance at me through the mirror a few times. His burning anger toward me makes my stomach drop. Ryland slides across the seat, moving closer to me.

"Don't fucking touch her," Thaddeus growls, and he instantly moves back onto his seat away from me.

Imogen is waiting out front when we pull in, and she rushes over, opening the door, crushing me in a hug. "Thank God you're okay; I was so worried when Thaddeus called," she says, pulling away and giving me a once-over. When she sees I am drenched in blood, her face falls. "Well, thank God for the healing properties of blood. I better tell your fathers to come home; they have been searching for her for hours," Imogen says, walking inside.

"I'm not staying, mom. I am taking my mates home where I can watch them," Thaddeus tells her.

Imogen looks back at him and nods. "Can you at least say goodbye to your fathers?"

Thaddeus nods, grabs my hand, and tugs me inside. I am shivering, and I don't know if it is cold or shock. Imogen races upstairs and returns with some clothes. She points to the bathroom, and I nod just as her mates answer the phone and she starts talking.

Walking in, I place the clothes on the sink. My clothes stick to my skin from the dried blood, and my hair is all matted. Peeling my clothes off, I turn the shower on when Thaddeus walks in with Orion. Thaddeus and Orion strip their clothes off and step into the shower behind me.

"Where is Ryland?" I ask; the only answer I get is a growl.

My hair is coated in blood. I wash it once before Orion takes over. I am exhausted mentally and honestly can't care less about what I look like. All I can think about is April and how I didn't notice what she had planned. Then my thoughts drift to Lana. What will come of her now? Thaddeus said April is alive still, but that means little. I know there are worse ways than death, so what did he do that he could walk away, leaving her alive? I can feel how much he wants to kill her. He wants to inflict the same thing I endured on her, yet he gives nothing away. I try asking a few times, but all he will tell me is she is alive.

Orion washes my hair, getting all the blood out. I barely even register their hands on my body. I am numb, completely numb. Yet, I welcome that feeling; it is better than feeling anything. Thaddeus washes my body while Orion is brushing my hair with his fingers. He is a little rough, but I don't care; the pain is my least worry.

My thoughts are eating away at me. I am pulled out of my head by the water being turned off. I feel like I am on autopilot; I can see everything going on around me, yet I feel nothing. The night goes by in a blur, and the next thing I remember is Thaddeus, stopping the car.

I look around, confused. I don't even remember leaving the house or saying goodbye to his parents. Don't remember anything about the trip. I do remember fog, though, yet I can't remember when it started, only realizing its absence when it suddenly lifts as Thaddeus opens my car door. The cool breeze of the night sweeps over my skin. We are home. Everything comes back to me startlingly clear.

"I should call Lana," I tell Thaddeus.

He shakes his head. "Not tonight," he says.

"I don't even know if she got home."

"She is home with April, Evelyn. She is fine, I promise," Thaddeus tells me. Yet, how does he know that? Confusion hits me; I don't remember him calling her; maybe he did because I don't remember anything since getting out of the shower. I feel disorientated.

"Come, Evelyn, I won't ask again," Thaddeus growls, making my eyes snap to him. I must have been staring off into space. I reluctantly follow him inside, Ryland tries to grab my hand, but Thaddeus pulls me away and growls at him.

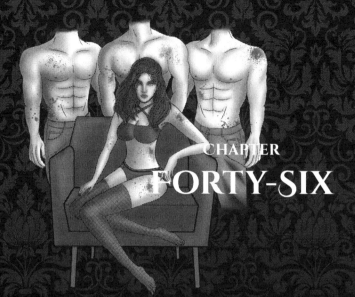

CHAPTER
FORTY-SIX

Ryland

All I want to do is touch her; we nearly lost her because I said she could go. However, I'm not entirely at fault, but still, I said she could go without us, disobeying Orion and Thaddeus.

Evelyn is to remain with someone until we change her, or until she agrees to be changed. Thaddeus is holding back, which I am grateful for; he wants to beat me senseless but doesn't because he doesn't want to scare her.

I would have preferred the beating; at least I would be able to touch her, hold her. This is worse because she is right in front of me yet so far out of reach.

Evelyn keeps stealing glances at me, her guilt hits me hard. She is in shock, that much I can tell; she doesn't utter a word the entire trip. Thaddeus drags her into the kitchen, plops her down in the chair, and rummages through the fridge. No one says anything, and the tension is so thick I can almost taste it. Orion and Thaddeus are angry at both of us.

I am almost tempted to say something, just to end the silence.

Orion and Thaddeus make grilled cheese and put it in front of her. Evelyn just stares at the plate. She isn't hungry. Thaddeus, I know, won't let her leave until she eats so I nod toward the plate, and she seems to understand as she bites a corner off, chewing slowly. Orion hands me a plate and offers Thaddeus one.

Thaddeus shakes his head. "I'm not hungry for food," he says, his eyes not leaving Evelyn.

Evelyn's fear hits me, and I can tell she doesn't want him feeding on her while he is angry; not after he hurt her last time. She has grown to fear his bloodlust, and that is wise. I also fear it; the number of times he has drained me is ridiculous. Draining a Lycan is worse than when he drained Orion. Orion snaps back faster. I, on the other hand, would be out for days, and Evelyn would be dead.

I move my chair back, and Thaddeus' eyes snap to mine; he raises an eyebrow in question. He knows I hate him feeding on me. Orion, I can handle, he is gentle, but Thaddeus can be cruel and makes it hurt intentionally.

"She is scared," I tell him.

"And you're not?" he questions, knowing exactly how I feel.

"Not as scared as her," I tell him as I step closer.

Thaddeus regards me carefully. "You're still not touching her." His eyes sparkle in mischief as he jerks me toward him, smashing his lips against mine. I groan. God, I missed him, every angry piece of him. He pulls away too quickly. Arousal floods the bond, and we both turn to see Evelyn watching us. Her thighs are pressed together tightly, and Orion smirks as he watches her reaction to us.

"You like when I kiss Ryland?" Thaddeus asks her, knowing full well she does like watching us.

Her face flushes at his words. Of course, she does, just like we all like watching her with each other. Her arousal is perfuming the room, such a sweet aroma. Thaddeus kisses my neck, his tongue runs over my mark, and I groan, pressing against him as I feel his magic wash over me, or the fog as Evelyn calls it.

His teeth sink into my neck as he tugs me closer, and I moan loudly. Pleasure rolls over me. Usually he doesn't bother when he feeds on me, yet he enjoys Evelyn's reaction to watching us. His tongue laps at my neck, yet I know his eyes are on her.

Thaddeus' teeth leave my neck after a few minutes; the euphoric feeling goes with it, and I miss his touch instantly. Desire courses through me.

"Later, if you behave," Thaddeus says, and my shoulders sag with disappointment. Orion, I can tell, doesn't agree; he wants me punished for what happened to her. I will take whatever punishment they want to dish out as long as I can have her.

Stepping away, I move to Evelyn. She looks up at me, and I can see the longing on her face. She reaches her hand up as I lean down, my hands on the back of her chair but then, she hesitates and looks between Orion and Thaddeus.

She knows this is how Thaddeus is punishing me, and she doesn't want to get me in more trouble. Thaddeus nods; her fingertips brush my cheek. Leaning down, I kiss her softly and Orion growls, stalking off out of the kitchen toward the living room.

"He is mad at me?" she asks, her voice sad.

"More me than you," I tell her, and she nods in understanding.

"That's enough; finish eating, Evelyn," Thaddeus tells her, and she looks back at her plate, frowning.

"I'm not hungry," she whispers, but picks up another piece anyway and bites into it.

Thaddeus turns around, turning the kettle on. "Coffee?" he asks, looking at me.

"I will make them," I tell him, and he nods.

Evelyn eats and puts her plate in the sink. She looks to Thaddeus, waiting, not wanting to piss him off any more than he already is.

"You can go."

She rushes out as soon as the words leave him. I can feel she wants to find Orion as she darts out, not looking back, which leaves me with Thaddeus.

"Be thankful Evelyn is here, Ryland, because right now, I want to kill you," he says, burning anger through the bond.

"You're not going to hurt her, are you?" I ask worriedly.

I can feel the darkness in him, but her presence seems to have a calming effect on him. He relishes everything about her; he is so caught up in her that I think he forgets he is mad at her, especially when she is like this, doing what he wants and not arguing back for once.

"No, I am angry, but I am relieved she is okay. Though, I would like to tan that ass of hers red," he says. An image of her, bent over his knee hits me, and I feel my lips tug at the thought, my cock twitching in my pants.

"That might not be a punishment," I smirk. Mates are made perfectly for us; if anything, it will probably turn her on.

"I would make it hurt," he says, as the same thoughts run through his head, and he adjusts his pants which are growing tighter.

"And April?" I ask.

He growls, sending a shiver up my spine. I'm not game enough to ask again. I know whatever he has done must have made her suffer. I am surprised he actually let her live. None of us could understand Evelyn's empathy toward the woman. She is too kind-hearted; she doesn't want to hurt Lana even though the bitch deserves nothing but death in my eyes.

Humans are odd things to try and understand.

Walking out, I find Evelyn on the couch with Orion; she is sitting on his lap while he traces circles with his fingers on the skin of her thigh. He seems calm enough.

I have never felt anger like this from him before. Orion is always level-headed, but I have broken his trust. Sitting in the armchair away from her, Thaddeus sits beside her and Orion. I turn the news on to fill the silence.

Thaddeus runs his hand up her leg, and she shivers, resting her head on Orion's shoulder, and I watch as he kisses her temple. She is exhausted and needs sleep.

"Sleep, Evelyn," Thaddeus tells her, but she shakes her head. Evelyn is unsure.

"What's wrong?" I ask her, confused when she tries to fight against it. She is completely exhausted, yet refuses to close her eyes; we can go longer without sleep, but Evelyn not so much.

"You're worried I am going to leave?" Thaddeus asks, her eyes dart to him, and she nods. "I'm not going anywhere, little one; not after today," he tells her. His hand runs up the inside of her thigh, and she shivers. Thaddeus' lips turn up in a smirk. His eyes sparkle as he watches her reaction to him. "Want me to help you sleep?" he asks, gripping her hips and pulling her on his lap.

E velyn

Thaddeus pulls me on his lap. My legs are straddling him, his hands run up the outside of my thighs. I grip his face, my palms on his cheeks, running my thumb underneath his eyes as they darken; veins sliver under my touch. I trace the lines of his face and down his neck. Thaddeus is letting me touch him. My fingers brush his neck when I notice where I bit him had healed, and my mark is gone.

"Where I bit you, it healed?" I ask, confused.

"Yes, you're human, Evelyn. You can still mark us, but it will only stay temporarily until we change you," he says, and I pull back.

Change me? Change me how? Turn me into one of them? The thought alone is enough to make my heart skip a beat. I don't want to live forever or feed on people, and I sure as hell don't want to turn into a furry creature and howl at the moon and shit.

"But..." I glance toward Ryland and Orion.

"It will happen eventually, Evelyn," Orion tells me.

"So, I don't get a choice? I don't want to live forever," I tell them, and Thaddeus' grip tightens.

"No one said right now, Evelyn. When you decide," Ryland tells me.

"No, I won't. It's not natural; I don't want to be a monster," I tell them before I realize what I have said. "I didn't mean...."

"It's fine, Evelyn. No offense taken," Thaddeus says, brushing my cheek with his thumb. "You still have plenty of time; no one will do anything until you say so," he says.

"What if I never want to change?" I ask, and I see Thaddeus' eyes darken.

His jaw clenches. "Then I will make a choice for you."

I shake my head and try to climb off his lap. "No. I won't agree to this, Thaddeus. You don't get to decide that for me," I argue, but his eyes go completely black as I am ripped off his lap. Thaddeus growls, and a shiver runs up my spine as I lean further away from him.

"And why the fuck not, Evelyn? Clearly, you can't make decisions for yourself," he snaps as he turns to glare at me. I know he is talking about me nearly getting myself killed, but he can't blame that on me. How am I supposed to know what others' intentions are?

"Because I don't want this life, I want a normal human life," I tell him, and he laughs.

"That went out the window the day you met us, Evelyn," he tells me.

"When you say human life, what do you mean?" Ryland asks, sitting forward and staring at me.

Thaddeus' head snaps toward him. "Don't even entertain the idea, Ryland," Thaddeus tells him, but I answer anyway.

"I don't know, just normal."

"You want kids?" Ryland asks, and Thaddeus and Orion both growl at him. Do I want kids? I'm not sure, but I don't want them now; I know that much.

"Maybe," I tell him, not knowing how I actually feel about that particular question. Ryland sits back, resting his head on the back of the armchair, looking up at the ceiling. "Why?" I ask.

"Because that's not possible," Thaddeus answers, though I can tell he is irritated that Ryland mentioned it.

"What do you mean?"

"You're human, Evelyn. Bearing one of our children could kill you."

"I don't understand."

"When a human gets pregnant with their mate or mates, the child isn't human."

"So?" I ask, not understanding.

"One of us can't knock you up. If you get pregnant, it won't just be one of our kids; it will be all."

"You have lost me," I admit, trying to understand what he tells me.

Thaddeus puts his head in his hands, trying to figure out what to say next. Orion steps in for him.

"If we were all vampires, it would work, but Thaddeus is a Tribrid, and Ryland werewolf. If you get pregnant, the baby will be a tribrid. When a mate falls pregnant, the baby is a mix of its parents. You have more than one mate because Thaddeus is a tribrid, so therefore the baby would have all our DNA."

"Why does it matter what it is?"

"Because humans can't carry a Lycan baby, Evelyn. It would kill them," he answers.

"But your mother is part human."

Thaddeus shakes his head. "No, my mother is a witch and has Vampire DNA. They thought she was human, but she isn't, and she did die having me. Her vampire DNA brought her back."

"So, if I have a baby, would it be all your child? And it would kill me?"

"Yes," Thaddeus answers.

I say nothing; what can I say? But suddenly, having that option taken away from me makes me want it. Getting up, I head for the stairs. Orion tries reaching for me, but I brush his hand off. I am just about to go up the first step when I hear the news anchor on TV mention the Parse hospital where Lana is. "Breaking News, we are outside the Parse Hospital, reporting on a domestic situation."

I stop, glancing at the TV, and everyone else also does, too. They go to a live stream inside the hospital, and my stomach drops as I see April come on the screen.

E velyn

The stream shows April, walking through the hospital corridors with a gun in her hand. April walks up the corridors and into a ward out of sight. The live stream continues to play when we hear a bang.

Ryland switches the TV off, and all eyes go to me as I walk over, grab the remote from Ryland, and turn the TV back on. My heart thumps against my chest as I flick through the channels to find the news report again. Ryland tries to take the remote from me, but I snatch it away from him.

I need to know; I need to know what happened. Where is Lana? My mind is racing, the cold tendrils of fear creep into me, my stomach drops as I instantly break out in a cold sweat. My hands are shaking as I clutch the remote and frantically flick past the channel. I press the back button, and a news anchor stands out the front of the hospital. Police block the entry to the hospital behind her.

The flashing of police lights flicker against the building as cops run around, trying to secure the hospital. People run from the building in complete chaos.

"What you saw on screen is the wife of the well-respected Sergeant Derrick Tanner. According to insiders, there has been a double murder and suicide. We believe the youngest victim of the double homicide is their adopted daughter, fourteen-year-old Lana Tanner. The girl resided with Mrs. Tanner while her husband recovered in hospital. It is unknown what caused these sudden events to unfold, but it is a tragedy we may never understand."

Three images come on the screen, a picture of April, one of Derrick in his uniform before the fire-ravaged him, and lastly, a picture of Lana. Her beautiful face is full of light, the picture-perfect girl next door.

My lungs restrict and my legs buckle underneath me as I stare at the screen. I can see the news lady talk, but there's no volume as I go completely dead to my surroundings. I can't hear a thing going on around me; can't think straight as I stare blankly into space.

This is my fault; I told Thaddeus not to kill her even though he wanted to. That was a mistake; I killed the only sister I ever had because I didn't want to live with the guilt of taking April away from her. But instead, April took her husband and Lana's life before taking her own.

I killed her; I set off the chain of events that led to her death. If only I would have listened to them. If only I never went to that house. If only I told Thaddeus to kill her, Lana would still be here.

My breath comes faster in short puffs when the realization dawns on me. I killed her; the closest person to family I ever had, is dead. The person I was willing to kill for died because I wanted to believe April still had good left in her, that her understanding was only tainted, and she wasn't to blame for her actions.

Thaddeus is right, April deserved death. But Lana didn't deserve this. This was never meant to affect her; I thought I was protecting her by letting April live because I was afraid she would end up in the system no child wants to be a part of. My idiocy killed her. My failure to see what she was capable of killed Lana. The little girl I fought to protect for an entire year, is now dead. Everything I did is for nothing, but more importantly, my mistake killed her.

O rion
The moment Lana's picture comes up on the screen, she buckles, her legs go out from underneath her, her nails dig into her palms so hard she is drawing blood. She looks hollow as she stares at the screen, eyes wide and a dead look on her face as the color drains from it.

The emotions coming from the bond tell us how destroyed she is inside, yet she doesn't say a word and is completely mute, trapped in her thoughts and guilt. She thinks this is her fault. Evelyn shuts down, completely shuts down. She is right in front of me, but with the look on her face, she might as well be a million miles away.

Thaddeus is a raging storm inside, the darkness creeps in. Ryland is the first to move. He hesitantly walks over to her frozen form, crumpled on the floor. We can all hear the erratic beating of her heart as it thumps against her chest, the shallowness of her breathing, like she can't catch her breath. Her bottom lip trembles as she bites down on it hard enough to draw blood. Evelyn is breaking, and none of us know what to do other than stare at her.

Ryland reaches his hand out to brush her hair from her face, but she moves away and stands up. The remote slips from her hand and breaks apart on the floor, the batteries falling out as she turns almost robotically. She is there right in front of us, but nobody is home. Evelyn moves more on instinct, like a zombie as she walks up the stairs on autopilot. She doesn't want anyone near her; doesn't want us to touch her, like she knows she will break if we do.

"I need to go; I can't be here," Thaddeus says, as the storm within him rages to magnitude levels. He looks to the stairs, wanting to go to her, but won't risk exploding near her.

He feels her guilt hitting him, along with his own. He never intended for April to kill Lana, along with Derrick. He wanted her to suffer, but he never imagined that Lana would also pay the price for what he implanted in her head. Not in a million years.

"Go," I tell him, and within a blink, he is gone. He is a ticking time bomb on the brink of exploding.

Ryland looks to the stairs, Evelyn's despair hitting us like a tidal wave as it crashes into us. I race upstairs only to see that she has locked the door. I twist the door handle until it snaps, falling apart in my hand, and we find Evelyn on the floor, broken.

She is screaming inside; you can see it on her face as she breaks. Tears roll down her face, her face turning red and blotchy as she wails, her hands rip out her hair as she loses it. She has completely lost the plot.

Ryland grabs her hands, stopping her from pulling chunks of hair out, her nails dig into her delicate skin, leaving scratch marks as she claws at herself, like she thinks she can claw away the pain she is feeling inside.

"Orion, do something!" Ryland yells to me as she loses control.

Ryland pulls her onto his lap, restraining her hands which are now digging into his leg above the knee. He rocks her, trying to soothe her while she weeps. Kneeling beside her, I grip her face, forcing her to look at me. Her eyes are red and puffy, dead, as she stares back at me. She is completely distraught. I let the fog slip over her, her breathing evens out, her tears slow, yet she still tries to fight against it as her body slowly relaxes and her hands unclench. Ryland's leg is bleeding with the little half-moon shapes of her nails.

"Sleep, Evelyn," I tell her, as Ryland brushes back the hair sticking to her face from her tears. She shakes her head, trying to fight off the compulsion. "Sleep, Evelyn," I repeat, and she goes out like a light.

Her eyes shut as I force her to sleep, her body goes limp in

Ryland's arms, and her head rolls back against his arm. He stands, clutching her to his chest and lays on the bed with her. I sit beside him, trying to think, but come up blank. Death is something we are used to; eventually, when you live as long as we do, you lose everyone you have ever known, which is the downside to the curse of immortality.

Everyone you have ever known will eventually die around you, but Evelyn has never experienced that; she never had a family, never stayed any place long enough to grow close to someone, so this is new to her; this is devastating. The closest thing she ever had to family is now gone. Even Derrick couldn't break her after what he did. Thaddeus couldn't break her. Lana's death, however, did. This broke her. I've never seen her look so frail. This is going to haunt her even more than that vile man.

FORTY-EIGHT

Evelyn

I wake early to my phone ringing next to my bed. It is on silent, and I can just make out the vibrating sound. I ignore it, not feeling like talking, and figure it must be one of Thaddeus' family members.

Stretching, I sit upright. The events of the past twenty-four hours hit me almost instantly. Thaddeus sits in the armchair at the end of the bed, staring off into space. Ryland is asleep beside Orion and me; I have no idea where his mind is, but he isn't in the room.

Lana is dead. My only family is now gone, and I just can't wrap my head around it; it is like a bad dream. Thaddeus is still as a statue; he doesn't move as I stand up, completely lost in his thoughts. I take my phone and look at the screen. Five missed calls from Lana. At the sight, my heart clenches. She will never call me again. I will never hear her voice again. I still can't believe April killed her, killed her own daughter. I quickly go to the bathroom, needing to pee. As I walk past Thaddeus, all he does is stare at the same spot on the ceiling; the look on his face is vacant.

After using the bathroom, I quickly wash my hands and walk out.

I wave my hand in front of Thaddeus' face, but he doesn't react. What is wrong with him? I touch his arm with no reaction, he is awake because his eyes are open, yet the look on his face is like he isn't aware of me touching him.

"Vampires do that sometimes; he is stuck in his head," Orion says, making me notice he is now leaning against the door. He comes over, wrapping his arms around me, and I wrap mine around his waist. Sparks move over my cheek where it rests on his bare chest.

"When will he come back?" I ask, looking up at him.

"When he figures out how to come back, or one of us pulls him from it," Orion tells me. "Are you okay?" he asks, and I nod.

I will be fine, unlike Lana. I'm still alive and breathing, guilt hits me at what happened.

"Hungry?" he asks. I shake my head. "Well, you should eat anyway. I will go make something," he says, letting me.

Orion glances at Thaddeus, and I can see the worry etched on his face for his mate. Orion walks out, and I am about to follow when I decide to sit with Thaddeus for a while. Ryland is still fast asleep, snoring softly. Climbing on the armchair, I sit on his lap, draping my legs over the armrest and grabbing his arm to wrap it around me.

Thaddeus being gone for so long was horrible; now he is back and stuck like this. His skin is warm as I lean against him. Using my fingers, I trace the lines of his face. His face feels rough with stubble, but he feels warm, like home. My phone starts vibrating again; I can't ignore it this time.

I grab it and sit back down on Thaddeus's lap. Looking at the screen, my heart skips a beat. Lana? I shake my head. I know she is dead already. I must be losing it; there is no way she can be ringing.

The news anchor confirmed three people are dead –they even put up her photo– so I have no doubt she is truly gone. My mind must be trying to find ways to cope. As I try to rationalize, I drop the phone on my lap and I nestle back into Thaddeus. My head is resting on his shoulder, my hand strokes his rough cheek. I love the way they smell, the smell of their skin, and how warm they are.

Suddenly, I feel movement; Thaddeus moves, making me look up at him. His big arms envelop me, crushing me against him and letting go slightly. Sitting up, I straddle him, wrapping my arms around his neck. His face goes to the crook of my neck.

"You're back," I mumble against his shoulder and kiss the side of his neck.

He growls softly, almost a purr. "You don't hate me?" he whispers, making me furrow my eyebrows.

"Why would I hate you?" I ask, confused, wrapping my arms around his neck tighter and pressing against him.

"Because of Lana," he says, rubbing a hand down his face.

"You didn't kill Lana. April did," I tell him, and he shakes his head. "Nothing you did killed Lana. That is on April. She pulled the trigger, not you. But I am fairly sure I am losing my mind," I tell him, and he pulls back, grabbing my face and looking at me. I hear my phone vibrate again.

"Why do you say that?" he asks, curious.

"Because I keep thinking I can hear my phone ringing and see her name pop up," I tell him. He kisses me softly and pulls away.

"Please don't keep punishing Ryland; it isn't his fault," I tell him, and I see his eyes dart to Ryland behind me. After a moment, his eyes settle back on me. He pulls me against him, resting his chin on my head.

My phone vibrates again, and I retrieve it from where it fell between us. Looking at the screen, Lana's name pops up again. Sighing, I drop the phone on my lap when Thaddeus picks it up.

"Ah, Evelyn, you're not imagining it, unless I have gone crazy with you," he says, looking at the screen.

Sitting up, I look at the screen. "You see it too?" He nods, and I take it from him to answer it.

My heart skips a beat, and a lump forms in my throat as I answer it, popping it on loudspeaker.

"Evie? Evie, you there?"

294

Shock hits me. Thaddeus nudges me with his arm, and I shake my shock off. "Lana?" I ask.

"Evie, I have been trying to call for hours! I need help, please! You have to help me," she says, and I can't help the tears of relief that she is okay. "Evie?" Her frightened voice comes again.

"Yes, I am here. I thought you are dead," I tell her. Silence on the other end. "Lana?" I ask when she says nothing.

"I think I am. I don't know, but I need help. I remember the bullet hitting me in the chest; then, I felt cold. I'm scared, Evie," she says.

Thaddeus stands up; I wrap my legs around his waist as he starts walking toward the door.

"Wait, where are you?" I ask her.

"I don't know; I am in some metal box. I can't move. The door is next to my feet, and I can't open it," she tells me. Metal box?

I look at Thaddeus, and he says one word. "Morgue."

Morgue? Thaddeus takes the phone from me while I try and wrap my head around what he said.

"Hi Lana, this is Thaddeus," he tells her.

"Argh, hi, where has Evie gone?"

"Never mind that for now; do you feel strange?" he asks.

"My throat is burning," she admits. Thaddeus kisses my forehead, and Orion comes over. I try to put my feet down and stand, but Thaddeus jostles me, making me remain where I am, his arm tightening around my waist, so I wrap my legs back around him.

"I am sending Orion to come to get you. You know Orion?"

"Yes, but why not Evie?"

"You will see Evie, but Orion is faster. He will come to get you and bring you here," Thaddeus tells her. He hands my phone back to me, and I answer it.

"Lana, you there?" I can hear Thaddeus and Orion whisper to each other but can't hear what they are saying. The next second, Orion disappears, the front door left wide open.

"Evie, is it true?"

"Is what true?" I ask her; she sounds so frightened.

"What April said, that Derrick...."

"Yes, Lana, but don't worry about that. Orion is coming to get you, okay?"

"My phone is dying," she tells me and the phone cuts out completely. I try to call her back, but it goes to voicemail.

"She is alive; April didn't kill her," I tell Thaddeus.

He shakes his head. "I think she did; you should prepare yourself. Lana may be different when she comes here," he tells me. I don't care if she is different as long as she is alive. Lana is alive. No matter how traumatized she is, she will get through it. But why is she in a morgue?

"Why would she be in a morgue?" I ask, as the realization of what Thaddeus said hits me. "Is she dead?"

Thaddeus nods.

"But how? I just spoke to her? She is human like me."

"Many people are walking around with vampire DNA, completely unaware, so when they die, we find out when they come back as the small amount of vampire DNA brings them back. We learned all this when my mother died having me."

"So, you're saying Lana is a vampire?"

"I would be willing to bet my life on it," he says. Either way, I don't care as long as she is alive. She will get through this.

Ryland suddenly starts walking down the steps, rubbing his eyes and yawning. "Morning," he grumbles, and Thaddeus lets me down. I rush over to him and jump on him. Ryland catches me, and I wrap my legs around him. "Why are you so happy?" he asks, confused, looking at Thaddeus.

"Lana is alive!" I tell him.

He looks at Thaddeus, who steps closer, pressing his chest into my back. Ryland looks at him warily, probably because he isn't supposed to touch me, but he slept in the bed, and Thaddeus didn't do anything. "Is she?" asks Ryland, looking at Thaddeus, wondering if I have lost the plot.

"Vampire, I think. Orion has gone to get her," Thaddeus tells him.

Thaddeus wraps his arms around both of us. Ryland leans into him as I get crushed between them.

I hear Ryland say, "I'm sorry," before I realize he says it to Thaddeus. Thaddeus pulls his face back as I look up at them both. Thaddeus' eyes drop to mine between them. He kisses my head and turns back to Ryland.

"I overreacted; she is fine," he says, pecking Ryland on the lips, only for Ryland to grab the back of his neck and deepen the kiss. My stomach tightens as I watch them together. Thaddeus chuckles, pulling away after a few seconds. "Come, I need coffee," Thaddeus says, turning toward the kitchen. Coffee sounds great.

"Is he okay?" Ryland asks, making me look at him.

"Yeah, why?" I answer. Ryland shakes his head.

"Because he? -"

"I told him it isn't your fault," I tell him, and he looks at me. Ryland quickly kisses my cheek.

"He almost seems happy," Ryland says, walking into the kitchen and sitting me on the counter next to Thaddeus.

"Do you think we should call Bianca?" Thaddeus asks Ryland.

"Might be a good idea; we don't know how she will react to Evelyn." Thaddeus nods and pulls out his phone. Their words confuse me. I have known Lana for years; I am no threat to her.

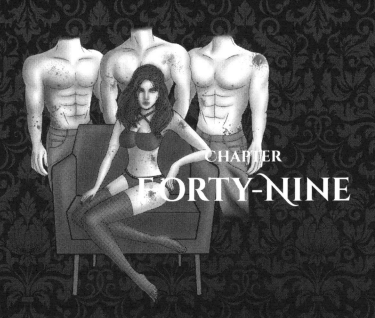

CHAPTER
FORTY-NINE

Evelyn

Thaddeus calls Bianca, and we spend around an hour waiting until I hear movement outside. I am sitting on the lounge with Thaddeus and Ryland when the front door opens, and Orion steps inside.

Standing up, I go to see Lana when Thaddeus pulls me behind him. Lana walks in, cautiously looking around the room until her eyes land on me. Her hair is messy, and she is wearing a hospital gown. Her eyes go wide when she sees me and rushes over to me, a little too fast, nearly knocking me over. If it weren't for Thaddeus holding my arm, she would have knocked me to the ground.

"Thank God you're okay," I whisper, hugging her back.

She sighs deeply, squeezing me tightly. Thaddeus, I can see, is watching her with a strange expression on his face, and I can feel his caution through the bond. I notice Orion standing behind her, his hand on her shoulder awkwardly, like he is worried something will happen.

Their worry through the bond makes me uneasy; why are they

acting like that? Is it Lana? Orion and Ryland have met her plenty of times; she isn't like April.

Lana steps back and looks around. "This place is nice. Do you live here with them?" she asks.

I nod as her eyes dart around the room quickly; all her movements seem jerky and too quick. "Come, I will get you some clothes," I tell her, grabbing her hand.

Thaddeus places his hand on my arm, stopping me when I am about to take her up the stairs. "Orion will get her some clothes," Thaddeus tells me.

"Why are you acting like this? It is Lana," I ask him. His eyes don't leave her.

"It's not safe," Ryland says, stepping closer.

"I am not going to try and leave again; I am right here," I tell him, but he shakes his head.

"We aren't worried about you doing anything, Evie," Ryland says, using Lana's nickname for me.

"I'm not going to hurt her," Lana exclaims, shocked by his words; she looks appalled that he would even suggest such a thing.

"You may not mean to, but it's a chance I won't take. Not with my mate," Thaddeus says, pulling me against him.

"You're being ridiculous; Lana won't hurt me," I tell him, but he doesn't let go.

"I will go with them, Thaddeus. Evie will be safe," Orion says.

Thaddeus reluctantly lets me go, and I grab Lana's hand, pulling her up the stairs. Orion is right on our heels. I rummage through the wardrobe, give her some clothes, and follow her into the bathroom and shut the door, but Orion's hand stops it. "Door stays open," he says.

Lana looks mortified at his words, as any teenage girl would be. "Not all the way, just so I don't have to knock it down if something happens," he says, confusing me. I turn the shower on for her, and Lana gets undressed. She seems different, almost perfectly fine, like nothing happened. Lana hops in the shower.

Sitting up on the sink basin, I notice her chest is covered in blood under the gown, and she has a scar where her heart would be. "Are you okay?" I ask her. Lana's head whips to me so fast, she nearly gives me whiplash just watching how quickly she moves.

"Yeah, fine," she says, her voice almost melodious.

"So, what happened?"

"I don't really remember; child services got involved. April had been acting strange the past week, and I was staying in a motel near the hospital. I was visiting Dad, and she came in crying hysterically; saying these horrible things, that dad raped you, that he is sick in the head. She was waving his gun around. Dad tried to get her to calm down. I heard a bang, and Dad fell off the bed, and I saw blood pooling, and the next thing I know, I heard the gun go off again, felt like I was punched in the chest. Then I woke up in the morgue; that's when I called you," she tells me.

I hate the way Lana calls him Dad, that she has an attachment to the vile man, but I also understand he was good to her; she never saw the parts of him I did.

"Orion wouldn't tell me if they are okay; he brought me here. Said I couldn't go home, said that I am a vampire now. Pretty cool, don't you think? I love the Vampire Diaries," she says excitedly.

Her attitude shocks me. So unfeeling, like she doesn't know the people who raised her, like she has no connection or emotion at all.

"Is it true what mom said? Did dad really do that?" she asks.

I cringe at the word, feeling disgusted hearing it leave her mouth. "Yes, Lana, what April said is true," I tell her.

She looks at me. "But you are over it, right? You're good now?" she asks.

Her words shock me. Is this the same Lana I knew? What happened to me is not something you get over; you just live with it, deal with it, or in my case, not deal with it, thanks to Thaddeus, who dealt with it for me.

I say nothing.

"So, what about mom? Did she get arrested?" Lana asks, and my lungs restrict. She doesn't know. She doesn't know they are dead.

"Lana..."

Orion pops his head in the door, shakes his head, and presses his fingers to his lips. He doesn't want me to tell her. "I am not sure," I tell her, turning back to her.

She is washing her hair. Why am I lying to her? What is going on? Lana's strange behavior and Thaddeus' sudden distrust of her runs through my mind, and nothing makes sense. Suddenly, the water turns off. I hand her a towel. She steps out, wrapping it around herself, the room full of steam.

"The hot water here sucks," she says, making me raise an eyebrow. The room feels like a sauna, the room is so thick with steam I feel like I am inhaling the water in the air. I open the door, intending to walk out, and the breeze from the open window brushes over me when she speaks again.

"What's that smell?" she asks, and just as I turn to face her, I notice her face twist into a demon, her eyes go blood red as she lunges at me, knocking me over and sinking her teeth into my shoulder.

I scream, and Orion is already ripping her off me, her teeth pulling painfully from my skin. Lana thrashes in his arms, a crazed look on her face.

"What the fuck, Lana! You bit me!" I say, shocked just as the door bursts open. Blood trickles down my chest where Orion ripped her teeth out of me.

She continues to thrash in his arms like a wild animal. "Let me have her!" she screams, fighting against him. Ryland rips me to my feet and yanks me from the room, his arm around my waist.

I see Thaddeus walk over to her and grab her face. "Enough!" he yells at her, and I see her freeze for a second before she starts thrashing again. Ryland drags me downstairs, my hand clutching my blood-soaked neck. He sits me on the lounge just as Bianca walks in. Her eyes dart to the stairs at the commotion above us.

"Upstairs," Ryland tells her, and she disappears in a fast blur. I hear banging and crashing upstairs, making me look up at the landing above us.

"What's wrong with her?" I ask him.

Ryland bites into his wrist and presses it against my lips to stop me from asking any questions.

"Drink it," he says, and I let my lips part, feel his blood coat the inside of my mouth, warm and thick, and I have to force myself to swallow. The sensation of my wound healing beneath my hands is strange.

"What's wrong with her?" I ask again. His blood coats my lips, and Ryland wipes it off with his thumb.

Ryland looks up and then back at me. "She is a newborn vampire; they feel everything differently or feel nothing at all. Your scent must have overwhelmed her," Ryland says.

"But Orion doesn't attack me like that?"

"He has had hundreds of years of practice to control his blood-lust. Even older ones sometimes slip. Lana has no control yet."

"But she will be okay, right?"

He sighs, running his hand down his face. He looks tired. He places his hands on my legs, looking up at me. "That is why Bianca is here. She will take Lana and look after her," Ryland tells me just as Orion comes downstairs, his clothes torn from the struggle.

"Lana won't go with her; she doesn't know her," I tell him.

Orion growls at me and sits down, clearly angered by something. "She can't stay here with you; she won't have a choice but to go with Bianca," Orion argues.

"And if she says no?" I ask.

"Then Thaddeus will kill her. She needs guidance; Bianca will look after her," Ryland tells me.

Thaddeus walks down with a limp Lana in his arms and walks outside. I get up to follow him to check she is alright, when Orion pulls me down on his lap, wrapping his arms securely around my waist.

Bianca walks down the stairs, fixing her outfit, which is wrinkled, and then comes over to me. "I promise to look after her, Evelyn; she is safe with me. Promise," Bianca says, looking to the door Thaddeus just walked out of. I like Bianca; she is always kind to me, and I know if my mates trust her, I can as well. Bianca is Thaddeus' aunty, after all.

"Can I at least say goodbye?" I ask them.

"She is unconscious; Thaddeus broke her neck," Bianca says, and I jump up, horrified by what she said.

Orion pulls me back down on him. "She is fine, love; it won't kill her," he whispers just as Thaddeus walks back in.

"I put her in Ryland's car; you can take that to get home." Bianca nods, and rushes outside.

"You broke her neck?" I ask him angrily.

"Be grateful I didn't kill her; usually, I kill any newborn vampire I come across. I didn't because she is your friend," he says, and I can feel his anger burning into me through the bond. I hear Ryland's car start and try to get up, only to be stopped by Thaddeus' grip on my arm. "You will see her again, but when you're not so breakable."

"Not so breakable?"

"Yes. You're human, Evelyn." His words anger me. He wants me to turn into a vampire and be uncontrollable like Lana? He just said he snapped her neck, for crying out loud.

"I have already told you I won't change, and seeing her like that reinforces that decision," I tell him.

"You won't have a choice; you will get older. Evie, you will decide, or I will decide for you!" he yells at me. The lights flicker in his anger.

"Fine, then I will change," I tell him. He seems shocked by my words. "I will change when you give up your magic!" I scream at him. If I have to give up my life, he can give up his magic like his mother wants him to.

"That's not happening," he growls.

"Then I am not changing," I tell him defiantly, crossing my arms and holding his glare, refusing to back down. I knew he would say that. We stare at each other for a few seconds until he storms out of the house angrily, slamming the door behind him.

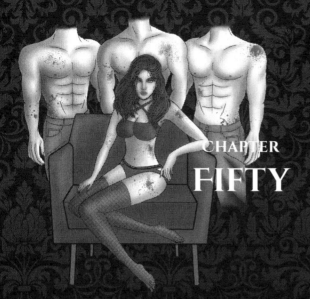

FIFTY

Orion

Once again, they are at each other's throats, though Evie has a point. She shouldn't be the only one to give up something. We watch him leave; he is angry that she even suggested it.

Evelyn is a bit upset, but she has a determination in her; his magic scares her. It scares all of us, but I can see the wheels turning in her head, and I know deep down, as much as he says he will force her, I know he never will, because part of him loves that she is so vulnerably human, though our little mate doesn't know that. Doesn't realize the change she has brought out of him.

Thaddeus is never one to back down, never one to walk away from a fight, but he walks out on her. Not because she demands something in return but because he won't risk hurting her, not again. He wants her to accept him, craves it. So instead, he leaves before his temper gets the better of him.

That's one of the strangest changes we see in him. Usually, he doesn't care about the darkness, and welcomes it. He relishes the power it gives to him and relishes our fear. But he doesn't want her to fear him; he wants to cherish her and love her; he is starting to realize the damage his magic does, realize how much it affects her. But can he really give it up for her?

Evelyn stares at the door and turns around to face us. Her fists are clenched by her side. Ryland has a smirk on his face at her words. He likes the fire in her and that she will stand up to him.

Honestly, so do I, but I worry that it might get her killed. She thinks we see her as weak, and in some ways, being human; she is. But she doesn't actually realize how much control she truly has over him.

Evelyn flops down on the couch beside Ryland and I. Ryland pulls her onto his lap. I growl at him, pulling her off and over to me; he is still in trouble for letting her go. I'm not so forgiving of what he did. Evelyn, however, doesn't blame him; she feels guilty for Ryland getting in trouble with us.

"Please stop blaming him," she says, looking up at me and touching my face with her fingers.

I kiss her fingertips. She is tired of fighting with us, tired of everything. I can never stay mad at her. With Ryland, though, I am determined to try, but the next words to leave her lips grind my gears because she knows I will give in to her; she knows how much I love her, and even though she doesn't realize most of the time, she sometimes plays on that. "If Ryland can't have me, neither can you."

I growl at her, nuzzling my face into her neck. "Is that so?" I ask, nipping at her neck as she leans back against me. Her arousal perfumes the room as I run my hand over her stomach and press it between her legs. Her hips move involuntarily against them as I rub her over the leggings she is wearing. Her chest is rising and falling as she loses herself in the feeling of my fingers teasing her.

"I can put you in a better mood," I tell her.

"You can try," she challenges, and I smile as I watch Ryland's eyes flicker to his beast for a second.

I move my hand back up to the waistband of her pants and slip my hand inside, my fingertips trace her slit. Her breathing picks up as I rub her clit in a circular motion. Ryland growls, and my eyes snap to his, his eyes are pitch black orbs, watching my hand move between her legs, feeling her getting wetter. I ram my finger inside her, making her gasp, then add another and curl them inside her. Her thighs open, allowing me more room as I fuck her with my fingers.

Ryland makes a strangled noise in his throat, his lips part, and I smirk. He wants her, the hunger clearly evident on his face, his hands dig into his knees, and he looks like he wants to pounce on her.

"Ryland," I snap at him when he tries to move. Her eyes flutter back open and go to him as she reaches her hand out to him.

He stares at it and looks at me. I sigh, and he knows I am giving her what she wants as a devious smile lights up his face. Ryland grips the waistband of her pants and tugs them down, revealing my fingers, moving in and out of her. I pull my fingers from her as he settles between her legs on the couch. Just as I do, he grabs my hand, sucking on my fingers, and I feel my cock jump in my pants at the sensation of his hot tongue, tasting her on my fingers.

Ryland's lips go to her thigh and he sucks on it. Her breath gets caught in her throat when he licks a line from her ass to clit, her back arches as her nails dig into my jeans. Ryland's lips devour her before I hear Thaddeus' voice flit through my head.

I know he only went outside to have a smoke, to calm himself down, and I have to try not to smile when I hear his voice as he forces himself into my mind. "Do you know how hard it is to stay mad at her when I can feel how turned on she is right now?"

"You're welcome to join us," I tell him, and he scoffs. "You know she won't stay mad at you; not while she is like this."

"No, I have something to do; I will be back in a few hours," he says.

My mind becomes my own again. Ryland's eyes are on me; he must have realized Thaddeus was in my head. I shake my head, and his eyes go back to her as he pulls her thighs apart further and plunges his tongue in her; she bucks her hips against his face. My hand trails down to her shirt as I peel it off her and unclasp her bra. Her full breasts bounce free and I palm one roughly, pinching her nipple, making her cry out at the sudden pain.

Ryland suddenly sits up, pulling her to him, and she pouts, jutting out her bottom lip. She doesn't want him to stop, and I can feel how close she is, feel how much she wants us to fuck her. Ryland kisses her and grips her around the waist to pull her onto his lap so I can remove my pants.

I bite her plump little ass and ram my fingers inside her. Ryland kisses her breasts as she moves her hips against my fingers. My thumb presses against the tight muscles of her ass right before I push it in, making her gasp and push back against my hand.

Ryland lifts his hips, pushing his pants down slightly, freeing himself, and I pull my fingers from her as he positions himself underneath her. She wriggles her hips and sinks onto him, letting him fill her. My fingers are slick with her juices, moving between her cheeks as I force them into her tight hole, making her moan as I slip them in and out of her and move her hips against him, riding his cock.

Ryland, gripping her hips, moves them faster as I kneel behind her, kissing her shoulder. I feel her shudder. Using my other hand, I rub her clit while pulling my fingers from her and positioning myself behind her. With one thrust, I push myself inside her, making her cry out at the pain before stilling. My fingers move faster, and I feel her start to relax, her muscles untensing. I can smell Ryland's blood where her nails dug into his shoulders.

Ryland thrusts up into her, and she lets out a breathy moan. Her head rolls back onto my shoulder, and I kiss the side of her face. "I'm going to move now," I warn her, and I feel her nod.

I pull out and thrust into her. Her eyes open, she bites her bottom lip and leans forward, using Ryland's shoulders to brace herself as I thrust into her again. Gripping her hips, I watch myself slip in and out of her, becoming lost in the feeling of myself deep inside her, her arousal building, and I feel her tense, her stomach tightening.

I can tell she is close as she keeps moving her hips to meet our thrusts. Her breathing gets harder. Ryland's teeth sink into her mark as he finds his own release, sending her over the edge as she milks his cock. I speed up, chasing my release, and I feel my balls tighten before spilling my seed into her.

E velyn
I wake coated in sweat; burning pain radiates throughout my chest, and I can feel alarm through the bond, making me sit upright. Ryland is asleep next to me. I can hear movement downstairs. Ryland suddenly sits bolt upright and a loud growl leaves his lips. His eyes are pitch black orbs.

I look to the door, and within the blink of an eye, he is gone; I feel air rush past me from his movement. As I chase after him, my heart is pounding in my chest. I race down the stairs, nearly tripping but catching myself before I roll down them.

I can hear things slamming around in the kitchen as I race toward it and freeze in the doorway; my blood runs cold. My entire body goes cold, and fear consumes me; my hands are shaking, and I feel the air become lodged in my throat. Thaddeus leans against the pantry door, drenched in blood, his chest rising and falling as pain ripples through me.

Orion has ripped his shirt down the middle, revealing his chest, which is riddled with what looks like bullet holes.

"Evelyn, get towels!" Orion screams as I stand there in shock.

Thaddeus' eyes snap open and he faces me as his chest heaves with each breath making a loud wheezing noise. "Evelyn!" Orion screams, and my brain kicks into gear, understanding what he is telling me to do.

I race into the hallway closet, grab whatever my hands land on first and rush back to the kitchen. Ryland's fingers are in his chest, trying to remove whatever is lodged in it, blood pools on the floor around him, and Ryland screams, yanking his hands away.

"What is it?" Orion asks.

Ryland shakes his head, digging his fingers back into the hole, hissing and jerking away.

Thaddeus' breath is getting shorter, and he looks on the verge of passing out. I have never seen him like this; he looks weak. Pushing Ryland away, I can see the tips of his fingers are cut open and bleeding, but they aren't healing. I bury my fingers into the hole in his shoulder that Ryland is working on.

Thaddeus is that weak, he doesn't make a sound or even flinch as I twist my fingertips into the hole and feel something pointed. I try to grab the edges when it slices straight through my fingertips like a razor. I cry out but grip the point. Thaddeus groans as I rip it from him, just as Orion rips another out of his stomach. I hold it up, looking at it. It is shaped like a Razor but has a clear middle with remnants of a green liquid inside.

I drop it on a towel, moving it onto another. Ryland watches helplessly, holding pressure on the holes that aren't healing as we continue to pull more from his chest, legs, and stomach.

By the time we are done, we have pulled twenty-three from him, my fingers bleeding and cut to pieces from the sharpness. I know I would be in pain if it weren't for adrenaline.

"Why isn't he healing?" I ask. Panic courses through me at seeing him like this.

"He needs blood, human blood," Orion says.

"He can feed off me," I tell him, but Thaddeus shakes his head weakly.

"He will be fine; I should have enough time to get some blood bags before-"

"That's hours away, Orion," I tell him, knowing he will run to the city, which usually takes him an hour to do.

"He can't feed on you, Evelyn, not while he is like this. He won't be able to control himself."

"And if he doesn't feed?" I ask.

Ryland and Orion look at each other. "I'm not sure. He has never been injured before, and we don't know the effects of whatever they poisoned him with." Ryland admits.

Thaddeus' eyes start drooping. "I will be fine, love," he chokes out, coughing up blood. They both look at him in panic. Getting up, I reach into the drawer to grab a knife. I'm not going to risk him dying. Through the bond, I can feel how weak he is, which alone scares me half to death.

"Evelyn, put the knife down," Ryland growls.

"Either he feeds off me, or I will bleed out into a cup. Choose," I snap at him.

Orion growls, trying to grab me, but I step back, running the blade across my wrist, crying out when I slice through tendons, not expecting the knife to slice through so easily as I press the blade as hard as possible. My hand is useless, but I hear Thaddeus growl, his eyes snap open as my blood starts dripping on the floor, and he holds his breath.

"Are you nuts?" Ryland screams, ripping me toward him.

He bites into his wrist, but I press my lips into a line, refusing, holding my arm out to Thaddeus. He shakes his head, but I ram it against his lips. He growls as the urge to feed takes over, and his teeth sink into my wrist and he grabs it. I don't know how long he feeds, but I can feel myself becoming lightheaded. Thaddeus growls loudly, and Orion rips my arm away from him, but Thaddeus doesn't let go, and I feel it snap; my arm breaks under the pressure, making me scream.

Orion pries him off me with Ryland's help, and I slump on the floor. Thaddeus is consumed with bloodlust, while all I want to do is sleep. I feel warm hands wrap around me and Ryland's wrist pressed to my lips. I let my lips part, his blood fills my mouth, and I have to force myself to swallow as if my body has forgotten how to.

Feeling myself heal as his blood races through me, healing my wounds, I feel my broken arm snap back into place with a loud crunch, making me whimper right at the moment I pass out.

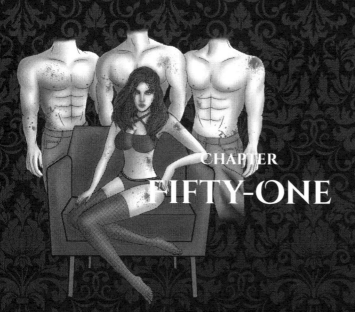

CHAPTER
FIFTY-ONE

Evelyn

I wake up to fingers trailing down my back, rolling over, I see Thaddeus lying beside me. I actually think I might have dreamed the entire thing. He looks perfectly fine, like nothing has happened.

But I know I didn't dream it when he pulls me on top of him. "Don't ever do that again," he says, as his voice shakes which is what makes me look up at him. I can feel his anger through the bond, but it is directed more inward than at me. "I could have killed you. Don't risk your life, not for me, Evie," he says, kissing my forehead, brushing my hair off my face.

"You were dying," I tell him.

"I don't care. Promise that you won't do it again."

I say nothing; that isn't a promise I am willing to make. They keep saying they won't live without me, but even though we fight, I don't want to live without them either. Yes, maybe it is the bond talking, but I am certain of that decision.

"Evie?" Thaddeus says, as his anger bubbles out of him.

"No!" I snap at him, and he growls. "I won't promise that. You needed help, and I helped," I add. Ryland and Orion walk in the next moment. Orion tosses Thaddeus a blood bag, and he catches it. I sit up, watching them as they come into the room. "How long was I out?" I ask.

"Not long. You passed out when your arm snapped back into place," Orion says, sitting on the end of the bed. He bites into the corner of the blood bag and I scrunch my face up at it.

Ryland shakes his head. "A blood bag grosses you out? You have drunk our blood and let them feed off you."

"It's different; it looks gross looking at it like that," I tell him.

Orion nods. "Because it is. Tastes nasty from a bag, but does the job."

As I turn to Thaddeus, I see that his eyes are pitch black. He is watching me as he drinks from the bag. The wounds on his chest have healed, but they have left scars all over his chest. "How come the scars didn't heal. What happened?"

"Not sure; it must be whatever is in the shrapnel."

"Shrapnel?"

Thaddeus nods his head, draining the bag and squeezing it like a juice box. "Hunters. I went to see my sister. I got to Leven's outskirts and stumbled across a base of sorts amongst the forest; I was curious, so I went and had a look. I tripped an alarm around their base and a bomb went off. Those things that you pulled from me were in it. I ran back here right after the explosion. But we need to move; they are a little too close for comfort."

"Why would they have a base at Leven?"

"I'm unsure, but I know we were spotted at Parse City. My father said he caught them lurking around the office; even had the security cameras hacked."

"If they know about your family, why haven't they done anything to them?"

"They aren't after them; my family lives peacefully. They are after me," Thaddeus states.

"His family have left town for a while till things cool down.

Thaddeus called them and told them to get out, so they don't use them against him," Orion adds.

"But you haven't done anything in ages; why do they want you?"

"They have been following us for decades, Evie. We aren't good people," Ryland chimes in.

"You mean I am not good," Thaddeus says with a growl.

"I have done my fair share of bad shit, Thaddeus; you can't take all the blame," Ryland retorts.

"Regardless, we need to leave. I think they may know about you now; we can't risk staying here any longer," Thaddeus says.

Orion grabs a suitcase from the wardrobe, and I can tell he has done this plenty of times as he starts grabbing things and putting them in. Ryland grabs another and starts filling it with my clothes and toiletries.

"What? Right now?" I ask as I watch them pack up necessities.

Thaddeus sits up, swings his legs off of the bed and stands. He walks into the bathroom and grabs a few things, like my makeup and hair straightener. I help him, pass him things, knowing his silence means we are leaving, and there is no room for argument. Not that I will argue over this after seeing what they did to him.

"You have time to shower if you want; we won't be ready for about half an hour," Thaddeus says, and I quickly strip my clothes off, hopping in and turning the faucets on.

I hear them rummage around and do things. I shower quickly, hop out, and I notice one of them has left one of their shirts and a pair of my leggings on the end of the bed. I quickly dry myself, slip them on, and pull my hair in a bun, only for my hair tie to snap. Quickly ducking into the bathroom, I look under the sink, retrieving another and grab the packet out. As I do, I notice the pads and tampons under the sink. I stand up, pulling my hair in a bun, trying to remember the last time I had my period.

Thaddeus was gone for over a month, and I don't remember getting them at Imogen's. Then, it dawns on me. I haven't had my period since the first week I got here, which means I was due for it to start around the middle of my time at Imogen's. That is like a couple of months ago, but I know that can't be right. We didn't have sex until I was marked. That was like six or seven weeks ago?

I have no idea; the only thing I know for sure is that I am late. My heart skips a beat as panic hits me. I lift my shirt, thinking I might notice a change, but I don't. Suddenly, the bedroom door opens, and Orion runs in; he must have felt my mood shift.

"What's wrong," he asks, staring at me curiously when he sees I am fine.

"Nothing." I shake my head.

"I felt you become scared," he says, looking around the bathroom.

"Just nervous," I lie, but I feel my heart skip a beat, and he cocks his head to the side, watching me. Can he tell I am lying? I know he probably can, but he says nothing.

"Come on, we are ready to leave," he says, escorting me downstairs and outside.

Thaddeus looks up when we walk out and keeps his eyes on me as I sit to put on a pair of shoes. "Where are we going?" I ask.

"Nowhere and everywhere," Thaddeus answers.

I shake my head; he doesn't even know. We all get in the car. Orion is behind the steering wheel and I stay in the back seat with Ryland. I doze on and off while driving, waking at each stop when they get fuel to stretch my legs.

"How much further?" I ask, getting tired of sitting in the car.

"We will find a hotel in the next city," Orion says.

Ryland pays and brings back some chips and drinks. I groan, hopping back in the car; this time, Thaddeus gets in the back with me. Ryland winds his window down and lights a smoke, offering one to me.

I shake my head, and he raises an eyebrow but shrugs. I see Orion's eyes snap to me in the mirror, and I quickly look away, putting my head in Thaddeus' lap. The next time we stop, though, it isn't in a city. It's a hotel on the outskirts of a town. Thaddeus and Ryland get out and both walk into the reception.

When I am about to get out, Orion flicks the locks on the doors, staring at me in the mirror. "You're hiding something," he says.

"No, I just want to get out."

"I know you are; your heart rate just picked up. Tell me now, Evelyn."

"Unlock the doors, Orion, please." He shakes his head and I see Ryland come out. My eyes go to him and Thaddeus as they walk toward the car. Orion's eyes don't leave me in the mirror. "Three seconds, Evelyn." I look between them all and he starts counting. "1... 2..."

"I will tell you, just not here; they will hear," I say, panicked as I see Ryland reach for the door. He pulls on the handle, but it doesn't open. He taps on the window, talking to Thaddeus. "Please, Orion," I whisper.

He sighs, unlocks the door, and I get out.

"Why are the doors locked?" Ryland asks, looking at me.

"I bumped the button," Orion says, and I let out the breath I was holding.

"You okay, hun?" Ryland asks, looking at me.

"Yeah, sore back," I tell him, and he nods. My back is actually killing from being cooped up in the car.

"Number 26," Thaddeus says, tossing a set of keys to Orion, who catches them.

Orion grabs my hand and tugs me after him a little too quickly. I have to jog to keep up with him. He unlocks the door and shuts it once we're in. Orion flicks on the light, grabs me, and presses me against the dresser, his arms caging me in. "Tell me!"

I am saved from answering when the door opens and Ryland walks in, shock clear on his features as he takes in Orion standing over me. "What's going on?"

"Nothing," we both say at the same time.

"Doesn't look like nothing," he says, stepping closer, and Orion straightens up.

"It's nothing, Ryland; I am just teasing her," he says, as a smile slips onto his face.

Ryland eyes him for a few seconds. Thaddeus opens the door, carrying the other suitcase, which distracts Ryland, and I use that opportunity to move away from Orion. I climb on the bed with its ugly floral pattern bedspread. It is a nice hotel; just the decor is ugly. The outside is modern and sleek; the inside looks like a flower bomb has gone off. Even the carpet has a floral pattern on it that is more suitable for the fifties, and the room has two queen-sized beds. Ryland grabs the bedside table that separates the beds and places it under the TV hanging on the wall and pushes the beds together.

"I am going to see if anything is open in town," Orion states.

Ryland heads for the bathroom, stripping his shirt off as he goes.

"Can you grab some movies?" Thaddeus asks, when he flicks on the TV and we see only static. Orion nods, looks at me, and walks out. "Wonder why he is in a bad mood," Thaddeus mutters, pulling me down on the bed with him.

FIFTY-TWO

Evelyn

    I fall asleep next to Thaddeus and Ryland. Orion brings back movies, and I don't even last through one. The next day I wake up, and Thaddeus and Ryland are gone. Sitting up, I find Orion on the bed next to me, reading a sheet of paper with a box in his lap.

"Good, you're up," he states, putting the paper down.

"Where did Thaddeus and Ryland go?" I ask.

"Out. Thaddeus needs more blood. Now tell me, and don't lie to me."

I look down in his lap at the box that sits there. It is a pregnancy test, and my heart rate picks up just by the sight of it.

"So, I guess I am correct in assuming that is why you were staring at your belly when I walked in and why you refused a smoke when Ryland offered it," he states. I say nothing, just look away from him. "Well, you can't be that far along. When was your period due?"

"The second, last week, we were at Imogen's."

"That would explain why you can't see anything yet."

"Yet?"

"Supernatural pregnancies are half the time, Evelyn," he says, sitting up and grabbing my hand. He pulls me off the bed and thrusts the box in my hand. "It says you need to pee on the stick and wait," Orion says. "Now, Evelyn, before they get back. And the door stays open, so I know you don't tamper with it."

I take it from him and walk into the bathroom. I try to close the door, but Orion walks in and closes it. "You can't watch me, Orion."

"I will turn around. Just hurry up; they won't be long," he says as he turns his back to me.

I suddenly get stage fright; I always need to pee first thing in the morning, but it is awkward with someone standing there. I quickly pee, thanking the gods pregnancy tests are done via urine sample and not a stool one. That would be humiliating.

I flush, hand him the stick with the cap stuck back on, and he sits on the basin, staring at it intently like it is some sort of experiment while I wash my hands. Three minutes feel so long, but then, I hear him growl. Orion grabs my hand and yanks me out of the bathroom. "Come on; we need to go."

"What?" I ask, confused.

"You're pregnant, Evie. We need to go now so we can get rid of it."

His words make my blood run cold. Get rid of it? I am not getting rid of it. "No, Orion," I tell him, pulling my hand from his and backing up. Orion makes a noise in his throat that makes goosebumps rise on my skin.

He turns on me, backing me into the corner. "You can't keep it, Evelyn; it will kill you!"

"I'm not aborting my child, Orion."

"You don't have a choice; I won't allow it to kill you," he says, grabbing my wrist and trying to pull me toward the door.

"No, Orion, let fucking go of me!" I scream at him as he keeps trying to get me to follow him.

"Look, we will get rid of it, then if you want something to look after, I will get you a puppy," he says.

I shake my head. "This isn't your choice."

"Like hell, it isn't; you're irrational; what part of 'it will kill you' don't you understand?"

"No! My body, my choice!"

Orion growls, grips my arms, and presses me against the wall. "I said no. It's simple, we get rid of it, then if you feel bad, I will get Thaddeus to erase it from your memory, get you a puppy, and everything will be fine."

"No!" I scream to his face.

Orion growls, hitting the wall above my head. Tears are streaming down my face; he wants to kill our baby, and I know deep down there is nothing I can do if he forces me.

"Stop crying; this is what needs to be done. Now, come with me before I call Thaddeus to get you," he says, grabbing my wrist. He yanks me toward him and I put my hand out to stop from smacking into his hard chest. "I am trying to be nice, Evelyn. Come with me now and do it the right way or I will get rid of it myself," he snaps.

His eyes turn crimson; I feel the fog creep over me and know he is going to try compelling me. I slap him, the fog instantly lifts. The growl that escapes him is menacing. He grabs me, but I go limp, escaping through his hands, dropping to the floor, cradling my knees to my chest.

"You said you didn't want kids yet! I don't see the big deal, Evelyn. Simple choice, either you or a baby; I choose you, end of argument," he snaps at me.

"I didn't want one yet, but I am not getting rid of it; it's our baby! How can you be so heartless?" I scream at him.

He tries to pick me up off the floor, but I kick and hit him, making it hard for him to grab me without hurting me.

Suddenly, the door bursts open.

"What the fuck are you doing, Orion?" Ryland yells, walking in with Thaddeus behind him. Shit, now I have three of them to go against.

Orion ignores him, and I can feel his anger hit me hard through the bond, making nausea roll over me. "Get up, Evelyn! NOW!" he bellows at me, reaching for me again, but Ryland growls when I pull away from him, slamming him against the wall.

"What the fuck has gotten into you? You're scaring her!" he screams at him.

Thaddeus steps into the room, assessing the situation. Orion shoves him back and walks into the bathroom. He grabs the box, walks to Thaddeus, and slams it into his chest. Thaddeus glares at him, grabbing it. "Talk some fucking sense into her," Orion snaps, walking out the door.

Thaddeus watches him storm out. Then, he stares at the box. Ryland walks over to him to see what Orion gave him, and their eyes snap to me.

"You're pregnant?" Thaddeus asks, wide-eyed.

"You can't keep it, Evie," Ryland says, walking over to me where I am frozen on the floor. My heart is pounding in my chest so hard I am finding it hard to breathe.

"I'm not aborting my child!" I scream at him, frustrated.

Ryland rubs the back of his neck, looking toward Thaddeus, who sits on the end of the bed, looking down at the pregnancy test in his hand. "Evie-" he starts, but I instantly cut him off.

"No! And I won't forgive you if you make me!"

Thaddeus looks at Ryland. Ryland looks between both of us and puts his hands up in surrender. "I am out; I ain't making her do anything she doesn't want to," he states, walking out of the room.

"Just let them calm down, then we will deal with this," Thaddeus says.

"Deal with it?" I ask as he rubs his hand down his face, his eyes softening.

"Yes, we will deal with it; you can't keep it. I will take it away; you won't even remember, Evelyn, be like it never existed," he says. I shake my head but can't even say anything around the lump in my throat. "Evie?" he says, getting up.

"No, just leave me," I manage to choke out.

Thaddeus sighs and walks out, closing the door behind him, leaving me a sobbing mess on the floor. They are going to kill our baby, take it from me. I get up and wash my face. My eyes are all puffy and they still haven't returned. Walking out, I notice the car keys still sitting on the dresser. Opening the door, I peer out.

We are on the second floor. The stairs are only a few yards away, and the car is parked right next to them. I just need to get to the car, but I'm not sure where they went. I duck inside and quickly close the door, tying my hair in a bun and slipping some clothes on.

Grabbing the keys, I dash for the car, stopping on the bottom step and pressing the button to unlock Thaddeus' car. It beeps once, the lights flashing. When I don't see them, I rush over, throw the door open, jump in, and start the car.

Reversing out and tearing off down the road for the highway, I have no idea where to go, but anywhere is better than the alternative. If I knew where Thaddeus' parents went, I would go to them, but they left the city, and I have nowhere to go. Trying to think of somewhere to go, I continue driving down the highway until suddenly, I notice a figure in the middle of the road. I am forced to slam on the brakes before hitting the person, only to realize it is Thaddeus. I slam on the breaks, barely missing him. Then, I put the car in reverse and looked over my shoulder to find Orion, standing behind the car.

CHAPTER
FIFTY-THREE

Evelyn

  Thaddeus stalks toward the car, making me panic, and I hit the gas. The car jolts backward but it stops, the wheels keep spinning but it's not moving. Looking back, I see Orion has his hands on the trunk.

He growls loudly as smoke from the tires spews everywhere, and I can smell burning rubber, but it is useless. How he is strong enough to hold the car in place is beyond me. I take my foot off the gas, not bothering to turn the car off. Instead, I dash over the seat and out the passenger door just as Thaddeus rips the driver's side door open and tries to grab me.

I run; it's all I can think of. I hear the car cut off right before my feet are knocked off the ground and out from under me. Arms wrap around my waist, tugging me against them. I thrash, kick, and scream, but Thaddeus doesn't let go. Instead, just tosses me over his shoulder, stalking back towards the car and throwing the back door open. I manage to kick backward, forcing the door shut.

"Evelyn, stop it," he snaps at me, but I don't. Instead, I continue to thrash. Tears roll down my face, and I cry and scream hysterically. They aren't taking my baby; they will have to kill me first. "Evie enough," Thaddeus says, spinning me around to face him and pressing me against the side of his car.

"No! No, you're not taking it from me!" I scream.

"It's too dangerous; we can't risk you," he says. I can barely even see his face through my tears as he pins me there, my feet not even touching the ground as I thrash, and I know it's pointless; I am not getting away. Not from them. "I'm sorry. I have no choice," he murmurs, pressing his face into the crook of my neck, and I go limp, giving up.

I will hate them forever if they make me do this. I can hear Thaddeus' hard breathing, his breath on my neck. Orion is standing behind him, looking away from the scene unfolding. I can tell neither of them want to do this, but they feel like they have no choice.

"I'll let you change me," I whisper.

My voice shakes but it's loud enough to get my point across. Orion's head snaps in my direction.

Thaddeus pulls back, looking at me. "What?" he asks, wondering if he misheard me.

"You can change me; I won't die. Please don't make me do this."

Thaddeus looks over his shoulder at Orion as he too walks over. "We don't even know how far along she is or when it will be born," Orion mutters, and I feel hope die out.

"It worked on my mother," Thaddeus answers him.

"Your mother had vampire DNA. Evelyn doesn't. Her heart could stop long before our blood takes effect and is in her system," Orion says.

"I can drink it every day, please, Orion," I beg.

His eyes soften as he reaches his hand out to stroke my face. "You will drink our blood every day, no complaining, no matter how gross it starts to taste?" he says, and I nod.

Thaddeus looks at him, and I can see the wheels are turning in his head. "C-section, if we keep her heart beating long enough by getting it out, she should survive?" Orion nods.

"Chances of finding a doctor once she goes into labor, Thaddeus-" Orion shakes his head, pinching the bridge of his nose.

"But if your blood is in my system, won't I just die and come back?" I ask.

"That's what we are hoping, but the baby will be tribrid; it might absorb everything. My mother craved blood during pregnancy," Thaddeus explains, and Orion nods.

I can see he is trying to think. "I'll do it," Orion says, making Thaddeus look at him.

"You'll do it; you'll really cut her open? Your own mate?" Thaddeus asks, incredulous. The idea nauseates me.

Orion nods. "Can't be that hard." He shrugs.

"I'm not saying it is; I'm just asking because I know you don't like hurting her."

"Well, I don't have a choice now, do I? She won't go through with it, so that's all we can do; you and Ryland can hold her down; I will cut it out while you feed her my blood." They both look at me, and dread consumes me; they are going to cut it out of me while I am awake and can feel it. They both stare, and I realize they are waiting for me to answer. I nod, even though the thought of it petrifies me. "And you do as we say. We have hunters after us, and until things die down, we can't stop, Evelyn, no matter how tired you get of moving."

"Please, I will do anything you ask, just don't kill our baby," I beg him.

He sighs, pressing his head against mine. "Fine, we can keep it," he whispers, and my heart skips a beat; they are going to let me keep the baby, our baby.

We stand there for a few seconds until I lose feeling in my arms from his grip. I wrap my legs around his waist, trying to pull myself up from the position and relieve the pressure on my arms. Thaddeus' eyes snap to mine. "I can't feel my arms," I tell him. He chuckles.

"Sorry," he says, letting go, and I feel the blood flow back to my throbbing limbs. He places my feet on the ground and steps back. His hand cups my cheek. "No more fighting us," he states.

"I won't fight you." He nods, opens the car door, and I climb in. Orion walks over to the driver's door and hops in while Thaddeus climbs in the back with me, pulling me against him.

"We need to get hold of Amara," he tells Orion, and I see him nod as he starts the car, turning it around, and heading back the way I came.

When we pull up at the hotel, Ryland is out the front waiting with our suitcases. Thaddeus looks at me as he opens the door. "Stay in the car." I nod, and he hops out, talking to Ryland.

My eyes follow them as Thaddeus opens the trunk. Ryland climbs in the back with me, and Thaddeus gets in the front. Orion pulls out of the parking space. "We are leaving already?" I ask.

"Yes, hunters are close; remember, no fighting us," Thaddeus answers, and I shut my mouth.

Ryland looks at me, confused. Then, he leans between the seats. "Did I miss something anyone wants to explain?"

Orion's eyes flick to me in the rear-view mirror, and I can tell he is smiling with the way his eyes crinkle, flickering red for a second. "We are having a baby," Orion states.

"We are?"

Orion nods, but Ryland looks to Thaddeus, who looks over his shoulder at him.

"Yes, Ryland. We are letting her have the baby," he says slowly, making sure he understands.

"Yes, yes, yes!" Ryland shouts, grabs his face, and smashes his lips into Thaddeus. "Aw, I hope it's a girl; we could dress her in cute little dresses," he says, letting go of Thaddeus and turning to me. I raise an eyebrow at his enthusiasm. He reaches for me, pulling me onto his lap.

"Seatbelt, Ryland," Orion says to him.

Ryland clips the middle seat belt around me, pulling me against him awkwardly. "We are having a baby," he whispers in a sing-song voice below my ear. I look up at him, his eyes sparkle. He is so happy. He kisses my nose, crushing me in his huge arms against him; I twist, putting my feet on the seat beside me, trying to get comfortable with the seatbelt latch digging into my backside and my hip.

We drive for what feels like hours, and it is becoming impossible to remain comfortable; I can barely keep my eyes open when I hear Thaddeus whisper to Orion. "We will do a loop around the state and cut back across. I can't get hold of Amara; I assume they went underground," Thaddeus tells Orion.

"What are we going to do now? She won't be able to run for long, Thaddeus."

"She won't have a choice," he says, moving, and I squeeze my eyes shut, pretending to be still asleep. I feel his gaze on me for a moment until I hear him turn back around. "I should never have killed all of those hunters back at Leven," Thaddeus says, making me confused.

"You led them straight to us, Thaddeus, and nearly died in the process."

"I was angry; I lost control. I didn't realize this would happen," Thaddeus admits, and I feel my heart skip a beat.

He said he stumbled across their base, but he went looking for them by the sound of it. Is he really that much of a monster that he would go looking to kill people? He said that sometimes people die, but he didn't mean it, that it isn't his intention to hurt them.

"This is why you need to give it up, Thaddeus; we can't keep doing this. Evelyn will get sick of running, and what will happen one day when she finds out you kill people because you like it? You think I don't know when the darkness takes you over that you want to hurt her? That you like it when you do. Even if you don't mean to, you still enjoy her fear?" Orion tells him. There is silence until Orion speaks again. "How many this time?" he asks.

"How many I killed or are still alive?"

"Both," Orion says.

"I think I killed around a hundred of them, but there are many more. I didn't realize it was a family base," he says and my stomach drops. A family base, does that mean there are children there? "It doesn't matter anyway; they would have turned out like their parents," Thaddeus answers with a total disregard for human life.

"You don't know that, Thaddeus; I am sick and tired of the blood on our hands for loving you," Orion snaps, his voice rising above a whisper.

"Then fucking leave! You don't like it? Leave, Orion. You knew who I was when you met me, and I am not changing."

"Not even for her? Or our child when it's born?" Thaddeus growls, but adds nothing. "Answer me, Thaddeus; I feel it. Feel it getting worse within you. I know you like the power, Thaddeus. I know you are addicted to it. Do you want to lose her?"

"You know I don't, so why ask? I fucking love her!"

"Then give it up for her; if you can't do it for yourself, do it for her."

"It's not that simple."

"What do you mean? Just get your mother and Amara to help you."

"It has attached itself to me, Orion, okay? It's a part of me now. I don't think it is possible any more. Why do you think I left? Do you think I want this for any of you? For myself?"

"We can find a way; there is always a way. But you have to want to give it up, Thaddeus. It attached itself to you because you let it. After all, you wanted it, too," Orion yells.

"Shh, you will wake her," Thaddeus whispers.

The car goes silent until I hear someone turn the radio up slightly.

Does Thaddeus really kill innocent people? Like he goes looking for them just to kill them? The thought sickens me; I know he is a monster but hearing this makes my stomach churn. Does he really want to hurt me and inflict pain on me?

I never realized how much of a struggle it is for him; sure, I feel him struggle against himself through the bond, feel his guilt after he does something that hurts me, but is he really enjoying it when he does it? Nothing Orion says makes sense to me; for the most part, Thaddeus is good to me or tries to be anyway, so why would Orion say that he enjoys it?

CHAPTER
FIFTY-FOUR

Thaddeus

A month passes quickly; we are still on the move. Evelyn becomes more and more uncomfortable as each day passes. She only has a month left. Pulling up at our next destination, I stop the car.

Evelyn is asleep beside me with the chair laid back while Ryland and Orion are crammed in the back. Morning sickness wracked her petite body a couple of days after we found out she was pregnant; despite the size of her growing belly, she looks frail and sickly and continues to lose weight. Her eyes are hollow, and her breathing uneven. We were right; the baby is absorbing everything we feed her.

I finally managed to get a hold of Amara, and she says she can't see Evelyn's future, which worries me. My mother told me not to worry; that when she was pregnant with us, her future couldn't be seen either, but still, with the way Evelyn is going, it has us all scared.

Our Evie is human, Bianca has been doing research for us and found out those carrying supernatural babies only live if they have vampire DNA. No human has survived before, not carrying a baby.

Most survive carrying vampire children, but no human survived werewolf children, and Evelyn is carrying a tribrid - a strong one at that.

I can already sense the magic radiating out of her, yet it isn't like my magic. I must have drawn the shit card when magic was handed out, hit with the bad stick, no scrap that I hit with the entire damn tree. The child Evie is carrying reminds me of Amara's magic, pure and good.

We try to keep it from her, not wanting to add to her worry. The darkness around me has worsened, and being near her is becoming uncomfortable. Amara thinks it's because I am picking up on Evelyn's distress. Evie has become wary of me, and sometimes I catch her staring, lost in thought like she can truly see the monster I am, yet she tries her best to cover it, but it doesn't go unnoticed by me.

"Babe, you need to wake up," I tell her, shaking her shoulder.

She moves to get comfortable, and I give up, instead, hopping out of the car, going to her door, and opening it. Ryland is grabbing our bags from the trunk while Orion goes to get the keys for the room. Scooping her up, she barely moves, her eyes flutter open and close again. I follow Orion to the room, Ryland right behind us.

When I place her on the bed, she rolls on her side.

"We can't keep doing this," Ryland says, looking down at her, and I agree; it is too much on her.

Every day she grows weaker; even walking is a challenge sometimes, though she has moments where she is full of energy, mainly late at night. She even craves blood sometimes, which always makes her sex drive spike after she has consumed it; the kid is going to come out with a head like a golf ball if she doesn't settle down. Her hormones are majorly out of whack.

One minute she is horny and has a burst of energy; the next tired and lethargic. Orion spends most of his time reading pregnancy books or surgical books, trying to find a way to help her.

"What do you want to do?"

"Maybe we should head home? It's been a month, and we haven't seen them for two weeks now," Orion suggests. I nod, maybe, or at least long enough for her to have the baby.

"It's up to you, Thaddeus," Ryland says, looking down at her again and brushing her hair from her face.

"We will head home tomorrow. I think that might be best. I will have Amara and my mother meet us there to set up some wards with me."

Ryland climbs on the bed beside her, rubbing his hand over her belly and kisses it.

Heading for the bathroom, I strip off and step into the shower. My mind is racing with what I should do, my thoughts consume me, and I feel the darkness creeping in. The whispers of my magic, calling me to use it, get louder. I try to tune them out and ignore them, but I know it is pointless; it will win as it always does. I shower quickly, shut the water off, and step out, wrapping the towel around my waist.

As I open my bag and take out jeans and a shirt, Orion raises his eyebrow at me. "Where are you going?"

"Out." I need to get away before it worsens and I attack Ryland again. Luckily, Evelyn remained asleep, dead to the world, because what I did frightened me and I couldn't stop until Orion pulled me off him.

"Thaddeus, don't do this; you're only feeding it when you give in to it," Orion tries to reason.

I know he is right but better I leave than let it hurt them. Ignoring him, I walk out the door, heading for the main street of this shitty town. The winter chill does not affect me as I continue walking, until I finally hit a gas station. For some reason, I look through the glass windows. A woman walks in the glass sliding doors, holding a little girl's hand.

It is late; for some reason, seeing the woman strikes me as odd. It is freezing out, and both of them have hardly anything on. I watch them when I see a shady-looking man walk in after her. I can tell by the way he walks that he is up to no good. Usually, I would continue on my way, but I find myself frozen, my eyes glued on the woman, unaware of the danger lurking in the gas station with her.

My thoughts go to Evie; what if that was her and our child? I am almost stuck in a trance until I hear the shrill voices of the woman screaming, and the girl's cries as her mother tugs her behind a shelf near the entryway. The man I can see is holding a gun at the teller, and I can hear his voice from where I stand.

The station attendant is holding his hands up when I see the man stalk toward the entry and grab the woman by her hair. The little kid looks on helplessly as he drags her mother away toward the register, pointing the gun at her head.

I blink, only to open my eyes and find myself next to the child in the store. My reaction shocks me; why did I do that? The little girl is sobbing, pulling me out of my tumultuous thoughts. My eyes go to her crouched behind the shelf sobbing, and I look toward the startled gas station attendant. He looks at me with alarm as the man turns, pointing the gun at me. He looks dirty; tattoos and piercings litter his face. He has a ratty, torn leather jacket on, looking every bit the piece of scum he is.

"Stay back, or I'll shoot the woman," he yells, pointing the gun back at her head. She has her hands clutching his as he yanks her hair. She might be in her thirties, maybe.

"Mommy!" the little girl calls, making my eyes dart down to her angelic little face.

"Close your eyes, princess," I tell her. The words leave my lips before I can stop them. What the hell is wrong with me? The little girl does what I say and I turn to look at the man, holding the woman hostage.

"I said stay back, man, I will fucking shoot her," he screams, and I can see the desperation on his face. He doesn't know what to think of me, but his instincts are telling him I am all kinds of wrong; his fear is thick in the air, and I feel my eyes bleed black.

I stalk towards him. His hands shake as he holds the gun and points it at me. He pulls the trigger.

The bang rings loudly through the shop and the bullet hits me in the shoulder.

"What are you?" he stammers, taking a step back.

I smile, digging my fingers into the hole and pulling the bullet out, examining it before dropping it on the floor. "Your executioner," I tell him, not giving him a chance to pull the trigger again. I snap his neck. The man's body falls to the floor at my feet. The woman screams, causing my ears to ring, and I feel a strong urge to kill her and drain her blood when I hear the little girl's voice.

"Mommy," her soft, unsure voice makes me turn around. The little girl runs to her mother, but I stop her by stepping in her path.

"Please, please, don't hurt my baby!" the woman cries, trying to reach for her.

Grabbing the little girl's face, I hold her chubby cheeks. My eyes focus on the vein that pulsates in her neck beneath her delicate skin. Hunger hits me and then, she touches my hand. Her tiny fingers tremble as she pulls me out of my bloodlust.

"You will not remember this man or what happened here once you leave the store. You came to the store with your mommy to get candy and left," I tell her. I watch her eyes glaze over, and she repeats my words. I let her go, handing her a chocolate bar from off the shelf.

"Please, I won't tell anyone; I know who you are. I swear I won't say anything," the girl's mother pleads.

"I am not going to hurt you. I just didn't want her to remember this day," I answer her mother, facing her. "Take her home; it is too cold for her to be out in this weather." She nods, scooping up her daughter. The attendant calls after her, but I wave her off. "I'll pay for it."

She nods, running back to her car. As I turn around to the attendant, he takes a step back. The blood drains from his face, and he puts his hands up in surrender. "You're the man from the news, the Dark One," he stutters.

"Can I get a pack of Marlboro blue 25's?" I ask, ignoring his question.

"You want smokes?" he asks, like he can't understand what I just asked for. I say nothing, staring at the idiot serving me. He grabs the packet and tosses them on the counter.

"The lady's fuel," I tell him, pointing to the register. God, do I have to do this shit for him? He hesitantly uses the register, and I give him the cash.

As I turn around and walk out, he speaks again. "What about the body?" he asks.

"Keep it, it's no good to me," I tell him, chuckling to myself and walking out the door. I shake my head, take a breath, and run back back to the hotel.

CHAPTER
FIFTY-FIVE

Evelyn

I am suddenly woken by arguing. As I sit up, I register that I am in bed. The last thing I remember is being in the car. As I look around, I see Thaddeus is arguing with Orion while Ryland is in between, trying to break it up.

"I told you not to fucking leave, and you still went. Why did you? We can't keep moving her around like this."

"It doesn't matter, Orion; we have to go before the police get called and come here," Thaddeus says. I can feel through the bond his darkness is seeping out of him though he seems pretty under control for how sickly twisted it feels through the bond.

"What's going on?" I ask. All their heads snap to me on the bed.

"Nothing, babe, we just need to leave," Thaddeus says, scooping me off the bed.

"I need to pee," I tell him. The baby feels like it is sitting on my bladder. He places my feet on the floor and my legs buckle under me from not having moved for so long. Thaddeus grabs my hand and holds me steady, but I push his hand away. "I'm fine," I tell him, and he lets go.

I'm not fine. I feel exhausted, ridiculously exhausted. My muscles are aching, even my bones are aching with every step I take. This baby has zapped the energy right out of me. My belly is so hard and round I can no longer see my feet. Just bending or moving slightly makes my lungs wheeze.

Quickly using the bathroom, I walk out to find the bedroom empty, apart from Thaddeus, sitting on the bed with his head in his hands. He looks up when I step out, walks over to me, and grabs me, obviously unwilling to wait for me to hobble down the stairs.

"Where are we going?" I ask, shivering when the cold chill of the air brushes over me as he steps outside.

"Home," he says, making me look at him.

"Really?" I ask, excited to finally not have to run anymore.

We have been on the move for ages, never staying in one place for more than a night. Orion opens the car door as we approach it and slides across the seat. Thaddeus places me in my seat and gets in on the driver's side to start the car.

I try clipping the seatbelt in, but it digs into my belly no matter where I try to put it. My skin is tender from stretching so quickly; every piece of me feels bruised even though there are no visible marks. Unclipping the belt, I try to get comfortable.

"Evelyn, seatbelt," Orion protests, trying to force it around me.

I swat his hands away, annoyed. "No, it irritates my skin," I tell him.

"You need to put it on," Orion growls, pulling me to his side and trying to wrap the middle belt around me.

"Orion, leave her," Ryland growls back at him.

"You know what? Fine, pull over," Orion says, angrily.

"I will put it on; just stop it, please," I beg him, trying to click the belt in.

Every day they argue over something; every day, we are trapped in this car; all they do is fight; I am sick of it. Thaddeus pulls the car over, and Orion hops out, slamming the door in my face as I lean over to stop him from leaving. Thaddeus gets out after him, and they start screaming at each other. I try to drown them out, sick of hearing the same bullshit.

"You okay, hun?" Ryland asks, as the headlights illuminate them while they fight on the side of the highway.

"No. They just don't stop. They are always at each other's throats."

Ryland reaches for me over the back of the seat, and I go to waterworks; stupid fucking pregnancy hormones. One minute I am fine, the next, either raging over nothing or crying. I miss my normal body, miss being able to see my own feet. When I wipe my tears, they are still arguing over God knows what. "What are they even fighting over?" I ask.

Ryland shrugs. "Thaddeus apparently killed someone, and he has been trying to explain something to him, but Orion is just an asshole and not listening and talking over him because he doesn't want to keep moving you."

Argh, this is a nightmare. "Who did he kill?"

"No idea, Orion won't let him explain."

I huff, annoyed at sitting on the side of the road. Climbing over the seat, I hop in the driver's seat. It is a tight squeeze between the two front seats, and I am sure I smack Ryland in the head with my bulging belly. "What are you doing?" Ryland asks.

"Leaving them and going home," I tell him, driving the car and taking off. Tears rolled down my face. Are they going to fight like this constantly when the baby arrives? I am over it. Thaddeus said we are going home, so that's where I am going; they can run home and sort out their problems.

Ryland's phone starts ringing, and I hit the gas harder. He answers it. "Hello, Orion," Ryland says, sounding bored.

I can only hear one side of the conversation, but I get the gist from Ryland's replies. "No, what do you expect? She isn't going to keep watching you fight. Sort your shit out and meet us at home," he says, hanging up, and I smile sadly at him.

"Slow down, love. Don't want to hit anything at this speed," he says, looking at the odometer and I release the accelerator a bit. I drive for a few hours until fatigue catches up to me, and I start yawning. I feel like all I do is sleep and eat.

Ryland speaks up after noticing my constant yawning. "Pull over at the next gas station." I nod and around twenty miles later, I finally find one. The highway is boring and goes on forever. That's what it feels like until I finally see the bright neon lights.

"Get in the passenger seat; I will drive." I climb out of the car, walk to the other side, and climb in. Ryland fills the car up and walks into the gas station. He returns with a bag full of potato chips and sweets. "They sold those tomato flavor chips you like," he says, pulling them out of the bag and handing them to me.

"Thank you," I tell him, open the packet, and start to eat them. I offer some to Ryland, but he shakes his head and starts the car. I eat my chips; the drive is peaceful because they aren't arguing, and I eventually fall asleep, only to wake up when the car stops again.

I sit up, stretch, and nearly cry in relief when I see our home. I missed this place, missed it so much. Thaddeus opens my door, picks me up and cradles me to his chest. I inhale his scent, placing my hand on his chest.

"I'm sorry. I didn't mean to upset you," he says, kissing my eyebrow.

I nod, not really caring anymore; I am over it. It is nearly daylight already; we must have been driving again for hours. Not that I really knew where we were in the first place before we got here.

"Where is Orion?" I ask.

"Inside, talking to my mother," Thaddeus answers, and I instantly brighten up. His mother is here; I kick my legs, wanting to be put down so I can go to her. "Settle down, little one; me carrying you will still be faster than you trying to run."

He is right; I am so much slower now. We step inside our familiar surroundings. The place smells like it has been locked up for weeks on end, which it has been. As soon as I walk in, I see Amara and Imogen talking to Orion. Imogen has a bag and some herbs in her hand. The chatter dies when I step in. Imogen's eyes go wide as Thaddeus places me on my feet. Amara's eyes run over my body worriedly.

"Hey, ma," I tell her, and she smiles, walking over to me and embracing me gently like she thinks she will break me. She gently rubs my belly and looks up at Thaddeus, and I can't decipher the look on her face. Amara hesitates, watching me closely like she is here but not seeing what is in front of her. Her eyes glaze over, and a dark expression takes over her face, her lips pursed together.

"Amara?" Thaddeus asks.

She shakes her head, snapping out of her trance. "Sorry," she quickly says, walking over and hugging me. She rubs my belly, a smile on her lips. "She is strong," Amara says. All of us look at her.

"It's a girl?" Ryland asks, stepping around me and into the room.

Amara nods, a huge grin on her face. "Can you feel it, brother? Feel her magic?"

"She is pure," Thaddeus answers, his voice choking up slightly.

His mother pats his back softly and he abruptly walks away. I can feel he is emotional through the bond, not sad but not happy either; it takes me a second to recognize it. It feels like loneliness. I stare after him, worried until Orion places his hand on my shoulder.

"I will check on him," he says, walking off after him. Hopefully, he does check on him, not argue with him.

"We brought you some things, some herbs to add to your tea. Orion said you're exhausted all the time; these will give you a boost. Oh, and this one will stop any pain you have; just don't take too much; they make you horny," Amara says.

Her mother smacks her up the back of the head, making Amara growl at her. "Amara was up most of the night, harvesting the garden for you," Imogen chuckles.

Ryland holds out his hand to put them away. He takes the bag from Amara, but as she puts the herbs in his hand, she tenses, jumps back, and her eyes glaze over. Her eyes dart to me, then back to Ryland, and I can clearly see the fear displayed in her eyes.

"Amara, what's wrong?" Imogen asks.

Ryland watches Amara when she suddenly grabs hold of both his wrists, her eyes turn white, and she gasps again. Her eyes keep moving like she is watching something. It is the eeriest sight to witness. "You can't let them do it," Amara gasps. Her eyes look frantically between us.

"What?" Ryland asks, looking at me.

"Promise you won't let them do it." Amara demands, her voice is almost frantic.

"What are you talking about, Amara?" Ryland asks.

"Thaddeus, he will end the world if she dies. It will doom us all," she gasps and her eyes roll into the back of her head. Blood starts running from her nose as Amara suddenly passes out.

Ryland grabs her in time just as she is about to hit the floor. Imogen looks lost, staring into space, while my heart is pounding so hard that I am struggling to breathe. I can feel a panic attack coming on, the room pulsates around me, and my vision begins to blur. What does she mean?

What did she see?

CHAPTER
FIFTY-SIX

Evelyn

Ryland moves Amara to the couch, placing her down gently just as Thaddeus walks back in with Orion. Imogen, Ryland, and I look at Thaddeus and my heart skips a beat as I remember Amara's words.

Thaddeus notices his sister on the couch and rushes over. "What happened?" he asks, looking at his mother.

Imogen stares at her son with fearful eyes, her eyes darting to me, but Ryland is the one that answers. "Nothing happened; she just passed out," he says.

I can tell Thaddeus knows he is lying. "What did she see?" he demands, looking at me, but I have gone completely mute; I can't even form a word. How can one person destroy the world?

Amara groans and her hand goes to her head like she has a bad headache. Her eyes are back to normal as they flicker to everyone staring at her. "What, brother? I just passed out. I am alright," she says.

"What did you see?" he asks again, but this time to her.

"Nothing you need to know. Things change; they will change," she says as her eyes dart to Ryland, who looks away, and then, at me.

Imogen looks lost for words. Exactly what do you say when the entire world rests on your son's shoulders and your daughter's visions?

"Well, we should be off. Make sure you use the herbs; they will help. The wards are set; everything is fine; just fine," Imogen says, her eyes not leaving Amara.

I can tell she is desperate to get out of here. I have no idea why they won't tell Thaddeus, but figure it can change the events of what Amara saw, what Amara warned Ryland about.

Thaddeus is about to protest when suddenly I blink, and they are gone; Amara must have misted out of here.

Thaddeus stares at the space where his mother and sister were before his eyes go to Ryland. "Tell me."

"You know I can't do that; Amara said things will change. I tell you, you will alter the future again, and maybe not in a good way."

Thaddeus breathes loudly, clearly not happy about being left out of the loop. Orion takes the herbs from Ryland and walks off into the kitchen. I look to the stairs, the shower is calling my name.

Thaddeus, noticing me looking at them, steps forward, his arms out. I reach mine up, and he picks me up awkwardly as I wrap my legs around his waist. My belly is making all my weight lean onto his arms, but he doesn't seem to mind as he carries me up the stairs effortlessly.

Then, he carries me into the bedroom and places me on my feet. I don't say a word as I walk to the bathroom and turn on the shower.

Thaddeus leans in the doorway, watching me. "Will you tell me?" he asks, and my mind goes to Ryland telling me things could change with Thaddeus knowing.

I shake my head. I don't want to be the one responsible for making things worse. Just thinking about it is making my heart race with fear.

Thaddeus steps forward, and my heart skips a beat. "Why are you scared of me?" he asks.

I'm not scared of him, just what he is apparently capable of. "I'm not," I tell him, holding my hand out for him.

He grabs it, steps forward, and wraps an arm around me, rubbing my belly. "What are we going to name her?" he asks.

I have no idea; no names are coming to mind at all. I actually thought it would be a boy, so now I am completely blank on names.

I shrug, not knowing, and slowly pull my shirt off. Thaddeus drops down, helping me pull my leggings down while I hang onto his shoulder. I can't even see his head underneath my belly but feel him press his lips to it as sparks rush over my skin.

He stands up, and I tug on his shirt, wanting him to shower with me. He complies, pulling it off, and I trace my fingers down his abs to the waistband of his jeans. Then, I turn away and step into the shower.

Thaddeus steps in behind me and adjusts the shower head, which is level with his neck, pushing it up higher and turning the other one on. Thaddeus dips his face under the water and looks down at me. "I love you," he whispers.

My heart squeezes at his words, and I rest my head on his chest. "I love you too," I tell him.

My hand reaches for a bar of soap and I start washing his chest and abs. He growls softly, almost a purr, which makes my eyes dart up to his, and he kisses my head. Once we shower, we walk downstairs, or more like Thaddeus walks because he gave up waiting for me and scooped me up. The problem isn't the stairs; it is trying to see them as I clutch the railing. Going down is easy, getting up is another story; I am always breathless.

Ryland is sitting on the lounge, flicking through channels, stopping on the news as I walk over to him and climb on his lap. Orion brings out a cup of tea, handing it to me. I sniff it, and it smells like grass, making me crinkle my nose.

"Drink it. Amara said it would help, and it will; she is never wrong," Orion says.

"But it smells nasty," I tell him. He folds his arms and looks down at me as Ryland moves my hand, trying to get me to drink it.

"Did you taste it?" I ask Orion, who shakes his head.

I huff, annoyed. How can he expect me to drink something he hasn't tried? I pass him the cup, and he rolls his eyes but takes a sip and starts gagging. His cheeks puff out, but he forces it down, trying to make out it doesn't taste that bad. I raise an eyebrow at him.

"You're drinking it," he says, handing it back.

"No, I am not, not after seeing your reaction to it."

Orion's eyes turn red, and he leans over the couch, his face next to Ryland's. "Drink it, Evelyn" I feel the fog slip over me, but I try to fight against it.

Ryland looks at him. "Don't use that on her; it's not fair to force her," he says, his hand rubbing my back gently.

"It's for her own good," he says, turning back to me. Thaddeus watches both of them, and I feel Ryland's chest rumble as I hear him growl. "Drink it, Evelyn, now," Orion says, and I can't help the urge to do as I am told.

Thaddeus sits on the couch beside me and glares up at Orion. "Stop it, now," he snaps at Orion, and I feel the fog lift. My trembling hand, holding the cup, stops.

"Can you try to drink it? Even some of it?" Thaddeus asks, and I look at the cup with disgust; the smell alone is bad enough.

I bring the cup to my lips, take a deep breath, and hold it as I quickly swallow some. I balk the moment it hits my tongue, forcing it down my throat. Ryland tips the cup to my lips again while I shake my head.

Orion is still watching me, and it is clear that it will start a fight if I don't drink it. I roll my eyes at him but drink it, chugging the last of it. It tastes like freshly cut grass and dirt. I shiver as I drain the cup and hand it to Orion, who looks in it as he walks off.

"God, he has been in a bad mood lately," I mutter, looking at Orion leaving the room.

Ryland pulls my head against him, and I rest it on his shoulder. Thaddeus sighs, grabs my feet, places them on his lap, and moves closer to Ryland. I feel a cold rush roll over me, making me twitch. My eyes widen, and for the first time in ages, I feel like I have been hit with a caffeine buzz, completely alert and awake.

Most of all, I notice my body isn't hurting; I feel rejuvenated, like I can run a marathon and also have an overwhelming sense to move. It is different.

"Well, that worked fast; look at her pupils," he says, nudging Ryland.

Ryland grips my chin, looking down at me. "Indeed, it did," he says, letting my chin go. I feel revved up and ready to go. Go where? I have no idea, but I suddenly want to move. What the hell did she give me?

My limbs are restless and twitching, and Thaddeus grabs my feet, holding them in place. "Maybe a little too much," he mutters, looking at me just as Orion walks out.

He leans over to kiss my head. "See? You feel better," he says. He is right, but I'm not sure if this is a better feeling anymore; I feel antsy.

"What is that stuff?" I ask, my words come out so quickly they sound like a squeak.

"Maybe a little less next time," Orion says, looking at Thaddeus, who nods.

"One herb is like an analgesic, the other like speed. Werewolves sometimes use it to speed up their healing abilities when gravely injured," Orion answers.

"Speed?" I squeak, looking down at my belly.

"It's natural and won't hurt our baby; Amara would never give you anything that would cause harm to her niece," Thaddeus says, watching my hand as I rub my belly and feel her kick, but it isn't painful like usual.

Usually, when she kicks, I feel like she is breaking something. Thaddeus watches my hand move, and I move it, lifting my shirt. Orion's eyes watch my belly move as I feel her roll. His cold hand touches my tight skin as it stretches underneath his hand.

"Not hurting anymore?" Orion asks, and I shake my head.

I feel nothing; more like I am given a local anesthetic, yet I can feel my limbs. But at the same time they also feel numb; it is a weird feeling, foreign to me.

"Any baby names yet?" Ryland asks, and I shake my head, looking to them to see if they have any. They, too, shake their heads.

"Well, she will just be Baby until someone thinks of something," I tell them, and they nod.

Orion's eyes snap to the huge TV for a second. A picture of a gas station comes up. "Turn that up," Orion says, and I look back at the TV.

Thaddeus sighs and gets up.

"Where are you going?" I ask as Ryland turns the volume up.

"I am not arguing over this again," he says and walks upstairs.

I look at Orion, who has a foul look on his face. Then, I turn back to TV to listen to what the news reporter is saying. Video footage inside the store shows Thaddeus, standing next to a child just in the doorway, and another man has a gun pointed at him. We watch without sound as Thaddeus turns, looks down at the child and says something to her. The picture is a little grainy, but she is obviously crying. My heart skips a beat as fear consumes me. Did he kill the little girl? It flicks to the service attendant, being interviewed, and the vision cuts off.

"He just appeared out of nowhere; he saved us, saved us all, then asked me for some smokes and paid for the lady's fuel," he says excitedly, and I can tell he is excited about being on TV.

Orion looks at me, shocked, and then his eyes dart to the stairs where Thaddeus went. The video flicks on again and the news anchor's voice starts playing in the background. "What you are about to see, some viewers may find distressing."

We watch as a man points a gun at the woman and then points it at Thaddeus' chest. He says something and the man shoots. Thaddeus pulls the bullet out and kills the man, letting the body fall on the floor. The woman appears to be screaming as the little girl rushes out from behind the shelf only for Thaddeus to step in her way and bend down to her level and grab her face. We don't hear what he says, but he then stands, hands her chocolate, and turns to the mother, who grabs her daughter and rushes out.

Thaddeus steps over the body and walks to the counter, getting smokes, and handing the frightened man cash. Then, as if nothing happened, he just walks off. I keep staring at the screen, stunned.

"See, everyone? An unlikely hero. Does this mean the Dark One has changed? Only time will tell, I suppose. However, we have recently learned of a new landmark for-" As she moves on to the next report, the TV flicks off.

We all stare, stunned, until I am hit with Orion's guilt. "I feel terrible," Orion mutters.

"And so you should," Ryland growls at him. I climb off Ryland's lap, walking to the stairs. Orion watches me but soon he follows, his head hanging guiltily. I climb the stairs to our room easily without losing my breath.

Thaddeus looks up as I walk in. "Look, I didn't mean to, okay? Can we not argue, please? We just got home," Thaddeus says, shocking me. Does he think he has done something bad?

CHAPTER
FIFTY-SEVEN

E velyn
    Orion clears his throat. Thaddeus looks up at him, and I can tell he is waiting for his wrath. Instead, Orion scratches the back of his neck, looking awkward and like it is causing him pain to apologize to him.

I step closer to Thaddeus, who is still waiting for Orion to yell at him. I grab his face and his eyes dart up to me. "You didn't do anything wrong," I tell him.

His brows furrow and he shakes his head. "I killed him. Aren't you mad?" he asks.

"You didn't do anything wrong, Thaddeus. Even the news anchor said you are a hero; you saved three people," Orion says, finally finding his voice.

At first, Thaddeus stares at him, completely dumbfounded. But then, as Orion looks away, I see Thaddeus' lips turn up. "You call that an apology?" he asks as Ryland steps into the room, leaning on the door frame.

Orion's eyes snap toward Thaddeus and I watch Ryland pull out his phone, making me bunch up my eyebrows. My eyes turn back to Thaddeus and Orion.

"I'm sorry, okay? I should have heard you out before going off at you," he says with a sigh, running his hand down his face. I think that is the first time Orion has had to apologize to Thaddeus by the look on his face.

"And I just got that on camera," Ryland announces, a devious smile on his face, making me laugh.

"Give me that," Orion snarls, trying to snatch the phone from him, but Ryland moves it away.

"Now we have proof that Orion isn't always right," Ryland taunts.

Thaddeus has a huge grin on his face, and I sit on Thaddeus' lap as we watch Ryland and Orion fight over the phone Ryland now has in his pocket.

"You're really not mad?" Thaddeus whispers, running his nose along my jaw.

I spin around on his lap and kiss him, biting down on his bottom lip. "Definitely not mad," I tell him. He kisses me; his tongue runs along my lip and then ravages my mouth, making me sigh as I melt against him. I wrap my arms around his neck and kiss him forcefully. I push him back on the bed to straddle his waist. Leaning down, I kiss and suck on his neck. My belly is getting in the way and makes it slightly difficult. Thaddeus' hands go to my hips as he rolls them against his hardening length beneath me.

"No, no, no, she is too far along now," Orion says, noticing us, trying to pull me off, but Thaddeus' grip tightens and I smack Orion's hands away. "What if her water breaks?" Orion says as I pull Thaddeus' shirt off, nipping at his neck, and suck on his hot skin.

"I will be gentle," Thaddeus mutters.

"Yeah, right, you're never gentle," Orion growls, trying to grab me off, which is hard from the angle I am at because he would have to grab my belly.

He steps closer, wrapping his arms around my hips below my

stomach, pulling me off Thaddeus. Thaddeus sits up, and I turn around in Orion's arms to rip his face toward mine and kiss him.

He exhales deeply and pushes me away, holding me at arm's length. "Don't be using your vixen voodoo on me. Not happening; you are too far along now," Orion says, and I pout.

My core is pulsating with need, and Thaddeus' arousal isn't helping at all.

"Well then, go downstairs if you don't want to participate," Ryland says as he steps past him and grabs me. He lifts me off the floor, my legs wrap around his waist as I feel my back hit the mattress and he climbs between my legs. He grips the waistband of my pants, pulling them off as he kisses me. I hear Orion mutter something and leave the room. My skin feels like it is on fire as his hands move over my skin.

Thaddeus peels my top off and removes his pants. Ryland sits up, and I climb on top of Thaddeus, his erection is pressing between my wet folds and hitting my clit.

I grab his cock as I position it at my entrance and sink down onto him. A guttural sound leaves me as I feel his cock fill and stretch me. I move my hips, and Thaddeus' fingers dig into them and he slams me down on his hard length.

"Thaddeus gentle!" Orion snaps at him, and I realize he has returned to the room. Thaddeus places his hands behind his head and sends a wink to Orion, who rolls his eyes, making my lips tug at the corners.

I find my own rhythm, moving my hips. My stomach tenses, and Thaddeus is about to move his hands, but Orion growls. Thaddeus freezes, and puts his hands back behind his head. He wants to touch me, plow himself into me, and I want him to.

I feel Ryland's lips go to my shoulder. I reach back, tugging on his hip, needing to feel him inside me, needing his touch. What is in that shit Amara gave me? She isn't wrong about it making you horny.

Orion comes over to the bed and sits next to Thaddeus' head. He leans over to kiss me and his hand goes to my breast as he squeezes it.

Thaddeus grabs his shirt, rips him toward him, and kisses him. My stomach tightens at the sight of them. Orion moans into his mouth, and I feel myself becoming wetter, needier as I watch them, arousal twists through me stronger as I pick up on their emotions.

Ryland's hand reaches around me, rolling my nipple between his fingers. I feel Thaddeus move his hand between my legs, rubbing my clit with his thumb just as I feel Ryland push inside me from behind. I moan at the overfull feeling of both of them moving inside me.

Feeling the bed dip, my eyes open to see Orion's face inches off mine as he grips the back of my neck, tipping my head back and sucking my lip into his mouth and biting down on it. Thaddeus' hands go to my thighs, pushing my legs further apart and taking all my weight as Ryland moves faster, making me bounce on Thaddeus. My fingernails dig into Thaddeus' chest as I feel my pussy flutter around him as I reach my climax. My skin becomes flushed as I find my release at the same time Ryland does. Thaddeus rolls my hips back and forth, his grip gets tighter as his nails break my skin, chasing his own release as I feel his cock twitch and feel his semen warm my insides.

I roll off him to lay on my side. Orion watches me with worried eyes as he gets up and walks into the bathroom to turn the shower on. When he returns, I groan; I don't want to move, completely relaxed as I catch my breath. Orion walks over to me, stands next to my feet, and holds his hands out to me. Ryland walks into the bathroom, followed by Thaddeus.

"Come on. Up," Orion says, grabbing my hands and hauling me to my feet. I reluctantly get up to follow him into the bathroom. Thaddeus is moving over as I step in. Orion strips off and hops in the shower. The shower feels squished now with nowhere to put my belly; I am bumping them everywhere I move. Ryland washes quickly and gets out, freeing up space.

I feel Thaddeus rub the loofah over my back while Orion steps forward and bites his hand, his blood runs out and drips on the floor. "Quick, Evie, before it heals."

He has been extremely pushy lately. I ignore him and smirk when his hand heels. He growls and rips me toward him. He spins me around, my back flush against his chest. He repeats the action, biting his wrist this time and pressing it to my lips. I let my lips part, let his blood run down my throat and grab it with two hands. The instant his blood touches my tongue, I can't get enough of the strange hunger, and I am getting used to it taking over.

"Good girl," Orion says, kissing my temple. Thaddeus is watching us as he washes his hair. His wrist heals, and I let him go.

"Give her more," Thaddeus says, watching me carefully, like he is looking for something. "Ryland, come here," Thaddeus calls out. Ryland walks in, looking at Thaddeus.

"Watch her eyes; tell me if you notice anything," Thaddeus tells him. Thaddeus nods to Orion, and he bites his wrist, bringing it to my lips. I drink his blood; the strange hunger becomes stronger as I drink from him. I hear Ryland gasp and look at Thaddeus, concerned.

Orion pulls his wrist away, looking at them.

"How did we not notice that before?" Ryland asks.

Thaddeus shakes his head. "Hang on; I want to try something. Ryland, give her your blood," he says.

"What's wrong?" I ask, starting to worry something is wrong with our baby.

"Your eyes change only slightly, but they change; I thought I imagined it at first."

Orion stands in front of me, wanting to see for himself. Ryland bites into his wrist and I feel the hunger come back, but tenfold; I can smell his blood before he even puts his wrist out. I grab it, but I shock myself when I actually bite into him, a feral sound escapes me as his blood rushes into my mouth.

Ryland grunts as my teeth sink into his flesh. My nails dig into him as I hold his arm. I feel crazed, completely overwhelmed by the taste of his blood, like I can't get enough of it. Thaddeus pulls me back. His hands go to my face as he pries my lips apart, looking in my mouth. My eyes are not leaving Ryland's arm, which is still bleeding, and I can hear his pulse pumping the blood through his body.

Ryland looks shocked at what I did. Thaddeus looks concerned, and so does Orion. Ryland rinses his arm under the sink basin and the intoxicating smell fades. I shake my head, coming to my senses.

"What is it?" I ask as Thaddeus pulls my top lip up, looking at my teeth.

"What did you feel when you just bit him?" Thaddeus asks.

"Hunger. It was weird; my throat felt like it was on fire; his blood soothed it," I tell them.

"That's not possible," Ryland says, turning the shower off behind me and grabbing a towel.

"Orion has been giving her blood daily for nearly two months; it's not impossible either," Thaddeus says, wrapping my towel around me.

"Can it be the baby?" Orion asks, staring at my belly.

"Also, another possibility, or-"

"Or what?" I ask, worriedly.

"Or maybe that's why you have been sick. If you are slowly turning into a vampire, drinking Orion's blood wouldn't be giving you what you need. Vampires crave human blood, and other species, not their own species."

"But if we both give her blood, what happens when the baby is born?" Ryland asks because the idea was to turn me into a vampire the entire time, so how will that affect me if I have both their blood in my system? Will I still turn vampire? Or will I turn Lycan?

"If you don't, she will become weaker, and she will die," Thaddeus says.

"And if we do?"

"I don't know. Hopefully, she turns into a vampire; if not, she might become a Lycan, or both."

"Or both? Is that even possible?" I ask.

"I guess we will find out. I thought the baby was absorbing it, but you have been drinking a glass of it every day; it kind of makes sense that it would start to change you," Thaddeus says, handing me one of his shirts.

"If she turns Lycan, Thaddeus-"

"I know, Ryland," Thaddeus snaps at him.

"What? What is it?" I ask, concerned by how he says it.

"If you turn Lycan, Evie, every bone in your body will break simultaneously," Thaddeus answers, and my heart leaps at the thought.

"Not only that, but every nerve ending will also be on fire. There is a reason nobody turns Lycan voluntarily," Ryland says.

"Did that happen to both of you?" I ask, horrified. I know bone breaking is a thing, but Ryland looks at ease when he does it.

"It only hurts the first time you shift, and no, only to Ryland. I am a hybrid. I don't shift completely into a wolf; I shift, but it doesn't cause my bones to break. It still hurts and feels uncomfortable, but not like a Lycan shifting. Your spine needs to snap and readjust to turn into a werewolf; I remain in this form, just grow fur and claws, my face distorts like when I attacked you," Thaddeus answers.

"Call Amara and Bianca, see what they turn up," Orion says, pinching the bridge of his nose. He looks stressed, really stressed. I reach out to touch his arm, and he looks up, pulling me to him and wrapping his arms around me.

"I will be fine," I tell him, and he nods, kissing the top of my head.

CHAPTER
FIFTY-EIGHT

E velyn
The next week goes by quickly; I start to feel more like myself. Amara's herbs help, but so does drinking both Orion's and Ryland's blood. Though Ryland's, I crave, and I sometimes need help to stop.

Ryland doesn't seem to mind, but I can tell everyone is worried about what will happen when the baby arrives. Honestly, I am terrified of dying, too, yet more petrified of coming back as a Lycan. They have explained numerous times what will happen if I do, and each time, it scares me more, to the point I have now stopped asking.

Amara seems to think I don't have long left, so today, Thaddeus and Orion are heading into the city to get some things. Ryland made the baby a crib by hand and it took him three days until he would even allow me into the shed to see it. Imogen brought over some of Amara's and Thaddeus's old baby stuff that she hung onto, and we have made a nursery next to our room, though we all agree the baby will remain in her bassinet in our room until she sleeps through the night.

We still haven't come up with any baby girl names yet, even

though they scour over baby name books every night, trying to find one they like. I don't care what they name her. I am dreading the time I actually go into labor. I am quite content with her remaining in my belly, too scared for her to come out even though I am so big now I am also uncomfortable.

Walking downstairs, I go into the kitchen where Thaddeus is making lunch. He puts a plate on the counter for me with a salad sandwich. "Mayo?" I ask, and he nods.

"Yes, and barbecue sauce," he adds, knowing my strange salad craving. I take a bite, and he hands Ryland one without the barbecue sauce as he takes a seat beside me.

"Orion and I will head into the city soon; will you stay here with Ryland?" he asks.

I nod, chewing my sandwich. Thaddeus kisses my head, and Orion walks into the kitchen, leaning on the door. "Call us if you need us," he says to Ryland, and Ryland salutes him. I laugh, but Orion rolls his eyes and walks over to kiss mine and Ryland's heads.

"We better leave. I don't like her being here with only one of us for a night," Thaddeus says, grabbing a bag and tossing it over his shoulder.

"She will be fine; just go," Ryland says, waving them off. They both leave but not before sending me nervous glances. I feel good, yet I have this nagging feeling in the back of my head, like they shouldn't go, that something bad will happen. Ignoring it, I finish my sandwich.

"What's wrong?" Ryland asks after they leave.

"Nothing, I think I am just getting nervous," I tell him.

"That's understandable," he says, grabbing my empty plate. "Come on; we will watch a movie," he says, holding my hand. I let him lead me to the living room room, and we watch a movie. After the second movie, I hear the pitter-patter of rain on the roof and jump up, running for the laundry.

Ryland jumps up, alarmed. "What is it?" he asks, following me.

"The washing is on the clothes line."

"Leave it; we will get it later," he argues, but I ignore him, grabbing the basket and rushing out the door to the clothesline. I start pulling the clothes off the line, looking nervously at the darkening sky as night begins to fall. Storm clouds move across the sky when I see lightning. "Just leave it, Evelyn; you and your nesting is driving me nuts," he says but helps drag the clothes off.

We end up leaving half of them as they become too wet, and Ryland runs the baskets back inside while I waddle toward the house, my clothes damp and sticking to me as I shiver from the rain.

Ryland walks out when I hear a loud alarm go off, causing me to look toward the house when Ryland runs at me.

I stand there, shocked, wondering what he is doing when his body suddenly lands on me, knocking me to the ground on the wet grass. He makes a gurgling noise before I feel something hit him, knocking the air out of his lungs. Ryland rolls off me, and a sharp pain radiates through my stomach, making me scream. Ryland tries to get up when I realize he is covered in little red dots. My eyes snap to our surroundings but I can't see anything when Ryland's voice chokes out.

"Run," he chokes, coughing up blood.

He pulls on my arm, sitting me up, and I can hear people running through the trees and the dirt driveway. He stands up, and I see his shirt is soaked with blood. His pain radiates into me through the bond, and I don't understand how he is able to force himself up.

"Ryland!" I squeal, pressing my hand on his wound, trying to stem the bleeding.

"Run, now, Evelyn!" he screams just as I hear guns start going off everywhere. Ryland shoves me, and I hear the bullets whiz past me as I stumble, get up, and run, bolting for the tree line of the forest.

I hear Ryland groan loudly and then hear a ferocious growl ring out, echoing off the trees. I don't dare look back; instead, I concentrate on running without falling. My hand is trying to hold my belly as I move; pain runs through my stomach and groin with each step.

I see the tree line get closer, I can hear people yell and scream when I feel it; feel like I have been punched in the shoulder. Ignoring the pain, I keep running when I feel my muscles go funny, my body becomes weaker, and I feel something hit me again, but this time in the lower back, making me gasp as I clutch at it.

My hand comes in contact with something, and I pull it out to look at it. I can feel my surroundings become a green blur as I stare at the dart I have just pulled out of my back. The dart slips from my fingers, and I see the ground rush toward my face.

My entire body goes numb, and I feel my limbs become heavy before I hear voices, the voices getting closer and closer until they sound like they are right on top of me. "Got her, bring the other one," I hear a deep male voice call out.

I try to open my eyes, yet they feel too heavy; even breathing feels hard as I fight to take each breath. I feel movement, my head rolls back as someone grabs me.

"Ryland," I breathe. I try to talk, but the words come out slurred and muffled.

"Hurry, we need to get back before their mates get back here."

I feel the darkness creep in, black swallows my consciousness as I slip into oblivion.

Waking up, I find myself on the ground. The cold concrete floor makes my limbs ache. Sitting up, my eyes are blurry, and I can smell a strong smell that reminds me of chlorine. I gasp when I see Ryland braced to a wall by cuffs holding his arms to the wall. His body slumps over, and I can see blood pooling around him. I roll onto all fours, trying to crawl my way over to him. Each movement sends searing pain across my stomach that takes my breath.

"Ryland," I stammer, trying to breathe through the overwhelming pain. I am weak; I have to lay down on the cold ground. My limbs are unwilling to do what I need them to do. "Ryland," I ask again, my voice cracking and sore as I try to speak. I hear him groan, and I turn my head to see him move his head before he suddenly starts jerking his arms trying to free himself. The braces don't budge.

I notice his wrists bleeding, and I can't help the sob that leaves my lips at seeing him so badly injured.

"Silver," he mutters, his eyes going to me. "Don't cry; I am fine," he says, though I can feel he isn't fine through the bond. His pain radiates into me with my own. He looks around the room and starts coughing. Blood sprays out of his mouth onto the floor, and his breathing wheezes when I notice the wound on his chest pouring with blood.

"You're not healing," I tell him, and he coughs.

"Don't worry about me. Can you get over to me?" he sputters out, blood dribbling down his chin.

I try to get up, falling face-first into the concrete, my limbs feel like jelly, but after a few attempts, I crawl over to him, putting my head on his lap when I feel it.

My legs are becoming saturated, and I feel like I have wet myself. "No, no, not now," I cry.

Ryland looks down at me and gasps. "Shit, your water just broke," he coughs out, as he tries to free his arms but fails.

He starts screaming out for someone. I'm screaming, trying to get their attention when I hear footsteps on the ground behind the steel door. Pain moves across my abdomen, so sharp my body jerks when I feel my insides tear, and I let out a bloodcurdling scream of agony. Ryland is screaming out when the door suddenly opens.

"Help her; she is in labor. You need to let me out, or she will die."

"Nice try, Lycan," says a voice, but I am lost to the pain, unable to concentrate on anything but the agony I am in. I feel someone grab my arms and legs. I writhe in pain, as the pain rushes throughout my body when I hear a sickening crack; my ribs break, and I scream as I feel her move within me.

"Get her to the infirmary now!" I hear an unfamiliar female voice call out as I am placed on something cold and hard.

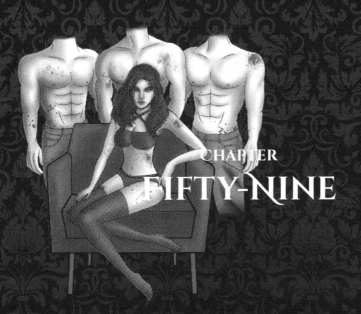

CHAPTER
FIFTY-NINE

Evelyn

    I can hear their voices around me, yet all I can see is darkness and the occasional flickering of lights above me. I know I am on some sort of trolley, feel the movement and jostle of the gurney they have me on, yet all I can think of is the pain. My insides are being ripped to shreds, and I have no control over it; my body jerks, and I can feel her savage movements as she tries to rip her way out of me.

"Hold her down," I hear a feminine voice yell before I feel gloved hands grip me. Panic courses through me as I try to thrash, unsuccessfully. I am choking on my blood, my lungs burn for air, and I am coughing uncontrollably as I feel warm liquid leave my mouth and run down my neck.

"Just cut it out; she is as good as dead anyway," I hear a male voice talking calmly, as if the very person they are effectively killing isn't lying and writhing in pain below them. The coldness seeps into my bones as I feel my life slowly draining from me.

"Once the baby is out, take it to the lab. I want its blood; then we need to move before its father comes looking for her."

"You are sure this is going to work?"

"He will come looking for her; then we will use her blood to kill him."

"What about the baby?"

"It's a monster. It will grow up to be exactly like its father. We only need its blood, then dispose of it."

My screams are dying out at their words as I focus on what they are saying and what they mean. I start thrashing, mustering any strength I have.

"I said hold her down. How is she still alive?" I hear the woman mutter, and then I feel something slash my stomach.

I feel the warmth of my blood run over the sides of my body as they cut me, yet all I can focus on is the sounds of my blood spattering on the floor, echoing loudly in my ears until I hear a shrill, high-pitched sound of a baby crying. Why am I not dead? I can still hear them, though the sound is becoming muffled, distant as I strain to hear; hear her cries, when suddenly, I feel no pain at all, just cold. Oh so cold as I listen to my heart thump one last time, the noise I will never forget: my dying gasp before I feel nothing.

Ryland

They take her away. They wheel her out as she lays writhing in agony. Her screams pierce my ears and heart as I watch on helplessly, thrashing against my restraints, and I can feel the silver bleed into my skin, my skin melting away under it.

I try to listen, but I am much too weak. I am unable to even focus on my surroundings long enough to focus on my hearing. Looking down, I am still losing blood, becoming weaker by the second as I pray my mates will get to her in time.

Amara's message rings loudly in my head, and the doom that

follows if I fail. I failed; I set a path toward a future that will be snuffed into existence. I feel my link to her grow weaker, weaker as the seconds tick by, and I know my mates can feel my failure.

My agonized scream echoes off the walls as I feel my teether to her snap painfully, like a hot poker is shoved into my chest, removing her soul as she dies. I can almost hear her last breath as I gasp. Tears burn my eyes, and I know I have failed. She is gone; our little mate is dead. They left her with me, trusted me with her, and I failed her.

Hearing footsteps outside the door, I look at it. The door opens, and a man in a lab coat walks in. He is young, only in his twenties, yet I can tell by the way he looks at me with pure hatred he has been raised a hunter, raised to despise anything that isn't human. His black glasses perch on his nose as he steps into the room.

He walks over, crouching in front of me. "I would say congratulations on your baby girl, but you will never see her. She is just a means to an end," he mocks.

I growl at him, thrashing, but he doesn't even flinch; he knows he has the upper hand in this situation. He knows I can't escape, and just to make sure, he pulls a syringe from his pocket. I identify the green liquid instantly as wolfsbane and brace myself for it.

He brushes his blonde mop of hair from his eyes. His hazel eyes glint wickedly. I thought Thaddeus was evil, but by the look in his eyes, this man is worse. They think we are monsters, yet he is here to get his jollies off over inflicting pain.

He stabs the needle into the bullet hole in my chest, squeezing the plunger as I feel the acidic liquid burn through my cells, gritting my teeth. He seems dissatisfied that he doesn't get the reaction he is hoping for; instead, he pulls a knife from his pocket. The blade glints under the dim light, casting shadows on the walls as he twirls it between his fingers.

"You think you're the higher beings of the earth. Little do you know you are just a pawn in our games. Thaddeus, your mate, will fall, and I will watch him die and gladly reap the rewards of being the world's hero," he says and pushes the blade into my stomach. The silver slices through my skin like a hot knife on butter and he twists it. His face contorts as he smiles, showing his teeth.

"You're all dead; every goddamn one of you," I spit at him, choking on my own blood.

"I don't think so," he says, as he turns and nods to the man standing guard at the door with a gun in his hand.

I hear the sound of a trolley and see another man in black armor push the gurney into the room, dripping with blood. He walks beside it, dumping the body wrapped in a sheet at my feet. Evelyn's limp, dead body falls to the ground with a thud; the sickening sound of her head hitting the concrete as she is dumped on the ground like garbage makes bile rise in my throat.

"Yet you react to her. What is so special about an insignificant human?" he asks, pulling the blade from my stomach and stabbing her in the chest. I thrash as I watch him mutilate her body, mutilate her face. The man in armor throws up on the ground near the door. The man in front of me looks at him over his shoulder and looks back at me, shaking his head in disgust. Tsk, Tsk, Tsk, he clicks his tongue. "Some don't have the stomach for this line of work," he states as he stands up.

"I will leave you with this," he says, kicking her body with his foot.

As he walks toward the door, I can't help it; I laugh. They have no idea what they have done or what is coming for them. The man in armor stares at me, yet I have tears rolling down my face from laughing. They talk of destroying him, yet he will destroy everyone and everything when he finds her, and he will find us. They have no idea what they have awoken, the hell that is about to rain down on everyone and everything.

They stop, staring back at me. The man in armor looks at his boss nervously.

"I would run if I were you. You have destroyed the last shred of his humanity. You have just awoken the devil. He will bring hell on earth for what you have done," I tell him as I break out into fits of laughter.

"Ignore him; fear does weird things to people," the man says, pushing the others toward the door and closing it while I continue to laugh. That's all I have left - the sick satisfaction of knowing Thaddeus is going to destroy them all, destroy all of us.

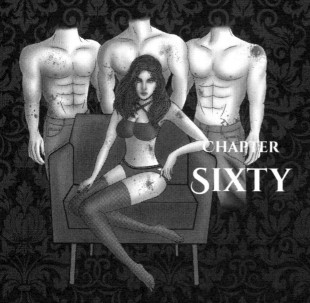

SIXTY

Thaddeus

Amara is the one who first alerts us; we are on our way back and have just stepped onto the busy main street when my phone starts ringing, making us stop. She utters one word like she has seen it seconds before she rings, seconds before agony tears through me.

"I'm on my way."

The phone is dead just as I am brought to my knees, and Orion, who is still walking, collapses violently in a heap. My veins feel like they are on fire as I feel Ryland's pain through the bond, taking my breath away. As I clutch at my shoulder, acid moves through my veins, engulfing everything in flames. Evelyn's fear hits us, pure panic kicking in, and I can feel that she is running. Feel her getting weaker as she, too, feels Ryland's pain and her own.

Orion is screaming on the ground, trying to put out the invisible flames consuming him while I try to breathe through it unsuccessfully. People wonder why two people are suddenly on the ground writhing in pain, yet I don't care; all I care about is getting to them.

Then, suddenly it stops, it stops just as quick as it starts. Orion's screams die out, and I roll onto my hands and knees, panting as anger courses through me and I stand up. People in the main street back up; the ground rumbles violently beneath my hands, the road cracks, along with the building around me as I feel the darkness trying to take over. But I need a clear mind, need to find them as I focus on them, focus on my mates.

Orion stands. Sweat coats his body and drenches his shirt, something I have never seen on him as he struggles to find his legs. My phone shattered on the ground from where it fell from my hand. Moving, I make my way to Orion, grab his arm, and haul him to his feet as his legs give way from under him.

"We need to move, come on," I gasp out, catching my breath. Frightened onlookers scatter as we stagger down the street and cars stop as we dart across the road and into their path.

"What did they use?" Orion coughs out, still trying to catch his breath.

"I have no idea, but whatever it is, it has to be ten times worse for Ryland."

"Evelyn?" he asks, his voice shaking with fear.

"The link severed," I tell him, knowing they must be unconscious.

We start running, forcing ourselves to move, heading home, praying we make it, and get to them in time. When we hit the concealed driveway, I get a burst of energy as the house comes into view. My Mother and Father, I can hear inside. The front door is thrown open while Amara comes running from the trees beside the house.

"They aren't here! I didn't get here in time," Amara says, fear on her face as her eyes scrutinize our surroundings.

"What did you see?" I ask, gripping her arms and shaking her as I force her to look at me.

"I saw Ryland fall. I knew something had happened, but then I lost it. I couldn't hold it, like they went unconscious," she says, shaking her head. I can tell she has been using her magic; her aura is weak. Weak like she has been overexerting herself, trying to see what happened.

"Head to Leven; they have to be at the facilities there," I tell them.

"Your fathers will check the military facility on the way," my mother says as I see them come out of the house. My father is trying to pick up any scents, but the place is clean. No scents at all, not even human scents, like they masked themselves somehow.

We race to the compound on the outskirts of Leven. Minutes feel like hours as we race to get to them in time, running past the sign bordering the town when I feel her wake. Evie's consciousness starts to wake, but it doesn't last long. By the time we get to the gated compound, I feel the bond break, feel her dying breath, and I snap.

A scream leaves my lips as I feel my soul shatter into a million pieces; the part of it that belongs to her dies with her. The ground moves in a wave as I approach the fence, feeling the volts of electricity ripple in the wire as I tear it apart with my hands. The barbed wire sticks to and catches on my clothes as I tear a hole through it; storm clouds brew violently as lightning sets the trees on fire.

She is dead; they killed her.

Raising my hands, I feel the darkness ebb and flow throughout my body, sickly sweet and sadistic. My eyes are bleeding black, and I feel the darkness consume me as I march toward the brick building on the hill. I hear horns blare when I am tackled to the ground.

Amara smacks me in the dead center of my chest, knocking me backward.

"Get off me," I scream, as I feel her trying to absorb my magic and take it from me, but they must pay. They must die for what they have done.

"You will bring the entire building down on them! Think, Thaddeus!" Amara shrieks.

"It doesn't matter if she is dead! She is fucking dead!" I scream at her, electrocuting her.

She growls as she is thrown off and Orion grabs my arms. I fling him off. The ground cracks in my anger.

"Your daughter is alive! You do this, you will kill her!" Amara screams, making me halt.

"You don't know that," I tell her, as my mother grabs my arm just as gun fire rings out.

We all duck for cover as I feel fire burn in my veins, igniting every cell in my body as it leaves my fingertips, lighting the surrounding buildings on fire. People run and scream as my fury takes over.

"I do! I can feel her! She isn't dead, and neither is Evelyn! You have been feeding her blood. They want you to walk in there. They will be expecting this!" Amara screams, trying to stop me as she blasts me with what little energy she has left, pinning me on the ground while chaos breaks loose.

They know we are here and are now getting ready as we fight with each other, wasting time.

"They are in there! You do this, you kill us all!" my mother says.

I can hear trucks leave the facility, making me look up. Armed vehicles leave in succession, barreling through the fences toward us. I watch my mother dig her hands into the ground and feel her energy leak out of her as the ground moves.

"You need to get me in there," I tell Amara.

"I can't! We could end up anywhere! I don't know what inside looks like! I can't just mist us in without seeing inside!"

The sound of metal on metal makes me look toward the four armored trucks as roots shoot from the ground, crushing the vehicles and bending them like paper origami. The entire place looks like a war zone as my mother uses her magic, wielding it like a weapon.

Orion moves quickly, killing anyone he comes across as well as those being thrown from the vehicles, while I am still stuck to the ground, held by the snares of Amara's magic.

"Let me up." She shakes her head. "I don't want to hurt you, but you give me no choice," I tell her as I let hellfire loose. The ground turns black as charcoal as it consumes everything in its path; a line heads straight for the facility that has my mates held hostage.

Her magic is wavering as she tries to hold it. She tries to stop me, but she is no match for me; her magic comes from life and needs the energy to empower and strengthen it. Mine is dark, mine comes from death, like a muscle it flexes. I am neither living or dead. Amara is life, and even she knows her power has its limits; mine doesn't need anything to draw off, whereas hers does. She gives a piece of her life essence to use hers, whereas mine takes from anything surrounding it, strengthening me, while hers weakens her.

"Thaddeus, you're killing her!" my mother screams.

"Tell her to let it go!"

"Amara, please!" my mother begs.

Sweat coats her face as she buries her hands further into the earth. Amara's magic dims, breaking under pressure, the entire ground turns black and burns. Everyone screams as the flames lick at them while I get to my feet. My mother is trying to stop the flames, creating a barrier, forcing my darkness around us, protecting them from burning along with the earth on which they stand.

"Get me in that building now," I tell my sister.

"We could end up anywhere, Thaddeus!"

"I don't care; just get me in there."

"It's a trap, Thaddeus!" Orion says, coming to my side, drenched in the blood of hunters, their fallen bodies lying on the grass and road everywhere, the smell of burning flesh and metal heavy in the air as I look around.

The entire place has gone silent except for the sound of the roller shutters closing on the entire building, blocking the entries and windows. The siren cuts off, and I know they are right, they want me to come in to get them. "You're right," I tell them.

Looking around, the entire place is a trap, and my mates and daughter are the bait. Orion lets out a breath, looking around for another point of entry.

"And that's why you're not going in there," I tell him. He looks back at me just as I snap his neck, his body falls limp against me as I catch him, sinking my teeth into his neck and draining his blood. I won't risk him; there is already enough on the line.

R yland
The first flicker of life is the twitching of her fingers. Her lacerations slowly close as our blood moves through her veins, closing and sealing every wound. I look around the room, trying to find something to free myself but only see concrete walls and a chain hanging from the ceiling in the middle of the room. The steel door is the only way out besides the grate in the ground that is much too small.

When I hear a predatory growl, my eyes are drawn to Evelyn on the floor, and I hear her heartbeat thump. Her body is trying to kick-start itself as I hear it again. It becomes steady, thumping in her chest as every cell in her body is awoken.

"That's it, baby. Wake up," I tell her, trying to nudge her with my foot.

She growls, the sound of a predator about to attack as her senses take over. I hear her sniff the air and see claws slip from her nail beds, tearing off her nails as she stretches her fingers. Yet, I don't hear bones snapping, don't hear agonized screams, nor does she smell like a vampire or Lycan, but something else, something close to her old scent, but slightly different. She isn't either, but both, and that becomes startlingly clear when her head snaps in my direction.

Her amber eyes stare back at me. Her lips curl over her top lip as fangs protrude, bloodlust takes over as her eyes scan the room and land on me. She sniffs the air, and I notice the crazed look on her face. I am the perfect prey, completely defenseless and at her mercy.

The bond reforms with renewed strength as she suddenly looks down, and I know she can feel it; feel it coming back. But it still isn't enough as she lunges at me. Her fangs sink into my necks and tear through my flesh. I let out a gurgled scream.

"Evie," I choke, struggling against my restraints as she starts draining me.

Footsteps outside make her pull her face away; her face snaps toward the door. "Focus on the noises," I tell her, trying to get her attention off me.

When the door opens suddenly, I see the man in armor race in, gun drawn. Shock registers on his gaunt face; his human blood is appealing to her more than mine as her attention goes solely to him, her head tilting to the side as she watches him.

His shock is wearing off as fight or flight kicks in; seeing her covered in my blood and her own, he tries to slam the door shut, but she is quicker as she lunges at him. Her legs wrap around him as he turns to run, her claws sink into his chest as he lets out a bloodcur-dling scream, his blood sprays across the walls as she sinks her teeth into him, her hands go through his chest as he staggers backward, back into the room as she drains him. The man goes limp under-neath her as she continues to rip him apart until he is left completely drained and in pieces.

Her eyes are clear of the haze as she realizes what she has done. His limbs rip from his body as it falls to pieces in her hands and she looks at them in pure horror. Evelyn kicks his body away from herself frantically, and I can hear the erratic beating of her heart.

"Look at me, love," I call to her.

Her head snaps up so quickly; if she were human, she would have

373

snapped her own neck. I watch the recognition register in her mind, her hands go to her belly before she starts clawing at herself, looking for our baby and the bump that is no longer there.

"Where is she? Where is she, Ryland?" Her voice breaks as she realizes she is no longer carrying our child.

"I don't know, but you need to get these braces off," I tell her.

Her eyes dart back to me as she gets up; within a blink of an eye, she has ripped them from the wall, the sound of metal hitting concrete sounds loud in this empty room. She hauls me to my feet, putting my arm over her shoulder as I lean heavily against her. The entire building starts to shake, the ground ripples under our feet, and we hear gunfire from outside.

"We need to find her before this building comes down," I tell her, as she half drags me toward the door, my breathing wheezing from the movement and the bullets lodged in my chest. She places me on the ground. "We need to move," I tell her when she suddenly holds her breath, tearing the front of my shirt.

I hiss as she digs her claws into my chest, pulling the razor-like bullets out. Green liquid oozes from the holes, down my chest, her fingertips sizzle as if acid was tipped on them. She grits her teeth, removing all five, her fingertips mutilated as the silver burns her flesh.

"We won't be getting anywhere with you like this," she says, and I realize she has been holding her breath the entire time as she draws a breath through her parted lips.

I can feel the wounds healing extremely slowly and can't heal around the wolfsbane that floods my system. She pulls me to my feet just as we are knocked to the ground when the building shakes again. Chunks of concrete fall from the roof around us, the lights flicker and swing as we make our way down the corridor to a door that leads to stairs, a green neon sign flickers above it saying exit.

Grabbing the railing, we make our way up, and I realize we are in some sort of basement. The entire place suddenly comes down around us. I feel my strength come back slowly but not fast enough, my wounds heal at an agonizingly slow pace. Evelyn's anxiety levels are peaking, and I can feel her mind is completely consumed with finding our daughter. When we reach a door, she lets go of me, hitting the door so hard it blows off the hinges, shattering to the ground as she starts going from door to door. I hear screams of people as she moves quickly from room to room; I stagger after her when a hole is blown in the side of the building, dust pours in, making the corridor fill with debris.

Reaching the first room, I notice the blood bath left in Evelyn's wake as she continues from room to room. I collapse as I feel the wolfsbane spread toward my heart, the bullets stopped its lethal spread, yet my body isn't healing fast enough to get rid of it now that they have been removed.

The loud bang of a gun going off makes me look in Evelyn's direction. Her body is flung against the wall when suddenly Amara appears in the corridor in front of me. Evelyn coughs, getting to her feet and spewing blood onto the floor.

Amara gasps as she vaporizes in front of me and appears next to Evelyn when we hear the faintest of cries. A woman steps out from behind a man coming out of the door behind him, our daughter clutched tightly in her arms. Evelyn lunges for her just as Amara touches her shoulder, and they disappear into thin air.

The man in the lab coat raises the shotgun, his eyes not leaving me as he uses the lip along the wall to walk across the hole in the floor, the floor breaking off under his weight as he presses his back close. The woman behind him looks at the gaping hole and looks to the room that is blown apart, trying to figure out how to get across, just as I hear the click and a bang sounds out.

My chest explodes in pain, sending me flying into the wall and along the floor. He reloads the gun as I try to get to my hands and feet, when I hear him scream for her to hurry up; the woman places my daughter on the ground and jumps across the gap, her foot slips on the loose rubble as she tumbles through the hole in the floor to the floor below. Her terrified scream echoes off the cracked rendered walls and then I hear a thud.

Blood is pouring from my mouth as I try to breathe while I drown in my own blood, when Thaddeus appears, jumping to the ledge from outside. His eyes go to our daughter next to his feet as he nearly steps on her; a menacing growl sounds throughout the entire building.

The walls shake and come down around us as the darkness consumes him. I watch the man fumble, falling on his ass as he takes a step back toward me. Thaddeus picks up the bundle of fabric covering our daughter when I hear the man laugh hysterically. Thaddeus' fingers zap with electricity when the man pulls a device from his lab coat.

"Either way, I win." He chuckles, looking toward the ceiling where I see cables running along the one side of the intact roof.

"Run!" I scream. Adrenaline pulses through me as I lunge toward the man; his deep, booming laugh reverberates loudly in my ears as Thaddeus registers what I said. He turns, jumps from the ledge and disappears out the hole in the wall. Everything moves slowly as I land on the man. His head is smashing against the concrete but not hard enough to knock him out when he speaks.

"My backup plan," he gasps out as he squeezes his hand into a fist, and I hear the click.

The entire building vibrates like an earthquake, deafening noise echoes as the entire building detonates, sounding like a freight train as I watch in horror as flames consume everything.

Overwhelmingly hot wind moves over me.

E velyn

Each room is empty, yet I can feel I am getting close, like a bond is tethering me to her, drawing me closer. Opening the next door, I find some scientists standing around some device. They jump as I burst through the door and leap into action, but the moment I think about it, I am on them, ripping them to pieces, draining them, and moving on to the next door. I can hear Ryland stagger through the hallway as I go from room to room until I'm knocked to the ground when the wall suddenly explodes next to me.

Debris hits my skin and slices me, but my focus is on her; I can feel her, which pushes me to keep moving through the pain and shock. Reaching the end door, I look back to see a hole in the floor from where the wall blew away and crashed through to the floor below.

Twisting the handle, I shove open the door to see a woman grabbing vials and shoving them in her pocket before snatching my baby from the table. My mind doesn't even register the other person in the room until it is too late, and I feel myself being knocked back.

My stomach feels like it is smothered in acid, the wind being knocked out of me as I am flung backward out of the room. I see a man walking towards me, a shotgun pointed at me as the woman uses him as a shield, hiding behind him. Her red hair sticks to her face as her head whips around, and she sees me on the floor.

Standing up, my stomach turns, and I projectile vomit on the ground, slipping on my own blood as I reach for the woman, wanting my baby. I feel a hand touch me and I feel motion like a stone is thrown in a pond, a ripple effect, the room disintegrates around me.

"My baby!" I scream, and I find myself outside.

Gun fire is ringing everywhere, and I have no idea how I got here. Jumping to my feet, I see Orion's body propped against a tree next to me. When I get to my feet, running across the field of dead bodies and blown apart trees and cars, I feel hands wrap around my waist, flinging me to the ground before being tackled and pinned.

"Thaddeus is getting them," Imogen's dirt-covered face hovers above mine. I know she is trying to reassure me.

Then I hear a groan, making me turn to see Orion coming to his senses and shaking his head. Imogen allows me to sit up, and I get to my feet. I can see a huge hole blown out the side of the brick building and a dark figure standing just inside the cavity. My eyes focus when I see them bend down to pick something up.

"Where is Amara?" Theo asks, looking around just as I feel the ground tremor like an earthquake and I'm being knocked backward by a gust of wind, seeing black as my head bounces off the ground from the force.

Sitting up, I rub my eyes filled with dirt to see the building has exploded, everything is on fire, and I hear the loudest screech as I start running toward the burning building as it starts to collapse in on itself.

Nothing but soul-shattering pain ripples over me, all-consuming pain as I reach the building. Ryland's agonized screams beneath the rubble rip my heart to pieces. The sounds of a baby's cry echoes around me as I try to find her. Trying to see her through the clouds of smoke billowing out, my ears ring when I see Thaddeus sit up. The cries get louder, pulling at my heart when I feel air blast past me, clearing the smoke until I hear things crash around.

"No, no, no!"

I hear her frantic screams as I find my feet, through the shock I see Orion, ripping pieces of concrete from the pile and tossing it as he digs through the wreckage. Tobias and Theo scrabble at the ground, channeling through it, while Imogen drops to her knees, clutching her stomach.

A heart-breaking hysterical scream tears out of her as she howls. As I run toward the remains, Thaddeus grabs my leg, nearly tripping me, and I look down to see my daughter cradled in his arms, covered in dirt and dust but unscathed. He pushes her toward me, and I grab her as he stands.

Thaddeus runs toward the crumpled structure and raises his

hands. Slabs of broken concrete, brick, and rubble move at rapid speed, being hurled into the fields and trees. Watching as the dust settles and my vision clears, I gasp as the air lodges in my throat.

I see them drop, Tobias and Theo fall to their knees, and Imogen's screams get louder. I stare in shock, not able to process what's happening when I see Orion pull Ryland off the ground, his entire body white with dust. As he sobs, relief hits me at seeing him when I feel a wave of air move through the trees as Thaddeus screams, clutching her limp body to his chest. She is unrecognizable by the dust and blood covering her body, but I have no doubt who it is by the sounds of the cries; the guttural cries of a parent losing their child; that soul-crushing pain as I look at Imogen's heartbroken face. Amara is gone, and I realize that is how I got outside, how Ryland is still alive; she sacrificed herself to save us.

Tears slip down my face as I watch Thaddeus clutch her body. Her head falls limp over his arm and her arms hang oddly as she lays limp. Tobias chokes on his sobs as he takes her from him, brushing her hair from her face and hugging her close like he can't bear to let go.

Imogen's cries go silent as he walks toward us and lays her next to Imogen. She clutches her daughter, rocking her back and forth, sobbing and humming. Her voice cracks, and all noise dies out except the sounds of her hums while she soothes her dead daughter like she can soothe away the pain of losing her.

Theo stands silently, staring off blankly, no emotion registering, like he just shuts down completely. I stare around, waiting to wake up from the nightmare we are trapped in. I'm praying I wake up, and this is all a dream my mind conjured up.

"She saved me," Ryland says, his voice breaking. Orion is the only thing holding him upright as he staggers forward.

Imogen looks up at him. Tears roll down her face in a steady stream, leaving tracks on her skin as they wash away the dust from her cheeks. "She saved us all," she whispers, and looks back down at Amara. Her thumb brushes her cheek.

Tobias takes Amara from Imogen, who clutches onto her, not wanting to let go of her. "Come on, hun, you need to let her go," he says, trying to take Amara from her, but she refuses to and shakes her head.

Thaddeus crouches down in front of his mother, grabbing her face and forcing her to look up at him. His eyes are watering as he fights against his own tumultuous emotions. He feels guilty, angry, every emotion ripples through him at war against the other. "You need to give her to me, ma; you need to let her go," he says, but Imogen shakes her head. "We need to take her home, ma; we can't stay here," he says, and I can feel him using his magic, see her eyes glaze over slightly as he nods to his father, who bends down, taking his daughter from his wife's arms. Imogen reluctantly lets go, staring at her now empty arms.

I look down as I feel a movement in my arms. My daughter sneezes and coughs; her little lips make a little O shape. Her faint cries make everyone look at the bundle in my arms as her face turns, searching for milk, searching for something as her mouth opens, sucking at air.

"She is hungry," Imogen says, making me look at her. Out of his daze, Theo steps closer, looking down at the baby in my arms.

She starts crying and I try to soothe her. Her cries get louder and fill the silence when Theo steps closer, his arms outstretched, wanting to take her. I stand, passing her to him, and he dusts off his hands on his pants before cradling her in his arms.

"We should head home; she will be hungry, and you won't have milk now that you're no longer human," Theo says, making me remember I also died, but came back.

Looking at Amara, I feel my heart palpitate, survivors guilt kicks in. I realize it isn't my guilt, but Ryland's, as he is staring at Amara in her father's arms. Imogen turns and flees; I hear that she is running toward our house and away from the destruction.

"Can we run with her?" I ask, worried, remembering how sick I always felt running while human.

Theo nods. "Yes, in short bursts. Bianca ran with Thaddeus when she kidnapped him," Theo says, and I look to my daughter who is suckling on his knuckle, knowing that's why she has gone quiet.

"Bianca did what?" I ask, confused by his words.

"It's a long story; one for later," Thaddeus says as he grabs Amara from his father. I notice Theo looks away like he can't see his daughter like that, like he doesn't want to remember her that way. I hear bones snap and see Tobias shift into a black wolf, taking off after his wife.

"I will take Ryland," Theo says, passing my daughter back and trading places with Orion, who still has a tight grip on Ryland's arms. Thaddeus takes off, leaving only Orion, Ryland, Theo, and myself.

I look down at our baby and pass her to Orion. "I am scared I will drop her," I tell him, and he takes her, his hand holding the back of her little head as he tucks her inside his shirt against his chest.

"Let's go home," Theo says, looking at what's left of the building and burning surroundings. I can hear sirens in the distance getting closer, see the flickering of the blue and red lights coming from the town.

CHAPTER
SIXTY-TWO

Evelyn
    I can't understand; nothing to me makes sense. I just can't fathom something as tragic as this happening to her. Never, in my wildest dreams, could I picture Amara being gone. It doesn't feel real, like a bad dream I am yet to wake up from.

When we get home, Thaddeus is nowhere to be seen, yet I can feel his heartbreak, his guilt. Nothing compares to the agony of his tortured soul. No amount of pain I have ever endured measures up to the feelings that swirl within him.

"What's taking him so long?" Imogen says while pacing around the living room.

Her tears look like they are permanently etched into her grief-stricken face. Looking at my daughter squirming in my arms, I can't imagine the heartache she is feeling. I have only been a mother for a few hours and know without a doubt I will lay my life down without hesitation for the baby in my arms. I will give up everything and everyone for her in a heartbeat.

"He will bring her back, love," Tobias whispers, pulling on a pair of pants Orion has handed him.

Theo stands staring out the window, lost in his thoughts. The air in the room is cold and empty despite being overcrowded. There is nothing but silence as we all wait for someone to wake us from this nightmare that I feel we are forever trapped in.

Ryland is sitting on the bottom of the steps, his guilt gnawing at me as I look over at him. Orion keeps giving him worried looks and approaches him. His wounds still aren't healing, blood drips onto the floor and stains it. The smell of his blood has lost all appeal to me; I am numb with shock.

The shrieking of our daughter's cries is the only noise to be heard when Orion walks over, holding his arms out, and I place her in them. He walks into the kitchen, and I hear him rummaging around for formula to feed her hungry belly.

Moving over to Ryland, I grip his arm, pulling him to his feet but he shakes me off. My temper flares at seeing him wallow in guilt. I understand his pain, yet she didn't die saving him for him to drop dead from his stubbornness.

"Amara didn't give up her life for you to bleed out on the floor. Now get up," I snap, my voice harsher than I intended as I try to contain my emotions. Imogen and Tobias' heads snap over to me, where I stand at his feet.

"Evelyn is right, dear; no one else needs to lose their life today," Imogen says, her voice shaking as she walks over to him and grabs his face, forcing him to look up at her. How she holds it together and doesn't blame him is beyond me. I wish I could be as soothing as she is despite how much she has endured today. "Amara wouldn't want you in pain; let your mate help you."

"She died for me, Ma; I can't live with that," he whispers, and places his head in his hands and starts crying. His body heaves as his words reverberate around the room, hitting him harder at the realization.

"I have lost one child already; I won't lose another. Now, get up and get cleaned up while we wait for Thaddeus to return," she tells him.

Orion walks back out with our daughter in his arms; I can hear her hungrily slurping on her bottle, gulping it down. Imogen looks over at him.

"Don't let her gulp it; she will bring it back up," Imogen says, and no sooner than she says it, she spews over the front of the blanket she is wrapped in. Orion stares down at her, his face worried as Theo walks over to him.

"Here, I will feed her. Hun, go find her some clothes and a diaper. Orion, go help Evelyn with Ryland," Theo orders.

Orion hands our daughter over, grabs Ryland, forces him to his feet, and hauls him up the stairs. Tobias and Imogen follow, but turn into the nursery, and I can see they need the distraction over everything that has happened; something to distract them from the pain. That is our daughter, but I'm not going to say no to them; they know what they are doing more than any of us.

Turning the shower on, Orion helps me strip off Ryland, and I push him in the shower, but he stands there, staring off at the tiled wall.

"I broke him," Ryland says, making me look at him, and I realize he is talking about Thaddeus, whose emotions are so strong that they are almost suffocating us.

"He just needs time. She was his sister," Orion whispers, and I notice he, too, is trying to keep himself together; he is just better at hiding his true feelings.

"I just don't understand how it's possible; aren't you all immortal?" I ask, hating that I can't understand any of this; maybe understanding would make it easier.

"She burned herself out. She used all of it when the bomb went off. After it went off, I couldn't understand why I wasn't burning until I looked up and saw her standing there taking it all, absorbing it, so it didn't touch me." Ryland chokes, and collapses on the ground in a heap, his head goes to his knees as sobs wrack his body.

"Amara's magic is tied to her immortality; Thaddeus' isn't. His is different. Like mine, it has a life force of its own; Amara's burned out, and so did she," Imogen says, leaning against the door frame. Guilt hits me that she overheard us talking. She must have read it on my face as she shakes her head, her eyes teary. "It's okay, Evie; I know you have questions. As sick as it sounds, I am all too familiar with death. I just wasn't expecting it to be my own daughter's," she says, looking up at the ceiling, willing her tears to go. "This is going to destroy him," she says, shaking her head, and I realize she is good at shoving her emotions back now that she is over her initial shock. She is stronger than I ever could be if our roles are reversed; I would prefer death than to be without my child.

Imogen's phone rings and she glances down at it in her hand; a hiccuped sob leaves her lips. "I need to take this; it's my sister," she says, and I can hear the unspoken emotion she is trying to hide as she continues to look at the screen. She answers it but says nothing as she looks to the ceiling, fanning her eyes with her other hand, taking a deep breath.

"Hey, sis," is all she says as she struggles to find the words to tell her sister her niece is gone. Imogen walks out, leaving us.

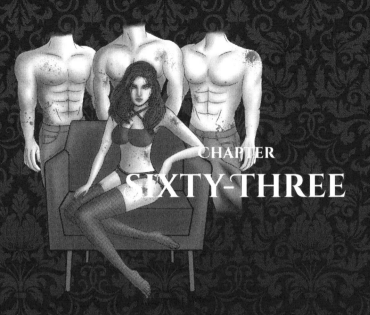

CHAPTER
SIXTY-THREE

Thaddeus

I run.

I don't know what else to do. My little sister is lying limp in my arms as I cradle her. Her bubbly, carefree, happy self is no longer with us. She saved him, gave her own life to save my mate because she knew I couldn't live without him.

But how does she expect me to live without her? She is my baby sister, we fight and bicker, but at the end of the day, she is always there. She is my first friend, and was my only friend growing up. We are each other's rock. She knows all my secrets, and I know she will keep them safe; nothing I ever do is unforgivable to her. She loves me despite my many flaws, despite the pain I cause her, she still loves me; loves me enough to throw her life away for me.

I sit on the mountain with her, which overlooks my home. My parents are there with my daughter and my mates, yet I can't bear to see the heartbreak on their faces. How do I face them, knowing I am the reason for her death? All my mistakes and grievances are coming back to haunt them and me, yet my sister paid the ultimate price.

A price that is for only me to take. I sit her on my lap; life is drained from her face, and gold veins litter her skin from where her magic bled out of her. She shouldn't have to pay for my sins; none of them should have to.

My mother, though, is the one I worry about having to face; how can she ever love me after knowing I am the reason for the death of the one child that is actually good, pure within herself?

Things can't end this way; I can't live with this void, forever lingering and haunting me for the rest of my life; live with the knowledge that she died for me; live without her. I will give it up for them. Before, I couldn't see how much damage I was causing, stuck within myself. It is selfish. It is selfish to think I could control the very thing my mother and Astral tried to protect the world from; I now know that none of it is worth losing her or my family over.

For the first time, my mind is clear; the usual ramblings of the darkness creeping over me are now nothing but distant whispers of my insanity. Now, I have found a new purpose, a reason to give it up and not just for Amara.

I am unwilling to lose anyone else to it, not my family and not my daughter. Nothing is more important than her, not even my mates, and for her, I will give it up. It is like trading my unstable insanity for a new sense of clarity, and it gives me a new will to live, only it is too late for my sister. But I can do this one thing for her. Nothing has felt righter than this decision because I made it myself.

Pulling my phone from my pocket, I look up my Aunt's phone number and dial it.

I wait.

Excitement bubbles within me as I hope for the best. It's something I haven't held onto for the longest of times. The phone rings a few times until she finally picks it up and answers.

"Thaddeus?" she asks, not hiding her shock.

"Have you still got Astral's grimoires?" I ask.

I just need to check one thing before proceeding; make sure I am correct, because I can't have the darkness taint my little sister; she won't be able to live with it.

"Yes, but you don't need them; I know them word for word. What happened?" she asks as concern laces her words.

"Say someone dies, and I use my magic to bring them back. Will it taint them or just disintegrate when it hasn't got a host to feed off?"

"What are you talking about, Thaddeus? Who died?"

"It doesn't matter because I am bringing them back. Will it taint her or disintegrate back to the realm it came from?"

"It should disintegrate. What are you doing? Who died?" Her frantic voice screeches through the phone. "Thaddeus, I swear if you hurt Evelyn, I will kill you myself!" my aunt screams at me.

"It's not Evelyn, Aunty B," I tell her. I can't leave her wondering.

"Who?"

"It's Mara," I tell her, using my sister's nickname, which I used when I couldn't pronounce her name properly when I was a boy.

I hear her gasp; a hiccuped sob leaves her. I wait, giving her a chance to register what I said, let it sink in. When she suddenly gasps loudly, I hear her rummaging around and hear the faint flicking of pages turning.

"I thought you said you knew it off your head?" I ask, suddenly worried.

"How did she die?" she asks, her voice rushed.

"She burnt herself out; she used all her magic," I tell her. The thought saddens me because to do that would have been extremely painful. It's not like overusing a muscle; it's like losing part of your soul, feeling the life sucking out of you.

"You don't have to give your magic up, Thaddeus. You just need to jump-start hers," she says.

"What?" I ask, now confused.

"You need to jump-start her like a battery. Amara isn't dead; she is like a petrified piece of wood or a drained vampire. She needs the energy to make power, energy for energy, a jump start," she says, and I feel hope bubble up within me. I hang up.

I have two options: give up my magic and awake her with necromancy or boost her. Laying her on the ground, I try the better alternative first. Placing my hands on her chest, I let my magic cascade over me, sickly sweet and cold, my eyes bleed black, veins of liquid darkness spread over my body, moving towards my hands where I let it build up; build until I can feel it vibrating over my palms. The sadistic whispers become louder, trying to feed off her remains, but I ignore them, focusing solely on her, not letting them creep back in, not letting it take over as they call out for me.

The sky darkens as storm clouds roll across the sky, thick and heavy; the air feels electrified as I channel the energy around me; the ground shakes beneath us. I see lightning whip and crack across the sky, angry and relentless, fueled by my magic as I continue to let it feed off the storm I brew, off the energy as it zaps through the sky. Then, I let it go, sending it straight into her. The ground turns black beneath her as it blasts straight through her chest and into the ground. The air thickens, and I can smell the burning, acrid smell of my dark magic as it blasts the earth before my magic decays into the earth beneath me.

I wait, listening for any sounds of life within her, feeling for the gold flecks of her aura, but get nothing, just silence and the sound of the raging storm above my head made by my tumultuous emotions. Minutes feel like hours as I wait. I decide to give it one more go before trying the other way, but nothing happens.

Pressing my hands to her chest again, I feel for sickly sweet power of my magic, letting it build when I hear it.

Thump.

Then nothing. Shaking my head, I am about to draw energy when I hear it again. It makes me stop, wondering if I imagine it when I feel her heart bump in her chest. Rhythm picks up as it turns into fluttering, sounding like that of a hummingbird's wings as it picks up speed.

Tears slip down my face when I realize she is alive. I can feel her heart beat beneath my hands. She suddenly gasps for air, her eyes fly open. She's bleary-eyed before life returns to them. She smiles, her hands go to mine as a strange look crosses her face. She looks down at my hands and her eyes dart to mine.

"Oi, hands off the merchandise; what's wrong with you? I am your sister," she says, shoving my hands off her, appalled they are on her chest.

I am too stunned to care about what she just said; instead, I grab her and crush her against my chest while she smacks at me. Amara tries to escape my death grip on her but then she suddenly relaxes and hugs me back. "God, I am so glad to have your annoying, whiny, bitchy ass back," I tell her, kissing her head.

"Get those filthy lips off me. I know you suck cock with those lips," she says, rubbing her forehead with her hand. "Thank you," she adds, resting her head against me, and I pat the side of her face with my hand as we watch the storm dissipate.

Relief floods me as she loops her arm through mine. "I need your help with something," I tell her, and she nods, looking up at me.

"You're doing the right thing," she tells me, already knowing what I have in mind.

"I should have done it years ago," I admit.

"Better late than never," she says, pulling her necklace from around her neck and holding her hands out to me. "Before we do this, I just thought I should tell you something, because I am your favorite sister."

"You're my only sister," I deadpan.

"Exactly, therefore, the favorite. And Amara makes an excellent name for my niece, don't you think?" She grins.

"No," I tell her. This girl doesn't have a serious bone in her body, does she?

"I like Amara. Come on, brother, it has a nice ring to it," she says, bouncing on her feet.

I shake my head, and she gets on her knees, begging, clasping her hands together and looking at me with the most deranged puppy dog eyes, making me raise an eyebrow at her. "Middle name, and that's it," I groan.

"Deal," she says, jumping up and grabbing my hands, a triumphant grin on her face like she just won the lottery. "Ready?" she asks. I let out a breath...

...and nod.

E velyn

Imogen has been pacing in the living room again. Something has made her nervous after her sister called. She won't say anything, but something has changed. Her tears stop as she nervously paces in front of the door, jumping at every noise she hears.

Ryland's wounds finally heal after he manages to wash the majority of the poison from them. Orion is staring off into space when I feel Thaddeus' mood switch, making Ryland look over at me, obviously feeling it too. Relief and happiness radiates out of him and into us.

Theo and Tobias are sitting on the couch, watching the fire crackle, completely silent. My daughter lays on Tobias' chest as he rubs her little back. Time seems to move so slowly, agonizingly slow, as we wait for Thaddeus to return to us.

Thaddeus' sudden shift in mood is alarming; one minute, he is almost happy; the next, I feel the tendrils of darkness flood into him, so thick that it makes my heart race faster. We can hear the storm brewing outside, and I have no doubt it is from him. What is he doing that he is using his magic? Has he officially lost it? Did he break, as Ryland said?

I can't understand the shift, but my anxiety is through the roof as I watch lightning light up the sky outside. Ryland gets up, pacing along with Imogen.

After a while, I no longer feel anything from Thaddeus, like he is suddenly blocking us out. That is almost worse. He cloaks himself and shuts off his emotions like a switch, leaving me with nothing to go on. Worry claws at my insides when my daughter suddenly starts crying, the lights flicker as she shrieks.

Tobias rocks her, trying to get her to calm down. Everyone freezes as we watch the power in the house surge until she suddenly quiets. A few minutes pass and the sound of the front door opening makes everyone look toward it.

Thaddeus walks in, and Imogen sobs in relief, throwing herself at him and embracing him in a hug.

"Thank goodness you're okay," she says, and I can feel his shock as he hugs her back. He is a wreck, his clothes all ruffled, yet he is unusually calm. Tobias and Theo get up and Thaddeus' eyes snap to the little bundle in his father's arms; his eyes tear up at the sight of her.

"Where is Amara? Where did you put her?" Theo asks, worried, and I realize she isn't with him, she isn't in his arms anymore; what did he do with her body?

"Didn't think you could kill me off that easily, did you?" her voice says behind us, making us all jump.

Ryland's head turns in her direction and a strangled noise leaves his lips as he charges at her. Scooping her up and squeezing her as he crushes her against his chest, relief courses through him at seeing her. His guilt moves to the back of his mind; it is still there, but now overshadowed by his immense relief.

"Amara?" Theo and Tobias say at the same time, as everyone runs toward her.

I stand shocked, looking at Thaddeus, who has a silly grin on his face; happiness radiates out of him as they all hug her.

"Now, where is this niece of mine? Hand her over," I hear Amara demand as she takes her from Tobias. "Isn't she the sweetest thing?" Amara coos. "Hi, baby girl," she says, kissing the top of her little head.

I rest my head against Thaddeus' chest, and he wraps his arm around my shoulders.

"You brought her back," Ryland says, turning around and looking at Thaddeus. He nods but says nothing, too busy watching his parents fuss over Amara and the baby.

Ryland walks over to him, and Thaddeus pecks him on the lips and hugs him. "I never blamed you," is all Thaddeus says, and Ryland nods, hugging him back, resting his head on Thaddeus' shoulder while Thaddeus rubs his back.

Amara passes our daughter to Orion; we really need to come up with a name for her besides 'the baby'. Tobias and Theo walk over, hugging Thaddeus with tears in their eyes.

"Thank you," Tobias says, squeezing him.

I step out of their way, moving toward Amara. She brings me into a hug, squeezing the air from my lungs. "I will be the best aunty," she tells me, and I nod.

"You're the only aunty; hard to compare," Thaddeus taunts her.

"Don't forget our deal, brother," she retorts, and he rolls his eyes.

"What deal?" I ask, confused.

"Doesn't matter. Here, Ma," Thaddeus says, holding out his hand to her.

Amara nudges me with her elbow, motioning toward Imogen, and I watch as his mother approaches him and Thaddeus hands her something. Imogen gasps, and I realize it's a necklace. "You're really giving it up?" she asks, and I try to figure out what she is talking about.

"Yes. Do what you want with it," he says, and I look at Amara, who has a huge grin on her face.

"What is it?" I ask. Then recognition hits me, and I cover my mouth. No wonder he seems so calm; I can't feel it, feel the darkness writhing through him. "Your magic?" I ask, and Thaddeus nods as I throw myself at him, wrapping my legs around his waist, hugging him tightly. Orion hands our daughter over to Theo as he and Ryland tackle us, making us all crash to the ground in a heap.

"No need to make a big deal out of it," Thaddeus growls, and I can feel he is a little embarrassed.

"So, about this name. I am telling you Amara is perfect. Look at her, she is exactly like me, perfection in a small bundle," Amara says, looking down at us.

"I said middle name only," Thaddeus growls.

"She said, he said, she said; Amara is perfect," Amara says, and I climb off Thaddeus, who is currently crushed beneath us.

"I'm not calling her Amara; we will come up with a name," he says.

"Come on, brother, look at her; isn't she the cutest, like me?" Amara says, holding our daughter closer.

"No. Middle name, and that's it," Thaddeus tells her, making me chuckle.

Amara pouts, giving him the evil eye and walking over to hand our daughter to Theo. We all sit up and find Imogen has placed the necklace around her neck for safekeeping.

"You are doing the right thing," Imogen tells him as she hugs him. He pats his mother awkwardly on the back as I realize he is starting to choke up; she gently rubs his face. "I love you, son. Always have, always will," she tells him, and he nods, falling silent.

"Coffee?" I ask everyone, knowing Thaddeus wants the spotlight off him. Ryland nods, walking into the kitchen.

Theo and Tobias get up and shake their heads at Amara's pouting, as they turn to us. "No, we should let you settle in with your daughter. We will come back in a few days," Theo says, handing our baby to Thaddeus.

I am a little sad to see them go, but I can tell they want to get

Amara home and to the safety of their house, and give us time to ourselves. I don't know what to do when they leave.

"What a day," Orion says, sitting on the couch next to me. He pulls me on his lap. Thaddeus sits just staring at our daughter on his lap, playing with her little hands.

"Why did you do it?" I ask him, and Thaddeus looks over at me.

"For her," he says, looking back down at her. She looks tiny in his arms as she squirms. Imogen has put her in a pink onesie and matching beanie. Ryland brings out coffee for everyone, placing it on the coffee table and sitting next to Thaddeus, looking at our daughter in awe.

"She is so tiny. I can't believe we made that," Ryland says, looking at Thaddeus.

He pulls me off Orion and onto his lap. I rub his stubble with my hand, and he softly pecks my lips. Thaddeus leans in and kisses me as Orion rushes over to take our daughter from him and walks upstairs to put her down now that she has fallen asleep again.

Thaddeus' tongue traces my bottom lip as he grips my hips and pulls me on his lap, his hand cupping the side of my face as he deepens the kiss. Orion returns, and I feel his hands remove my shirt, pulling it off me. His hands go to my breasts from behind; they no longer feel cold to me. Thaddeus turns to kiss Ryland. I watch as his tongue slips into his mouth and arousal hits me at the sight of them. Orion grips my chin from behind, forcing me to look at him as he kisses me. Reaching up, my hand slips into his hair, and I feel Thaddeus' lips go to my nipple. Ryland's hand moves to the other. Orion releases me as Thaddeus kisses me and pulls back.

"I love you; love all of you," he says, pressing his face into my neck. "Everything I need is here with you. All I need is our family," Thaddeus whispers.

SIXTY-FIVE

One year later
Thaddeus

She got the damn name, my sister managed to sink her claws into Evelyn and Ryland. And honestly, I am sure Ryland would have let her name our daughter whatever outlandish name she could conjure up.

Today is one year since she was born, one year since my sister died and returned to us, one year since I gave up my magic, and one year since our lives truly began. Everything is good and right in the world. Well, as right as it can be anyway.

No more news reports have crossed the nightly news of the Dark Ones, no more fear and hysteria surrounding us. I miss it sometimes, miss my magic, but they always manage to bring me out of the darkest parts of my mind, remind me of why I did it, remind me of what I have gained in return.

I always thought I never needed anyone, never needed anything, that fear was all I sought, when what I truly sought was bigger than that, bigger than myself. No, what I truly craved was a sense of belonging, my place in the world, and that place was with my family all along, with my mates.

Evelyn showed me a life I never knew I wanted before, one I needed. I used to think I was all-powerful and mighty before her, and had control of the world in my sadistic hands. Thought that I was the strongest out there, when in reality, her forgiveness and compassion and everything she endured at my hands was stronger than me. Still, she forgave me and proved she was the stronger one; I always thought forgiveness and mercy were weak, but that is where I was wrong; forgiveness isn't about being weak. It's about showing you everything has no control over you, not how someone makes you feel, not what they do; forgiveness can only be given by those who truly know themselves; it is given not because they think they should give it but because that's how they move on with their lives, showing they truly have control of their life.

Evelyn forgave me for my past sins, and once she did, I forgave myself for my misdeeds and apologized for my wrongs. She gave me the sort of freedom that comes from forgiveness, and being forgiven is liberating. And that is when I realized what truly matters. Looking at my daughter, Amara Emery Madden-Kane, I realized this is what matters: protecting her from the world.

Loving her taught me to love myself.

Although, I do feel sorry for her when she starts school and has to spell that mouthful of a name. I shake my head at the thought; we should have called her Amara Alphabet.

I know her happiness is all that matters to me now, and I can't wait for our son to be born in the spring as our little family is blossoming.

Amara luckily inherited my sister's magic. My boy, though, is yet to be determined, and I now understand why my mother took my magic when I was a baby. Evelyn's mood swings are worse with this pregnancy, and her bloodlust is a force to reckon with.

She surprisingly adjusted to being a hybrid quite well. She has managed not to kill anyone since she left the hunters' facility.

Though, sometimes she gets these urges to kill and hurt people, she always fights them. It's in a vampire's nature to kill; her being hybrid means she gets the Lycan temper to fight against, too. Lana, her friend, is staying with my aunt. Lana has struggled deeply, she is almost uncontrollable, and Evelyn took it hard when we told her we have no choice but to keep her locked up until she can control herself or we may have no choice but to kill her.

Evelyn, in the end, chose to have her locked up and visits her every month. Now that she is getting so far along, though, she probably won't see her until after the baby is born. He is a mystery; Amara says it feels like he has dark and light magic, a mixture of both. None of us know what that means, but we will do what is necessary when the time comes. It seems the male gene tends to have a darker, more sinister side to their magic.

Grabbing my daughter's birthday cake, I walk outside towards her cheeky angelic face, my entire family gathering around as we all start singing to her. She claps her hands excitedly, wriggling in her seat as I place it on the table, making sure to cup my hands around the flames, so they don't blow out on her.

"Dadda, Dadda, up," she says, holding her arms out for Orion to pick her up.

We thought it would be confusing for her to have three dads and only one mom, but I honestly don't think she notices she is different from other kids. I watch as she blows out her candles. My mother helps start cutting the cake while I wrap my arms around Evelyn's growing belly as she sits on Ryland's lap.

Rubbing her belly, I can feel him moving around and hear his little heart thumping within her. Evelyn looks up at me with a smile on her glowing face. I kiss her softly and her hands find their way into my hair, deepening the kiss.

"Get a room!" Amara screams over at us, and I pull back, chuckling.

"You wait until you find your mate; you won't be able to keep your hands off them either," I tell her, and she shakes her head.

"Nope, don't need one; I am content with my player ways," she says.

"I can't wait till you find your mate. I hope it's a man too," I tell her, and she looks appalled, disgusted even, as she scrunches up her face.

"Eww, don't even say that! No cock is coming near these lips," she says, making kissy faces like Evelyn.

I growl at her, and Evelyn chuckles. I know she would never, but my sister does fancy her, and she only does it to piss me off. "Huh, Evie? I reckon I could show you a better time than my brother," she says, sending her a wink.

"I don't doubt that for a second," Evelyn says, making me huff.

"Got yourself a little competition there, brother," Amara retorts, and Ryland growls at Amara.

At the same time, Orion, who is used to our bickering, rolls his eyes as he passes Amara to, well, Amara.

"Hey there, my princess. Aunty got something for you," she says, walking off to the table with the presents.

"You know she is only playing," Evelyn tells Ryland and me.

"She isn't playing; she likes you, has always liked you, but I know she would never act on it," I tell her, and I watch Evelyn's brows furrow in confusion. She appears to be blind to Amara's affection, thinking she is just mucking around. She doesn't truly understand Amara isn't just mucking around. I sigh and shake my head.

My grandfather comes over to me. "Will you be back at work tomorrow?" he asks, looking up at me.

"Yes, Orion is coming with me. Is the council meeting still going ahead?" My grandfather nods; he is head of the newly reformed council. I am now on the board with Orion, much to my shock, and I actually enjoy it.

I never thought I would see the day when I enjoyed community events and management. Ryland works with my fathers and Amara. The business is booming, and Evelyn, when she can, works at the cafe she now owns with my mother, seeing as she has been waitressing and managing that café she worked at. She wanted something to do, so we helped her open her cafe. She has a few employees that work there now that she can no longer work every day, but she still loves it.

"Make sure you are early tomorrow, then. Bianca wants to show you around the new council chambers we built," he tells me, and I nod. He pats me on the back, going back to my grandmother.

"You're going back tomorrow?" Evelyn asks, looking up at me. Her sadness hits me through the bond. Her emotions are all over the place with this pregnancy; she is more clingy and doesn't like being on her own. I think she is scared after the last time, scared of being by herself when the baby comes.

"You can come to work with me, love," Ryland says, kissing the side of her mouth. She sighs, wrapping her arms around his neck and pressing her face into his neck, inhaling his scent.

Her bloodlust hits me as she suddenly moves at an alarming speed, jumping off his lap. I blink to find her now sitting on the steps, away from everyone, trying to control herself. Her marking Ryland was a nightmare, we literally had to pry her off him. A shiver runs down my spine at the memory; she almost killed him, and to this day she still apologizes over it.

"She can feed in front of us; none of us care," my mother says, and Ryland chuckles, making my mother and fathers look at him.

"Believe me, you don't want to see that, Ma," Ryland tells her, and she squeezes her eyebrows together.

My father understands instantly but it takes a moment for mom and once she understands too, she gasps. "Oh right, yes, definitely don't need to see those parts of my sons and daughter," she blurts when she realizes Evelyn wouldn't just feed on him. "Some things are best behind closed doors, away from my ears, thank you," mom says, and my father chuckles as Amara sings out.

"You should take your own advice, mom! Some things your daughter doesn't like to hear, too."

"You shush! Why are you even listening?" my mother snaps at her.

"Bit hard not to when you're screaming their names," Amara retorts; my mother growls and Amara takes off, laughing as my mother hunts her down.

"Wouldn't be a family get-together if Amara didn't piss at least one person off with that witty mouth of hers," my father says.

"Like mother, like daughter," says Orion walking over with Amara in his arms. She reaches for me, and I take her from him, kissing her chubby cheek as she plays with the toy Amara got her.

"Pop-pop," she says, showing them her robotic dog.

My father, Theo, brushes her dark curls behind her ear as she shows them her toy. She looks like Evelyn, and is gentle like Evelyn. She is the sweetest little girl and is loved by everyone.

"I'm going to start the grill," Ryland says and kisses our daughter's head.

My grandfather follows him. "I will help. Caroline, dear, can you help Evelyn get the table set?" he calls out, looking for her.

"Already on it," my grandmother sings out, and I can see Evelyn, my mother, and her through the window grabbing all the food they have prepared to bring out to the table.

This is life. Everything falls into place, and I couldn't be happier with the way everything turned out as I watch my family laugh and taunt each other as everyone is having fun. This is what it is to be part of a family; this is happiness.

This is pure bliss.

Authors I Suggest

Authors I suggest.

Jane Knight

Want books with an immersive story that sucks you in until you're left wanting more? Queen of spice Jane has got you covered with her mix of paranormal and contemporary romance stories. She's a master of heat, but not all of her characters are nice. They're dark and controlling and not afraid to take their mates over their knees for a good spanking that will leave you just as shaken as the leading ladies. Or if you'd prefer the daddy-dom type, she writes those too just so they can tell you that you are a good girl before growling in your ear.

Her writing is dark and erotic. Her reverse harems will leave you craving more and the kinks will have you wondering if you'll call the safe word or keep going for that happily ever after.

https://www.facebook.com/JaneKnightWrites

Available on Amazon:
Wild and Blood Thirsty
Wild and Untamed
In his Office
Hers for the Holidays
Mistaken Mates
Her Fae Lovers
Dark Desires

By the Sea
Owned by the Dragons
Her Dominant Dragon
Her Trapped Dragon
Repaying the Debt
Savage Mates
Savage Hunt
Savage Love

Moonlight Muse

Looking for a storyline that will have you on the edge of your seat? The spice levels are high, with a plot that will keep you flipping to the next page and ready for book two. You won't be disappointed with Moonlight Muse.

Her women are sassy, and her men are possessive alpha-holes with high tensions and tons of steam. She'll draw you into her taboo tales, breaking your heart before she gives you the much deserved Happily Ever After.

Dark and twisted, she'll keep you guessing as she pleasurably tortures you with her words, making you ready for the instalment.

Available on Amazon
The Alpha Series
Book 1 - Her Forbidden Alpha
Book 2 - Her Cold-Hearted Alpha
Book 3 - Her Destined Alpha

Magic of Kaeladia Series
Book 1 - My Alpha's Betrayal: Burning in the Flames of his Vengeance
Book 2 - My Alpha's Retribution: Rising from the Ashes of his Vengeance

His Caged Princess

Instagram:
Author.Muse
https://www.instagram.com/author.muse/?utm_medium=copy_link
Facebook
Author Muse
https://m.facebook.com/login.php?next=https%3A%2F%2Fm.

facebook.com%2Fprofile.php%3Fid%3D100068618567349&refsrc=
deprecated&_rdr

Muse Linktree

https://linktr.ee/Author.Muse

Also by Jessica Hall

Join my Facebook group to connect with me

https://www.facebook.com/jessicahall91

Enjoy all of my series

https://www.amazon.com/Jessica-Hall/e/B09TSM8RZ7

Hybrid Aria Series

Book One: Hybrid Aria

Book Two: Alpha's Unhinged Mate

Book Three: Fight Between Alphas

Book Four: Alpha King's Mate

Made in the USA
Monee, IL
14 December 2024

73771820R00240